I'm Looking

Sabrina Waldorf is an Upper East Sider and hopeless romantic. After years of looking for her real-life man in finance, she decided to put pen to paper and create her own trust fund baby instead. When she's not heading out for bagels or taking a stroll around Central Park, she can be found curled up in her apartment with a good book.

I'm Looking for a
Man in Finance

SABRINA WALDORF

PENGUIN BOOKS

PENGUIN BOOKS

UK | USA | Canada | Ireland | Australia
India | New Zealand | South Africa

Penguin Books is part of the Penguin Random House group of companies whose addresses can be found at global.penguinrandomhouse.com

Penguin Random House UK,
One Embassy Gardens, 8 Viaduct Gardens, London SW11 7BW

penguin.co.uk

First published 2025

001

Copyright © Ally Busdeker, 2025

The moral right of the author has been asserted

Penguin Random House values and supports copyright. Copyright fuels creativity, encourages diverse voices, promotes freedom of expression and supports a vibrant culture. Thank you for purchasing an authorized edition of this book and for respecting intellectual property laws by not reproducing, scanning or distributing any part of it by any means without permission. You are supporting authors and enabling Penguin Random House to continue to publish books for everyone. No part of this book may be used or reproduced in any manner for the purpose of training artificial intelligence technologies or systems. In accordance with Article 4(3) of the DSM Directive 2019/790, Penguin Random House expressly reserves this work from the text and data mining exception

Set in 12.5/14.75pt Garamond MT Std
Typeset by Six Red Marbles UK, Thetford, Norfolk
Printed and bound in Great Britain by Clays Ltd, Elcograf S.p.A.

The authorized representative in the EEA is Penguin Random House Ireland, Morrison Chambers, 32 Nassau Street, Dublin D02 YH68

A CIP catalogue record for this book is available from the British Library

ISBN: 978–1–405–98191–0

Penguin Random House is committed to a sustainable future for our business, our readers and our planet. This book is made from Forest Stewardship Council® certified paper.

I'm Looking for a Man in Finance

1

Hallie

I was in love.

I moaned.

The bagel to cream cheese ratio . . . perfection. The smoked salmon . . . delightful. The addition of capers . . . genius. The flavors exploded across my tongue with every bite. The rumors were true, and I knew my review of this place would get a lot of attention on social media.

This cute bistro had popped up in the West Village over the weekend and there were whispers they could be contenders for one of the best bagel spots in Manhattan. With such high praise already, I knew I needed to be one of the first to review it for myself. I snapped a photo of the bagel with my perfectly manicured fingers framing the logo of the bistro. A beautiful stoop of someone's house added just the right vibe to the shot.

As soon as I hit post my phone started to buzz as the likes and comments flooded in. I'd carefully crafted my food review page on social media over the past few years, which now reached nearly ten thousand followers and counting. Not exactly influencer status, but not nothing either. I watched the notifications pile up and wondered, not for the first time, if one viral post could tip me from underrated to undeniable food influencer overnight.

My blog started off as a way to stay sane during my intern days at *Sophisticate*, the magazine I'm so proud to still work at nearly three years later, now as a full-time journalist, but it had become something more—my creative playground. I covered hole-in-the-wall dumpling shops, farmers' market pop-ups, boozy brunch spots in Williamsburg, and everything in between. I never missed a chance to pair my bite with the perfect backdrop. Maybe in another life it wouldn't be just a hobby.

The bustle of NYC continued around me as I stared at my phone, bagel still in hand. The West Village was a brunch-stained love letter to chaos. Flower carts spilled tulips onto the sidewalk. I dodged a golden retriever in a raincoat, sidestepped a painter dabbing at a canvas on the sidewalk, and nearly collided with a guy on a Citibike who yelled, "Nice fit!" before vanishing down Bleecker.

Just another day.

I started walking again, weaving past a man in a three-piece suit as he argued with a pair of twenty-somethings that were filming something in the middle of the sidewalk in front of a vintage bookstore. This was my neighborhood. Messy, vibrant, loud, and beautiful.

The rumble of the subway vibrated up through the ground as I hurried down the stairs to catch my train. I swiped up on my lock screen to look through the incoming notifications when a new post on my feed caught my eye. Victoria, the food critic for *Sophisticate*, was posing on the streets of London with Big Ben in the background.

I am so excited to dive into the food scene of London, well known for its variety of old and new flavors over this upcoming year . . .

I stopped walking mid-stride, barely registering the curse words flying toward me from the person behind who narrowly missed plowing into me. My finger hovered over my screen as my brain took off at light speed.

It couldn't be . . . That meant . . .

With barely any time to spare, I slipped into the subway, my eyes locked on the phone in my hands. Victoria was *gone*. Not just on vacation. Gone-for-a-year kind of gone. That post was more than her career update—it was a shining light for me. A slow hum of realization started in my chest and spread through me like a tidal wave. If she was moving to London for the year . . . her job—the job I'd dreamed about since freshman orientation at NYU—was officially open.

My heart stuttered. The rattling subway car faded into the background. I'd studied Victoria's reviews like gospel, analyzed her tone, the rhythm of her critiques, the way she made even a side of roasted carrots feel profound. And now . . . could I be the one to fill that role? Could *Sophisticate* even *consider* someone like me?

I didn't go to Le Cordon Bleu. I certainly hadn't spent my childhood in Michelin-star restaurants that my parents ate at on a regular basis like Victoria. I was a girl from a small town in Ohio who ate cereal for dinner more often than I'd like to admit. I'd moved to Manhattan with a dream of living in a place where dreams came true and where I could dine at the kind of places I used to read about in blogs growing up. I'd also built something from scratch—my social media account, all ten thousand followers and counting. Reviews that people trusted. A voice. A perspective. Maybe it wasn't fancy, but it was mine.

But was that enough?

The train lurched forward, and I gripped the pole next to me, the phone still in my hand, screen glowing with Victoria's smile frozen beneath Big Ben.

My world had just shifted—and I wanted it badly enough; this could be the moment everything changed.

I glanced up at the looming skyscraper across the street from the subway station as I climbed the stairs back out into the city. The building housed *Sophisticate*, a women's magazine known for covering any topics from sex and relationships to health and politics. It had become a part of the very fabric of American culture, devoted to the concerns of women and their lives.

From the moment NYU's journalism program accepted me, I dreamed of working for *Sophisticate* and still felt grateful every day to walk through those glass doors. There was only one piece of the puzzle missing from my dream—writing as *Sophisticate*'s food critic.

When I applied to the magazine out of college, I knew it would take some time before I was qualified to apply for a position that wielded such power within New York's food scene. So I worked myself nearly ragged for two years as an intern, fetching coffees and teaching my boss how to convert a PDF, before I finally landed my column—"Overheard in NYC". It was a tiny column at the back of the magazine, barely two-hundred words per week. But it was a step toward my dream job, covering the most exquisite cuisines across the city.

My notes app was full of one-off comments I'd heard from people around me—on the subway, in my favorite coffee shop on a Sunday, or on my morning run through Central Park. I covered anything from the juiciest celebrity sighting to the newest sex position I overheard some girl telling her friend she'd tried with her partner. I was grateful to even have "Writer at *Sophisticate*" on my résumé, but my passion was to write about food.

A text message from my best friend, Roxie King, popped up across the top of my screen.

Roxie: What does this evoke for you?

Attached was a photo of a rounded sculpture that looked nothing short of phallic. Roxie worked at a famous art gallery on the Upper East Side where she sold art and sculptures just like this one to people that had more money than they knew what to do with.

Hallie: Confusion? Of the penis-shaped kind?
Roxie: I should have known better than to ask a sex magazine columnist . . .
Hallie: Hey! I write about more than just sex . . . speaking of which.

I sent her the link to Victoria's post and stepped off to the side to avoid the morning commuter rush on the sidewalk.

Roxie and I were roommates during our freshman year in college and bonded over our mutual love for food—with my dreams of becoming a critic and hers of photographing the most beautiful plates of food in the world. But neither of us had cracked the code of the restaurant scene yet, relying heavily on our own social media accounts to make a name for ourselves within the industry. Now we were roommates once more, living together in our tiny apartment in the West Village, as we tried to chase our career dreams.

My phone dinged with Roxie's reply.

Roxie: Are you going to apply?
Hallie: Why? So they can smile and say "how cute"?
Roxie: You know exactly why. You're just as qualified to apply for the position as the next person. So why the hell wouldn't you?

The lobby of *Sophisticate* was always buzzing—sleek black-and-white marble floors, artfully arranged florals, and a rotating collection of cover stories displayed in gold frames near the elevators. Roxie's words rang in my head as I stepped through the revolving doors. I was immediately greeted by the scent of espresso and expensive perfume, the hum of heels on tile, and the distant ding of the elevator arriving. There was a certain magic in walking into a building that felt like the nerve center of modern womanhood.

I rode the elevator up with a group of writers and staff, all in various stages of caffeine dependence. One of the girls from the fashion team complimented my boots, and I made a mental note to text Roxie a thank-you—she'd convinced me to splurge on them during a sample sale last month.

When I reached our floor, the open-concept office hummed with energy. There were half-eaten croissants on the community kitchen counter, mood boards pinned up on the walls, and a fashion assistant dragging a rolling rack of outfits behind her like it was her oxygen tank. Someone in editorial shouted about a missed deadline while another person ran past holding three coffee cups like a juggler in the circus. It was a chaotic, caffeinated dream, and I loved every inch of it.

I dropped my tote on my desk and booted my computer, sipped the last of my bodega coffee and snacked on the last few bites of my bagel. My desk was small, tucked between two other junior writers, but it was mine. A framed photo of Roxie and me at graduation sat beside my monitor, next to a stack of colorful notebooks and a candle I wasn't *technically* allowed to burn.

"Morning, Hallie," came a voice from the desk beside mine. It was Janelle, one of the other junior writers, typing furiously with one hand and balancing a blueberry muffin in the other. Her oversized glasses slipped down her nose as she glanced at me. "Tell me you saw Anthea's heels today. God, I want to be her."

I laughed, setting my coffee down. "I haven't yet. But I can imagine. I swear she floats instead of walks."

Janelle leaned closer, lowering her voice. "Okay but real talk—did you see the job board this morning? Everyone's buzzing about Victoria's position opening up."

I nodded slowly, the glow of my computer screen reflecting in my eyes. "Yeah. I was thinking of applying."

Janelle froze mid-bite, muffin halfway to her mouth. "No. Way. Hallie! That's huge! Wait—do we celebrate this with lunch, drinks, or those cupcakes from that bakery in Chelsea?"

"Maybe all three? But only if I work up enough courage to submit it."

She grinned. "You've got this. You're basically the only one in here who could write a review that makes me want to lick my screen."

I smiled at her, the nerves in my stomach calming just a little.

I had an article to finish—something I'd overheard this weekend from an heiress discussing an exclusive club in Hell's Kitchen—but I kept glancing toward the top corner of my screen, where the company's internal job board icon glowed like a neon sign.

Maybe Roxie and Janelle are right. Maybe I am just as qualified as the next person. What's the worst that can happen? They say "no"?

Without a second thought, I logged onto the job board and pulled up my updated résumé. I moved to this city for college to chase my dreams. How was I ever going to reach them if I never took chances?

Victoria's open position was sitting at the top of the list as the newest opening and before I could change my mind, I clicked into it and applied. Taped to my computer screen sat a picture of my family. I traced my fingers across my mother's soft smile, then my father's sun-worn face, and finally my younger sister, grinning wide on her wedding day. They hadn't understood my enthrallment with New York when I first told them of my dream of moving to the city—they all still lived in the small town in Ohio I'd grown up in, just down the street from each other. To them, life was a quiet neighborhood where everyone knew your name, and Friday nights were reserved for potlucks or high school football games.

But I craved the unfamiliar. The kaleidoscope of languages on the subway. The pulse of yellow cabs and flickering crosswalks. The smell of halal carts and roasted peanuts wafting through every other block. I wanted more than comfort—I wanted color. Energy. Flavor.

They might not have understood my new life, but they were still proud. My very first published column in *Sophisticate*—a two-paragraph "Overheard in NYC" piece about a woman breaking up with her boyfriend over a taco truck order—was framed in my parents' living room, right next to my sister's ultrasound picture. That's how much it mattered.

And now . . . maybe this next step could be even bigger.

Still buzzing from the decision, I clicked over to my current column draft. Deadline looming, lunch forgotten, I chewed nervously on a pen cap and reread the opening paragraph. Last week's piece had gone unexpectedly viral—and by viral, I mean our traffic spiked just over 3,000 more clicks than usual. But in digital publishing? That was basically a cultural moment.

I had been on my way to pick up a coffee last Wednesday morning when I overheard this twenty-something corporate girl talking to her friend outside the coffee shop near my apartment, while they sipped on their matcha lattes.

"I just go to Whiskey Locker; you know, the bar on West 55th Street? Down in the Financial District?"

Her friend nodded enthusiastically, dressed head to toe in

Lululemon. They were clearly on their way to a Pilates class or coming from it.

"And I wait for any guy in a vest and a button up to ask me out. Financial analyst, investment banker, you know, I'm not picky." The girl flipped her perfectly highlighted blonde hair over her shoulder. "Sure, they all have been fuckboys so far, but eventually one of these finance bros has got to stick around long enough to buy me a Birkin . . ."

After the "Overheard" article went live, our *Sophisticate* notifications had lit up.

@nycchronicles: I heard this exact convo outside Devocio in FiDi. She was serious as hell. But I can't blame her. Those finance guys are HOT! #OverheardinNYC

@financebrosanonymous: Whiskey Locker is where careers go to thrive, and dignity goes to die LOL

@lululemonwarrior: Was she telling the truth? Asking for a friend.

Even Anthea Sparks herself had reposted it to her story. I'd nearly passed out when I saw that notification come across my phone. That was the moment I felt it. Not just excitement—recognition.

For a few glorious hours, I had floated through the newsroom like I was wearing invisible heels, three inches taller. I wasn't just the girl scribbling snarky eavesdroppings into my notes app. I was seen. I was heard. And not just by the audience of *Sophisticate* readers scrolling through columns during their lunch breaks, but by the woman who had built the entire damn empire.

I felt like I had finally cracked the glass ceiling of irrelevance.

People in the office smiled a little longer when they passed my desk. Someone had even scribbled "future Pulitzer winner?" on a Post-it and stuck it to my monitor. I left it there. A little tacky, a little ironic, but still—not *entirely* impossible now.

It wasn't just the clicks, though I checked the analytics way too many times. It was the comments, the reblogs, the DMs from friends I hadn't heard from since college:

> This is hilarious, Hal. More please.
> You're basically Carrie Bradshaw now.
> Remember me when you're famous.

I went as far as to order an overpriced cappuccino just to sit outside the same coffee shop, wondering if lightning might strike twice. I even brought a notebook, pretending to look busy while hoping someone nearby would say something column-worthy again. No such luck. Which left me with an old note I'd overheard at a workout class that didn't feel nearly as punchy for my next article.

Before I had time to analyse it further, Anthea Sparks, my boss and editor-in-chief of *Sophisticate*, walked past my desk. She was wearing Carolina Herrera and sporting Gucci platform sling-backs that were yet to even hit the runway. She was the definition of "boss bitch" in the very best way and had turned *Sophisticate* from just another women's magazine into one that shaped every aspect of female culture.

As she passed me, I barely caught the words, "Hallie, do you have a minute?"

"Oh, yes. Right, absolutely." Anthea was already sweeping into her office as I quickly closed my laptop and hurried after her. My heart was pounding. This was the first time she'd ever specifically called me into her office. It wasn't like my boss didn't know who I was, but I assumed I'd always been just another face in the crowd. Maybe this was the moment that would change everything—or the moment I'd screwed up entirely.

Anthea's office overlooked Manhattan, as if she were a queen surveying her kingdom. The skyline was framed in the background, the sun highlighting the opulence of my surroundings. It was the perfect blend of luxury and industry. She covered her walls with the pages of *Sophisticate*'s next edition. Anthea's bold handwriting covered each page in sticky notes, detailing her thoughts on the tiniest points. A Peloton bike sat propped in the corner of her office and a clothing rack filled with the pieces the magazine was planning on covering in various articles was overflowing near her back wall.

I stood for a moment in the doorway, unsure if I should sit or wait for her to acknowledge me. Her assistant, a woman with impeccable style and a clipboard permanently attached to her side, rushed by carrying a cup of coffee.

"This isn't hot enough," Anthea told her as she took a sip, causing all the blood to drain from her assistant's face. Anthea glanced up, her icy green eyes narrowing as she sent a signal, dismissing her assistant.

Anthea didn't acknowledge me, her fingers still tapping out an urgent message on her phone, as if she hadn't just invited me to her office. I could feel the pressure building, the soft hum of the air conditioning filling the otherwise silent room.

I used the moment to survey Anthea's office, the perfect décor, the plush velvet couch, the floor-to-ceiling bookshelves with countless binders, the sleek coffee table covered in glossy *Sophisticate* magazines. A wave of envy washed over me. Was this what success looked like? I wondered if I'd ever make it to a point where I was calling the shots like she did.

I swallowed, trying to suppress the knot in my throat. This was Anthea Sparks. This was the person who made *Sophisticate* what it was today. And here I was, just another writer hoping to get noticed. That was if I made it out of this conversation with a job. Because who the hell knew why she'd called me in here.

Finally, Anthea put her phone down and looked at me. She didn't smile, didn't offer a pleasantry. Instead, she leaned back in her chair, folding her arms across her chest, her expression unreadable.

"I wanted to talk to you about your 'Overheard in NYC' column from last week," Anthea said, cutting right to the chase. She wasn't a woman that afforded herself the luxury of wasting time.

For a moment, I froze, unsure of what was coming next. Was she going to tell me I'd gone too far? Had she changed her mind after sharing it and thought the article wasn't to *Sophisticate* standards, after all?

I had to brace myself for whatever came next. She was the picture of composure, like she had all the time in the world. "And it obviously resonated with a lot of people. So, I was thinking . . ." She trailed off for a moment, as if letting the words hang in the air, before continuing. "This whole 'finance guy' thing. It has some legs to it. I want you to take it further. Let's call it 'Love on Wall Street', where you write a series of articles trying to find a date with the most eligible bachelors on Wall Street."

My mouth went dry, and I blinked a few times, trying to process what she'd just said. Was she serious?

"Wait, sorry—dating? Finance guys?" I stammered, completely thrown off.

Anthea's gaze was sharp as ever, unwavering as she observed me. "Yes, that's what I just said."

I couldn't breathe. My mind short-circuited as I processed the idea. Dating for a column? This was a whole new level of personal exposure. I was supposed to go on dates, to share my life, my privacy, for the sake of a story? I hadn't signed up for this.

But I couldn't help but wonder if I was overthinking it. I had been scrambling for something, anything, to make an impact—something more than just my "Overheard in NYC" fluff. And this idea? This could blow up. It could make me.

"I . . . I don't know . . ." My voice was small, unsure. My gut tightened at the thought of dating guys I already found distasteful. Wall Street types? They were everything I despised: arrogant, superficial, heartless. And women like me, just a little too smart, a little too ambitious? We were nothing but objects to them.

But then I remembered the application. Being a food critic had always felt out of reach, just a glimmer in the distance. If I said no to this, I could kiss any chances of getting that position goodbye.

My first instinct was to figure out a way to backtrack out of this conversation and pretend it never happened. Anthea must have seen the look on my face because she narrowed in on the challenge I was presenting her.

"You know, I saw a notification come across my inbox earlier today." Anthea pushed off her desk and circled to drop into her chair. Not a single piece of silky black hair moved as she leaned back in her office chair. "I didn't realize that you were interested in our food critic position."

"Wait—hold on," I said, frowning, confusion clouding my thoughts. "I thought we were talking about a dating column. What does this have to do with the food critic position?"

Anthea didn't even flinch. She simply leaned back in her chair, her posture smooth and commanding, the faintest hint of a smile playing on her lips. "You're right to be confused. I wasn't planning on explaining it just yet." Her eyes narrowed, piercing through me. "But I'll make it clear. If you can pull this off, write a series that resonates and brings in even more traffic than your last piece, I'll consider you for the food critic role. It's yours for the taking. But first, you must prove you can write a story that captivates."

If I had been speechless before, my brain had simply forgotten the function of speech at this point.

I blinked at her, trying to wrap my head around her proposition. A dating column for a chance at my dream job?

"You'd let me go from writing about finance bros to

covering Michelin-star restaurants?" I asked incredulously. Even I thought that was a bit of a stretch, despite my own delusions in hoping for the position.

Anthea didn't seem phased by my surprise. She simply leveled me with her piercing gaze. "You have talent, Hallie Woods. Even if it may be raw and could use some refinement. And *Sophisticate* didn't get to where it is without putting talented people in positions to succeed. If you feel you'd succeed the most in our restaurant critic spot, then I might just put you there. But first you must prove it." Anthea lifted one perfectly plucked eyebrow at me.

The compliment, however backhanded, nearly made me miss the rest of what Anthea had offered. I had always dreamed of working with Anthea and would have done almost anything for a compliment from her, as would anyone else here, but could I do *this*?

Was I going to take the offer? Or was I going to walk away?

My mind raced through the possibilities.

Pros: This could be my chance to prove myself, to elevate my career to something bigger than the "Overheard" column. Anthea herself had said she'd consider me for the food critic role if I succeeded.

Cons: I'd be using my own life as content. Could I really put my personal dating life on display for thousands of readers? It felt ... exploitative. And what if my dates actually turned out to be not half bad? How was I supposed to throw them into the fishbowl too?

I tried to picture it, sitting across from some Wall Street bro in a posh bar, pretending to enjoy his stories about IPOs and mergers while inside I was cringing. I could already feel the mockery of it. And even worse the judgment from my peers.

Would they think I was *selling out?*

I glanced back at Anthea, whose green eyes were locked onto me, expectantly waiting for a response. She had probably seen the wheels turning in my head.

"Are you still with me, Hallie?" she asked, her voice colder now, a slight edge creeping in.

I hesitated for just a second longer, my mind running in circles, filled with uncertainty, but I couldn't deny the thrill that pulsed through me. This was my chance to step up and prove that I belonged here. That I wasn't just some girl who wrote about nonsense but someone with real potential. Someone who could write about the most delicious food this city had to offer.

"Okay," I finally said. "I'll do it. But just so we're clear—what exactly are you expecting here? Dates with actual Wall Street guys?" I couldn't help but add the last part with a bit of sarcasm.

Anthea's lips curled into a satisfied smile. "Exactly. One a week. But the key, Hallie? You need to make it compelling. We're not looking for a *dating column*, we're looking for a *story*—your story, your journey into the world of finance guys. We want details. Make them feel real."

A mix of excitement and dread surged through me, but I nodded.

"Alright, I'll write the first one. But—" I hesitated again. "What if they're all ... not great? What if it's a disaster?"

Anthea leaned forward, her smile tightening. "That's not an option."

I felt a flutter of unease. Would it be worth it? What was I willing to sacrifice for success? I was about to find out.

"When do you want the first article by?"

Anthea's eyes glinted as she checked her watch. "Two weeks. Don't disappoint me."

As I turned to leave, the weight of her words hit me again. The pressure, the challenge. My stomach was a storm of nerves, but the truth was, I had never felt more alive. This could make or break me. And I was choosing to make it.

2

James

Whiskey Locker provided the best Friday happy hour in all of New York City. Everyone from Wall Street would migrate from the southern tip of Manhattan up toward Central Park to loosen their ties, leaving behind the high-rise offices full of people dealing with the cash flow of the wealthiest people around the world.

This bar drew nearly every crowd in New York—models within the fashion industry, Wall Street mongers, celebrities, musicians, influencers—you name it. They lounged around the dimly lit velvet booths that provided privacy for its patrons. But a crowd like that always drew in curious onlookers, those that wanted to breathe the same air as those with the power to influence industries. Men and women leaned against the bar, hoping for someone sitting in those booths to pluck them out of anonymity and deem them worthy of their time and energy.

But despite the various groups mingling together, there was one profession that had always reigned supreme at Whiskey Locker. They were unmistakable—the tailored suits, perfectly pressed vests, and glinting luxury watches set them apart. These were the investment bankers, financial analysts, hedge fund managers, and everything in between—the true backbone of this establishment.

Or what social media now kindly referred to as "finance bros". The bar had always belonged to them—to us. And I was proud of it.

"Are you going over to Michelle and Elliot's for dinner tonight?" Sebastian, my best friend and heir to Whittaker Holdings—the biggest fashion conglomerate on the planet—asked me.

"I was planning on it," I told him as I tapped my ring inscribed with my family's crest against my whiskey glass. "Are you?"

Sebastian shook his head. "Not tonight. I have a meeting with an upcoming designer. I'm hoping to close a deal with her tonight."

"Business or pleasure?" I gave Seb a knowing smirk as I took a sip.

Sebastian Whittaker was many things—a fiercely loyal friend, a business shark, and an exceptional flirt. It wasn't unheard of for him to mix the latter two for his own personal means. He'd been tossing ethics out the window since I met him back at Princeton, a true hedonist at heart. But that didn't mean he wouldn't earn the title of CEO of Whittaker Holdings when it was time for him to take over the company from his father.

Of course, there were always whispers—the "nepo baby" allegations followed him wherever he went as people watched him play the charming playboy. They liked to call him a product of privilege, a rich kid who had coasted through life on his father's name. But anyone who knew him, anyone who had watched him put in the long nights and fight for his place in the cutthroat world of business, knew that Sebastian had earned everything that came to him.

"Business. Strictly business on this one." Seb smoothed a hand over his dark hair, the tattoos on his hands stretching. "Elliot wasn't happy to hear I'd be missing out again tonight. He told me he was going to leave me off the invite list if I didn't make it to the next one."

"You know how Elliot gets," I told him. "He doesn't want to feel like his relationships are purely ornamental. And he's not wrong. You haven't made as much of an effort lately to show up to things."

"I've been busy." A muscle flexed in Seb's jaw. I knew that he'd had an enormous amount of pressure on him as he prepared to take the helm of his family's company, but he never shared enough for me to know where his head was at.

"Right."

Elliot Granger was the last piece that completed our Princeton trio. The three of us had been inseparable in college. We couldn't be more different. While Sebastian partied almost constantly and I networked to climb the Wall Street ladder before graduation, Elliot secluded himself in his apartment to learn about the cryptocurrency market. By the young age of twenty-two, he'd become one of the most successful cryptocurrency wallet managers in the world, changing the game for hedge fund managers forever. He was on track to be one of the youngest billionaires in the world. Between all of that, I'm still not sure how he snagged Michelle during our time at Princeton. She was effortlessly beautiful, with a sharp mind to match, and always had a way to make everyone around her feel like they were the most important person in the room. Elliott was a goner the second he laid eyes on her.

My phone chimed with another automated email analysing today's market. Ignoring the sigh from Seb across from me, I reached for it.

"You could use a little less business and a bit more pleasure, I think."

With a final sip of my whiskey, I declined.

"It's been over a year since Cassidy, man. You haven't even spared a glance at another woman."

"And I don't plan to anytime soon."

At one time, I had thought Cassidy Lark was the love of my life. From the first moment I spotted her working behind the counter of my favorite coffee shop, her energy had enraptured me. She'd been so charismatic, so magnetic, so completely different from every girl that I'd grown up with, that I'd fallen head over heels. I had thought I'd found the love my parents had—strong enough to conquer even the deep lines between social classes. That was, until I'd stumbled across the thousands of dollars she'd siphoned off me over the course of our relationship and the entire thing came crashing down.

"You're going to have to, eventually." What I loved about Sebastian was his stubborn persistence until it was directed at me.

"Who says?"

"I know you, James." Sebastian leveled me with a look, his gray eyes narrowed. "You crave that kind of connection. If you don't seek it out, it's going to find you."

"We'll see about that." I tossed a hundred dollars down on the table to cover our drinks and a tip. "Have fun tonight."

"Always do."

*

I paused in the hallway when I heard shouting on the other side of my parents' apartment door.

What the fuck?

The pounding of my fist echoed off the marble in the entryway foyer of their penthouse apartment on the Upper East Side. Their building's grand windows overlooked Central Park. When I was a kid, I sometimes forgot I lived in a concrete jungle with that view. The soft hum of traffic from below barely pierced the thick walls of their upscale, meticulously decorated home. Shuffling and faint shouts came from the other side, then the door opened to reveal my mother—Eloise Rossi.

She was dressed in luxuriously simple cashmere, the kind that only a few select designers ever seemed to get right, paired with silk lounge pants. Her blonde hair was styled in a French twist, and her makeup was impeccable, not a blemish in sight. Although I got her blue eyes and high cheekbones, my dark hair and thick eyebrows came from my father's Italian ancestry.

I wrapped my arms around my mother's petite frame, the familiar scent of her perfume grounding me. The warmth of the hug was comforting, but something about the raised voices I'd heard from the other side of the door unsettled me. I pulled back slightly, glancing at her with a raised brow.

"What was that yelling?" I asked as soon as she opened the door. I peered over her head, unsure of what I'd find.

"Oh, it's your father." She waved a hand dismissively, stepping aside to let me in. "Don't worry about it. We'll talk later." She was already pivoting toward the kitchen, gesturing for me to follow. "Come in. I have a snack laid out for us."

I could tell by her calm demeanor that whatever had caused the shouting was either no big deal or something she'd seen a hundred times before. My mom had always had this ability to make things seem smaller than they were—an admirable skill, especially given how differently she and my father had been received by each other's families when they first got together.

She'd grown up in one of those families where power and wealth were inherited, not earned. Her father had disapproved of my father for years, seeing him as little more than a blue-collar guy from a family that owned a pizza joint in Brooklyn, not someone who belonged in the same circles. But my mother had persuaded my grandfather anyway, throwing caution to the wind in a way that would've been unthinkable for most people of her background. Eventually, her family had come around, not wanting to lose their only daughter.

"You look good, sweetheart," she said, steering me toward the kitchen, where she'd set out a plate of olives and prosciutto. If there was one thing Eloise Rossi loved to do, it was host. "How's everything?"

"Good," I said, reaching for an olive. My mind kept circling back to the shouting, but I tried to push it aside. "Dad's alright?"

"Your uncle called." My mother pursed her lips. "There seems to be an issue with the restaurant. Your father's your father. He'll calm down. Don't worry about it."

"What do you mean?"

She sighed, collecting another jar of olives from the pantry. "It's the same old story. The restaurant's in trouble again."

I raised an eyebrow as I reached for a slice of cheese. "Trouble? What kind of trouble?"

"Your father's family hasn't updated anything since they built the place. They still run it the way they did back then—no website, no marketing. Just hoping people will walk in." She shrugged as she dumped more olives out for me. "Your father thinks some changes need to be made, but your uncle always sides with your grandparents, doesn't want to make waves."

I nodded, having heard this song and dance before. The pizzeria had become something of a neighborhood institution over the years. But my grandparents' reluctance to adapt to the changing times had left them struggling in a market that had long moved beyond traditional family-run businesses.

"And Dad's had enough of it?" I prodded, reaching for another olive.

She motioned to the plate of snacks, urging me to eat. "Let's leave it to him to handle. He'll figure something out. Eat first. You're too thin. Those long hours at the office are not doing you any good."

"I have a dinner later," I told her, but she waved me off and edged the plate closer. I plucked yet another olive from the plate to appease her.

"What is Dad going to do?" My mother shrugged a shoulder—I wished I could strive for her level of unbothered.

"Enough talk about business. That's all we do in this house . . . business, business, business." She let out a long sigh before mischief filled her eyes.

"Oh, no." I shook my head. "I know that look."

A smile played at the corners of her lips. "I ran into Nora Lauder at brunch this morning."

I knew this was going in a direction I would not like.

"She mentioned that her daughter, Felicity, is back in the city from her time in London."

And there it was.

As did everyone who grew up on the Upper East Side, Felicity and I had frequented the same circles growing up—between balls, dinners, and society events. The two of us knew each other well. Which was how I knew she'd been in London for a "gap year", even though she was years out of college. It had been more of an attempt to find an eligible bachelor overseas because Felicity Lauder had scared off nearly every man that came from a family with status. Let's just say, "high maintenance" was a vast understatement when it came to her.

"Did she now?"

"I think you should reach out to her," my mother continued, oblivious to my disinterest. "Ask her to lunch."

"That's a nice thought," I murmured.

She reached out to wrap a hand over the top of mine. "I just want you to be happy again."

"I am happy." My hand turned over to squeeze hers.

"Felicity could be a great option. She comes from a wealthy family."

"Why does that matter?" I asked. Money had never been in the conversation before with who I dated. "You didn't marry for money."

"No, I married for love." My mother looked toward the study where her husband was finishing up his phone call with the kind of adoration in her eyes that people made movies about.

My father, Giacomo, walked into the room looking much happier than I'd heard from him through the front door earlier. He walked over to give his wife a kiss, even though he'd seen her minutes ago, and reached across the counter to shake my hand.

"Well, look who finally made it home," he said, his deep voice warm, the anger that had been audible moments before nowhere to be found.

"Hi, Dad," I said, returning the handshake. "You okay?"

He shrugged, his demeanor shifting to something lighter. "Of course I am. Everything's fine."

But he couldn't fool me. "What happened with the restaurant?"

He hesitated for a moment, glancing at my mother. "It's the same thing again, James," he muttered, rubbing a hand through his thick dark hair. "They're going to run the business into the ground. I've been trying to get your uncle to see reason, but . . ." He trailed off, looking away.

"You both are stubborn. It's in the Rossi blood," my mother chimed in, not missing a beat. She moved to pour herself a glass of wine, as if this conversation was already old news to her. "The two of you are far more similar than you are different."

I crossed my arms, leaning against the counter. "How bad is it?"

"This is the third month in a row that we've had to float some cash into the business to keep them out of the red," my father said, his voice now quieter, tinged with frustration. "I don't know how much longer we can keep doing this."

"I'll help," I said, without thinking.

Both of my parents turned to look at me.

"No," my father said quickly, shaking his head. "You've got your own life to worry about. We'll figure it out."

But I was already firm in my decision. "I can't just ignore this. It's been a part of this family since the fifties. You're not going to let it fail, are you?"

He ran a hand through his hair again, clearly exhausted. "I'll handle it."

"I'm not going to let it fall apart, Dad. Let me help."

My mother placed a hand on my arm. "Enough about business. It's not good for you to get worked up."

But I couldn't let it go. My family's restaurant had always been a part of our lives, and I wasn't going to let it slip through our fingers without trying to do something about it. Despite my father's protests, I stood my ground.

"I'll find a way to help," I insisted.

He sighed. "Alright, but don't say I didn't warn you."

I nodded, then glanced at my watch. "I've got to go, but we'll talk more about this soon."

As I headed toward the door, my father's voice called out, a hint of pride in his tone. "It was good to see you, son. You should come around more often."

3

Hallie

"Think of this as a celebration for your new think piece," Roxie whispered in my ear as we climbed the staircase of her client's home in the Upper East Side to the kitchen, where the sounds of clinking glasses and soft conversation floated down to greet us.

Roxie looked like she belonged here.

She had pulled her dirty-blonde curls into a sleek twist that somehow made her look both editorial and effortless. Her Vivienne Westwood dress—a structured plaid number with a nipped waist and dramatic neckline—was vintage, yes, but *intentional* vintage. Fashion-editor vintage. She carried herself like someone who regularly dined on rooftops under string lights, not in our shared apartment where the radiator never worked properly, and the walls were thin enough to hear our neighbors' nightly arguments.

The doorman had greeted her like she lived here. Not in the building, but in the neighborhood. Like he expected her to glide past velvet ropes and into penthouses scented with Diptyque candles and generational wealth. Like he somehow knew she drank her espresso black, owned real pearls, and knew instinctively which fork to use at a seven-course dinner.

We'd stepped out of the cab into a part of the Upper East Side that looked like it had been airbrushed. The buildings were limestone and pre-war, with those ornate iron balconies that made it feel like Paris if Paris had hedge funds and legacy admissions. The sidewalks were unnaturally clean—like someone power-washed them every morning just in case a billionaire might stroll by.

The trees were wrapped in white twinkle lights, the kind you usually only see in wedding vision boards, and they gave the whole block this ethereal glow, like the evening had been staged just for us. Or rather, just for the people that lived on the Upper East Side. The kind who knew how to navigate a cocktail hour with charm and a touch of well-timed eye contact. The kind who didn't flinch at coat check or get self-conscious about ordering the cheapest glass of wine on the menu.

A line of town cars idled out front, their chauffeurs leaning against the doors in crisp uniforms, talking quietly into earpieces like they were coordinating a discreet rescue mission. A woman in a camel coat walked by with a tiny dog that probably had its own monogrammed carrier and a social media following. Even her leash was designer.

The awning above the entrance was forest green, embroidered with gold script that spelled out a name I'd only ever seen in real estate listings I clicked on for fun—way past midnight, usually, when I was feeling particularly reckless. Inside, the lobby was marble and moody lighting, with a chandelier that looked like it had once belonged to someone with a title and a minor palace. A man in a tuxedo had held open the door, and I was pretty sure he'd mistaken Roxie for a socialite. Or a model. Or both.

And honestly? I didn't blame him.

Me? I'd done my best to keep up. My dress was a second-hand find from a shop in the East Village with no label and a mystery origin story. The corseted bodice hugged my waist just right, and the hem skimmed my calves in a way I hoped looked more "quiet luxury" than clearance rack. I'd paired it with the only heels I owned that didn't destroy my feet—still not convinced I'd make it through the evening without blisters—and a clutch I'd found on deep discount at Barney's.

I'd spent the entire cab ride rehearsing how to look like I didn't care about fitting in—even though I did. The women here would be dripping in silk and old money, with manicures that matched their handbags. I'd curled my hair into loose waves and swiped my signature red lipstick to make up for the fact that nothing I was wearing had ever been written up in *Sophisticate*.

This was Roxie's zone, despite not having grown up in this world. She lit up around rooms like this—her laughter a touch louder, her smile a little sharper. I was just hoping to make it to dessert without knocking over a glass of wine or accidentally insulting someone's hedge fund.

"A celebration with people I don't know who don't know that I am writing an article on dating finance guys on Wall Street?" I lifted a perfectly filled-in eyebrow at my best friend.

"You know Michelle," she countered. I'd been at the art gallery with Roxie on more than one occasion when Michelle Granger had come in to buy a new installation for her home or to use at a charity auction she was hosting.

Michelle was one of those rare Upper East Side women

who was warm without being fake, generous without needing applause. She had a sly sense of humor that could disarm even the prickliest person, and she and Roxie hit it off immediately when Roxie sold her a ceramic piece titled *Woman Smoking at Sunset* and told her, with full sincerity, that it reminded her of Michelle.

Roxie smirked, her eyes gleaming with that mischievous sparkle. "And you never know—maybe there's a hot, eligible finance guy here tonight. You could knock two birds out with one stone. You're due for a little action," Roxie whispered in my ear as we stepped into the kitchen, where men in Armani and women in minimalist cocktail dresses lingered around a long marble island, sipping on drinks that were being served by a bartender in a black button-down.

I couldn't help but roll my eyes. "I'm here to write about them, not date them."

She just grinned wider. "Same difference." Then she took a deep breath as she prepared to blend in with the crowd. I didn't mind her leaving me. Observing others was part of my job, and I was more than content to play the wallflower for a little while.

This was Roxie's prime—getting to rub elbows with people in a different tax bracket than us. She could shmooze her way into a royal wedding, I was sure of it. Add a little alcohol to the mix and she could either become the life of the party or a liability—there was no in between. But she was my soul sister despite her few flaws, and there was no one I'd rather walk arm-in-arm with into a party at a mansion on the Upper East Side.

"Roxie!" Michelle swept across the room in a floor-length

black dress. Her flaming red hair shone brighter than almost all the perfectly curated art in the room. "I'm so glad you made it. Hallie, it's lovely to see you again."

Michelle leaned down to give me an air kiss on either cheek. I'd been around my fair share of wealthy people at Roxie's art gallery and the double kisses would never be something I'd get used to. "Hi, Michelle."

"Please, make yourselves comfortable. Grab a drink. Dinner will soon be served." Michelle squeezed each of our hands. "Elliot is around here somewhere. I will make sure he says hello."

And just like that, she disappeared back into the crowd of guests.

"Come on, let's grab a drink," Roxie said. Despite how much reassurance Roxie gave me or I gave myself, I could never stop that inky, black voice from sliding in from the depths of my mind to remind me that I didn't quite fit in and would never amount to other women. Which was part of the reason I liked to avoid functions like this entirely.

Armed with a drink in my hand—part liquid courage, part social armor—I finally felt brave enough to scope out the other guests that were here tonight. Most of them were people I'd seen around the gallery or knew from the gossip tabloids. That was until my eyes locked with a pair of deep-blue eyes from across the room.

Damn.

He was the definition of tall, dark, and handsome. With his long legs crossed casually at the ankles, he leaned against a kitchen counter. He'd left the top few buttons of his dress shirt undone, revealing sunkissed skin and a gold chain that twinkled under the overhead lighting. A Rolex flashed on his wrist and the golden signet ring on his pinky rested against the glass he was holding.

Well-dressed, mildly good-looking men were a dime a dozen in this town. But then there was *him*.

His gaze lazily flicked toward my feet before trailing back up my body. There was a fire roaring in the sitting room off the kitchen, but it felt like I'd thrown myself directly into it.

"Hallie?"

"Yes?" I snapped my gaze away from the man across the room and glanced over at Roxie, who was looking at me like I'd suddenly fallen ill.

"Michelle asked us to take our seats?" Roxie gestured at the rest of the group as they made their way into the formal dining room. I glanced back over toward the kitchen to see the man still leaning against the counter, his gaze still locked on me like he had all the time in the world.

"Sorry, just spaced for a minute," I told my best friend, who seemed to buy my excuse for the temporary lapse of attention.

"You're sitting across from me," Roxie whispered in my ear as she spotted our place cards on the dining table. Michelle had sat us toward the end of the table, which I was thankful for. It gave me fewer people to keep up appearances with, even though I knew Roxie could hold a conversation for the both of us.

As I rounded the table to take my place across from Roxie, a hand appeared from behind me and gently pulled my chair out. "Looks like we'll be sitting next to each other tonight."

The voice was deep, sending goosebumps across my shoulders as I followed the hand up to see the stranger from before smirking down at me. A single dimple appeared on the left side of his full lips, the kind that could make you forget your own name if you looked too long. And, from this close, I could see different shades of blue in his eyes, like layers of the ocean. So easy to drown in.

My pulse stuttered, and the world seemed to narrow to just the space between us— intimate and impossible to ignore. I looked away, heart hammering, and slipped into the chair that he had pulled out for me. His body heat kissed the skin of my back as he pushed my chair in. The fireplace at the far end of the room crackled, but the flush creeping up my neck had very little to do with the flames.

"I'm James." He extended a hand, still standing beside me.

I hesitated for half a second before placing mine into his. His fingers curled around mine—firm, warm, sure. A shiver zipped up my spine.

"Hallie."

"How do you know Michelle?" James asked me as he picked up the bottle of wine in front of us. "Would you like some?"

"Please," I told him. He poured a glass for me, then one for himself, as if this was just a dinner party and not a moment that had completely knocked the breath out of my lungs.

Was the bar really that low, Hallie?

"My best friend and roommate," —I gestured toward Roxie— "is Michelle's art gallerist."

James glanced over at Roxie, who had now garnered the attention of our entire half of the table, except for the two of us. "Ah, yes. Michelle loves her art."

"How do you know the Grangers?" Somehow, I was keeping up a conversation with him without flubbing my way through it. I wasn't sure if I'd gained a newfound sense of confidence or if it was the way he was giving me his full attention, like he truly cared about what I had to say.

"I went to college with them at Princeton." *Definitely from a different world than me.*

While I was sure that he had gotten into Princeton on a legacy admission, I had gotten into NYU through a grant they gave out to those who couldn't afford to go there without help.

A group of waiters appeared to deliver the first course of the night and the table's conversation turned to quiet murmurs about the food.

"Dear lord, I need five of these," Roxie groaned across the table as she finished the last bite of her tiramisu.

I laughed at my friend as I savored the last bite of mine.

"I think I may sneak a few home in my jacket pockets," James added, and I laughed.

We'd spent the past hour bantering back and forth about each course—comparing notes on flavors, debating wine pairings, swapping favorite restaurants in the city. He actually knew what a millefeuille was and had passionate thoughts on duck confit. It was . . . fun. Easy. Like we were two people enjoying dinner together and not two strangers from entirely different worlds.

Every time our eyes met, there was that unspoken something—an energy, a spark. It wasn't loud or overwhelming, but it was there. I could almost picture him asking for my number by the end of the evening, or suggesting we go for a drink afterwards—anything to keep the conversation going.

"Oh, wait! Hallie, we should toast to you!" Roxie lifted her glass a little unsteadily. Everyone else around us was caught up in their own conversations.

"Toasting for what exactly?" James asked, lifting his own glass and glancing at me with that same quiet intensity. His gaze was a heat lamp, and I was wilting under it—in the best way.

Before I could be self-deprecating, Roxie swooped in—knowing that I would never admit my successes myself. "Hallie was just offered a feature piece at her job," she stage-whispered. "She's a writer at *Sophisticate*."

James looked genuinely impressed. "Wow, I didn't know I was sitting next to a rockstar."

It was a simple compliment—like something someone would say to be nice—but the way he said it, like he actually meant it, made something flutter low in my belly.

"What's the article about?" He shifted his entire body toward me. His thigh brushed mine beneath the table. He didn't move away.

"It's about her trying to find the *hottest* finance guy on Wall Street," Roxie interjected, grinning proudly.

James's expression shifted, eyebrows lifting in surprise. "Really?"

"It's stupid, really," I hurried to tell him, feeling the need to explain why I had agreed to the project.

James's smile softened. "Why?" he asked, genuine curiosity in his voice.

I shrugged, suddenly feeling a little defensive, like I had to explain myself. "I'm just trying to write something that'll get me closer to my real goal—becoming the food critic for *Sophisticate*."

The shift in his gaze was subtle, but I noticed it. A quick, thoughtful pause. Then, he leaned in a little, as if to hear more. "So, you're doing this . . . to get your dream job?"

"Exactly." I studied my wineglass, trying not to sound too self-conscious. "It's not about the dates or the guys. I'll probably never actually date them. They are *not* my type. Couldn't be further from it actually. I just need the piece to get my foot in the door."

James chuckled. "Please, you must tell me what you find so repulsive about men in finance."

The hand gripping my chest slowly eased as I realized maybe I *hadn't* stuck my foot in my mouth. With renewed confidence, I reached for my glass of wine. "Well, I have a pros and cons list. I have to give credit where credit is due," I admitted, giving him a playful shrug. "Typically, they dress well, and they have a finger on the pulse of the NYC food scene. Not to mention the free financial advice."

There was never a doubt that I would see a finance bro at the newest restaurant that I was reviewing, or a group of them, all carbon copies of each other—the same Rolex shining on their wrists, the same slicked-back hairstyle, the same loafers, and the same five expensive suit brands that they always circulated.

"But between their 401(k) talk, the constant scrutiny of credit scores, or the way they think a fancy watch makes them interesting, it's hard to choose a top choice. I'd rather eat plain bagels for the rest of my life than listen to another round of 'what's your net worth?'"

James smirked. "You've really thought that out, haven't you?"

"Of course," I said, the tension in my shoulders loosening. "It's the most predictable thing in the city. They're all the same."

"And yet, you still need them to get your dream job," James said, his tone almost teasing now.

"Well, yeah. Sometimes you've got to play the game." Despite James's interest in the conversation, the flash of his signet ring on the stem of his wineglass reminded me how different the two of us were. While I was rambling about a ridiculous article that I wouldn't have even chosen to write, I did not know what this man did. But before I could ask, James was already carrying along the conversation.

"And what exactly is the goal this article is getting you to?" Being the center of his attention was like a lightning strike to my body; every nerve ending was on fire and I wanted nothing more than to remain in his spotlight.

"*Sophisticate* is well regarded in the food industry. The kinds of opportunities that would open for me, I couldn't get them anywhere else. It's my dream company to work for."

"So this is all a means to an end?" James supplied.

I nodded. "Exactly. If this finance bro article helps me slip that final puzzle piece into place, then so be it. At the very least, I'll have a few dates and some nice dinners out of it on their dime."

"Even if, as you said, you do not intend to really date these men, and you'd just be stringing them along?"

"They're big boys. They can take it. Surely they have to be to work in such a money-hungry, cutthroat world? Honestly, I see this as payback for how often I hear about a man in finance treating a girl poorly." I gave him a one-shouldered shrug. "What about you? What do you do?"

But before he could answer, his phone buzzed. He pulled it out of his pocket, glancing at the notifications on his screen. Already the party felt slightly dimmer without his gaze on me.

"I'm sorry, it looks like I have some fires I need to put out." James stood up from his seat, leaving me to stare after him in confusion as he made his way toward Michelle and Elliot. One second, he was sitting next to me, enraptured by our conversation, the next he was breezing toward the exit.

"You're not staying for a night cap?" I heard Elliot ask.

"Duty calls," James replied.

Was he a doctor? That would explain the expensive clothing. He must be like a neurosurgeon.

James hugged Elliot and gave Michelle a kiss on the cheek, then headed for the stairs without sparing a glance in my direction.

"Hey, are you okay?" Roxie leaned forward into my view to grab my attention. It was what I loved most about her. We could be in a crowded room like this, and she'd never fail to notice when I was slipping away, retreating into myself, caught up with that voice in my head as it berated me.

I kept my eyes fixed on the staircase where James had just vanished, my chances of seeing him again fading. "I guess I'm a little surprised he didn't ask me for my number."

Roxie pointed her fork at me. "I thought the two of you were really hitting it off."

"So did I," I said.

Roxie shrugged nonchalantly before eyeing the tiramisu on the plate of the person sitting next to her. "He probably has a girlfriend or something."

"Maybe." I swirled the remaining wine in my glass.

I told myself it was just a fleeting connection, one that didn't mean anything. But I couldn't shake the nagging feeling that it might have been something special. Something rare that I'd never get the chance to explore.

4

James

Well, that was disappointing.

I really thought there was a spark between Hallie and me tonight. A spark I couldn't ignore.

From the moment she walked into the Grangers' kitchen with her extremely loud friend, I was drawn to her. Even with the room already humming with people, she stood out—not because she was loud or trying to command attention, but because she didn't need to.

While Roxie turned heads the second she entered, all striking features and effortless allure, Hallie had a quieter kind of presence. The kind that lingered. Roxie moved like she was born to be the center of the room, Hallie didn't need the spotlight—she just showed up fully, completely herself.

When everyone else tried to appear how they *thought* the world wanted them to appear, Hallie was refreshingly real. And maybe that's what pulled me in the most. She didn't try to impress. She didn't have to.

She had that effortless beauty that others spent thousands of dollars trying to achieve. Her eyes and hair were a rich chocolate color, her skin was a creamy porcelain, and her small frame made her appear almost doll-like.

But even if she didn't come from the same place that the

women I grew up with did, she was no different. They were all the same. All of them looking for someone with a trust fund that could support the lifestyle they wanted—take them to fancy restaurants or buy them a Birkin. At best, they hoped they'd find a man that would get down on one knee with a ring from Tiffany's and a family house ready to be passed down to them on the coast in Connecticut.

I'd already faced disappointment once, and I didn't want to experience it again.

I hadn't lied when I said I needed to leave. When my phone had gone off during dessert, I'd expected an automated notification on the markets after they'd all closed. Instead, I'd gotten a cryptic message from someone I hadn't expected to hear from—Theodore Drake.

The Drake family owned Rooster, the world's first search engine. They were one of the most powerful families in the country and probably the world. They had grown their small family tech business into a world-renowned gladiator that now led the way in multiple different fields. All the message said was that he had some important, time-sensitive information for me that would apply to Berkley Williams, the company I worked for, and one of the largest investment firms on Wall Street. Theo and I had met in passing at various parties. We barely knew each other, but in investment banking, connections were key.

And the message was too tempting to pass up. If Theo had valuable information, it could not only avoid a potential disaster for the firm and its clients, but it could boost my career. It could even help me get one step closer to opening my own investment firm. If Theo's message was as big as I predicted it to be, my intervention tomorrow could sway the loyalty of some of the firm's clients to me.

Theo had asked to meet at The Nest, one of many of Manhattan's private clubs, known for its exclusivity and privacy. Staff checked phones at the door, and the club's board hand-selected new members. They picked their clientele on a variety of factors that were a mystery to the public, but many guessed it aimed to create a diverse space for its clients for both business and pleasure.

The lobby was nondescript and appeared more like the lobby of a hotel than a club housing some of the wealthiest and most influential people in the world. The concierge greeted me with a lockbox, which I placed my phone in before they gave me a card that would grant me access to the floor Theo was on—one of the many bars in the twenty-thousand-square-foot facility.

The room was dimly lit by gold wall sconces, lavishly decorated with round velvet booths that provided privacy, high-top tables in the middle of the floor if one wanted to be seen, and a bar that took up one entire wall serving clients looking to make business deals or simply decompress from the day's events.

In the darkest corner of the room, Theodore Drake reclined in a booth. His hair, a light blonde, was short on the sides and messier on top. Tattoos snaked up his neck, peeking out from his collar. He was the exact opposite of what a leader of the largest tech company in the world would look like, which is probably why his brother Peter was the CEO while Theo worked as a vice president.

"Theo, it's been a while." I slid into the booth. A waiter appeared moments later to take my order. Theo was nursing a glass of scotch already, the sweat on the outside of his glass showing he'd been there for quite some time.

"It has." Theo brought his glass up to his lips for a sip. "I've been debating all day on whether I should even do this. What we are about to talk about could be considered illegal. It's in a definite gray area. But the topic itself is far more illegal than this mere warning will be."

I had to school my features lest I give away my surprise at Theo's bluntness. People knew him for being aloof.

The waiter dropped my Old Fashioned down in front of me. "I'm all ears."

"My brother will complete a deal tomorrow that will make Rooster a monopoly. It won't be obvious, but it *will* be a monopoly. Tonight, I'll be breaking the news to the press. I have a reporter coming after I meet with you."

Measuring my thoughts, I tapped the side of my glass with my ring.

Tink. Tink. Tink.

"Why are you telling *me* this?" I asked. In this business, information like this never came freely.

"Because I know that you've been aiming to open your own investment firm. Leveraging information like this could gain you the upper hand within your firm and its clients."

Theo's blue eyes were nearly clear—icy like his demeanor could be—and as sharp as knives as he studied me. But instead of feeling like his prey, this felt like a lone wolf pairing up at the most opportune time.

"What do you want in return, Theo?" I took another sip of my drink. "Information like this never comes free. You and I both know that."

Theo's gaze was predatory. He took his time watching me from across the booth. Unable to resist playing with food, even if he had no intention of eating this time. "I'm gathering favors for when the time is right."

"What company will be there to take over if you saddle it with antitrust lawsuits?" I asked, my brain already working on how to mitigate the fallout at work with Rooster's stocks sure to plummet.

"That's my worry. Not yours, Rossi. Rooster is so large that it can afford to have some limbs cut off to remain intact. Peter will have to step down and finally allow the company to step into a new age. Rather than repeating past successes without adding anything new, Rooster needs innovation.

Then, like a snake uncoiling, Theo stood from the booth and re-buttoned his jacket. "Now, I have the reporter waiting for me upstairs. I presume we're finished here?"

"Sure." I left my glass half-drunk on the table and stood. "It's a pleasure doing business with you, Theo."

"I look forward to the future." Theo gave me one more meaningful look before disappearing into the club.

As I watched him leave, I knew with certainty that Theodore Drake was cutting the head off the king, only to take the crown for himself. But not before leaving me with his sword to use for my protection.

"Your stop," the cab driver barked from the front seat as the taxi pulled up to a Dumbo warehouse someone had converted into a nightclub. Lights pulsed inside, visible from the windows on the top floor. I wanted to be anywhere but a new club in Brooklyn on a Saturday night, especially because I was nearly done writing my Rooster piece for Monday's market reopening. But I'd gotten an S.O.S. text about my cousin Brandon.

It was his twenty-first birthday, and I figured I was going to be walking into a fire in need of putting out. Instead, they ushered me to the VIP section, a gift from my father to his nephew. Brandon was surrounded by his degenerate friends with a hostess perched on his lap. Now I understood my uncle's text message asking me to keep Brandon out of trouble.

"James!" Brandon hoisted an entire bottle of champagne in the air, his other arm wrapped around the waist of the hostess. "You made it!"

The bottle came dangerously close to smacking the head of his friend next to him.

"Woah, there!" Before any damage could be done, I snagged the bottle out of Brandon's hand. "Maybe let's keep the drinks on the table and out of the air."

"You're no fun when you're sober. You know that, right?" Brandon looked at the hostess still perched on his lap. "Can you get my cousin a drink? He needs to catch up. You still drink Old Fashioneds, James?"

"I'm good—" But the hostess disappeared before I could wave her off. If I was going to have to babysit my drunk cousin, Old Fashioneds weren't a luxury I could indulge in tonight. "Thanks."

"Isn't she great?" My cousin yelled over the sound of the thumping bass that was already rattling my eardrums.

"She's something," I replied, my voice already starting

to grow hoarse from shouting to be heard above the music.

Brandon huffed out a laugh as he took another swig straight from the champagne bottle. "You've barely entertained a single woman that's looked your way since Cassidy. It's been over a year."

Annoyance settled in the bottom of my stomach. "Is everybody counting or something? I'll date someone when I'm ready and find someone that wants me for *me* and not my wealth."

My cousin lifted his hands up in mock surrender. "I was only trying to look out for your happiness."

A flash of the conversation I had with Hallie at last night's dinner flashed into my mind. I had never had as much fun having meaningless conversation with a stranger through a dinner or getting to know her over dessert.

But if she'd realized you're just another finance guy on Wall Street, she'd have dismissed you as arrogant and repulsive like the rest of them.

"I can handle myself." As I leaned back in my seat, I remembered the fiery conversation I'd heard about between my father and his brother yesterday as I stopped by my parents' apartment. "What's going on with the restaurant? Dad seems tense lately."

Brandon wiped a dribble of champagne off his chin, his eyes glossy with too much alcohol. His dark eyes—just like our dads'—carried that typical Rossi fire and he had the same sharp features that I did. We were often mistaken for brothers rather than cousins. "Uncle G and Dad sat down last week to look at this year's projections based on the current traffic the restaurant has seen so far this year. It's not looking good. With the price of goods going up and fewer customers coming in the door, Dad thinks we have a year tops before we go under."

The full Old Fashioned now in my hand was looking more appealing with every word Brandon said.

"It's that bad?"

"Well, you're off wearing your fancy suits and managing billions of dollars. I would guess he wouldn't want to bother you with our menial family problems. Besides, what do you care? You're the only one who doesn't help at the restaurant. Even Emilia comes in on the weekends when she isn't studying for some test or playing volleyball."

That jab stung. It wasn't lost on me that my younger cousin, with his Rossi features and his reckless enthusiasm, had put in more hours at the restaurant than I had. Even his younger sister beat me in that regard, and she was still in high school. But making pizzas and cleaning tables had never been my dream.

"Hey, Brandon. Just because I'm not slinging pizzas every night doesn't mean I don't care about our family and its legacy." I took a swig of my drink, nearly downing half of it to take the edge off the conversation—and the music that seemed to be shaking my skull. "An argument tonight won't get us anywhere, and it certainly won't help our dads. I'm not here to fight."

Brandon sighed dramatically, leaning back in his chair with the bottle in hand. "Can I give the restaurant a lump sum?" The question felt ridiculous coming out of my mouth while my cousin was on his way to being wasted.

"Sure," Brandon shrugged. "The restaurant would use it. But that still won't solve the issue. We need to get more customers in the door. I've suggested concentrating on social media, but you know how our parents are. They think that it's a waste of time and wouldn't work. What we really need is the pizzeria to go viral."

Brandon might have been young and dumb, but he was on to something. Money wouldn't solve the problem outright. It would just prolong the inevitable. The only solution was to make the restaurant a New York City staple. It might have been my younger cousin's idea, but I knew I had to be the one to figure something out to avoid my family's legacy being taken away.

5

Hallie

As I walked through the doors of *Sophisticate* on Monday morning, I hit post on a new review to my social media page. A taco truck had opened on my usual route into work, and I knew it needed to be featured the second that chorizo hit my tongue.

One of my favorite things about reviewing food was how it could change lives. It's the universal love language that everyone understands. Despite our differences, we all know when something has an explosion of flavors or delivers a warmth that settles into our souls. When the food is good, it's made as a labor of love. People that delivered delicious food like that deserved to be celebrated, and I knew that sometimes that recognition could change their lives forever.

"Hallie, have you got a plan for your first finance bro article?" Anthea breezed past my desk wearing a deep purple power suit that let everyone know she meant business. I swiped out of my account and dropped my phone down on my desk, trying to buy myself a few seconds to collect myself.

"Yes!" I exclaimed. Anthea raised an eyebrow. "I think this series can be sustainable for about two months. That should give me enough time to find the most eligible Wall

Street bachelor and date him long enough for the piece to be both entertaining and meaningful."

"Yes. That sounds great and all," Anthea mused, "but how are you going to do it?"

"Well, according to my sources," I started. My "sources" being Roxie, but Anthea didn't need to know that. "Tuesdays are the new Fridays in New York. So, I'm going to head down to Whiskey Locker tomorrow night. We both know finance guys love to work late. Their happy hour is more like eight o'clock, rather than five. Then I'll try to secure my first date."

Anthea gave me a nod of approval. "You need to do more than just *try*, Hallie. You need to succeed." She leaned in close and dropped her voice to a volume only she and I could hear. "This series can boost the magazine's numbers, and I'm counting on it." With that, she breezed toward her office, showing off her custom Nikes. Because she was the person who pulled off a power suit and sneakers.

"God, I want to be her," Janelle sighed next to me.

"Maybe matcha latte girl led you astray," Roxie said as she stirred the tiny straw around in her drink.

I sighed. "But there were so many comments on my article seconding what the girl I overheard said. Maybe this is just the wrong night. I could have misremembered what I wrote."

There were only a few patrons inside of Whiskey Locker and it was nearly eight already. A few men had come in, briefcases in hand, for a drink at the bar. But none of them had seemed interested in the handful of women lingering at the high-top tables, including Roxie and me.

"Let's give it another hour and then we can leave. Maybe I need to consider a different bar," I sighed, thinking about how I would report this to Anthea when she asked for an update. I had no idea how I was supposed to tell her I'd already hit a roadblock.

There goes the restaurant critic position and your dreams.

"If this place is still dead in an hour, I am dragging you to that new club near our apartment. We didn't get all dressed up on a weeknight for nothing."

"Roxie, you host parties on weeknights at the gallery regularly. This is nothing new for you." I eyed my best friend. She was the only girl I knew that could make a pair of latex pants look stylish and not like something out of an adult movie.

"Exactly, but *you* rarely go out. So I'm not wasting this opportunity to have drinks on a weeknight with my best friend." Roxie reached out to clink her glass against mine.

As if on cue, the doors to Whiskey Locker opened and a squad of well-dressed men walked in together—expensive watches glinting on their wrists and country-club-style vests providing them some break against the chillier evening air, suit jackets already ditched.

"I take it back. Matcha latte girl did not lead you astray," Roxie leaned over to whisper in my ear. "Fair warning, I'm overdue a long night with an attractive man."

"Noted," I replied. That was Roxie's way of letting me know that if the opportunity presented itself, she would leave with someone. But only if I was comfortable.

The group of men stopped at the bar first, and as if it were a rite of passage to complete their finance bro look, each of them ordered an Old Fashioned. With their drinks in hand, they began scanning the bar for their entertainment for the night.

A man with short, neatly trimmed auburn hair caught my eye. He was engaged in a conversation with his friends, likely discussing the news that had broken this morning about Rooster. According to an anonymous insider, the world's first search engine had become too large and too driven by profit. The source leaked details about a deal the CEO was finalizing today, which could potentially lead the company into legal trouble. Social media had been going crazy all day about the plummet the company's stocks took.

But despite the deep conversation he was in, he flashed me a smile and excused himself from his group.

"Incoming," Roxie whisper-sang as the man approached us.

Blue eyes.

A small scar on his left eyebrow.

A full beard that matched his hair.

Wait? Was that a small silver hoop in his left ear?

"How are you doing?" He leaned one arm on the table next to me, Old Fashioned still in hand. "I'm Mark."

"Hallie." I stuck my hand out for him to shake.

His hand wrapped around mine and I waited for the same shiver to run down my spine when James had first shaken my hand last Friday night. It had been a while since I'd dated seriously in New York. I'd always found it wildly impossible before. So, I took my interaction with James as mere excitement to be putting myself back out there again.

But no shiver ever came.

"Hallie. That's a beautiful name," he said as he slid into the open seat next to me.

"What do you do, Mark?" I asked, even though it was painfully obvious. Nevertheless, Mark's eyes lit up as he explained to me he was an investment banker. Within a matter of ten minutes, I learned that he'd attended Brown and was a member of Delta Sigma. By the time he finally took a breath, I'd drained my entire glass of wine.

"Can I get you a refill?" Mark asked me.

"Please, a Riesling," I told him, suddenly thankful to be sitting in silence once more. Without the article looming over me, there was no way I'd even let this guy get me a drink, never mind be hoping he'd ask me out on a date. I would probably pass out from boredom before we even shared a kiss. Maybe this assignment was going to be harder than I'd originally planned.

A few of Mark's friends patted him on the back as they walked by, their eyes glancing back toward me and Roxie. One friend hiked his head in our direction before making his way over, smiling at Roxie.

"It's about damn time," she huffed. "I look way too good to not get at least a little flirt in tonight."

"Maybe switch to an espresso martini," I suggested. "Nudge me if you hear me snoring over here."

"Oh, please. I have no plans to let this man talk about work." Roxie fluffed her dirty-blonde hair before turning on her megawatt smile. It was mesmerizing watching Roxie suck the poor guy into her vortex, charming him like a snake whisperer.

He doesn't even know what's coming for him.

I glanced back toward Mark to see where he was at with my glass of wine, only to find him wrapped up in a conversation with someone eerily familiar.

Tall.

Dark.

Handsome.

Unmistakable blue eyes that I could see from here.

"You've got to be kidding me."

James caught my eye over Mark's shoulder and gave me a quick wink—like we were in on something together, even though I had no idea what it was. Then he turned his attention back to who I had *hoped* would be my first potential date and cuffed him on the shoulder as if they were old friends.

The bartender placed my fresh glass of wine before Mark, who was now fully distracted by James.

Of course.

After James had vanished from Michelle's dinner party without leaving so much as an email address or social media handle, part of me wished to never cross paths with him again. That he'd just be another blip in a long string of strange New York encounters. But now, here he was, standing in front of the one person I'd made an effort to connect with tonight, siphoning off his attention with a wink and a pat on the back.

Why was he even *here*? This place wasn't exactly known for its moody cocktails or understated charm—it was packed wall-to-wall with Patagonia vests and high-yield egos. The kind of bar where the drinks were overpriced, and someone was always bragging about Series C.

I pushed away from my seat, catching Roxie's eye for

only a second. She was fully immersed in her conversation, effortlessly commanding the attention of the man sitting next to her. She had that gift—blending in effortlessly, like she belonged wherever she landed. It was a trait I envied. I always felt like I needed an instruction manual just to get through a conversation with a stranger.

Roxie's eyes slid from mine to look over toward Mark and widened when she realized who he was talking to.

I moved closer, my heels clicking louder than I intended, just in time to overhear Mark say, "Seriously, man, your market report on Rooster was genius."

Rooster?

I paused mid-step.

All the news could talk about was the leadership shake-up the company was facing and an investor freak-out on Wall Street today.

James tilted his head modestly, and I suddenly noticed the way his suit fit just a little too perfectly. Not trendy, not flashy—expensive in a way that whispered instead of shouted. His whole vibe was easy confidence. Cool competence. The exact energy I'd learned to associate with boardrooms and Bloomberg terminals.

No.

No, no, no.

"Oh, Hayley! Here's that glass of Riesling for you," Mark exclaimed once he noticed me standing next to them.

"Thank you." I took the glass of wine from him and tried my best to avoid making eye contact with James. "And it's Ha—"

"You saved nearly a billion dollars across our

portfolios today with your write-up on the situation. I'm not sure anyone in the firm's history has ever done that before." Mark was staring at James like he was the second coming.

My fingers tightened around the stem of the wineglass. The words tumbled out of Mark's mouth and hit me one by one, each heavier than the last. Portfolios. Write-Up. Billion dollars.

Oh my god.

James *was* a man in finance.

And I'd spent the other night—an entire meal—casually dragging men in his profession to his face.

Nice one, Hallie. And this is why you're still single.

"I just wanted to make sure our clients' investments were safe." James lifted one shoulder in a half-hearted shrug. "You know, I thought I noticed you could have shifted a few of the accounts you manage today."

The simple comment leeched all color from Mark's face and after a long pause, he glanced down at his watch. "This has been great, James. But I just remembered I have some work left to do." And without a glance in my direction, he hurried out of Whiskey Locker like the place was on fire.

As he left, I could feel James's eyes on me now, his attention unshakable and intense. It was like he was pulling me into his orbit with every passing second. I wanted to look anywhere but at him, but my body betrayed me, as my gaze lifted to meet his.

God, how tall *was* he? Six-four? Six-five, maybe? He made Mark—who I'd mentally filed as "tall enough"—look like a teenage boy who hadn't hit his growth spurt yet.

"Did he just . . . ?" I muttered, more to myself than to the man standing next to me—who I wasn't entirely sure just potentially thwarted my lead for the evening on purpose.

"At least you got a drink out of the situation." James's voice slid through the air like velvet as he clinked his Old Fashioned against my wineglass. "It's not a complete loss of an evening."

"What are you doing here?" The clink of our glasses taking me out of my shocked stupor.

A smirk curled at the corner of his lips, slow and sure. "I'm just enjoying a nice evening out." His eyes darkened as they held mine, lingering. "I think the better question is what are *you* doing here?"

It was clear what James was getting at. With most of the clientele of this bar being men who worked in the financial district, that simple quirk of his eyebrow told me he knew *exactly* what I was doing here.

I let out a long sigh, the weight of rejection settling heavily in my chest. I'd tried to brush it off in the days since the dinner party, but it was still lingering. I'd thought we'd hit it off—our conversation had flowed so easily, so naturally. It had felt simple, like the beginning of something. I'd expected a contact exchange, maybe even a suggestion to meet up again. But instead, he left me stunned, slipping away from the Grangers' house without so much as a goodbye or any way to reach him.

And now, standing here in a bar full of finance bros, I realized something I hadn't before: he never told me what he did for a living. Not once. And I, brilliant in my red lipstick and righteous opinions, had offered my unfiltered thoughts on men in his exact profession—to his face.

Of course he'd taken it personally. How could he not?

I just hadn't realized it then.

So why do I want to try having another conversation with him?

Before I could subject myself to more embarrassment, I looked for the quickest escape route out of this conversation. "Roxie and I were just about to leave, actually. I figured I'd cut my losses since that's now two men that have run from me in the last week."

I should've just walked away. But something about the tension between us made me want to face it, if only to get it over with. Maybe it was the look in his eyes—cooler now, unreadable in a way they hadn't been at dinner. So I didn't sugarcoat it.

"And if you were going to ghost me, you could've at least waited until we finished dessert."

James let out a laugh, low and quiet, but the warmth from the Grangers' dining room wasn't behind it anymore. The spark I'd seen was gone. He'd built something between us now. A wall. And I couldn't tell if he was waiting for me to climb it or back away.

"Are you sure you were leaving with your friend?" James didn't even look bothered by my comment as he glanced over my shoulder toward where Roxie and I were first sitting at the bar. "I don't think she got that memo."

I turned to see two empty seats where Roxie and the other guy that had approached her had been. With one glance at my phone, I saw a text from her telling me she'd hit it off with "Greg" and was going to grab a bite to eat with him, but to let her know how my search for my first date goes.

"You've got to be kidding me . . ."

As if this night couldn't get any worse. While I was happy for Roxie, the best chance I had at securing a date before the end of the week when my first article would be due was now slim to none tonight. Maybe I should have written about her escapades and passed them off as mine.

"Better luck next time." The wink James gave me nearly sent me over the edge.

"Apparently, my luck has dried out." I laughed bitterly, feeling the wine in my system loosen my tongue more than it should have. "First you leave without giving me your number after I thought we had a rather great conversation over dinner. But now it makes sense, because I probably offended you the entire time. Then I get ditched by my first potential muse for my series. Why am I even surprised? I am trying to write an article about finding the most eligible bachelor out of a group of workaholics."

There was a long stretch of silence once I'd finished my rant. I could feel the tension thickening the air around us like a fog. James's brow furrowed slightly as if my bluntness had caught him off guard. He cleared his throat, looking uncomfortable for a second, before speaking again, his voice softer this time.

"The reason I didn't ask for your number," he began, his eyes avoiding mine, "is because you seem to have rather strong opinions about men in the financial sector and while it's perfectly alright for you to have those opinions . . . I didn't think they would suit us well if we had moved forward with the night."

The moment his words left his mouth, I wanted nothing more than to crawl into a hole. Of course, I'd been too honest with him. I could feel my face heating up with the realization of how easily I'd let my feelings spill out, and now I was standing here, feeling like a fool.

I took a deep breath, trying to steady myself. "That doesn't mean my opinions would have applied to you."

James offered a small, almost regretful smile. "Well, I'm not a fan of your plan to use my coworkers and peers for your own personal gain and plaster it all over a magazine."

I let out a frustrated sigh. As much as I hated being called out for this assignment that I also did not want to do, I understood where he was coming from. But that didn't mean I wasn't going down without a fight, seeing that he had just crashed my entire evening, knowing full well what this article meant for me.

I crossed my arms, trying to hold my ground, but I couldn't help the flush creeping up my neck. "You can't deny that every man that works in finance that comes to this bar is intending to meet someone."

James's eyes softened, his posture loosening a bit. "Even if that were true," he said, "they aren't asking for their conversations to be exploited for the world to read."

The tips of James's ears had turned pink over the course of our argument, and if I wasn't mad, I might have found it cute.

It's not like I enjoy writing articles about my dating adventures. I'd much rather write about the new restaurant in Hell's Kitchen that had the best jalapeño poppers in the city or the bakery with scones so moist, they melted on your tongue.

I crossed my arms over my chest. "We all do things we don't want to do sometimes and it's not like you can stop me from having a conversation with *every* man in the financial sector at *every* bar they frequent."

James lifted one perfect eyebrow. "Try me."

6

Hallie

"Honey!" My parents' faces appeared on my computer screen, far closer than they needed to be as the video call connected. "It's so good to see you. Does she look a little thin to you, Richard?"

"Mom, I'm fine."

"Molly, she looks the same as she did last week," my dad grumbled.

"Have you been eating, sweetie? I know it's expensive out there in New York." My mother leaned into the camera, trying to get a better look at me while giving me a better look at the inside of her nostrils. "You know you can always come home if things get too hard."

"Mom, I promise I'm doing fine." Our weekly calls always started out much the same. My mother would have some unwarranted concern that would prompt her to suggest me moving home, and my father would grumble in the background, telling my mother that I was fine.

"I liked last week's 'Overheard in NYC', Hallie." My dad cut my mom off from continuing even further on the rant.

"Thanks, Dad." Every week, my dad would send me his notes on my tiny column. Giving his thoughts on everything I overheard around the city. Sometimes I toyed with the idea of pitching an "Advice from Richard Woods" section because of how unintentionally funny he was with his feedback.

Just last week he'd equated online dating to a build-your-own boyfriend machine.

"Oh, add that bagel place you reviewed to the list of places you need to take me the next time I come visit," he added. "That might have been my favorite one you've done on that social media page of yours."

"How's Roxie, honey?" My mom cut back in. "Are the two of you staying safe when you go out?"

I loved my parents. They were good people, and they meant well. But the most they'd ever known was the small town in Ohio that I grew up in. I still remember the confusion on their faces when I told them I wanted to go to NYU instead of one of the state schools in Ohio. Then again, when I graduated, and I told them I wasn't moving home. New York City was a large, unknown danger that they had no concept of despite the tourist excursions they'd taken whenever they visited.

"We're doing good, Mom. Thanks for asking."

"Have either of you gone on any dates?" My mom tried to take on an air of nonchalance despite the fact she asked for an update on my dating life at least once a month. It didn't help that my younger sister was already married with a baby on the way. In my mother's eyes, I was behind the eight ball.

Dating had never been my strongest suit. I'd spent most of my twenties focused on my career, and the few relationships I had were either too brief or fizzled out before they could really go anywhere. My mom never let me forget it—always asking, gently, but persistently, when it would be *my* turn to bring someone home to meet the family.

"Actually, I've been dating more than usual," I admitted. "It's for a new series my boss asked me to write."

"Like a bigger column?" My dad asked excitedly.

"What series are you writing about that requires you to go on dates?" My mom asked at the same time, her voice laced with concern. Honestly, me and her both.

"Yes, a bigger column and it was a request from my boss. I couldn't really say no, and to be honest, my career depends on it."

I glanced at them through the screen. They were frozen. My dad's expression had gone completely blank, while my mom's face twisted into something dangerously close to skepticism.

"If I write this column, I get a shot at my dream job."

"The restaurant critic position?" I could always trust my father to be overly excited for every opportunity that came my way.

"Yes, the restaurant critic position."

Despite my parents' inability to see the love I had for this city, for the work I wanted to do here, they both looked thoroughly excited for me.

"That's great, honey." My mother's smile was wide and genuine. Growing up, they'd watched me develop my love of food. Two regular parents that tried their best to provide their daughter with as many cultural food experiences as their predominantly white community had in store.

"How's Kate?" I asked.

With my little sister being pregnant with her first kid,

and me being hundreds of miles away, we'd had little time to see each other. Doctors deemed her pregnancy risky early on, eliminating air travel as an option. It had been nearly two years since I'd taken the time to fly back to Ohio. Every time my parents picked me up from the airport and we pulled onto the two-lane road that led into my old hometown, I felt cast into limbo. No longer the little kid that played on the playground in the town's only park. No longer the teenager that had her first kiss in the tiny drive-in movie theater with one screen. Not even the fledgling adult that packed up all her belongings and left all she knew behind for whatever lay beyond the town's limits.

The person I'd become no longer fit into the constraints of my hometown. While a part of me would always belong there, that person no longer existed.

Sometimes it was easier to just *not* try to fit myself back into that old body, the previous version of me that no longer felt right.

"Kate's doing well. Her doctor will probably make her bedridden starting next week. They said she has preeclampsia. So better safe than sorry." My mother sighed. "It would be nice for you to visit before the baby arrives."

"I'll try my best." It was the same excuse I used every time they asked. "I will definitely be there after the baby is born."

My phone buzzed on the table next to my laptop.

Roxie: Whiskey Locker in an hour?
Hallie: Wrapping up a call with my parents. I'll meet you there?

> **Roxie:** Tell Richard and Molly I said hi :)
>
> **Roxie:** Wear something hot tonight. We're getting you a finance bro one way or another.

"I've got to run. Roxie's waiting for me for . . . dinner tonight. I'll talk to you guys next week?" My parents nodded and waved as I disconnected the call.

Roxie was right. After striking out on my first attempt at securing a date for "Love on Wall Street" because of James's intervention, the only solution was to try again. Show up on a different day and hope that my very attractive arch-nemesis had somewhere else to be tonight.

Tonight called for the leather jacket that was collecting dust in the back of my closet. I wasn't about to let the opportunity of a lifetime slip out of my grasp just because I ran into a roadblock. Even if that roadblock had the warmest blue eyes I'd ever seen, a smile that made my stomach flip, and a stupid dimple. Did I mention he was really, really tall?

"What about them?" Roxie pointed toward two men casually leaning by the dart board in the far corner of Whiskey Locker. Both had their suit jackets draped over their chairs, sleeves rolled up to reveal well-toned forearms. They looked nearly identical—perfectly styled hair, clean-shaven, expensive watches, shoes without a single scuff on them. Each of them held an Old Fashioned.

They were just what I needed.

Without allowing enough time for my mind to talk me out of it, I slid off my stool and sauntered across the bar, with Roxie following closely behind.

"You know, I've always found people who can play darts so impressive." I hated how my voice rose in pitch, as if I suddenly shared matcha latte girl's personality. "Every time I even attempt to play, I never get a single one on the board."

The only difference between the men standing in front of us was their hair color—one dark and the other fair. Except for that, from their suits to their watches, their shoes to their clean shaves, they were pretty much interchangeable. The blond guy had posed to throw his dart, but dropped his hand and gestured for me to step forward.

"I can help you, if you'd like." He smiled, a row of gleaming white teeth shining back at me. "I'm Graham."

"It's nice to meet you, Graham. I'm Hallie," I told him as I stepped in front of him to the white line on the ground. Graham was average build, average height, without a single blemish on his face. Everything about him was *average*. But that didn't stop me from ever so slightly enjoying the feel of him behind me as he drew close.

All it took Roxie was a sly look as she tucked her hair behind her ear for Graham's friend to pull a chair out for her and slide into the free one across from her. The two already diving into their own conversation.

"It's all in the wrist," he murmured. He handed me a dart, his breath tickling my ear, and gently guided my hand upward. Unlike James's rich timbre, his voice was much lighter. It barely tickled my eardrum, where James's voice sunk deep into my bones.

Why the fuck are you thinking about James? Pull yourself together. That's the last person you should think about right now.

With Graham's hand guiding me, I pulled my arm back

slightly before throwing the dart toward the board, fully expecting it to bounce off like every other time I'd ever played.

Instead, it stuck. In the far upper left of the board, but it stuck.

"Oh my gosh!" I jumped for joy, completely caught up in the moment. "I did it!"

Graham laughed as he watched me bounce on the balls of my feet. "You did it!"

"Only because I had an excellent teacher." Graham's smile deepened and his mouth opened as he prepared to respond but was quickly interrupted. Every ounce of hope that had grown in me over the past five minutes evaporated in an instant as my brain registered the voice.

"I'll take next."

James.

He stood a few feet away. Tonight, he was in a navy suit that complemented his tan skin perfectly and if I didn't find the man infuriating, I would have allowed myself to acknowledge how attractive he looked.

What the *fuck* was James doing here again? Didn't this man have any other bars to spend his happy hours at? Or late hours to work as he sold his soul to capitalism?

James better thank his lucky stars that we were in a public place. That was the only reason I wasn't letting him have it right now.

"Sure, man." I wanted to scream with frustration as Graham gestured for James to take his spot. Blood drummed in my ears and the corners of my vision grew fuzzy as I stared at the smirk on James's face.

The last thing I wanted was to let him think he'd

swooped in and thwarted my evening once again. If James wanted to play, then we were going to play.

"Graham, do you mind getting me another glass of wine?" I asked lightly, offering him my glass with a smile. He didn't hesitate, sliding out of his seat almost eagerly. I got some sort of sick thrill from the way James's eyes narrowed.

"It would be my pleasure."

I knew I was playing with fire, but I felt strangely brave tonight. Bold, even. Maybe it was the wine, or maybe it was the sting of James's intervention still lingering like cheap perfume. Either way, I wasn't going to let him thwart my plans a second time.

"What a fool," I heard James whisper under his breath as Graham made his way through the throng of people toward the bar.

"What was that?" I asked innocently, batting my lashes in his direction. James's expression hardened, and I wasn't sure which one of us was going to crack first.

"Ladies first." His voice was low as he finally looked away, gesturing to the waiting dart board. Satisfaction bloomed in my chest as I stepped forward. My shoulder brushed against his chest, and I felt the sudden tension in his body before he stepped back, creating space between us.

Following the same tips that Graham had given me earlier, I pulled my arm back and let the dart fly. It bounced off the board with a sad little thud.

"Damnit," I hissed. Despite having the finesse of a baby deer on ice, I *really* didn't want to lose to James.

"You didn't put enough behind that one." He moved

in closer, and my pulse slowed as the air seemed to warm between us.

"I don't need your help. I already have Graham's."

His jaw tightened. From this close, I could see the different shades of blue in his eyes—far too distracting for my own good.

"Graham's an idiot and is currently chatting up the bartender," James said flatly.

I glanced toward the bar. Sure enough, the bartender was leaning across the bar top and Graham looked like he was trying very hard not to drool directly into her cleavage. My empty wineglass was still in his hand.

Refusing to give James the upper hand again, I shrugged. "He'll be back."

A smirk tugged at his mouth. "Oh, he'll be back—to let his friend know he's staying put until the bartender's shift ends and skipping the next bar entirely."

"You are *infuriating*," I snapped. "You're quite full of yourself, you know that, right?"

Time suspended for a moment as James stepped closer, until his chest hovered just a breath from mine. Our inhales and exhales lined up, synced like some cruel kind of duet.

And then, I heard it—a quiet sound from deep in his throat, like he was swallowing a curse or a groan—before he backed away again. The air between us cooled instantly.

"I'm simply stating facts." That maddening smirk was back. "You know, if I didn't know any better, I'd say you aren't putting up much of a fight in this game of ours."

Without breaking the moment, he raised a hand, flicked his wrist, and sent his dart flying.

Bullseye.

"Maybe you need a new teacher, Hal."

The nickname caught me off guard. People used to call me that when I was a kid—back when I had scraped knees, wild hair, and zero interest in impressing anyone. It was something my sister shouted across the soccer field, something my dad used when he ruffled my hair before dinner.

No one had called me that in years.

And yet, from James, it didn't sound childish. It sounded intimate. Like a shared secret. Like he'd reached back in time and plucked a piece of me I didn't even know I'd left behind.

Worse still? I hated that I didn't hate it.

Then he tipped back his drink, polished it off, and disappeared into the bar—leaving me flushed, frustrated, and not entirely convinced it had anything to do with losing.

7

James

"Did you see the news about Peter Drake stepping down as CEO of Rooster?" Sebastian asked me over drinks at Whiskey Locker the following Thursday after work. "There're whispers that Theo Drake has put his hat in the ring for the selection of the new CEO."

My friend stared at me expectantly, but my mind was elsewhere. The last thing I wanted to talk about was work. I'd spent the last couple of days talking about the tech giant and its stocks. When they'd rise again. If they'd keep dropping. When we should reposition our portfolio back under them.

Instead, I watched the door, scanning each new patron as they walked in—waiting for a certain brunette to appear. I'd been buried in work until nearly ten last night and by the time I finally left the office, all I wanted to do was collapse into bed and sleep until the sun forced its way through my blinds. But still, I stopped by my favorite bar—just in case Hallie was there, working her charm and trying to seduce one of my coworkers into spilling details they'd probably rather keep to themselves.

"You know, Berkley Williams came out relatively unscathed in this complete debacle with Rooster." Sebastian's voice trickled back in over my thoughts of Hallie, which had been recurring over the last few days.

I'd spent the better part of the night after I ran into her on Tuesday reading through her biography on *Sophisticate*'s website and scrolling through social media for any signs of a Hallie Woods. All I found was a food blog that covered local eateries around the city. Each review was thoughtful and done with an intention that sought to elevate the restaurant in front of more people. Plus, she seemed to get really great engagement on there. I told myself I was only trying to find different ways to protect my friends by staying up until three in the morning scrolling through every review. But in truth, I was also curious. This was a completely different perspective of the woman I'd been convinced was calculated and ambitious.

"We managed to position our portfolio for minimum damage," I replied. "That's our job, after all."

Sebastian studied me from his side of our booth. We'd known each other long enough to know when the other was being purposefully vague.

I glanced down at my watch, ignoring the curious look my friend was giving me. It was nearly nine o'clock. If Hallie was planning on coming here tonight, she would have already showed up. I was certain of it. It was quite possible that she'd taken my threat seriously and tried her hand at a different bar to avoid me.

"Do you want to grab a night cap at McGuire's tonight?" McGuire's was another regular haunt for many of the people I worked with, though not nearly as popular as Whiskey Locker.

"We haven't gone to McGuire's in a long time," Sebastian said slowly, and I could practically see the wheels turning behind his green eyes. But because Sebastian never turned down a good time, he didn't argue when I flagged down the waiter, handed over my card without blinking, and stood to grab my coat.

McGuire's was only a few blocks away from Whiskey Locker. After a long day at the office, most of my coworkers didn't want to venture far for a drink. Whiskey Locker was newer, flashier, and definitely more upscale—but McGuire's was the kind of place that didn't need polish to have charm.

The floors were a little sticky, the bar a bit cramped, but the beer was cold and the company was good. No one came to McGuire's to be seen—they came to unwind.

Which, if I was being honest, was exactly why I'd suggested it. I hadn't been able to shake Hallie from my mind, and something told me if she hadn't already called it a night, this could be where she'd end up.

So it wasn't a surprise when I walked in and immediately spotted Hallie tucked into a corner booth with a man I didn't recognize, but could tell just from his suit that he worked for another investment firm. Roxie sat opposite her, laughing at something a second guy was saying.

Hallie's cheeks were flushed like they'd been the other night, which I now knew meant that she was a few drinks in. Tonight, she wore a short, fitted dress under a tailored blazer, the hem riding high on her thigh above sleek, knee-high boots. The dress was deep green—soft, silky-looking—and it clung in all the right places. It made it impossible not to look twice.

She looked good. Really good.

Too good.

And though I didn't want to admit it, not even to

myself, there was something about the way she laughed at whatever the guy she was with had said, the way her eyes sparkled under the dim lighting, that made it hard to breathe for a second.

I heard a throat clear from behind me. "Are you going to continue into the bar there, James?"

"Yeah, was just scoping out an open spot," I told him, despite half of the bar being completely open. To Sebastian's credit, he said nothing.

"Can I get an Old Fashioned and can you send a glass of Riesling over to that woman in the corner?" I asked the bartender as soon as we settled into a pair of chairs.

"What's gotten into you today?" Sebastian asked, his attention fixed on Hallie. "I didn't think you had it in you to go after another man's woman."

"Who's saying that's her boyfriend?" I shot back, doing my best to keep from staring as she laughed at something her companion said. Especially after the twinkling sound of her laugh made my dick twitch.

I've got to get laid.

The bartender walked over and set the glass of wine on Hallie's table. I watched as she scanned the bar, trying to find the culprit. Her mouth dropped open the minute her eyes landed on me.

I winked.

Hallie's lips moved, and I was certain she was cussing me out under her breath. Without a second thought, I pushed back from the bar and sauntered over to them.

"Who's that from?" I overheard Hallie's date asking her.

"Oh it's no one—"

"Harsh, Hal. I would think you'd place a little more importance on someone you dated for four years." I placed a hand over my heart, feigning hurt.

Hallie's jaw dropped, and those beautiful lips, painted in a dangerous shade of red, parted in disbelief.

"What are you talking ab—"

"You guys dated?" Hallie's date for the night asked. He'd combed his auburn hair over to hide a growing bald spot, I suspected, and his teeth desperately needed whitening.

I slid into the open seat at their table with a grin. "Oh yeah. We met back in college when we both attended—"

"NYU," Hallie grumbled, clearly playing along, which meant her evening must've been going worse than I initially thought.

"Yes, NYU! Hallie here was studying journalism, and I was studying finance."

Her date's interest piqued. "Finance? Where do you work now?"

"Just down the street at Berkley Williams." I narrowed my eyes playfully. "Don't you work at BAT?"

Hallie tracked the unfolding scene, her eyes darting between us.

"Excuse me, everyone," Sebastian's voice broke in as he placed a hand on my shoulder. "I figured I'd join the party since my friend here so rudely ditched me at the bar."

Sebastian fell into the last empty spot next to Roxie and her date for the evening. Before throwing an arm across the back of Roxie's seat, he shook her date's hand. Seb's accidental touch made Roxie tense up.

"Sebastian Whittaker." Seb extended his free hand to her, flashing a smile that could disarm anyone. I swear that man could charm a nun away from her lifelong commitment with just a smile. What caught my attention, though, was seeing Roxie—who I'd watched so easily win people over at the Grangers' dinner—become visibly flustered under Seb's focus.

"Roxie King." Roxie recovered after a few seconds of free fall and placed her hand in Sebastian's.

"Well, now it's a party." Sebastian tossed a wink at Roxie and she immediately turned the color of a ripe tomato, clearly caught off guard, before he motioned for the bartender to bring the group another round of drinks. He reached into his jacket pocket and pulled out a sleeve of Cuban cigars—Seb's favorite vice.

"We were kind of on a date," Hallie cut in, motioning to the two men at the table. Roxie's date looked to be engrossed in whoever he was texting on his phone while Hallie's date was far more interested in having a conversation about the market trends with me than asking her any stereotypical first-date questions.

So, what do you like to do in your free time?
What's your favorite movie?
What's your dream job?

I was certain Hallie hadn't shared her hopes of becoming a restaurant critic for *Sophisticate*, because that would require admitting why exactly she was on this date in the first place.

"Are you sure about that?" I shot back, relishing the frustration that pinched her forehead as Seb and I made no effort to leave.

"You've got some explaining to do." Sebastian leaned over to whisper in my ear once the bartender dropped off another round of what everyone was drinking. I gladly took the cigar he offered me, needing something to calm my nerves. For some reason, Hallie flirting with this guy was making me edgy. Between this week's encounter at Whiskey Locker and tonight, I was more tense than Wall Street on the morning of a market crash.

"There's nothing to explain," I told him. Because *what would I even say?*

I met this girl at the Grangers' last Friday night. She hates everything about men in finance and is writing a piece for work on what it's like to date us. So now I've made it my personal mission to make sure she has the least amount of material to work with.

I'd sound like a raging lunatic, and even Seb would start to worry about me.

"What are you doing?" Hallie's voice cut through the haze of cigar smoke, tinged with disapproval.

"I'm enjoying a drink with good company, Hal."

"Don't call me Hal," she hissed.

"Why not? I think it's a rather cute nickname." The twitch in her left eye said otherwise, but I didn't let up.

"It reminds me of Dennis Quaid in *The Parent Trap*." Hallie crossed her arms over her chest, her date now completely forgotten. But I wasn't sure he minded because he was now chatting happily with Roxie's date.

"And that's a bad thing?" I asked.

"Yes, because *The Parent Trap* is one of my favorite comfort movies and you don't get to ruin that for me."

A lazy smile spread across my face. I wasn't about to feel bad for messing with her. Especially when doing so meant she had those big, beautiful brown eyes locked on me, giving me more of a challenge than I had bargained for.

"Maybe we both just have great taste in movies."

Hallie rolled her eyes and turned her body toward me. Her leg brushed mine under the table, and I forced myself to ignore the way my stomach flipped.

She's an attractive woman. It's not your fault your body responds like that to her.

"Don't flatter yourself. It's not cute." She tossed her hair over her shoulder, and the floral scent of her perfume washed over me.

This Hallie was a far cry from the woman I'd met at the Grangers'. When I first saw her walk into their kitchen she'd been a little shy, reserved, and waited for Roxie to take the lead. Now? She was giving as good as she got.

"You didn't mention at dinner on Friday that you have a food blog," I said, and Hallie lit up, only for a moment.

She had her guard back up, but I'd seen that brief glimmer at the question about her blog and I liked it.

"How do you know about that?"

Logic told me I couldn't possibly admit that I'd spent far too many hours since we'd first met searching for as much information as I could find about her on the internet. Because if I did, I wasn't sure I had an answer if she asked *why*.

So instead, I listened to my good sense and lied my ass off.

"I was looking at reviews for this new bagel place in the West Village I'd heard about, and I stumbled across a post that featured someone I recognized." The lie felt clumsy, but I was rewarded with a small smile on Hallie's face.

"You should go. Those bagels changed my life." But her smile disappeared as fast as it came, as if Hallie remembered that the two of us were squaring off like two cowboys in the Wild West.

"Eli?" Hallie directed her attention back to her date. I'd forgotten he had even been there. "Do you want to go grab a quick bite?"

The sweet smile she gave him would have probably brought me to my knees. But just as she flashed it to him, Eli's phone buzzed on the table. He glanced at the screen, his face falling slightly. "I'm sorry, I've got to head back into the office. This was a great time, though. I've enjoyed chatting with you all." He shot a half-hearted smile before standing up and quickly making an exit.

And then he was gone.

Hallie took a deep breath. When she finally spoke, she looked squarely at me. And, if I'm being honest, maybe it was a little fucked up that I found it hot.

"This isn't some game, James. You can't keep trying to sabotage my article. It's going to get written, no matter how hard you try to stop it." Hallie stood up suddenly from the table, her frustration crackling in the air.

"You're 0–3, Hal." I couldn't resist throwing in one more jab, reminding her of every conversation that I'd interrupted.

"0–4," she muttered under her breath.

"What was that?"

Hallie swallowed, and I couldn't help but follow the

movement. "I'm 0–4 on getting asked out. Struck out last night, even without your interference."

A smug grin crept onto my face. "So, if this *were* an actual game we were playing, I'd be winning?"

I had more important things to focus on—my family's restaurant, my dream of opening my own investment firm—but, honestly, nothing seemed as entertaining as messing with Hallie Woods.

Hallie grabbed her purse. "Roxie, I'm out of here."

Roxie quickly jumped from her seat next to Seb, looking like she wanted to put as much space between the two of them as possible. She and Hallie disappeared out of the pub and into the night, leaving Seb and me with Roxie's date, who was still sitting at the table, casually scrolling through his phone, blissfully unaware that his date had just left.

"How did we both strike out tonight?" Seb asked, staring at the door where the women had just exited, looking genuinely perplexed. "That doesn't even seem possible."

"I didn't strike out tonight, Seb," I said, settling back into my seat and sipping my Old Fashioned. "I hit a home run."

8

Hallie

"How much do you have left to write?" Roxie asked me as she clicked away on her computer. The gallery had received a new shipment of art over the weekend, and she'd spent the better part of the day logging it into the system.

One of my favorite things about being a journalist was the freedom to do my job from anywhere, so today I decided to work from the gallery with Roxie. It also helped me avoid running into Anthea at the office. The last thing I needed was for my boss to ask for an update on the article that was due to be in her inbox by the end of the day—the one detailing two failed dates I'd spun into something more acceptable, but I could only imagine what Anthea would say.

"I'm doing my last read through now." This article was the introduction to the entire series. It *had* to be good—not only for the sake of readership, but for the sake of my career.

"Didn't you already say you were doing your last read through an hour ago?" Roxie leveled me with a knowing look over the top of her laptop.

I sighed. "Okay . . . this is my *final* read through."

The article felt like it was missing something, but I

couldn't bring myself to admit that the missing piece was James. Arguing with him had been the most entertaining part of the two nights he'd ruined.

"Okay." Roxie closed her laptop. "Spill. You never second guess your work. What's going on?"

Roxie's radar for bullshit was always spot on. Especially with me. The two of us became inseparable through college—sharing our first heartbreaks, surviving our first hangovers, and figuring out how to grow up. There was nothing I could get past her.

"Well, when I should be writing an article about a flashy finance guy and him asking me out, I have no material but two failed attempts to get a guy to stay past one drink." I dropped my head into my hands and let out a long sigh. Why was the cosmos dangling my dream job in front of my face, only to make it feel just out of reach?

"Shall we ignore the obvious reason those dates didn't work out?" Roxie asked innocently. "Because of a certain man?"

My frown deepened as my thoughts drifted to the frustratingly handsome enemy I'd somehow ended up with. "I don't even know his last name. All I know is I opened my big mouth and offended a financial analyst that can hold a grudge."

Roxie chuckled and then leaned back against the counter. "You know, I love my job. But I can't wait for the day I can just focus on food photography full time. That's the dream. It always has been. I'd give anything to have my own shot like you do now. You have the opportunity to leap *now*, Hallie. Don't let it slip through your fingers."

The door to the gallery opened and Michelle Granger swept in, postponing our conversation.

"Michelle! I didn't have you down for an appointment today." Roxie rounded the gallery's desk to greet one of her biggest clients.

Michelle took off her sunglasses with a pair of silk gloves as she took in the gallery. "Oh, I was just in the neighborhood and wanted to stop by. I'm looking for a new piece for the dining room."

"Above the fireplace?" Roxie asked, slipping immediately into her work mode. She gestured toward one of the newly installed pieces. "You've styled that room wonderfully. It is moody, eclectic, rich. I think you need something like this with colors which will only enhance that theme, not something that will become an accent piece."

"Oh, this would definitely be an option," Michelle mused as she analyzed the piece. "I didn't have time to catch up with either of you after dinner last week. How was your evening?"

"It was lovely, Michelle." Roxie reached over to squeeze her arm. "Thank you for inviting us."

Michelle directed her attention to me. "Hallie, how was James Rossi? I wasn't sure how sitting you two next to each other would go."

Rossi.

Roxie snorted and quickly tried to cover it up with a cough. I floundered for a second. "It was . . . something."

Michelle glanced between the two of us. "James is a good guy. He comes from a rather well-known family."

That was rich people code for "his family is loaded",

which explained the signet ring he always wore. Only people that came from old money would wear something like that as if it were just a normal accessory. I should've known he was a finance bro—everything about him screamed it. The way he carried himself, the smug charm that never seemed to falter. All the signs were staring me in the face.

"I was hoping the two of you would hit it off," Michelle continued. "From what Roxie had told me about you, I thought you would work well together. James needs a woman that's down to earth and established in her career."

Michelle wasn't far off with her matchmaking attempt, with the sparks that flew over dinner—before my big mouth had completely ruined the mood and shut down any remaining chemistry between us.

Honestly, I was thankful that whatever had been brewing was killed. James had an uncanny ability to mess with my head, make me second-guess everything, then act like I was the crazy one calling him out on it. So yeah, the article might've been a disaster, but at least it had spared me from getting any further involved with him before I regretted it.

I received a look from Roxie that screamed *keep your mouth shut about one of my biggest client's best friends.* "And why is that?"

"Well, James has had a rough go of it with women." Michelle gave us a sad smile. "He has a big heart, always putting those around him first, and it bit him in the butt with Cassidy."

"Cassidy?" Roxie asked, flashing me a curious glance.

"She's his ex." Michelle waved her hand through the air

as if this piece of information she just gave us wasn't the fodder I needed. "He hasn't gotten over it. She really did a number on him."

"Roxie, put this one on my account. See if you can have it delivered this weekend." Michelle studied the art piece one more time before giving us one more serene smile. "It was lovely chatting with you both. I'll have to invite you both to our next dinner party."

With a wave that was far more elegant than anything I'd ever be able to achieve, Michelle was gone.

"Why is James Rossi suddenly everywhere in my life?" I asked as soon as the door closed. Within a week, this man had not only become the bane of my existence, but he'd wormed his way into every crevice of my mind. For whatever reason, he seemed determined to ruin my chances. He was infuriating, impossible to figure out, and yet I couldn't stop myself from fantasizing about him.

Teeth biting a lip. Messy kisses. Sweat-slicked skin under cool sheets. Cries that disappeared into the night.

What has gotten into me?

Roxie dropped onto the gallery couch next to me and wrapped an arm around my waist. I leaned over to rest my head on her shoulder. "Is that such a bad thing?"

"I would say that his current wish to disrupt my life is certainly negative." After straightening up, I glanced at the article, awaiting my boss's approval.

"Many women would likely think that having an attractive, eligible man's undivided attention is positive." Roxie placed a kiss on top of my head before she shoved me up to my feet. "Please send that article to Anthea now. There's a new ramen place in Soho that I want to try."

I clutched a hand to my chest. "A woman after my own heart."

The Economics of Finding the Most Eligible Man in Finance

By: Hallie Woods

If they chastise the bartender for putting scotch in their Old Fashioned instead of bourbon, they aren't actually mad. *They just know the importance of getting it right the first time.*

If they answer a work call in front of you, get used to it. You might even consider it foreplay.

For Christmas, it's safe to assume a new Rolex watch would be a suitable present.

When they tell you they just have to send one more email before EOD, plan to entertain yourself for approximately two hours.

The allure of men in finance has struck deep into the hearts of the women of New York City. Was it the impeccably tailored suit? Or the manicured nails and perfectly kept hair? Or maybe it was the copy-and-paste handsomeness they seemed to have obtained? When one rejected you, you could just move on to the next. Whatever it was, I was enthralled by the idea of finding out more about what made them tick.

Many of my preconceived notions proved true on my first outing, much to my disappointment. Finance Man #1, let's call him Mr. Red Head, ordered an Old Fashioned at the bar for himself and a glass of white wine for me. We chatted about work—me, barely getting to mention I was a writer before being subjected to an hour of market analysis that I didn't ask for. He mentioned he'd attended Brown and was in a fraternity. How he still had monthly dinners with some of his fraternity brothers and how his dream was to climb the ladder of investment banking and to become, for lack of a better term, a "wolf" of Wall Street.

By our second round of drinks, I'd quickly realized that there wouldn't be a second date. Why is that? Because the second round of drinks never came as Mr. Red Head became caught up in a conversation with a peer about work that would derail the entire date.

But nevertheless, I was on a mission to find the most eligible man in finance, and I wouldn't settle until I found him.

After I hit send, I realized the details I added to improve the chemistry weren't necessarily based on the guys but had more to do with a certain 6'5", blue-eyed investment banker who I just couldn't get out of my mind.

9

James

As I entered my family's restaurant, the familiar scents of garlic, tomatoes, and warm pizza dough enveloped me. It instantly transported me back to being nine years old, standing on a stool in the kitchen next to my Nonna and Nonno. I could almost hear Nonna's soft Italian lullaby of instructions as she showed me how to knead the dough just right, whispering that it was a secret—one I could never share with anyone but family. I could taste the salty-sweet sauce simmering on the stove and feel the heat of the oven warming the kitchen, everything coming together into the meals that shaped my love for food. That scent always made me feel like I was home, no matter how far I'd wandered.

Rossi Pizzeria was situated just under the Brooklyn Bridge, in a corner building that was once a bank in the late 1800s. Much of the architecture remained—the large arched floor-to-ceiling windows, the stamped gold-tin ceiling, and a handcrafted staircase in the back of the restaurant that took you up to an event space. Red-checked cloths adorned the tables. A mixture of black-and-white stills of Brooklyn and family photos hung proudly on the walls. Repurposed wine bottles formed chandeliers hanging from the ceiling. This place had gone through many iterations in its time. A cramped, diner-like space that my father and his brother had then remodeled into the open-floor elevated dining space that it was now. Patrons could see the kitchen from the dining room, watching pizza makers toss pizzas into and out of the brick ovens. Or watching my grandfather, still the only one to put the final garnishes on top of each pie.

On a Sunday afternoon, only a few people occupied tables—a far cry from the bustling restaurant it once was. Times had changed. People had moved out of the neighborhood and flashier places had popped up round the corner, taking customers away from Rossi's despite it being a Brooklyn staple.

My father seemed to have realized that it was sink or swim for the pizzeria. My aunt, uncle, and grandparents still believed that the legacy they had already built would carry them on.

"James, hey!" Brandon bussed one of the few dirty tables in the restaurant. A white apron tied around his waist. He worked a shift nearly every day to help him pay for tuition at NYU. He was studying business, intending to take over this place from his parents one day.

I only hoped it was still around then.

As I walked in, I noticed his younger sister, my cousin Emilia, carrying a tray of drinks to a table near the back. She was wearing a simple black apron over a volleyball t-shirt, the same shirt she wore to every shift after coming from practice. She had that quiet determination about her that made me respect her work ethic more than she probably knew. Even though she was still in high school, Emilia was a fixture in the restaurant, always helping when she wasn't on the court.

"Is my dad in?" I shifted my satchel farther up on my shoulder, glancing at Emilia as she made her way past me.

After Brandon's twenty-first birthday party, I'd been thinking about how I could make a difference to my family's restaurant. I'd put together an entire business proposal that I was certain my father and uncle couldn't say no to. Especially when they saw the projected figures I'd worked on for revenue. Money was a language everyone could understand. Even if my father and uncle specialized in the art of pizza.

She flashed me a quick smile before heading to the kitchen. "Dad and Uncle G are in the back office," she called over her shoulder.

"Thanks." I nodded before turning my attention back to Brandon.

"It's been a slow day," he said, adjusting his apron as he wiped down another table. "Do you want me to put an order in for you?"

"Sure," I told him before I made my way toward the back of the restaurant.

Today's visit was unannounced. I hadn't told my father or uncle what I'd been working on. More to avoid hearing a no before I could even get started. Because if there was one thing the Rossi clan was good at, it was being stubborn with asking for help.

Voices that spoke in hushed tones on the other side of the door quieted when I knocked.

"Come in," my father's heavily accented voice came from the other side.

"James!" Uncle Antonio exclaimed when I opened the

door. Both my uncle and my father wore mirrored looks of surprise.

Nowadays, it was difficult for me to come all the way to Brooklyn to visit the restaurant. Most weekdays and some weekends I spent in the office crunching numbers and analysing market trends. But that didn't minimize how important my family was to me. No client was more important than my family's well-being and happiness.

"What are you doing here, son?" My father sat forward in his chair behind the only desk in the cramped office that was covered in so many bills and various pieces of paper that I wasn't sure how he could tell heads from tails.

"I wanted to talk with you and Uncle Antonio. Here's a proposal I've prepared for you both to review." I took my satchel off my shoulder to grab my laptop with all my notes.

"A proposal?" When I looked at my father's confused face, I saw myself thirty years from now—thick eyebrows with different shades of gray, thick curls that were turning from silver to white, wrinkles around his eyes and mouth that hinted at a life full of laughter and happiness.

"I know how we can keep up with the current social media trend in the market." Uncle Antonio let out a chuckle as he settled back into his seat, his eyes bouncing between my father and me as if he knew he was in for a show.

My father waved me off as I set up my laptop and pulled up the presentation I'd made. "We are fine, *figlio*."

I'd come prepared for a fight. Brandon had already mentioned how little importance our parents placed on social media and how little they believed it could get meaningful results. But numbers don't lie, and surely they would both see that.

"If you'll just let me show you what I was thinking." Opposition was nothing new to me. I faced it daily in the office. There was a reason people nicknamed players in finance "sharks" or "wolves". When they smelled blood, they went in for the kill. Everyone around me wanted to be the pack leader, the one on top, and they'd do anything to make sure that you didn't succeed so they could.

I was used to dealing with stubbornness—especially from my father.

To his credit, he leaned back in his chair and allowed me to continue. I laid it all out—hiring a social media manager, hosting a night for influencers to come in for a meal on the restaurant in exchange for a review, using social media to stay on trends and reach more customers, hiring a food photographer to create a curated page that would have thousands of followers tuning in to the colorful feed. I even laid out the numbers it would take to franchise the restaurant or work with major manufacturers to create a frozen pizza option that could be in grocery stores. Every suggestion I made was supported by data and actionable steps.

But when I finished and was met with silence, I knew they would ignore my suggestions.

"This is great, son. But we don't have it in our budget to hire a social media manager or pay a photographer." It took everything in me to keep my face neutral and not show my disappointment. I'd taken the time to show my father and uncle how they could rearrange their expenses to fit this into their current budget.

My father's excuse wasn't a reasonable one. He leaned forward and pressed his forefinger into my chest. "Have faith, *figlio*. We are in the business of making food with love. People will recognize that."

"But Dad—" My retort died on my tongue when I saw the look in my father's eyes. He had made up his mind; his decision was final.

Uncle Antonio, who had been quietly observing, finally spoke up. "James, the business you're in is very different from ours. We don't run numbers, we run ovens. Food is about bringing people together, not spreadsheets. You're good with those numbers, but here, it's about the heart. Focus on your work, leave this to us, and we'll fix it the way we always have—by making the best damn food in Brooklyn."

"I'll just leave this here." My fingers fumbled for the printout amidst the towering avalanche of papers on my father's desk, each rustle a potential threat to its survival. "In case you change your minds."

"I'll see you for dinner tonight?" My father asked as I stood to leave. Hoisting my satchel back on my shoulder, I gave him a terse nod before exiting the room.

As I re-entered the dining room, Brandon placed a pizza, freshly removed from the brick oven, upon one of the many unoccupied tables. Emilia was clearing a nearby table.

Brandon studied my face, a thoughtful frown creasing his brow. "Didn't go well?"

I shook my head in defeat.

Emilia gave me a quick nod, her ponytail swishing as she walked past me. "The food's still the best part of the place, right?"

My cousin pulled out a chair for me, then sat next to me. Not a soul remained in the restaurant. If what Brandon had shared at the club in Brooklyn a week ago was true, this place couldn't afford too many more empty days.

"I tried to give them some numbers on the benefits of hiring a social media manager."

Brandon snorted as he bit into a slice of pizza. "Now I understand why it didn't go well. I'm sure you droned on about facts and figures. By the time you were done, Uncle G gave you some sad excuse that you'd already disproven in your presentation because he'd zoned out as soon as you started talking about ROI."

"Were you listening through the door?" I joked, taking my first bite. An explosion of flavors burst across my taste buds. I wasn't being biased when I said Rossi Pizzeria was one of the best pizza places in all five boroughs. The food spoke for itself.

"Did they give you some speech about how the right people will find this place?"

I laughed, shaking my head. "Yep. Same old story."

I used to think Brandon was irresponsible, his constant partying and inability to find a job outside the family restaurant a testament to his immaturity. I believed a portion of his past hostility toward me resulted from his misunderstanding of my non-participation in the family restaurant. But when it came down to it, the two of us weren't all that different. We both cared enough to see this place last—whether that was against our parents' better judgment or not.

Emilia came over to join us, a tray in hand with a fresh batch of drinks. "Don't worry, James. We'll figure it out.

Maybe we can start by getting some influencers in here—get people talking."

My phone dinged in my pocket. Two notifications—one for *Sophisticate* and one for Hallie's food blog. I'd set up web alerts earlier this week, as I told myself it was only to keep tabs on the articles that she put out. But as I read her latest piece, a chuckle escaped me. Her wit was as sharp as ever, and the playful jabs she threw in were a testament to the humor I'd come to expect from her. Each article highlighted the latest guy she was trying to get a date from, using witty nicknames, and ending with some sort of interruption. Only she and I knew the source of that disruption.

Her blog post featured a list of the best ramen places in Manhattan. It was full of clever quips, intelligent remarks, and clear expertise on what made good food. But what I found the most compelling about her writing was her ability to highlight the story *behind* the food—whether that be the chef, the cultural impact of the restaurant, or how a family-owned chain became a giant. She didn't just review food; she told its story.

Wait.

Why hadn't I thought of this before now?

"Emilia," I exclaimed, leaning over to drop a kiss to the top of her head. "You're a genius."

"I already knew that," she said.

Maybe my father was right, and the right people would love this place if they just knew it existed. Luckily, I knew an infuriating, annoyingly beautiful aspiring food critic who could help make that happen.

10

Hallie

I was a month into my "Love on Wall Street" column. I'd written four articles, each depicting the same thing: the introduction of a carbon copy of a man I'd written about the previous week, a date with stale conversation that fizzled out or was interrupted before we could discuss a second date.

The only saving grace of this series was how so many women had found the material relatable, adding their own personal accounts of their run-ins with the men of Wall Street. But with every failed date—every interruption from James Rossi—I was seeing the chances of obtaining the magazine's restaurant critic role slowly slip away. That feeling only compounded when I sat down at my desk on Monday morning and opened my company inbox to see an email from Anthea sitting right at the top.

SUBJECT: YOU SEEM INCAPABLE OF SECURING AN ACTUAL DATE

The entire body of the email was blank. There was only the subject line glaring back at me. Anthea's taunting email in my coffin of self-doubt. My stomach clenched with dread; the weight of missed opportunities pressed down on me, leaving me with only one last desperate gamble.

Hallie: Want to go to Whiskey Locker tonight? Operation "Get Hallie a Date" needs to begin.
Roxie: I think I may skip out on tonight. I'm tired of gracing those Wall Street men with my presence when they don't know the opportunity they have at their fingertips.
Roxie: But you've got this. I have a good feeling about tonight!

Honestly, if I were Roxie, I would have given up on tagging along to watch my best friend crash and burn a long time ago. So later that evening after work, I made the trek to Whiskey Locker by myself with a newfound determination to secure a date to write and finally stop disappointing Anthea.

This experience had led me to the conclusion that the dating scene was overrated. Sipping wine (again!), scoping the room for a date (again!), I thought, seriously, why does anyone do this?

"How are you tonight, Hallie?" Joey, the bartender, asked. The two of us had shared far too many conversations since I'd started coming here. I wore the fact that we were on a first name basis as a badge of honor—or at least that was what I told myself to make myself feel better.

"The usual, Joey. The usual."

"Hey, I noticed you were sitting by yourself and I don't want to intrude . . ." The universe must have taken pity on me and was on my side for once, because a rather handsome man was leaning against the bar next to me.

Thank you, I said up to the heavens, hoping I'd stay in the universe's good graces.

"You are definitely not intruding." I gestured to the open seat next to me, which he quickly slid into. After giving myself the quickest pep talk of my life, I stuck out my hand and plastered the flirtiest smile I could muster onto my face. "I'm Hallie."

"Henry." The most adorable dimple appeared as Henry enveloped my hand with his own and, for the first time during this entire charade, my stomach swooped.

I noticed the beer in Henry's hand. *Not an Old Fashioned. Already straying from the norm.*

Henry's gray eyes studied me thoughtfully. "Well, Hallie, what brings you to the Financial District?"

"What if I told you I'm looking for a man in finance?" I wasn't sure who this woman was that was taking over my body, actually flirting, but I was more than happy to let her take the lead.

And to my surprise, Henry seemed to like it. A melodic laugh blended in with the alternative rock music that Whiskey Locker loved to play.

"Then I'd say that you've just found one."

Henry ran a hand through his hair, tousling it in a way that had me wondering what he looked like underneath his perfectly pressed dress shirt and suit.

Would that be a conflict of interest?

Anthea never mentioned I couldn't have sex with the people I dated . . .

Hell, that was a pretty crucial part of dating.

"I'm sorry, that was an awful joke." Damn, even the way he blushed was attractive.

Almost like a reflex, I scanned the room, searching for a familiar handsome face that was plotting my demise. It was about right now when he typically appeared—like a pop-up thunderstorm on a summer evening, a dark cloud out of nowhere to ruin an otherwise perfect day. But his deep-blue eyes and signature smirk were nowhere in sight. I pushed away the sinking feeling that crept in at his absence, choosing to ignore how it felt far too large to unpack. Especially when I had an attractive man beside me, genuinely interested in what I had to say.

"Are you hungry?" I asked him, trying to force James from my mind. "Because I'm starving. I don't remember the last time I ate."

Henry flagged Joey down. "We can't have that, can we? Can we get an order of mozzarella sticks and pretzel bites?"

I pressed a hand to my chest. "A man after my heart. Mozzarella sticks *and* pretzel bites?"

"It's sacrilegious to not have both when you're at a bar." The two of us shared a smile, and I was already mentally taking notes on everything I wanted to write in this week's article. Surely this article would blow Anthea away.

"So, Henry, I'm assuming you work in FiDi." I gestured to his suit as evidence.

"You have exceptional deduction skills, Hallie." Henry glanced down at his attire with a chuckle. "I'm the Chief Financial Officer at Young Investments."

"A CFO of an investment firm? I feel like that's like an inception of the financial realm."

"That's the best response I think I've ever gotten to my job title." Joey dropped off our order, which Henry immediately dove into. "Normally, I get glazed eyes and incoherent nods. And what do you do, Hallie? I'm sure it's something far more impressive than being another unit in the FiDi."

"Oh, I'm a writer for *Sophisticate*." Henry's expression shifted in surprise, and I braced myself for the usual dismissal I was accustomed to. The only guy who had ever truly acknowledged my accomplishments without brushing them off was . . . James.

But Henry surprised me once more. "That's impressive. Writing and the entertainment industry are wildly fast-paced, and *Sophisticate* is definitely a leader in that space. So, I'd say that makes *you* an industry leader."

A guy who knew good bar food and could dish out compliments. It was about damn time.

"This may be forward," Henry added, his smile widening. "But do you want to go grab a bite to eat sometime? Get to know each other in a place that isn't looping the same seven songs?"

I couldn't help but laugh. "You noticed that, too?" Then, before I could second-guess myself, I added, "Actually, how about now? I could go for something more filling than mozzarella sticks and some pretzels."

Henry raised an eyebrow, taken aback for a moment, but then he nodded. "Now? Well . . . sure."

I couldn't believe it. It felt almost too perfect, too easy, and I knew I couldn't let the opportunity slip away. Who knew how long he'd stick around? Or if *he* would show up at any moment, turning everything upside down again. There was no time like the present.

Henry offered me his hand to help me off the barstool before handing me my clutch. "A culinary expert and a real visionary. I'm intrigued."

I was already thinking about how I could nail two birds with one stone—write the killer article Anthea was expecting by the end of the week while highlighting another restaurant that I'd had my eye on.

"After you." Henry gestured for me to lead the way, and I couldn't help but enjoy the feeling of a man following closely behind me. Lost in my excitement, I barely noticed the person entering Whiskey Locker from the corner of my eye.

"Oof—" Strong hands reached out to steady me as I pitched toward the side.

"Woah! Easy there."

Wait, I knew that voice. Perfect timing, as always. Right on cue.

"Hallie! You're already leaving?" Bright blue eyes twinkled down at me once I regained my balance. James glanced over my head at Henry, who was still right behind me. His lips pressed into a hard line and his hands, which were still on my arms, gripped me a little tighter. "Henry."

"James! It's nice to see you, man. How are you?"

Suddenly I was in a finance man sandwich that I'd never asked for.

I swear, if this article isn't a hit, I'm going to reconsider all my life choices.

"I'm doing good, man." Oh God, was that animosity I detected in James's voice? "How's your *wife*, Henry?"

I stiffened.

Surely, I'd just misheard James. Surely, he hadn't just asked Henry about his *wife*.

Henry had taken a few steps back, putting some distance between the two of us.

"She's doing well." The flirty finance man that I'd just sat next to at the bar was gone, replaced by a buttoned-up douchebag. "Thanks for asking."

James still hadn't removed his hands from my arms and was now moving toward me, tucking me into his side. His body pressed against mine, a jolt of electricity arcing between us, and I gasped.

Henry's face was now suddenly a deep shade of red as James continued to stare him down. After a few more awkwardly tense seconds passed, Henry cleared his throat and pushed past James out of Whiskey Locker.

My shoulders sank as my best shot at writing about an actual date walked out of the door.

11

James

I'd grown more and more restless as the last meeting of my workday stretched into the evening. Eight o'clock came and went, yet we were still in the thick of our investment review. Yes, I was physically in the boardroom, but my mind had wandered three blocks away, to a certain brunette likely perched on a barstool, instead of focusing on the market analysis we were discussing.

It had been over a month of our little game—if you could even call it that. I'd been relentless in my attempts to sabotage Hallie's articles, determined to throw her off her rhythm. But no matter what I did, she kept publishing pieces week after week that were hilarious, witty, and full of heart. Despite myself, a twisted sort of amusement bubbled up. Her audacity was almost . . . admirable.

Every Monday morning, like clockwork, I poured myself a cup of coffee and anxiously awaited my online alert for Hallie's article. I told myself I only read them to make sure I was doing a good job in deterring her from eviscerating finance men everywhere and not because I was actually interested. I definitely wasn't counting down the minutes of my workday just to see her again, or because I was genuinely excited to. That would be ridiculous. And I certainly wasn't replaying the way she glared at me with those sharp, beautiful eyes—or how it felt like a personal win every time I managed to make her laugh at one of my terrible jokes. Even if she tried her hardest not to.

Definitely not.

I pushed these thoughts out of my mind as I hustled over to Whiskey Locker, hoping I hadn't missed her tonight.

"Oof—"

"Woah! Easy there," I exclaimed as a woman ran straight into my chest just as I entered the bar.

Familiar wavy brown hair.

A floral scent I'd committed to memory.

"Hallie! You're already leaving?" I asked as I reached out to steady her. My pulse pounded a fierce rhythm that mirrored the alarm flashing in those beautiful eyes. If it weren't for the man standing so close to her, I wasn't sure I would have ever looked away. But the second I registered who it was—his light hair, those gray eyes, that smug presence—I felt rage boil in my veins. Fury surged, sharp and sudden, and the urge to pull her beside me was overwhelming, but I expected her to object to such a chivalrous gesture. Still, I couldn't help the edge in my voice. "Henry."

Panic filled Henry's eyes as he realized who had just caught him attempting to cheat on his wife. "James! It's nice to see you, man. How are you?"

"I'm doing good, man," I replied mockingly. "How's your *wife*, Henry?"

Hallie stiffened, her muscles tense beneath my touch, while a furious red haze clouded my vision. Henry Edison was notorious for trying to pick up unsuspecting women in his free time. Despite my reservations regarding his behavior, I had never interjected in something so trivial before. It wasn't my business.

Until now.

His gaze flickered between me and Hallie before a look of realization crossed his face. Henry wisely decided to take three giant steps backward, putting some much-needed space between him and Hallie.

"She's doing well." The CFO slipped back into place, completely professional. "Thanks for asking."

But when Henry didn't take the hint, instinct took over. My arm wrapped around Hallie, pulling her firmly against me. The air thickened with tension as we stood there, locked in a silent standoff. A few long seconds passed before Henry finally got the message and turned to leave.

"I need a drink." With a sigh, Hallie slid off my arm and onto a vacant barstool.

I braced myself for her usual fire—sarcasm, sharp retort, maybe even a shove. What I didn't expect was for her to slink off in defeat as if she'd lost all hope.

"Why so sad, Hal?" I asked carefully.

She didn't answer. Instead, she stared straight ahead. "Why do you always drink Old Fashioneds? Are they that good? You know what? Fuck it. Joey, can I have an Old Fashioned, please? I might as well see what all the hype is about since I've been writing about them for a month."

Joey gave a mock salute and turned away to make her drink.

I tried again, softer this time. "Hallie, are you okay?"

She didn't look at me, just rested her forehead on the

bar top. Her shoulders trembled slightly, and not from laughter. The dimly lit bar seemed to offer little solace as the noise of the crowd swirled around us. I reached out, resting a hand lightly on her arm, hoping to offer a sliver of comfort.

"Of course I'm not okay!" she shot back up. Instead of the angry glare I expected, defeat etched her face. "This entire series is a disaster."

Making his way back to our spot at the bar, the bartender served us our Old Fashioneds. With two large, somewhat desperate gulps, Hallie drank half of it, then wiped her mouth with the back of her hand. Not wanting to be too far behind her, I downed mine and motioned for Joey to grab us another round.

"Why are you so set on ruining my articles?" she asked me softly. "A normal person would have moved on by now. *Sophisticate* is a big magazine, but it's not like it's a highly respected news publication. These are supposed to be fun and light-hearted pieces, but you're acting like I'm going to ruin lives by publishing my articles. Why do you care so much?"

Why *did* I care so much?

I already knew the answer. Unlike most things in my life, this wasn't business. It was personal. Two years ago, I'd fallen for a woman that had been doing her own hunting for a man on Wall Street, much the same as what Hallie was doing now. I hadn't realized it at the start, but she'd wanted nothing more than to find someone that could bring her status and wealth. She cared more about the material things I could provide for her than my actual feelings.

I waited until Joey set down another drink in front of me so I could down half of it before I continued. "My ex-girlfriend," I finally replied as Hallie sat patiently, waiting for me to give her a logical answer to her question. But my answer was far from logical.

"What does your ex-girlfriend have to do with this?"

"To all intents and purposes, she was a lot like you. Looking for a man in finance, someone with money, that could provide her with the lifestyle she'd always wanted. She used me. At first it was just a Dior purse. Then it was a trip to Italy. Then came the listings for homes in the Hamptons. The final straw was realizing she had raided my safe, taking thousands for a shopping spree. The last thing I want is for any of my friends to have to deal with that, too."

Hallie's jaw dropped open in surprise. I waited for the look of disgust I'd grown accustomed to receiving, the look I hated. But it never came. Instead, she reached over to squeeze my hand. "I'm sorry that you had to go through that, James. No one ever should. But I am not Cassidy. I'm not going after these men for their money."

"So, what are you doing this for?" I asked her. She'd made it abundantly clear the first time I'd met her she didn't hold a very high opinion of people like me. Yet here she was, trying night after night to date the very men she detested.

"For a promotion. For my dream job. You know that."

I arched a skeptical brow as I finished the rest of my drink. For someone claiming this was all just for a promotion, she was sure putting in an awful lot of effort.

"Oh, come on. We all do questionable things to achieve

our dreams." Hallie downed the rest of the Old Fashioned. "You know, these aren't so bad after all. I might write a review on them. Maybe Whiskey Locker has the best Old Fashioneds, and that's why everyone loves to drink them. Perhaps I haven't been open-minded enough."

"The Nest has the best Old Fashioned in the city," I replied. Her skin took on that familiar pink flush, accompanied by the faint scent of alcohol on her breath, a clear sign she was well beyond tipsy. How many drinks had she had before I got there?

Joey was already ahead of the curve and dropped another glass in front of me, but water in front of Hallie. As I took a sip, I felt the pleasant warmth of alcohol settle in, a nice buzz humming through me. It was just the right kind of buzz—enough to say things I might not otherwise, but not enough to cloud my judgment.

"I heard that place is amazing. I've been wanting to review it for ages, but I haven't found my way in yet. It's far too exclusive, maybe even for *Sophisticate*."

"I can get you in."

Hallie's eyes widened. "Really?"

"I know people." I raised a shoulder in a shrug. "But not until you tell me why you're *really* chasing finance bros across every bar in the FiDi. Why is getting this promotion so important to you that you're doing something you obviously can't stand?"

Maybe it was the alcohol loosening her tongue or maybe it was the electric charge crackling in the air between us tonight. Whatever it was, it made her lower her guard.

"I love writing, stringing together words to create something beautiful, and telling stories. But my genuine passion lies in writing about food. On the morning of the dinner party at Elliot and Michelle's, I'd discovered that *Sophisticate* would soon have an opening for their food critic position. Despite only having experience with a social media food blog, I thought fuck it and applied anyway. My dream is to write about the glamorous Michelin-star restaurants and savor the incredible dishes prepared by the world's top chefs just as much as it is to shine a light on the lesser-known family-owned establishments that often go unnoticed yet serve some of the most amazing food. I've always hoped that one day, my name would be at the top of those articles."

It occurred to me I wasn't sure I'd ever heard Hallie speak for this long, except maybe on the night we met. A fiery passion had ignited in her eyes, pulling her beautiful lips into the first smile I'd seen tonight—radiant and unforgettable. The alcohol, mixed with the sheer delight of sharing her love of food, brought a deep flush to her cheeks, a vibrant contrast to her skin. I was so captivated by her energy that I nearly missed what she'd said.

"I used to write this small section in the back of our magazine that would cover snippets of conversation I would hear all over the city. I heard this one girl talk about trying to pick up a man in finance at Whiskey Locker. My boss loved it so much, she wanted me to expand it into a months-long column. So now I'm here, drowning my sorrows in a drink I've been making fun of for the last month as my dreams slip through my fingers."

Her hand shook as she lifted her drink to her lips, the liquid sloshing precariously. Tears welled in the corners of her eyes, and a wave of icy panic clenched my chest, stealing the breath from my lungs.

"Hey, hold on." I swiped a few napkins from a holder and gently laid them down in front of her. "Don't cry."

Her shoulders jerked with a hiccup that slipped out of her mouth. "I'm simply mourning the loss of a career I'll never have."

A long silence stretched between us, and I hesitated before responding. "What if I have an idea that would be mutually beneficial for us both?"

Her eyes drifted to mine, a single brow rising in curiosity. A small voice in the back of my mind told me this wasn't a good idea, that I'd regret it later. But I silenced it, ignoring the warning, letting curiosity and something dangerously close to attraction steer me straight toward her.

"What if *I* take you on a date?"

Hallie spluttered, her breath catching as some of her drink went down the wrong way.

Once she managed to regain control, her face shifted into a look of complete disbelief, as if I'd just suggested something utterly absurd. And, honestly, maybe I had. "Excuse me?"

"Hear me out," I said, raising my hands in an attempt to keep her from cutting me off. I needed to get this idea out. "Five dates. One per week. You can use each of them for your articles. I'm sure it's getting old writing about trying to find love in the same bars every week. You'll get wined and dined at the best restaurants the city offers. It benefits everyone involved."

"You still haven't explained how this is *mutually* beneficial." Hallie's wide brown eyes stared at me with a mix of disbelief and suspicion. But I didn't mind. As long as she was looking at me at all.

I took a deep breath before continuing, my voice a little more serious. "My family has a pizzeria in Brooklyn. It's been around since the fifties—my grandparents started it. Now my dad and my uncle run it, but profit has been shrinking because they can't sustain a customer base."

Her indifference shifted. There was an unmistakable spark of curiosity in her gaze. "Here I was thinking you were nothing more than a trust fund baby. I guess you still have surprises up your sleeve. Do they market on social media?"

I shook my head. I wouldn't count the poorly maintained social media account my aunt remembers to post on a handful of times a year as "marketing".

"Have you talked to them about the importance of social media?"

"Let's just say I've come to realize that I'm going to have to take matters into my own hands. Which is where you come in. After our five dates, you can cover my family's restaurant so we can try to stir up some new business. Enough that I have something substantial to bring to my father." To convince my dad about social media, I had to prove its importance beyond a shadow of a doubt.

Hallie didn't respond immediately. A thoughtful expression crossed her face as she silently considered my proposition.

"Five dates over five weeks?" I nodded, trying to keep my excitement in check. I told myself it was all about helping my family, but the thought of spending more time with her was almost impossible to ignore.

"We need ground rules," Hallie said, her tone suddenly serious, as if we were negotiating the merger of two billion-dollar companies and not a mutually beneficial arrangement.

"Ground rules?" I asked.

She nodded, ticking off each point on her fingers. "This is purely an arrangement. We're not pretending to be friends. No strings attached. Absolutely no kissing. And each date needs to be extravagant—got to make sure my boss is happy with the material."

I quickly mulled over her requests. While none of them were outrageous asks, *absolutely no kissing* rang around in my head for reasons I wasn't ready to explore yet. I reached out my hand for her to shake.

"You drive a hard bargain, Hallie Woods. But you have yourself a deal."

After what felt like ages of silence, Hallie finally asked, "What will I call you?"

"What do you mean?"

The bartender slid another Old Fashioned in front of me, and Hallie's attention shifted to the glass. Her eyebrows arched in surprise. Then, a dazzling smile illuminated her face, a smile that was far too radiant for any camera to do justice.

"You'll need a cover-up name in my article, obviously. Mr. Old Fashioned. I'll call you Mr. Old Fashioned."

12

Hallie

"Do you think it's too much?" I asked Roxie as I stared at myself in our floor-length mirror that we had scavenged from the side of the curb a few blocks over when we first moved. New Yorkers take that saying "one man's trash is another man's treasure" *very* seriously. I thought I'd won the lottery when I stumbled across an only gently used couch on the Upper East Side that I later found out was worth over ten thousand dollars brand new. Asking Roxie if we could borrow the gallery's delivery truck to get it home had been totally worth it.

Tonight, I was going on my first date with James Rossi, also known as Mr. Old Fashioned, and I was only mildly embarrassed by the fact that I had spent nearly two hours trying on my entire closet in search of the perfect outfit. Not that I cared what he thought, obviously.

"There's never a thing as too much. You look stunning, Hal," Roxie said as she lay on my bed wearing an off-the-rack dress that had premiered in last fall's Fashion Week, with no intention of leaving the house to be seen in it. "Where did he say he was taking you?"

It was a Friday night, and I hadn't heard from James after our conversation at Whiskey Locker until this morning. I was starting to think he was having second thoughts about our deal, when an extravagant bouquet of roses and a note were delivered directly to my desk at *Sophisticate*.

Around lunchtime, Anthea walked past my desk, the huge mass of roses enough to catch her attention, and everyone else's, before she saw the note signed "Mr. Old Fashioned". She looked at me with an eyebrow raised. "I'm excited to have this week's article in my inbox Sunday night." Then she was gone as quickly as she had appeared.

Seven o'clock, formal wear—that's all the note said.

Thus, I was standing in front of my second-hand mirror in a Valentino dress from Roxie's closet which she'd found at a thrift store for a fraction of the original cost. The black silk, trimmed with delicate lace, clung to my curves, its thin straps rested lightly on my collarbone. The fabric felt cool and smooth against my skin, while tiny embroidered butterflies in vibrant colors added a touch of whimsy to the otherwise elegant piece. I silently thanked the universe not only for Roxie and I being the same size, but also that her eye for beauty extended beyond art. The most formal thing I owned was a plain red cocktail number that paled in comparison to this masterpiece.

"The card didn't say where we're going, just that I need to dress formal and be ready by seven," I said, glancing at Roxie as she sprawled out on my bed, a dreamy sigh escaping her lips.

"The one time I decide not to tag along, and all the fun stuff happens," she muttered.

I recapped the lipstick tube and slid it into my clutch. "It's not like this is a proper date."

"Says who?" Roxie sat up, giving me a bewildered look. "The chemistry between the two of you over the past month is palpable. I'll be surprised if you end up going home alone tonight."

"Roxie!"

"What? Who says you shouldn't indulge a little?" Roxie grinned and gave me a suggestive shoulder wiggle as I finished buckling my heels. It was three minutes before seven.

But just as I began to explain exactly why I shouldn't *indulge*, the buzzer for our apartment rang. With unprecedented speed, Roxie leaped from my bed to let James up.

"Roxie," I warned as I followed closely behind her. But once my best friend got something in her mind, there was very little that would stop her. Roxie ignored me and reached for the doorknob.

James Rossi appeared in the doorway of our small apartment, his perfectly cut tux a striking sight against the worn walls. His dark hair, usually neatly combed, was styled with extra care, each strand perfectly in place. Time seemed to stand still as the two of us took each other in. A thrill, warm and electric, shot through me as his eyes lingered on me, sending heat licking up my spine.

"Well, suddenly this has grown quite awkward," Roxie spoke up, breaking the trance that had descended between us. "I'm just going to go crack open a bottle of wine and watch *How to Lose a Guy in 10 Days* for the millionth time."

James's gaze remained fixed on me as he directed his comment to Roxie in the kitchen. "Matthew McConaughey was fantastic in that."

Roxie paused, glancing over at him, clearly amused. "I didn't think you'd be into rom-coms, James." She pulled a bottle of wine from the fridge and began hunting around for the opener—one of the few kitchen utensils we had, seeing as it was an essential. "Men like him in romantic comedies are a dying breed."

"I have my moments," James said with a chuckle, before turning his attention back to me. "Are you ready?"

I was accustomed to seeing James in his impeccably tailored suits, but the sight of him in this midnight-blue tuxedo was nothing short of a feast for my eyes. The fabric hugged his frame flawlessly. The faint aroma of his luxurious cologne mingled with the air and I could already feel the anticipation swirling around us.

Unsure if I could trust my voice to remain steady, I gave a silent nod and left the apartment, my palms sweating.

"You two kids have fun tonight!" Roxie called from the kitchen, her voice sing-songy as I closed the door behind us.

With James and me suddenly standing in the hallway of my tiny apartment building dressed like we were about to walk a red carpet, everything was becoming far more real. Out of the corner of my eye, I saw James fidgeting with his bowtie, his fingers uncharacteristically clumsy. He stole a brief glance my way, a nervous blush creeping up his neck. This was already starting off far more awkward than any first date I'd ever had before.

The tension between us was apparent, and James cleared his throat nervously. "Uh . . . a car is waiting downstairs."

"Right." James's towering frame took up most of the hallway as we made our way down the stairs.

A town car waited outside, and a driver opened the doors to the rear of the vehicle as we approached. "A driver?" I whispered.

"You wanted the full experience." James extended his hand as I lowered myself into my seat. Only once he was sure I was comfortable did he lean in, his lips grazing the shell of my ear. "And you look stunning tonight, Hallie."

His words were gasoline, igniting a furious blaze within me, the sound of the car door slamming a futile attempt to contain the inferno.

James Rossi is a charmer, you know this. You're just falling victim to his tried and tested scheme.

But the reassurances died in my mind the moment his hand landed on the seat between us, his pinky brushing against mine.

The silence in the car was heavy, and I could feel the tension in the air as we both fidgeted in our seats. James opened his mouth at the same time I did, then quickly shut it when our words collided, an awkward laugh escaping his lips. We both fell quiet, the hum of the engine filling the gap between us.

Outside the window, the city was alive. Manhattan's skyline gleamed like a collection of dreams stacked high into the night, neon lights flashing by in a blur. Streetlights painted the pavement golden. I'd seen these streets on television, watching as Carrie Bradshaw made a crosswalk look more like a catwalk. I'd spent my teenage years reading about some of the biggest fashion names in magazines, but never in a million years did I think I'd be here—hurtling down these very streets, next to a man whose name seemed to command attention, while mine barely made a ripple.

How had I gone from that little town in Ohio to this

fast-paced city of ambition and excess, with one of the richest men in the city in the seat beside me?

I shook my head, trying to focus on the present. Focus on the mission. But the soft brush of James's pinky against mine had me questioning everything I thought I knew about control.

I was in over my head. And yet, somehow, I couldn't help but wonder if I was starting to enjoy it.

After another long stretch of silence, James cleared his throat as he focused on his cufflinks. I could see his fingers shake slightly, just a hint of unease creeping into his usually confident demeanor.

"I think we're both pretending to know what we're doing," he said, his voice suddenly more vulnerable than I expected. "Maybe we should just . . . let it be?"

I gave a small, almost reluctant smile, the weight of the night sinking in. This wasn't a date. It was a performance, one we were both learning how to play.

The city outside the window kept rushing by, a reminder that time was moving faster than either of us was prepared for. When the car finally rolled to a stop, I had to do a double-take to make sure I was seeing things correctly.

"This is—"

"*Crepitio*," James supplied, offering me his hand with a confident smile.

"But the reservation list is months long," I blurted, my fingers grazing his—a spark of excitement shooting through me.

The attraction to James Rossi was undeniable. He was incredibly handsome, charming, and, as I was beginning to see, surprisingly thoughtful.

Don't forget, this is just for the article.

That didn't mean a girl couldn't have some fun. Right, Cyndi Lauper?

I stood at the entrance to a newly Michelin-starred restaurant, so exclusive, you either had to *be* someone or *know* someone to get in. Not even *Sophisticate* had covered this place yet.

"But how?" I asked as James led me through the front door where a smiling hostess greeted us.

James gave his name to her before leaning in close and whispering in my ear, "I know people, Hallie. Did you forget?"

I did my best to look unphased as we were seated in the corner booth—a section for exclusive clientele only. As I settled into the plush seat, I caught a glimpse of Theodore Drake dining in the center of the room, the rumored next heir to Rooster.

How had James pulled this off?

Once we were seated, and the waiter delivered our drinks, the reality of the situation hit me. This wasn't a game anymore. James wasn't lurking in the corners of Whiskey Locker plotting my demise for the night, and I wasn't attempting to gain the attention of whichever giletclad man in the bar would have me. James was now the subject of my article, and to make this believable, we were going to have to treat this as an *actual* date.

It was beginning to seem like he was coming to a similar realization. A slight tug of his collar, followed by a deep breath. His face flushed a little, a pink hue creeping up from his neck to his jawline. It was a subtle shift, but it didn't escape me. He was usually so composed, but now there was a tension in his posture, something almost . . . vulnerable.

His fingers lingered around the edge of his glass, gripping it just a bit tighter than necessary, like he was searching for some stability. I saw his eyes flicker toward me, only for a second, before he quickly looked down at his menu, his brow furrowing as though he were trying to concentrate.

I wondered if he, too, was struggling to process the uncharted territory we had just entered. The way he had leaned in earlier to whisper in my ear, the soft way his words had brushed against my skin, felt different now. There was an earnestness in his manner that hadn't been there before, as if this moment, this night, was suddenly more important to him than he'd let on.

"It's not too late to abort the mission," I told him, realizing neither of us knew how to operate around the other when we weren't on opposing teams. Now that we were working toward the same goal, we were each learning about the other for the first time.

Our table's silence was so thick, even the waiter noticed, looking from one stiff back to the other.

"You want to give up an opportunity to have dinner at *Crepitio*?" James looked at me with fake dismay. He was right. I had become entangled in this exact dating scheme, all for the chance to write about the very same food I could be eating for dinner tonight.

"This," I gestured between us, "is quite awkward. Neither of us intended on *dating* the other and sparks will not be flying off the page of my article if sparks aren't flying during the date."

James slowly lowered his menu, a confident smile tugging at the corners of his mouth as he leaned back in his seat. "Shall we start over and get to know each other? Who knows, maybe we'll have a good time while we're at it."

His words were casual, but there was a nervous edge to them, a hesitation that revealed more than he probably intended. James Rossi, with all his confidence, was as out of his depth as I was. It was strangely comforting to know we were both navigating this new dynamic for the first time.

Then, just like the first time we met, James reached for the bottle of wine he had ordered for us. The way he poured the wine—slowly, deliberately—felt like a small gesture of intimacy. He was acknowledging the connection that was forming between us, however complicated it might be.

"I'm James Rossi, financial analyst at Berkley Williams. I'm twenty-seven. I grew up on the Upper East Side, but my father's family is from Brooklyn. They run a pizzeria that has been passed down from my grandparents and is in dire need of an overhaul into the twenty-first century. And I am the luckiest man in this room right now to be dining with you."

My heart thudded heavily against my ribs, each beat erratic and wild, as if it were trying to escape. James's gaze burned into me like molten lava, and I grabbed my glass of wine, the chill of it a welcome contrast to the heat rising in my cheeks.

"I'm Hallie Woods, column writer for *Sophisticate*. I'm twenty-five and I grew up in a small town in Ohio where my parents and younger sister still live. I currently live in the West Village with my best friend Roxie, in an apartment that's probably the size of the shoe closets of some of the other diners in here."

I didn't dare add that I *knew* I was the luckiest girl in the room tonight. Not only because I was living out my dream of eating at a place like this, but because James Rossi was undoubtedly the hottest man in the room. He was the hottest man in most rooms, to be honest.

"With that settled," James mused, reopening his menu as the waiter approached to take our orders. "You have a sampler on the menu. A six-course tasting menu? That way we can get a flavor of every item?"

"Yes, sir." The waiter nodded his head. "Is that what you would like? It would most definitely feed two."

"Let's do that. I know we'd like the full *Crepitio* experience."

My mouth ran dry, my throat tightening as I scanned what James had ordered. In a hushed tone, I leaned in closer, trying to make sure the waiter couldn't hear. "But there's no price. James, when there's no price, that means it's out of the range of my wallet."

"Who says you're paying, Hal?"

Once again, there it was—that nickname. I had initially wanted to despise it, to despise him for uttering it. However, whenever he flashed that silly half smile at me, I forgot about hating him altogether.

13

James

Dining with Hallie Woods was a completely new experience. It was almost like I'd never truly *enjoyed* my food until I shared a meal with her. She savored every bite. The way she talked about palates and flavors reminded me of how I talked about different financial markets. It was electrifying even getting to witness it, and I knew she was more than deserving of the food critic position at *Sophisticate*—finance bro article be damned. Not to mention the little moan she let out when she truly loved the taste of a dish. I can't lie, it left me more than a little turned on.

"What are you doing?" Hallie looked at me like I'd lost my mind between the filet mignon and the gelato as I took a picture of her staring at her dessert like she was in love. Was it possible to be jealous of gelato?

"Memorializing this moment for you." I checked the picture to confirm that she did, in fact, look like she was glowing even through the camera lens. "You know, for your blog? You haven't posted this week."

Hallie regarded me. "You've looked at my blog?"

Fuck.

I hesitated, suddenly feeling heat rise to my cheeks as I fumbled for an excuse. "Well . . ." I shifted uncomfortably in my seat, before letting out a long sigh. I'd already dug myself the hole, might as well jump into it. There was no point in denying it now. But I could at least save some of my dignity. "Of course I looked at your blog. I looked up your work for when you cover my family's restaurant."

Her lips curled into a sly smile, her eyes sparkling with satisfaction as she saw right through me. "Sure, if you say so," she teased, her voice light but with a mischievous edge.

I leaned back in my chair, trying to maintain some semblance of composure, but the way she was looking at me—half playful, half triumphant—made it clear that she knew she'd caught me in a small lie.

Hallie smiled, watching me squirm just enough to make it interesting. "I'll admit, I'm impressed. Not everyone goes digging through my blog to prep for a date." She took a bite of her gelato, her expression softening as she enjoyed the taste.

"You're good at what you do, and I found your reviews to be entertaining." That was only mildly true considering I had worked my way through every one of her posts and now had alerts on for when she posted.

"Well, I guess that makes us both snoops, seeing as I learned you are the youngest person in your firm's history to become a financial analyst." Hallie averted her gaze as she spooned some more of her gelato into her mouth. My attention drifted back to her lips, painted in deep velvet red, as they closed around the spoon. My blood seemed to pound in my veins, as my mind wandered to places it probably shouldn't have. Wondering what it would be like to kiss her, to taste the sweetness lingering on her mouth. What she would sound like when I ravished her.

Okay, was something on this menu an aphrodisiac, or was this really just the effect Hallie Woods had on me?

"James?" Hallie asked, peering at me curiously.

I snapped back to reality, my pulse quickening as I realized what I'd just thought.

"Did someone check up on me?" I asked, pressing a hand to my chest, trying to play off my thoughts with a grin. "Please, enlighten me on what you found."

"Nothing that I hadn't expected," Hallie replied, ticking each item off on her fingers. "Pictures of you at your prestigious private high school. Lacrosse, by the way? Very predictable of you. Then the newspaper article announcing the finance award you won at Princeton and your bio at Berkley Williams."

I raised an eyebrow. "I feel flattered."

"It wasn't a compliment," she shot back, her tone sharp, but there was an almost imperceptible smile threatening at the corners of her mouth.

"It sure feels like one. Going out of your way to stalk me." I winked, watching her squirm in her seat.

With a dramatic stab of her spoon into the gelato, Hallie looked away.

"What did that gelato ever do to you?" I asked.

She finally met my eyes again, the playful tension between us crackling. "I'm just frustrated."

"Why?" I asked, genuinely curious now. "What's going on? I thought we were having a good time."

She sighed, long and slow. "Because I'm enjoying myself."

"And that's a bad thing?" I asked.

"No." She mulled over her next words for a moment. "I suppose it's not."

When the last of the wine was finished, I was almost disappointed. The evening had turned out to be more than I expected—more enjoyable, more engaging, and for once, not all business. I can't remember the last time I truly laughed over a nice meal with someone who wasn't wearing a suit.

I stood and extended my hand to help Hallie out of her seat. Her dress shimmered as she stood, the soft fabric brushing against her legs, and I took the moment to openly appreciate the way it hugged her in all the right places.

I want nothing more than to touch her. To let my fingers trail over the delicate fabric. To feel the heat of her skin beneath it.

The thought crossed my mind before I could stop it. I pulled myself back, forcing my mind to quiet, but when I helped her into her coat, the brief touch of my fingers across her shoulders nearly made me forget we were standing in the middle of a restaurant.

She looked up at me, her eyes soft, and for a moment the rest of the world disappeared.

"Thank you for dinner, James," she said, her voice warm, and that single sentence wrapped around me like a gentle, unexpected embrace.

I didn't trust myself to speak right away. I just nodded, and then, without thinking, I reached for her hand to tuck it into the crook of my elbow as we walked toward the door. The feeling of her hand against mine felt so natural. I almost wished I could hold her a little closer.

As we left, I noticed the glances we drew, the stares from other diners who couldn't help but look at Hallie as we passed. I didn't blame them. I wasn't lying when I told her I was the luckiest guy in all of New York tonight. I tried to ignore the possessive feeling curling inside of me, wanting her just for myself.

The easy banter during the car ride back dissolved as I walked Hallie up to her apartment door; I suddenly felt nervous. Would we kiss? Did she want to kiss me, despite her ground rules? What about a hug? Was that too far? The bravado I normally possessed evaporated as Hallie searched her clutch for her keys, each second dragging on like an eternity. Awkwardly, I stood behind her, hands in my pockets, unsure of what to do or say. This was new to me, but then again I'd never been on a not-really-a-date before.

Would a high-five be too weird?

"Thanks for tonight." The key finally turned in the lock, but Hallie hesitated with her hand on the knob. "It was amazing. I have so much I want to write about. Between the finance bro article and the food, I'm sure I'll be up late. I can't believe I get to review that food. It's like a dream come true. So, thank you, truly."

I smiled, trying to cover my nervousness. Somehow, I felt like I was being transported back to high school and this was my first time on a date with an attractive woman. "That was only our first date. Just wait until you see what I have planned for the second one."

She looked at me with a playful glint in her eyes. "So, I'll see you next week?"

"Of course," I said, my voice a little firmer now. "We have a deal, remember?"

"I'm just making sure you haven't changed your mind."

"Think what you want about finance bros, Hallie, but

in my line of work, we take deals very seriously. I never go back on my word."

She chuckled softly, then extended her hand toward me, her expression playful. "A handshake to seal the deal, then."

I looked at her hand for a moment, my disappointment blooming quietly inside me. A handshake. After the connection we'd shared over dinner, after all that chemistry crackling between us, this was how she chose to end the evening? Maybe she really did just want to keep this professional. Stick to the agreement.

I took her hand, and she gave it a firm shake. The touch of her skin against mine only made me want her more.

"Good night, Mr. Old Fashioned," she said with a teasing smile, her voice light, but there was a hesitation there. One that made me wonder if she felt the same pull I did and part of her wished for something more.

"Good night, Hallie," I replied, watching as she stepped inside, leaving me standing there with a heavy, bittersweet feeling. I hadn't expected any of this. I figured once a week, the two of us would meet up, try our best not to kill each other, and that would be it.

So why did it feel impossible to walk away from her apartment?

"What are you reading?" Seb asked, finishing the laces on his tennis shoes with a firm tug. Sunday morning had arrived, and with it, Hallie's article—published a day sooner than usual. I'd just changed in the locker room at the country club when the notification popped up on my phone. I couldn't resist opening it right away.

"Just give me a minute," I murmured, turning slightly away as Sebastian grabbed his tennis racket and started bouncing a ball against the ground in that annoyingly steady rhythm of his.

"First you bail on drinks Friday night, and now you're cutting into our court time?" he said. "What gives?" He stepped closer, trying to peek over my shoulder. "Wait . . . is that *Sophisticate*? Dude, why the hell are you reading a women's magazine?"

I swatted his hand away, but it was too late—his interest was piqued.

"There's a woman, isn't there?" he said, his tone sharpening with suspicion. "Has to be. That's the only reason you'd be reading that."

Before I could stop him, he lunged and snatched the phone out of my hand.

"Seb—come on. I wasn't done!"

But he was already skimming the screen, backing away as I chased him onto the court. I vaulted the net after him, but he stayed just out of reach, holding the phone like a trophy.

"Why are you reading some article about dating men in finance?" Seb continued to scroll on the phone. "Wait . . ." Seb trailed off as his eyes quickly raced over the screen, going wide. "Didn't you tell me that you got in at *Crepitio* on Friday?"

I stopped mid-chase, heart pounding, watching the realization already dawning on his face. Seb stopped running and finally looked at me. He'd known me for almost ten years. To my frustration, it was nearly impossible to hide anything from him. "Is this article about you?"

Day in and day out I could play the corporate game and spin a reality to be something it wasn't, but with my best friend glancing between me and an article that Hallie had just written, calling me "charming" and "a true gentleman", there wasn't a chance I was getting myself out of this one.

Mr. Old Fashioned truly is old-fashioned. He walked me to my door and bid me farewell, promising a second date that I'm actually looking forward to. Maybe on this one we'll see if Mr. Old Fashioned can turn up the heat.

I read the final paragraph again, slower this time, letting the words settle into me.

She's looking forward to a second date.

She wants me to turn up the heat.

Did she mean that? Or was it just good copy? A clever line to wrap the piece, to keep readers invested in the next installment of whatever this was between us?

I kept circling back to that moment outside her apartment. The way her hand lingered in mine after the handshake. The pause before she turned the key. The way her lips parted like she was about to say something else instead of good night.

I'd convinced myself I imagined the flicker of disappointment in her eyes when we didn't kiss, but now I wasn't so sure. Maybe it was real. Maybe she wanted it as much as I did.

"You didn't even kiss her?" Seb exclaimed after he finished reading Hallie's closing line. "Why didn't you tell me about her? I tell you about every girl I'm with."

Sebastian wasn't lying. He told me about *every* girl he took on dates or simply hooked up with. And this man had been with *a lot* of women. He'd recount his escapades to me over drinks, often giving me far more in-depth detail than I cared to know.

"It's not anything serious. It was a first date."

The rest of the truth I kept to myself. Seb had met my family and eaten at the pizzeria on countless occasions over the years. But telling him I had only brokered this deal with Hallie for the greater good of the restaurant was not only complicated, it felt like a lie. If I were honest for just a minute, I'd admit that Hallie Woods fascinated me. Not only was she incredibly beautiful, remarkably intelligent, and hilarious, but she was also incredibly talented, as evidenced by the article Seb had just finished reading. And maybe that fascination was turning into something else. Our date had a far-too-convoluted explanation, so I kept our agreement to myself.

"Did you know you were dating a columnist?" Seb handed me my phone back. "Did you know she was going to write an article about your date?"

"I met her at the Grangers' dinner party that you skipped . . . again. And she told me she was a writer for *Sophisticate* that night. She doesn't name me, so I don't think there's any harm in it."

I shifted uncomfortably under Seb's narrowed gaze. His smile spread slowly, too smug, too knowing. The kind of smile that was a neon sign warning of danger ahead.

"We should go on a double date."

I shook my head, hard. "Absolutely not."

There was no chance in hell I was going to subject Hallie to Seb in that kind of setting.

"Besides," I added, raising a brow, "which one of your

current roster would you even bring? Or are we going with the classic 'whoever texts back first' strategy?"

Seb grinned. "That depends—do I get bonus points for bringing twins?"

I groaned. "This is exactly why you're not coming anywhere near her."

Seb clutched his chest like I'd wounded him. "That's not fair. You met a girl who's not only hot but *cool enough* to write an article calling you charming, and I don't even get to meet her? What kind of best friend are you?"

I ran a hand down the back of my neck, debating whether to come clean. "You already have."

Seb's eyes widened with realization. "No way. The girl from the bar? The one whose date you *sabotaged*? Oh, this just keeps getting better."

I'd had enough. The last thing I needed was Sebastian's commentary on my dating life. I grabbed my tennis racket and walked to the far end of the court. "We're cutting into our court time."

Sebastian's booming laugh echoed through the high stone walls of the court, punctuated by the rhythmic *thwack* of tennis balls from other players. "It's nice seeing you like this."

"Like what?" I asked. We stood at opposite ends of the court, the silence thick before Seb's serve. Then a grin spread across his face.

"Happy. Defensive, sure. But happy."

14

Hallie

"That article was incredible."

Janelle popped around the corner of my cubicle, eyes bright as she leaned in. "I was fanning myself by the end. I can't imagine what your next date will be. Mr. Old Fashioned sure knows how to show a girl a good time."

I laughed, heat rising in my cheeks.

After James had walked me to my door and said goodnight—leaving me far more affected than I cared to admit—I'd barely made it inside before Roxie called for the full post-date interrogation. By the time I'd finished spilling every detail and finally kicked off my heels, I was so inspired I sat down and wrote the entire article in one go.

It was in Anthea's inbox before midnight. To my surprise, I woke Saturday morning to an email from her.

SUBJECT: NOW THIS IS WHAT I HAD BEEN HOPING FOR

Posting tonight instead of Monday morning, so it gives this piece an extra day in circulation.

Coming from Anthea Sparks, that was practically a standing ovation. Early publication was almost unheard of—it had only happened to a handful of writers since she'd taken charge of *Sophisticate*.

So by Sunday morning, my article featuring Mr. Old Fashioned was at the top of the digital site for all to read. When I opened my social media later that day and saw that nearly a thousand people had already shared the piece—far more than any of my previous columns—I knew I'd achieved something special.

Women everywhere were swooning over the wining and dining I'd got from Mr. Old Fashioned ... and I mean, sure, it had been swoon-worthy. The food had been to die for. But I was mostly excited because it *finally* meant I had good material for my article.

The weekend only got better when I received a text from James on Sunday after brunch.

> **James:** The article was fantastic. Looking forward to your review of every course on your blog.
> **James:** 2134 Center Street, see you at 7 on Friday.
> x Mr. Old Fashioned

If he kept choosing places like *Crepitio*, I'd have enough material to last me weeks. Because that was all this was. Another article. Another dinner. Another opportunity to show Anthea I could write something people actually wanted to read.

The fact that James had signed off with an "x" didn't mean anything. Obviously.

A loud crash echoed from the break room—followed by someone shouting, "I'm fine!"—and I blinked, dragged back to the present with Janelle staring at me expectantly.

"Thanks, Janelle. Our next date is on Friday. Fingers crossed it's as good as this past Friday."

"It better be. I'm vicariously living through you. I can't even imagine being treated like that by a decent man." Janelle slumped against the wall of my cubicle, her long, dark hair falling over one shoulder in a messy braid. She had that effortlessly chic style going for her, with a mix of high-end designer pieces and the kind of casual flair that always made her look like *she* belonged on the pages of *Sophisticate*.

She stared off into space, her deep-brown eyes narrowing as she sighed, clearly worn out by the New York dating scene. "Every time I strike up the courage to go on a date in this city, I'm dealing with a man with Peter Pan Syndrome or someone who's married to their job."

Before I could respond, a voice cut through the hum of the office. "Hallie!"

Anthea. Of course.

Interns scrambled to make themselves look busy, and a few writers exhaled in relief that it wasn't their name being called. Janelle, not wanting to stick around for the storm, disappeared as quickly as she came.

I straightened up, trying to steady my nerves as I made my way toward Anthea's office. I admired her more than anyone else at *Sophisticate*, but the woman was terrifying—like I might be devoured by the beast herself.

I hesitated in the doorway as Anthea studied the rows of magazine mock-ups on her wall. I knocked lightly, and when she waved me in, I took a deep breath, steeling myself for whatever was to come.

She couldn't be telling me she hated the article. Not after she emailed me that she liked it, right? Right?

"Sit," she said, gesturing to the chair in front of her desk, without waiting for me to say a word.

I lowered myself into the chair, feeling the weight of her gaze on me. "The article has been a big hit," she said, without preamble. "This is exactly what I had in mind for this series. But now we need to up the ante. You know what they say, 'sex and love are sticky'. I expect to see something hot in my inbox this weekend."

I swallowed. Did she just say hot? What did she mean by hot?

Before I could form a coherent response, she was already waving me out of her office with a single flick of her wrist. "You've got the audience's attention. Don't waste it."

Something hot?

As soon as I get one win in Anthea's book, she moves the goal posts. Pushing my dreams just that much further out of my reach. Because not only was I asking James to take me on dates as fodder for my articles, it seemed like I might now have to kiss the man, too.

The only problem was, as much as I'd like to deny it, to me the idea was just what Anthea wanted, *hot*.

I followed my phone map to the address James had sent earlier in the week and found myself looking up at a newly developed warehouse in Upper Manhattan. I buzzed the intercom; a moment later, the door opened silently, as if guided by an invisible hand. No irritatingly handsome investment banker in sight.

Was this all some wild scheme to murder me once we got to the second date?

I wandered into a quiet, empty lobby, the only sound the gentle hum of the air conditioning, as a polite-looking receptionist sat at a desk, her fingers tapping lightly on a keyboard. Her smile was bright, and when she looked up at me, I couldn't help but wonder if I was one of the few people she'd spoken to all day.

"Are you Hallie?" the receptionist asked me. She stood up from behind her desk and circled around to shake my hand.

"I am," I hesitantly responded.

"Great!" The receptionist's cheerfulness struck me as odd; surely, serial killers weren't this chipper. "They're waiting for you right through those doors."

They?

With a flourish, she gestured toward the gleaming double glass doors, revealing an expansive industrial kitchen beyond. The polished stainless-steel countertops were lined with vibrant ingredients, while two pristine aprons hung up on the wall.

"You found it," a rich voice came from the opposite side of the room. Distracted by the kitchen of my dreams, I completely missed the seating area where James reclined in a plush chair.

I nearly did a double-take. I was so used to seeing James in a suit that the sight of him dressed down felt like catching a glimpse of a different person entirely—unexpected, and if I was honest, a little thrilling. He was wearing worn jeans and a dark green button-down shirt, the sleeves rolled up to reveal his muscular forearms.

He looked impossibly good, so good, in fact, that if

someone hadn't walked in right at that moment, I probably would've kept staring like an idiot.

"You're both here! Fantastic. Shall we get started?" Melody Garrett, the world-famous restaurateur, entered in her chef whites, and I did all I could not to pass out right then and there. I looked back over at James, eyes almost falling out of my head, to find him simply smiling at me, eyes sparkling.

"W-what's going on?" I managed to ask.

"I know how much you love good food, so I thought what better way to experience it than to have a cooking class from one of your favorite chefs."

He strode toward me in five long, confident steps and stopped just short of touching. The warm, spiced scent of cinnamon, cloves, and cardamom drifted from him, making my mouth water. Then—unexpectedly—his hand found mine. Just a brief squeeze, warm and solid and sure, before he let go.

I blinked, stunned. Since when was James touchy? He wasn't supposed to be touchy. He was supposed to be all business and banter and well-planned reservations . . . not this.

And I wasn't supposed to feel anything about it.

Except I did.

Which was a problem. A big, cinnamon-and-clove-scented, annoyingly charming problem.

"How did you know she was my favorite?" I asked, almost breathless. If the prospect of learning from a culinary legend in this incredible kitchen was surreal, then the simple touch of his hand was the thing that truly overloaded my senses.

"I noticed you reviewed quite a few of her restaurants on your blog." James shrugged. "So, I took a shot in the dark."

A wave of warmth washed over me, a feeling like sunshine on my skin.

I was already surprised by how personal our first date felt.

But this . . . this felt overwhelming. And yet, somehow, totally natural.

He hadn't just picked another amazing restaurant. He hadn't Googled "best date night ideas in Manhattan" or gone with a flashy scene to impress me. He'd chosen something thoughtful—intentional. He'd paid attention. The kind of gesture that made my chest tighten.

"Are you ready to learn how to prepare Chicken and Shrimp Laksa?" Melody asked, unaware of the thousands of other questions racing through my mind. James shoved his hands deep in his pockets and arched an eyebrow at my frozen state. He watched me, a mixture of amusement and anxiety in his eyes, waiting to see what I would do.

I reached for the apron, deciding to ignore my racing heart, and pushed forward, determined to make the most of every second we had with Melody. *The* Melody Garrett.

"Are you much of a cook?" James asked as he pulled his apron over his head and tied it around his waist with steady hands. Somehow, he managed to make that simple white fabric look like a designer brand.

"There's a reason that I enjoy reviewing food that's cooked by someone else," I said with a crooked smile.

Cooking wasn't exactly my strong suit, but the chance to watch Melody prepare her signature dish up close? That was worth burning a few shallots for. Her Chicken and Shrimp Laksa had put her on the map, allowing her to open her Asian-fusion restaurant that had sent waves across the food scene in New York City.

As Melody began walking us through the steps, I tried to absorb every word, every flick of her wrist as she added spices or stirred the broth. James, of course, took to it like he was born in the kitchen, while I mostly tried not to light anything on fire or accidentally julienne my fingers.

By the time we were plating, I was sweaty, flour-dusted, and maybe just a little more in awe of people who could do this professionally. After thirty minutes of trying not to burn my fingers, I stared down at my bowl, a far cry from Melody's incredible creation. Next to me, James was putting the final garnish on his own dish that was a pretty much exact replica of what Melody had plated in front of her.

"How did you do that?" I asked, staring at the perfectly poached shrimp and chicken, perfectly fried shallots, and the rich yellow color of his broth. Even the handmade noodles were perfect. "Did you miss your calling?"

"I grew up rolling pizza dough at my family's restaurant," James teased as we carried our bowls to the table. We thanked Melody (probably a little too effusively on my part, given how long it took me to let go of her hand) and she left us to eat, just the two of us.

"You expertly managed to create a critically acclaimed dish, and you're equating that to slinging pizza dough?" I asked as we took our seats.

"Hey, don't let my Nonno hear you say that. Slinging pizza dough is an art form. Plus, I'm sure yours isn't that bad," James said, smiling as he quickly swapped our meals, taking my travesty and giving me his plate of perfection.

"Are you sure you want to do that?" I winced as James inspected my Chicken and Shrimp Laksa. As much as Melody had tried to guide me, the broth was the wrong color, the chicken and shrimp had been overcooked, and the fried shallots had come out more burnt than fried.

But James carefully spooned a bit of the suspiciously brown broth into his mouth, and I waited, my eyes fixed on his, for the expected grimace.

"Just needs some salt."

"Oh, come on," I said with a laugh. We both knew that the dish required significantly more than salt to be palatable. "You don't have to eat that."

James stuck a hand out, keeping his bowl firmly in front of me. "So, Hallie Woods, future restaurant critic of *Sophisticate,* review me. Tell me how I did."

My heart did an annoying flip, which I promptly ignored. This wasn't real. Not in the way it was starting to feel. This was about mutual benefit—an article for me, good press for his family's restaurant. That was the deal. That's all it was supposed to be.

But between the private cooking class with my favorite chef and the thoughtful way he kept handing me chances to shine, it was getting increasingly difficult to pretend I wasn't swooning just a little.

I picked up my spoon, humoring him. The first sip hit like a revelation. The chicken and shrimp were juicy, the herbs were fresh, and the noodles were perfectly cooked.

"I really do think you missed your calling," I said, moaning as I went in for another bite. "Split this with me."

James was still attempting to eat my monstrous creation without flinching, bless his heart. I slid his bowl into the middle so we could share.

"In other words, a five-star review?" he teased, his signature smirk which I loathed playing on his lips.

"You'd get my most glowing review for this." Little did he know, I didn't just mean the dish in front of us.

15

James

"Tell me about your family." Our fingers lightly brushed while we walked—a simple touch, yet it sent tiny goosebumps up my arm that I couldn't ignore.

The energy between us seemed to intensify with every step we took. Every second that passed tonight made it harder to believe this was just an arrangement.

Central Park was nothing short of gorgeous at this time of year. The leaves were impossibly green, the spring blossoms popped like watercolor against the evening sky. Somehow everything seemed more vivid, like the park had tuned itself to the same frequency within me.

I'd started to second guess choosing a private cooking class with Melody Garrett as I waited for Hallie to arrive earlier. Not because I didn't think she'd enjoy it, I knew she would. It felt too thoughtful. Too revealing. Like I was showing my hand when I wasn't supposed to. But I'd taken a chance anyway, and used my connections to ask Melody to do a class for us. She just happened to be a friend of my mother's, who'd been visiting her restaurants for years. If that exposed my growing feelings for Hallie, then so be it.

This wasn't meant to be real. She was writing her articles. I needed a good review. But somewhere between her jokes at the bar and the way she looked at me when she ate the first bite of laksa, I'd started to see Hallie in a different light.

I didn't think she saw it that way, though. For Hallie, this was probably still just a series of interviews wrapped in dinner dates. Good content. A career move. But knowing that didn't make it easier to resist the way I wanted to get to know her more.

"Well," she started, as we dodged a crowd that had formed to watch a street performer play their music. "They're good people. They still live in my childhood home. My dad retired last year from the United States Postal Service and spends all his free time doing DIY around the house. I think he finished standing garden beds last week for my mom. My mom is a math teacher at the high school I went to and is beloved by all her students. My younger sister got married a few years ago and is pregnant with her first child. She and her husband, Devin, live down the road from my parents."

I nodded, taking it in. "How did they feel when you moved to New York City?"

"They didn't really understand it. They still don't, really," Hallie said, slowing as we reached the Bethesda Terrace. I stood back and watched as she approached the fountain, her shoulders rising and falling with a thoughtful breath. "They're perfectly content with their lives in Terry, Ohio. They've got great friends there and don't see themselves leaving that community. But, amazing as they are and as much as I love being at home, I'd always felt restless. I knew there was more out there for me. I couldn't see myself staying there for the rest of my life."

"So, you chased your dreams," I said, watching her.

It was admirable, moving across the country to a place where you had no family or connections. All to chase a dream. While I had followed the path of so many generations of my family before me.

She turned, her expression lightening, "I just figured why not make the big move in my twenties. I can always move back. Not that I think I will now. New York has my heart. Besides," she added with a grin, "Ohio bagels just don't cut it."

God, she had a great smile.

"What about you? I don't think you've talked much about your family outside of the restaurant." Hallie dropped down onto a bench, and I sat beside her, stretching my arm across the back. My fingers nearly skimmed her shoulder, but I hesitated. The impulse to touch her was almost instinctual, but I wasn't sure if it would be welcome—or just another part of the illusion she was maintaining.

"Well," I started, willing my voice to sound steady, "I'm an only child. My mom and dad met when they were in their early twenties. My mom comes from a finance family—big Wall Street legacy, lots of expectations. But my father grew up in Brooklyn, working for the family business."

"How'd they meet?" she asked, completely unaware of how tightly I was wound beside her, like a thread ready to snap.

"At a bar, in Brooklyn. My mom had gone out with some friends for the evening, and they'd decided to get out of Manhattan for the night. She met my dad and, as the story goes, they hit it off instantly. But my mom's family didn't receive it well, initially."

A frown creased Hallie's face. "Why not?"

"Well, my dad didn't come from money and my grandfather hadn't thought that he was respectable enough for my mother. He was worried that he was after her wealth."

Hallie shook her head, strands of her beautiful brown hair falling across her face. "That's terrible."

"Despite his harsh assumptions, my grandfather was just trying to protect my mom. He regretted it later on. He and my father grew to have a fond relationship before my grandfather passed."

Hallie let out a thoughtful hum. "It's a bit like Romeo and Juliet, isn't it?"

"Except they ended up with a happy ending," I said, with a smile.

As if on cue, a wave of disappointment washed over me when Hallie shifted forward, putting more space between us. My hand had been a hair's breadth from resting on her shoulder, and the sudden distance made me feel like something was slipping through my fingers.

"Do you enjoy what you do?" She stared thoughtfully at me with her elbow propped on her bent leg and her head cradled in her hand. "Being a financial analyst, I mean? Or did you just become one because you thought you should follow in your family's footsteps?"

I could see why she'd ask. My career path might seem predictable, especially in comparison to hers. But it wasn't quite that simple. My parents had always made it clear I could do anything I wanted, but I still gravitated toward numbers.

During school, I'd been the typical high achiever—getting good grades, playing multiple sports, doing my fair share of extra curriculars. But I'd spent my free time working at Rossi Pizzeria, and at one point I had thought I would become a business owner myself or even take over from my uncle and father when the time came. It wasn't until college when I took my first economics class that everything fell into place for me.

"I love it," I said, my voice a little more passionate than I intended. It was true. I wanted to make a difference in finance, build something of my own. "And I hope to one day have my own firm."

"Married to the job," Hallie mused, leaning back again. Right into my waiting hand.

It wasn't much of a touch—a mere brush against her back—but it felt like an electric shock, sending a jolt straight to my chest. My heart slammed against my ribs, and the awareness of her, of how close she was, made it hard to focus on anything else.

"Working in finance takes more dedication and time than the average job. I'm aware of that. But until I have someone in my life that means more to me than numbers, I'll be dedicated to my job."

Hallie seemed lost in thought for a moment, and I wondered if I'd said the wrong thing.

"I suppose I understand it," she said after a beat. "Dating in the city hasn't gone particularly well for me. So, I threw myself into writing and trying to move my career along."

I could hear the resignation that seemed to hang around her words. Part of me understood the feeling of putting the rest of life on hold to chase a dream. But as much as I understood it, I wanted to resist that kind of isolation.

"I don't particularly want a job that consumes every

aspect of my life," I admitted, almost too quickly. Hallie's shoulders stiffened under my touch, and I knew it wasn't just the contact that was making her tense. It was what I had said, the truth in it maybe. I got the feeling that I'd surprised her, that the sentiment didn't quite fit into the picture she'd painted of me before.

The sun had almost completely sunk behind the horizon, daylight slipping away from us. "I think it's time we got you home." As much as I didn't want this date to end, I didn't want to borrow more time than I was being given from Hallie.

I hailed a cab to take us to the West Village and the two of us slid inside. One question echoed around my mind as the cab rolled forward.

What are we even doing?

The excitement I got from disrupting Hallie's dates over the past month was nothing compared to what I felt right now. My heartbeat was a full-blown marching band, banging around inside my chest as we drew nearer to Hallie's apartment.

This was just an obligatory date. Simply part of our deal. I wasn't supposed to feel like *this*. Seb's teasing comment from last Sunday floated through my mind. *It's nice seeing you like this. Happy.*

Hallie's leg bounced up and down next to me. *Was she that eager to get out of the cab? Away from me?*

"So do you feel like today's date will be enough for another article?" I asked, trying to keep the conversation light. My hand splayed out on the seat next to us, brushing against her upper thigh by accident. That same frenzy of energy surged through me. She glanced at me, her lower lip pulled between her teeth, like she was weighing something in her mind.

"It was amazing. I can't wait to get home and write up the article. I think people everywhere will die at the personal touch you put into this. So, thank you for that."

"It's the least I can do. I'll make sure to really step it up for our next one."

"Right." Hallie took a big breath before.

"Are you alright?"

"Yes! I'm fine." Hallie turned, offering a wide smile, but her eyes betrayed a hint of something else. She closed her eyes briefly, then opened them again, glancing at me. "It's just my boss has put a lot of pressure on this upcoming article."

I gently reached out to take her hand in mine and tried my best to ignore the flames crackling inside of me. "How so?"

Hallie's eyes searched mine, and as we neared her apartment building, she spoke again. "She was hoping for this article to really heat up."

"Heat up?" A strange intensity filled the cab, the silence punctuated by the rhythmic tick of the meter and the driver's occasional sharp cough.

"Like a kiss or something like that." Hallie waved off her words, as if they were trivial, then reached for the door handle. "But we agreed there would be no kissing. I didn't think I'd have to worry about writing something like that into any of these articles, but my boss is full of surprises. So, I guess this is just me warning you about a fictional kiss that I'll have to conjure up for this week's article."

The flames inside me roared even hotter, nearly boiling the blood running through my veins as Hallie gave me a sympathetic smile and slipped out of the cab. I was frozen to my seat, paralyzed, watching her walk toward the stairs of her apartment building. The same images I had of kissing Hallie during our first date played in my head once more.

"Well, are you going to go after her?" The cab driver's voice snapped me out of my stupor. The older man looked at me as if I was a total idiot through the rearview mirror, his bushy eyebrows raised as if he couldn't believe I was letting a beautiful woman walk to her apartment door alone after a date. To be honest, I couldn't believe it either. She wasn't just beautiful—she was smart, funny, and had just told me she needed a kiss for her article. I needed to stop second guessing myself. *Hallie is not Cassidy.*

"Right. Yes. Thanks." I threw some bills in his direction and quickly climbed out after her. She was unlocking the building's front door when I bounded up the stairs behind her.

"James? Did you forget something?" Hallie asked, glancing over her shoulder as she pulled the door open.

"I did. Forget something." Before I could think better of it, I slid my fingers against the smooth, warm softness of her cheek, then slipped them around to the back of her neck, my fingers finding purchase in her soft hair. With one more step, I closed the space between us.

The pounding in my ears became deafening, and I wasn't sure if I was hearing her heart or my own as I lowered my head. Just before my lips touched hers, I realized I didn't want Hallie—I desperately *needed* her.

Only when her arms snaked around my neck, did I think that maybe she felt the same way.

I didn't care that we were standing on the stoop of her apartment building for the world to see as I kissed Hallie Woods for the first time. The softness of her lips, the lingering taste of red wine on her tongue, and the sharp intake of her breath as I deepened the kiss.

I backed Hallie up against the cold, damp brick wall. My hands trailed down her sides, savoring the feel of her curves—the soft give of her skin, the gentle heat radiating from her. She was *incredible*.

When we finally broke apart, I looked down at her, trying to figure out if I'd taken it too far.

She was so fucking stunning it nearly hurt to step away from her. I barely registered my mind reminding me that these dates were supposed to be obligatory, that Hallie could walk away at the end of it.

She said nothing at first, but she offered a shy smile. "By the way," Hallie said before she shut the door behind her, "when should I come by for the visit to Rossi's? I've been meaning to check it out, but I wasn't sure when to fit it in between all the articles."

I smiled, still trying to shake off the heat of our kiss. "Whenever you're ready. Maybe after a few dates—my family is always eager to meet anyone who's willing to write about their pizza."

Hallie's eyes twinkled. "I'll definitely make it happen. Can't wait." The warmth behind her eyes as she disappeared behind her apartment building door ignited a spark of hope within me.

16

Hallie

"So, he kissed you up against the wall outside and now you can't stop thinking about him. Did I get that right?" Roxie asked as she settled down on the couch next to me with a bowl of popcorn. A movie played on the TV, but we hadn't paid attention to a single minute of it.

"That about sums it up."

Roxie had been home when I returned from my second date with James. She'd taken one look at my mussed hair and swollen lips and immediately screeched like a kid on Christmas morning. She'd insisted on a full debrief over a glass of wine. It was normally Roxie giving these debriefs, so it felt strange that the situation was reversed for the first time.

"I can't say I told you so because I never actually told you so, but I *knew* this was going to happen." Roxie tossed a piece of popcorn toward me. "Was it hot? Spicy? Steamy? What chili rating would you give it? Oh, please give me the details. I *have* to live vicariously through you right now."

"It was . . ." *Sexy. Hot. Dangerous. The kind of kiss I'd be replaying in my head when I pulled my vibrator out of my nightstand.* "Really nice."

Roxie rolled her eyes at my scaled-back answer as she twisted her dark-blonde hair and resecured it with a hairpin. Tonight was one of the few nights that she had off from the art gallery and instead of going out, she'd decided to stay in and watch romance movies.

"I'm sure that Anthea will be happy with the magic you twist this date into on the page." If tonight's kiss wasn't spicy enough for my boss, I wasn't sure what would be. My only worry was whether Anthea would expect me to write something even hotter next.

I'd been so determined to prove I deserved the food critic position, so willing to do whatever Anthea asked, that I'd never stopped to consider what I'd do if I developed feelings along the way. I pulled a worn, crocheted blanket from the couch and threw it over our legs as if it could ward off those feelings.

"What's on your mind?" Roxie asked me, her legs tangling with mine. "I can see those wheels turning in that beautiful head of yours."

I mustered a small smile. "I'm worried about continuing these dates with James."

"Why?" Roxie asked. "You get to go on extravagant dates that a guy actually puts thought into. Have a little fun. Kiss a little. What more could a girl want?"

Roxie was right. What more *could* I want? James had put so much thought into both dates, pulling the little details he knew about me and crafting a night I'd enjoy. The problem was, everything James had done so far was perfect.

He was perfect.

"I'm worried that I'm maybe, possibly, having some feelings for him." My voice was barely above a whisper and Roxie had to lean in to hear me fully.

Her eyes searched mine as she set the bowl of popcorn and her glass of wine down on our coffee table. She reached out, taking my hands in hers. "Is that a bad thing?"

A lump formed in my throat.

Roxie pulled me into a hug. "Remember what our favorite movie to watch together is about? *Eat, Pray, Love*? I think it's your turn to experience life. Indulge in good food. Find yourself and maybe someone else along the way."

Roxie might have been right, but I couldn't shake the uncertainty about tonight's kiss. Was it because of his feelings for me, or was it just part of helping me fulfill Anthea's request about this week's article? The lingering taste of his lips only added to my confusion.

"What if we started our own blog together?" The idea had been bouncing around in my head for a while. Roxie and I had tinkered with it back in college but had ultimately decided we couldn't afford to start a business without some experience in the industry first.

Roxie pulled away from me, her brows nearly up in her hairline. "Where is this coming from?"

I reached for the bottle of wine to refill both of our glasses before I dove into my idea. A little liquid courage couldn't hurt.

"Come on, it was our dream back in college, and I've been thinking about it again recently." I span the stem of the wineglass between my fingers as Roxie considered my offer. She loved her job at the art gallery, but it had simply been a place for her to make connections until she could break into the food photography industry.

"What about the food critic position with *Sophisticate*? You're so close to getting it."

Becoming a food critic for *Sophisticate* had always been my dream. I'd started out as an intern, delivering coffees and becoming the queen of the copier machine. Then, when the opportunity came for my own column, I jumped at it. So, when Anthea had offered the promotion for "Love on Wall Street", I didn't see the harm in it. But now I was wondering if it was worth it. It was taking over my life, and I wasn't sure how comfortable I felt with my boss telling me who to kiss, even if the kiss she'd dictated had been nothing short of earthshattering.

"There's no guarantee. I could write this entire series and still have Anthea decide to not give me the position." It was time I took matters into my own hands. Maybe I wouldn't have the *Sophisticate* brand behind me and my reviews, but that didn't mean I couldn't make a name for myself on my own. I'd already proven I could create my own community with my social media, so why not take it a few steps further?

"What about you? What's your plan for getting from the gallery to food photography?"

Roxie sighed as she leaned back on the couch. "I'm not sure. My time at the gallery has been great. The clients there are wonderful to me. I've made great connections. But I'm still no closer to leaving than I was when I first took the job. Plus, the owner's an asshole."

"What if we did a dream board? Like we did in college whenever we wanted to plan our lives. We can lay it all out to start. We don't have to decide right now."

Roxie chewed on the idea for a moment. Back in college, she'd always been the one to jump into opportunities feet first while I'd just dip a toe in to test the waters. Her hesitation now was out of the ordinary.

"Okay, we can do a dream board. I think that's fair. I'm just worried that now isn't the right time."

"What do you mean? Why wouldn't the time be right?" Roxie's eyes softened as she reached for my hands again.

"Honey, the last thing I want is for you to be *this* close to the food critic position at *Sophisticate* and you don't see it through. Yes, you could write this entire 'Love on Wall Street' series and Anthea could still pass you over, but why wouldn't you at least give yourself a chance for it rather than counting yourself out before you even take your first swing?"

My phone buzzed on the coffee table, and James's name flashed across the screen, making my heart stop.

"That kiss must have really been something if he's texting you only an hour after he dropped you off," Roxie said with a knowing look.

> **James:** I had the best time tonight. Would you want to grab breakfast tomorrow? I know that we only agreed to our five dates . . . so I understand if you don't want to. But I wanted to speak with you about an idea I had for our next date.

I stared at the message, my thumb hovering over the keyboard. I wasn't sure what to say. On one hand, I wanted to see him again. On the other, I wasn't sure if I should blur the line between this ridiculous arrangement and something real. Was I getting caught up in the moment?

I looked over at Roxie, who had been watching me closely. "How should I respond?"

She leaned forward, setting her glass of wine down, her eyes narrowing in thought. "Well, for starters, stop second-guessing yourself all the time. I don't know what it is with you and overthinking everything, but it's holding you back. Whether it's James, the article, or your job application—if you want something, just go for it."

I took in her words, letting them sink in and ignoring the initial sting of them. Roxie was right. I'd spent so much time second-guessing every step I took, especially with this whole "Love on Wall Street" series, and now I was doing the same with James.

Taking a deep breath, I finally typed out my reply.

Hallie: I'd love to. Can I choose the place tomorrow?
James: I was hoping you'd say that. I want Hallie Woods' best breakfast suggestion in all of New York City.

Were we breaking yet another rule that I'd laid out before we started all of this? Yes. Did I care? I fired off the address of my favorite breakfast spot over on the Upper West Side, only realizing the stupid grin on my face when I looked up to see Roxie staring at me with raised eyebrows.

"What?" I asked.

Roxie raised her hands. "I'm not saying anything."

"Your face is saying something," I argued. But instead of responding, Roxie crammed her mouth full of popcorn and reached for the remote to find something else for us to watch. But her message was loud and clear when she settled on a movie about a woman that hired a man as her date to her brother's wedding, only to fall in love in the end.

"How long have you been waiting here?" I asked James as I slid out of the taxi. He was standing on the curb in front of my new favorite breakfast spot. I was starting to love seeing him dressed down in a pair of designer jeans, a gray sweater over a collared shirt, and loafers.

There was something different about him—warm, approachable charm that made my heart flutter in an unfamiliar way. His business-like demeanor softened, replaced by a smile that crinkled the corners of his eyes.

What doesn't this man look good in?

"I live a few blocks from here." He offered me his hand as I stepped onto the sidewalk. "I've walked by this place a hundred times since it opened, but I've never stopped in. I should have known that it was good, judging by the line out the door."

I imagined James' apartment would be dark wood, minimal, modern furniture, floor-to-ceiling glass windows high in the sky, with only a few personal touches. Not that I'd ever get to see it. Of course not.

"We have reservations." I said, shaking the thought off.

We passed the long line snaking out the door, and I gave my name to the hostess. She grabbed two menus and ushered us to one of the last open tables at the back. An awkward silence hung between us now that we were alone. The air seemed to hum with the unspoken memory of last night's kiss. It had consumed my thoughts ever since I'd fumbled for my keys, trying to unlock my door and still reeling from how James had pressed me against the building. His kiss, raw and urgent, had made my skin burn with a longing I couldn't explain.

I tugged at my collar, feeling suddenly too warm.

"Maybe one day you'll have a permanent table at places like this." James pulled my chair out for me. His unexpected acts of kindness outside of our dates threw me off every time. Was this a date? How was I supposed to act? What did this mean?

The questions whirled in my head as I glanced over the menu, trying to distract myself. I already knew what I wanted, but reading the words helped me avoid any eye contact.

"Maybe," I mused, inhaling the rich aroma of freshly brewed coffee as the waiter placed a ceramic pot, complete with tiny creamers, on the table.

"So, what's good here, Miss Expert?" James asked me as he studied the menu.

Sitting here with him, surrounded by the sounds of sizzling bacon and the cozy hum of Saturday morning, felt unexpectedly intimate.

"Their chicken and waffles are some of the best in the city but huevos rancheros are my favorite," I offered, trying to sound casual.

The waiter returned and took our order—two huevos rancheros and an order of bite-sized pancakes to share.

When she left, I turned back to James. "You mentioned you had an idea for our third date?" I asked, clearing my throat as I fought to regain my focus.

James poured himself a cup of coffee as he nodded. "Yes. I wanted to run it by you first instead of surprising you, because it would be a couple of overnight stays."

My eyebrows shot up in surprise. The mere mention of an overnight stay with him sent a rush of nerves through me. It meant that we would spend more time together than we ever had before. I tried to suppress the flood of questions. Would he expect to share a bed? Where was he taking me? Was it just the two of us?

"Memorial Day is this weekend, and I thought there's nothing more extravagant than being whisked away to the Hamptons." James's voice pulled me back to the present. "I figured we could invite Sebastian and Roxie too. My parents are renovating their place, but it should be usable enough for all of us."

"You want to take me to the Hamptons?" The thought hit me harder than I expected. The Hamptons? I'd been there once with friends, but we'd stuck to a few dive bars and local joints. This was different. The magazine could eat it up, though. I could practically hear Anthea's voice in my head, praising clicks and shares this article would generate.

I hesitated, the nervous tightness in my throat growing. It felt like too much. But then I thought about Roxie, who would jump at the chance to go if she were in my place.

"It's too much," I started, but James's face fell, and his cheeks flushed pink as he assumed I was turning him down.

"I can figure out something else to do in the city," he said quickly, but I reached out, placing a hand over his.

"No," I quickly interjected. "I would love to go to the Hamptons with you."

A visible sense of relief washed over his face, the tension in his shoulders easing. He gave me a smile that melted something inside me.

"Oh. Okay, great," he said.

His gaze lingered on me, warm and steady, and I squeezed my thighs together as a sudden heat surged between them. My mind flashed to the conversation I'd had with Roxie.

"I'm worried that I'm maybe, possibly, having some feelings for him."

"Is that a bad thing?"

"I think I'm going to have to make sure I'm going to the gym if we keep up these dates," James joked, as the waiter brought our appetizer of mini pancakes out. "If food is your love language, I may put on a few pounds trying to make you happy."

He laughed, digging into the pancakes, and divided up the appetizer between us. But my mind was reeling from what he'd said. Trying to make the other person happy? That's what people on proper dates do, right? Or was there something else going on here?

Maybe this wasn't about the article and the review for his family's restaurant after all. My mind kept circling back to that kiss. To the way James looked at me, like he was actually . . . interested. I'd hoped to keep this professional, but if I was being honest with myself, there was a small part of me that *wanted* to see if there was something more.

"Would you prefer a lot of syrup, or just a little?" James asked while I stared at him, dumbfounded.

"A lot," I rasped, my throat suddenly dry.

One kiss had sent me spiraling. And now, the idea of spending an entire weekend with James in the Hamptons left me both exhilarated and terrified. How was I possibly going to survive?

17

Hallie

SUBJECT: ARTICLE DUE BY MONDAY NIGHT

I'm feeling generous. Since it's Memorial Day weekend and we are off on Monday, I expect to have your article in my inbox by Monday night. It will be on the digital site on Wednesday. I hope to see something spectacular for the long weekend. Come see me before you leave.

Anthea's email hit my work inbox just as I was packing up my bag around lunch time. James had suggested we get on the road a bit earlier in the day to beat the traffic heading out to the Hamptons. One way in and out could back us up in traffic for hours.

I sighed as I closed my laptop and shoved it into my work bag. When Anthea had first proposed this idea, I'd been less than thrilled to write it. At first, it hadn't seemed like much—just a fluff piece, a lightweight assignment that I figured would only cost me a couple of sleepless nights. How very wrong I'd been.

Anthea was walking on her treadmill in a pair of heels when I knocked on her office door. "Hallie, come in."

The door clicked shut behind me, and I stood there for a moment, debating whether to sit or stand. It felt incredibly awkward to sit as she continued walking on her treadmill, so standing it was.

"You did a great job highlighting how personal your last date was so the reader could understand your love of food." Anthea's ability to multitask was admirable as she flipped through her tablet resting on her treadmill. "I can't even imagine how much money Mr. Old Fashioned shelled out to secure a private cooking class with Melody Garrett. You know, I may need you to slip me his number when this is all said and done."

The unexpectedness of Anthea's comment caused me to nearly choke, my eyes widening with surprise.

"It's incredibly difficult to find someone who can treat a woman right in this city." Anthea trailed off for a moment, lost in her own head before clearly remembering I was still standing in her office wondering why the hell I had been called in here. "Right. Well, I wanted to speak with you about the critic position."

Anticipation tightened my chest, making my breaths shallow. Was this it? Was this the moment I'd been waiting for ever since I'd applied to *Sophisticate*?

"I think it's only fair that I let you know we have another candidate for the position that the board wants me to interview."

Wait, what?

Had I heard her correctly?

Anthea's words echoed in my mind, a confusing bunch of half-understood phrases. Every hope I had drained away like air from a punctured lung, the weight of the realization crushing me. I'd been stupid to think that it would be this easy. That Anthea would hand over such a prestigious position to me if I'd only written a few articles.

"It's not a done deal. I told the board I already had another candidate that I was seriously considering, but I can't really turn them away when they want something. I wanted to let you know that I really liked what you did with this last piece and how you discussed the food elements in it. It was insightful, thoughtful, and your voice really shone. I think you'll have a promising career in the industry."

I might have floated on air after her compliment if she hadn't just crushed my dreams.

"You've got skill, Hallie. And you are very much still a contender for this role. But you're also doing so well. As editor-in-chief, I have to consider whether giving you a column in the magazine and on digital would be a better position for you. Maybe something on dating. I'm still experimenting with it."

Each word was a blow, a sharp sting that chipped away at my resolve. I suddenly found myself facing a double-edged sword by following Anthea's instructions. Ironically, my current achievements put my future at risk. I shouldn't have felt surprised that I was being passed over in my career. It happened in every aspect of my life, so why not this one? Like when my parents praised my sister when she got engaged and then turned to ask me if I had found anyone yet. Or when we went out and men looked at Roxie before they looked at me because she was exotic, unusual. And I was just . . . me.

"I'm excited to read your article next Monday night.

I'm sure it won't disappoint. Just keep raising the bar with the glitz and glamour. It's really kept the readers engaged."

A wave of numbness washed over me as Anthea dismissed me from her office, and I nodded, the stale air heavy in my lungs.

Janelle popped into my cubicle as I finished packing my bag, wanting to get far away from the office now as quickly as I could.

"So, what do you have planned for the weekend?" Janelle asked, seemingly oblivious to the tension that still clung to me after the conversation with Anthea. "Please tell me Mr. Old Fashioned is treating you to something *amazing*. A quick trip out of the country? Somewhere warm? A shopping spree? I can only imagine what it would feel like to shop with a no-limit black AmEx card."

I paused, trying to force a smile, but it came out more as a strained half-grin. "Actually, we're heading to the Hamptons for the weekend," I said, the words sounding strange coming out of my mouth.

Janelle's eyes widened in surprise. "The Hamptons? That sounds incredible. Have fun. I can't wait to read all about it."

I nodded, trying to ignore the way my stomach turned at the idea of having to share whatever happened this weekend. I didn't want to think too much about it—just needed to get out of here.

Roxie: Are you on your way home? James is picking us up in thirty minutes!
Hallie: Coming.

The weekend ahead suddenly felt pointless as I ducked

into the subway station that would take me back to the West Village. Why would I go to the Hamptons for an article that could secure me a column talking about something that I had no interest in writing about?

Because you actually want *to spend a weekend away with James.*

Despite my better judgment, even though he tried his best to derail my article, I couldn't help but feel amused by the sheer absurdity of his schemes, waiting to see what he'd try next. Those beautiful blue eyes, filled with warmth, made me feel truly seen for the first time in my life. Maybe that was why I kept my conversations with Anthea to myself.

When I walked into the apartment, Roxie was already sitting on the couch, phone in hand, scrolling through something that looked like a food blog.

"How was your day?" she asked casually, still distracted by whatever she was looking at.

I hesitated, glancing at the clock. "Uneventful," I said, a little too quickly before disappearing into my room to pack a few last items. The truth was, I didn't want to talk about the pressure from Anthea, or how I was struggling to figure out exactly why I was excited about James being in my life.

As I bent down to grab my suitcase from the floor, I heard a knock echo through the apartment. My heart skipped a beat, and I froze. That was it. The weekend had begun.

Roxie called from the living room. "I'll get it."

I stood still, trying to prepare myself for whatever came next. A slight shift in the air—his presence—was enough to make me question my packed bag and my rapidly growing anticipation.

Then, as if the universe had been waiting for this moment to catch me off guard, I rounded the corner out into the living room. And there he was.

James stood in the doorway, dressed in linen pants and a partially unbuttoned short-sleeved shirt, revealing the same gold chain I'd seen the night of the dinner party we met at.

"Hey," he said, with an easy smile, one that seemed unburdened by anything that the world could throw at him. It was the most relaxed I'd ever seen him.

"Hey."

James reached for my bag and slipped it from my shoulder. His fingers brushing the exposed skin there. Warmth pooled in my veins, turning thick like honey. At this rate, I'd turn into a gooey mess before we even made it to the Hamptons.

"I picked up some bagels from that little stand down the street for when we hit the road," James said, and Roxie's eyes flickered to mine, her eyebrows raised in surprise.

"The one that Hallie reviewed a few months back?"

"One and the same." James grabbed Roxie's bag with his free hand before turning to look at the two of us. "Are you both ready? Sebastian is meeting us there. He said something about some sort of work emergency with one of his designers."

Beside me, Roxie tensed, her face draining of all color.

"The city is already emptying out. So I'd prepare for a little extra time in the car." James disappeared back out of our front door, leaving me standing just as frozen as Roxie was next to me.

"Are you ready?" I asked her, despite being unsure of the answer to the question myself.

As Roxie straightened, her uncertain look was replaced by a smile. "It's a weekend in the Hamptons. Why wouldn't I be ready?"

"Are you going to be okay spending the weekend with Sebastian?" I reached out to pull Roxie to a halt as she started for the front door. "I know the two of you only spoke briefly at the bar the one time . . ."

Tension tightened Roxie's shoulders. She took a deep breath before turning to smile at me. "Of course, this weekend should be fun!"

"We're nearly there. The house is just around the corner." James steered his car past "houses" that were better classified as estates. Rolling green yards stretched out before me, each meticulously maintained with vibrant, professionally landscaped trees, flower beds, and bushes. Ten of my childhood home made up one of these mansions. Even the garages were massive, capable of sheltering at least five cars, if not more.

As I rolled down the car window, a rush of fresh air enveloped me. Unlike the city, there was not even a hint of smog, car fumes, or the stench of garbage. Instead, the salty scent of the ocean filled my nostrils, carried by the gentle breeze. In the distance, I could hear the rhythmic crashing of waves against private beaches.

"It's beautiful," I breathed, turning to smile at James.

"Beautiful, indeed." James's intense gaze held mine

captive, and only pulling into the driveway of an enormous house dragged me from the depths of his ocean-blue eyes.

"Oh my goodness. Is this it?"

Roxie leaned forward onto the center console, her eyes wide. "Holy *shit*."

"Holy shit," I agreed.

Tall, lush hedges, with their vivid green leaves, stood sentinel on either side of a beautifully crafted wrought-iron gate, partially concealing the magnificent house. We drove through the gates, past the charming cedar shakes, framed by pristine white windows and adorned with elegant black shutters.

"It's been in the family for generations. My great-great-grandfather bought this place nearly a hundred years ago."

"And no one's using it this weekend?" I asked as James pulled the car down the brick driveway that curved toward an attached garage.

"It's been undergoing upgrades for nearly a year. I think we'll be the first people to use it since then. I'm not even sure if everything's done yet." James put the car in park.

"Did you come here a lot before the renovations?" I couldn't imagine spending my summers running around a place like this. You'd need an entire staff to keep everything in order. The closest my family ever came to a butler or a maid was my grandmother coming over and not thinking the house was clean enough, so she did it herself.

"I spent nearly every summer here." James opened his door before rounding the back to grab everyone's bags.

"Every summer?" I asked as I took my bag from him.

"My mom wanted me to get out of the city. She thought

it was good for me to have experiences outside the concrete jungle."

Roxie snorted as she took her bag. "She didn't want you to spend all your time rubbing elbows with the rich in the city, so she brought you here to rub elbows with the rich out of the city?"

James chuckled at the ridiculousness as we headed toward the front door. "Come on, let's get inside. You can pick your rooms."

"As long as mine has a view and a bathtub, I don't care." Roxie pushed her sunglasses on top of her head and marched inside. "And as far away from Sebastian Whittaker as possible," she whispered under her breath so only I could hear. "Can you point me in the direction of the closest bathroom?"

"Just down there, second door on the right." James motioned toward the hallway on our left. Once we were alone, he turned back to me and gestured toward the stairs, "After you." James bowed, that same relaxed smile from earlier still shining on his unbelievably perfect face.

18

James

"I thought you said we'd have our pick of the rooms?" Hallie asked me as the two of us stared at the only two rooms that were in any condition for someone to stay in.

"I didn't think this many rooms would still be out of commission." The only rooms that had been finished were a room with a queen and the primary. Two beds for four people. "You and Roxie can take the primary. Sebastian and I will take the queen."

"Are you sure? We can take the queen." Hallie nervously chewed on the inside of her cheek, her eyes darting around the room. I had to fight not to imagine pushing her up against the wall of the hallway to kiss all the worry from her face. My hands on her hips. Gripping her curves. Our tongues dancing. The gasp that would escape between her lips as I pulled her inside one of these rooms.

In reality, I would stop myself before we ever got to that point, out of respect for Hallie and our agreement. I wasn't even sure it was what she wanted, since she hadn't once acknowledged our kiss. But the images in my head didn't stop. In my head, I tugged Hallie into the primary bedroom. Kicked the door shut behind us and pulled her down onto that large four-poster bed to kiss every inch of her. To relish in the sounds she'd make. To worship at the altar of her.

I knew that vision in my head was only that... a vision. But it didn't stop me from wishing that it were real. My pants felt snug around my groin, and I desperately hoped that Hallie wasn't paying attention.

I cleared my throat. "I insist. You two are my guests. Seb has been here a hundred times. He won't mind sharing the queen with me."

We stepped inside the primary, and sunlight streamed through the giant windows, illuminating the four-poster bed with its private curtains and the cozy reading nook in the corner, my mother's favorite spot. Hallie looked around, and I wished I could see it all through her eyes. Hell, I wished I could see where *she* spent her summers. Did her family take any trips anywhere? Or did they stay home? Did she have friends on her street that she spent hot Midwest summer days rolling around on bikes with? Did she go to summer camp, or did she stay at home to take care of her sister?

Hallie Woods was like a brand-new market to me and I wouldn't stop until I understood all the numbers perfectly.

"This is amazing, James. Thank you for bringing me here." Hallie dropped her bag off on the bed. "Now, I think we should find Roxie before she gets herself into trouble."

I tossed my bag into the room next to Hallie's and followed her back down the hallway. "I'm not sure what kind of trouble she could get herself into."

"In a place this big and knowing Roxie as well as I do, the possibilities are endless."

Voices drifted from the foyer as we descended the grand staircase, hushed and annoyed. Roxie stood in the foyer, arms crossed over her chest and eyes narrowed as Sebastian Whittaker smiled at her.

"We're in the primary at the end of the hall on the right, Rox." Hallie interrupted whatever stare-down the two were having.

"As long as I'm far away from him," Roxie huffed as she grabbed her stuff from the bench in the entryway. She shoved her way past Seb and bounded up the stairs past us.

"About that . . ." Hallie winced. "The only two rooms free are right next to each other. We're sharing the primary. Sebastian and James are in the room next door."

"Great." Roxie gave Hallie a forced smile.

"Oh no." Sebastian's voice took on a fake air of sincerity. "How terrible for you. I hope you brought earplugs, darling. I snore."

Roxie rolled her eyes before disappearing down the hall.

"Is this going to be a problem?" I turned to ask my best friend.

Seb gave me a smile that could have resembled a shark. "Why would you assume there'll be a problem?"

"Because you're you. And there's clearly something going on between you and Roxie."

Seb ascended the stairs, then paused to give me a clap on the shoulder. "This is going to be *fun*."

Hallie leaned over to whisper in my ear as she watched Sebastian's retreating figure. "Do you think . . . ?"

"We'll keep an eye on them."

Hallie tossed one more concerned look toward her best friend as she finished ascending the stairs to the main floor. "I'm not sure what their problem is, but they can bicker all they want. *I* am going to enjoy this beautiful house, this beautiful weather, and soak up all the relaxation I can get."

Sitting across from Hallie at brunch after our date last week had been torture. I could barely go a minute without having our kiss flash across my mind. Our week apart had done little to stifle the feelings of desire growing inside me—for her, for more. And now I was walking into three days with her. Uninterrupted time. No need to say goodbye at the end of the night. Just her and me (and Sebastian and Roxie, but I think they'll keep themselves busy).

Somewhere between her quick wit and that damn kiss, everything shifted. The article and the deal we'd made no longer seemed like my priority. I wanted her to see me for more than the guy trying to protect his family's legacy. I wanted her to see *me*, all the messy, imperfect parts I hadn't let anyone get close enough to see before.

"I want to give you some time to enjoy the backyard. We have a pool and a private dock for our sailboat. But I also planned a few things to show you around the area." I'd spent every summer here, but Hallie was experiencing it for the first time, so I aimed to make it special for her. We couldn't cram everything into these next three days, so a tiny part of me hoped that this wouldn't be the last time she stepped foot on my family's Hamptons property.

"I'm assuming food will be involved?"

My mouth twisted into a grin. "Of course there will be food involved. What a silly question."

Hallie sighed dreamily. "I bet there are so many amazing places here. I really hope Roxie brought her camera."

"Her camera?" I asked. I knew Roxie worked at the art gallery that Michelle Granger frequented, but I didn't realize that she was an artist in her own right.

"She's a photographer. She takes all the photos that I showcase for my blog. We had a dream once of starting our own food blog together." Hallie followed me through the living room to the kitchen. Carefully, she traced the fine details of the furniture—the worn edges of the mahogany desk, the faded floral pattern on the armchair.

"Once? Not anymore?" I opened the fridge, trying to figure out what we were working with. There wasn't an ounce of food inside, and I was certain the pantry looked the same. Clearly, at the end of the season, once Labor Day had passed, my mother had the housekeeper clean all the food out.

"Now's not the time." Hallie's words sounded rehearsed, as if she'd had this very conversation not so long ago.

"I think it could be the perfect time," I countered. Ultimately, we were here today because she wanted a career in the food industry. I'd known her long enough to realize she found the series merely an exercise to reach her goal. So why not take matters into her own hands?

But Hallie waved me off as she watched me double check the pantry was as empty as the fridge. "Looks like we'll need to make a stop at the store."

"We can run into town to grab a few things. I'll see if Seb and Roxie want to join."

Roxie came back down the stairs wearing a coverup over her swimsuit. She was making a beeline for the backyard, a beach towel tucked under her arm and her book dangling from her hand. "I'm good. I'm going to lie out by the pool with my book."

Seb bounded down the stairs, no longer in the suit pants and dress shirt he'd shown up in. He looked at home in a pair of linen shorts and a matching button-up shirt. "Seb, do you want to go into town with us to the store?"

Sebastian's head bobbed as he pretended to consider my offer. The subtle shift in his eyes toward Roxie lounging by the pool, however, betrayed his decision before a word left his lips. "I think I'm going to catch some sun. I've been stuck in the office for too long."

"When was the last time you actually went *in* to the office?" But he was already halfway out the door and no longer paying me any mind.

"I guess it's just the two of us." Hallie slid off the stool at the kitchen island. "Lead the way, my esteemed tour guide."

"You don't have to tell me twice. But let's take a different car. My dad has his whole collection here."

Which was how the two of us ended up cruising back toward town in my dad's favorite classic convertible. Hallie's laughter floating along the wind whipping through her hair. My phone pinged with another update on the current state of the market. They wouldn't close for a few more hours. I could count on one hand the number of times I'd left work before the market closed—maybe twice?—but when I'd asked for time off this weekend, I had promised myself I wouldn't let it pull me away.

The chance to spend this weekend with Hallie was too good to pass up. Despite the insistent itch in my fingers to check for urgent investor updates on my phone, the device remained stubbornly in my pocket. I wasn't about to waste a moment of this.

"How does even the grocery store look as luxurious as the houses?" Hallie asked as I pulled the car into the parking lot. The white-accented shaker-style architecture of the local store mirrored that of many houses in the area.

"I don't think we need much," I told her, grabbing a cart as we headed inside. "We have dinner plans every night and one breakfast reservation. So, we just need enough for two breakfasts, lunches, and snacks."

Hallie walked alongside me, the two of us throwing items in the cart as we circled the store. Her eyes widened comically as I reached for my cereal of choice, the shock evident on her face. "You're picking Cheerios over Cinnamon Toast Crunch?"

"They're good for your cholesterol. Says so right there on the box."

Hallie snatched the box from my hands only to put it back on the shelf, replacing it with Cinnamon Toast Crunch. "We're on vacation, James. Live a little."

"So now my cereal choice isn't exciting enough?" I teased, as we continued through the store. "First you think I'm a carbon copy of everyone else that works on Wall Street and now even my breakfast is boring? Should I get Raisin Bran instead? Really live up to the Mr. Old Fashioned character?"

Hallie tensed. Her knuckles whitened as her hand tightened around the handle of the cart.

"I never thought you were boring, James." Looking up, a heavy weight of regret settled in her eyes, clouding their usual sparkle.

It looked like both of us were working through a jumble of confused emotions. Breaking down preconceived notions. Venturing back into previously avoided territory. And neither of us knew quite what to do about any of it yet.

"Let's get some lunch meat for sandwiches and then I think we should be good. We should probably get back to make sure that Sebastian and Roxie don't kill each other."

The easy camaraderie we'd shared since arriving in the Hamptons had vanished, replaced by a tense silence. We'd transported ourselves back to those first few weeks where we were on opposing ends. But I no longer wanted to put on the boxing gloves and go a few rounds in the ring. Sparring with her was starting to feel like taking a swing at myself.

19

Hallie

Guilt. It's a terrible thing. It starts as a subtle discomfort, a tiny seed, but with each passing day, its tendrils wrap around your heart, growing larger and more painful. Until it consumes you and there's nothing left but that ugly vine inside of you.

My stomach churned as we drove back to the house from the supermarket. I could still hear James's laughter in the background, his easy-going attitude just as infectious as ever, but all I could focus on was the feeling gnawing at me. The guilt over how I had unfairly judged him before getting to know him. My discomfort intensified when I realized I was trapped between continuing articles that unjustly portrayed the finance-man archetype and missing out on a once-in-a-lifetime career chance.

We finally made it back to the house, and as I carried the bags inside, my thoughts only became more muddled. My heart pounded when James was near, a sure sign of my undeniable feelings. But I wasn't sure I wanted to feel this way. By Monday morning, my boss would expect a detailed article in her inbox, covering every aspect of the weekend's events.

Were the stakes worth the reward? James had made it clear he didn't mind being the anonymous subject of my articles, but the more real our dates felt, the more like a fraud I became.

"What's going on in that big, beautiful head of yours?" Roxie leaned over to ask me quietly as we sat in the back of yet another of James's father's fleet of cars, on our way to the dinner reservation that James had planned for the evening.

"I'm just thinking about all the great food we are about to eat."

Roxie narrowed her eyes at my deflection, seeing straight through me. "Spill," she whispered.

I stole a glance at James in the driver's seat, his laughter echoing over the sound of the engine as he chatted animatedly with Sebastian, completely engrossed and oblivious to us in the back.

"I think I'm having regrets."

Roxie's touch was firm but gentle as she reached for my hands and gave them a reassuring squeeze. "Regrets over what?"

"'Love on Wall Street'."

Roxie inhaled knowingly. "You're feeling guilty writing about James."

I nodded.

"You can always stop, or just make it up." With a comforting squeeze, Roxie wrapped an arm around my shoulders and pulled me in for a hug.

"I wish it were that easy," I sighed.

"Why can't it be?" That was the thing with Roxie. She never encountered a problem she couldn't solve. There was never a situation that she couldn't just back out of.

Nothing was ever too permanent, and there was *always* an opportunity to try again.

Her optimism was part of the reason I wanted to be her friend so badly back in college. She made everything seem so easy. As if making a choice were as easy as flicking a switch, not an agonizing process spanning days. Despite her chaotic tendencies, I knew she would always have my back. When life went sideways, she'd always be there to pick up the pieces with me.

"If I just stop writing 'Love on Wall Street', I could lose my job. Plus, I need the experiences to be real. Anthea is such a pro, she'll see straight through it if I start fictionalizing my dates."

Roxie shrugged her shoulders, as if the prospect of unemployment wasn't that big of a deal. I guess when you had constant freelance gigs lined up, it didn't seem like a big deal. But that was just who Roxie was. With her carefree spirit, she never let the small things get her down. Somehow, she always remembered that even the worst, most daunting moments were temporary.

"Weren't you the one that was just suggesting we start our own blog?"

"Weren't you the one that was hesitant over agreeing and wasn't sure if it was the right time?" I fired back.

"I've had some time to think about it," Roxie mused. "And maybe going off on our own wouldn't be such a bad thing. There's a lot that both of us would need to do, but maybe it's doable."

"What are you saying?" I asked her, pulling away to look at her.

"Let's just enjoy dinner tonight. I brought my camera."

Roxie gave me a wink right as James pulled the car into the restaurant's parking lot.

"How does seafood and Italian sound?" James jumped out of the car and opened my door, offering me his hand.

"It sounds perfect."

The warmth of James's arm enveloped my hand as he gently folded it into the crook of his elbow. A wave of comfort and security washed over me, making me forget the predicament the two of us found ourselves in. "Great, because this is the hardest reservation to get here. I had to pull a few strings for us. For you."

James's intense gaze reminded me of our date last week when he stalked toward me from his cab, culminating in one of the hottest kisses of my life. I'd imagined that kiss a hundred times over the past week. The way he transitioned, in a flash, from the gentle, soft-spoken man he'd been all evening to almost primal as he unleashed some of his raw need for me. A deep, throbbing ache pulsed through my body, a relentless rhythm that stole my breath.

James led me into the bustling restaurant, the sounds of clinking glasses and chatter washing over me as Roxie and Sebastian trailed behind, pointedly keeping their distance. The restaurant was bursting at the seams with people.

"Wow. You were right. This is the place to be in the Hamptons. Everyone on their vacation must be spending the evening here."

"Oh, don't be fooled," Sebastian replied. "There are deals being cut around this room as we speak. Just because everyone's traded their suits for linen doesn't mean that work stops."

As if to emphasize his point, Sebastian's phone vibrated.

"The rich never truly take time off."

"How sad it must be," Roxie quipped back at Sebastian, "to not slow down and savor even one night of life."

James and I exchanged uneasy glances.

"Roxie's right, Seb." James slid his phone from the table and into his pants pocket. "No phones."

"You're turning off your lifeline?" I asked jokingly.

"I can go an evening without work." James studied the menu in front of him. "I turned my phone off when we got to the grocery store."

"James Rossi can go twelve hours without checking his phone?" I reached over to feel his forehead. "Are you feeling alright?"

Darkness consumed the rich blue of James's eyes, the pupils dilating as he glared, but there was a hint of playfulness there. "You're infuriating, you know that?"

"I think it's my best quality," I joked, batting my eyelashes at him. "Don't you?"

The challenge in James's eyes was clear in the narrowed gaze and tightened jaw. My knees knocked against the underside of the table as his shoe, rough against my skin, scraped gently down the back of my calf.

"Are you alright?" Roxie asked me.

"Peachy," I murmured back as I caught the smirk on James's face.

That smug asshole.

Now it was Sebastian and Roxie's turn to share a look.

Careful not to attract attention, I subtly slipped my hand beneath the tablecloth, my fingers brushing against James's leg and his spine straightened instantly, his muscles tensing.

"You okay, James?" Sebastian asked.

"Just got a cramp," James replied through clenched teeth.

I pressed my lips together to keep the laugh bubbling inside of me from escaping. Two can play at that game.

When the waiter came over to take our orders, James leaned over. "You're going to regret that later."

A hand swept up my leg, going much further than I had dared to. His fingertips dancing dangerously close to the hem of my summer dress. Heat, like a sudden, burning brand, ignited between my legs, eliciting a sharp gasp. I only hoped the lights were low enough to hide the blush that was spreading from my chest up to my cheeks. His chuckle, a deep resonant sound, vibrated through my chest.

Back at the house after dinner, Sebastian began searching the liquor cabinet, which was stocked with alcohol older than me. "I think I'm going to have a night cap. Roxie, would you care to join me?"

I half expected my best friend to give Sebastian the finger and head to bed, but to my surprise she shrugged one shoulder. "Sure."

James and I watched the two of them wander out by the pool with a couple of beers.

"What do you think is going on between those two?"

"You know Sebastian better than me. But with Roxie, it's hard to tell. I'm not sure if she hates his guts or likes him."

James snorted. "I think that's fair to say for both of them."

"Do you—"

"I think I'm—"

"You first," James said.

"I think I'm going to take a shower and head to bed," I told him. Really, I was hoping a shower would wash away this overwhelming need growing inside of me to climb him like a tree. "It's been a long day between work and traveling here."

James shoved his hands deep in his pockets. A curt nod accompanied the sideways twist of his mouth. "Sure, yeah. I'll see you in the morning?"

"You can count on it."

I gave him an awkward wave and hightailed it toward the primary. What the fuck was I doing? I remained disoriented after dinner. Just the tickle of his breath against the shell of my ear had sent me into a tailspin. The private smiles he shared with me over dinner as he watched me eat one of the best meals I'd ever had were like a match to kerosene.

I wanted James Rossi, and I wasn't sure I could control myself around him tonight if it was just the two of us alone.

As I pulled my toiletries out of my bag, a knock sounded on the door. Roxie must be done with her drink by the pool with Sebastian. That lasted longer than I thought. Sebastian probably pissed her off before he could even pour her a drink. "It's unlocked!"

The door opened and when the silence stretched on for longer than I knew Roxie could manage, I turned.

James stood in the doorway, still not having crossed the threshold into the room. A flicker of something unreadable, a hint of desire perhaps, or maybe conflict, shone in his eyes.

"Did you forget something?"

James shook his head, taking one small step into the room. "No, I didn't forget anything." His voice was barely above a whisper. But it was his eyes, their piercing gaze sending shivers down my spine. So intense and locked on me.

"Then what is it?" My voice trembled, a shaky whisper barely audible, as James took another step closer.

I could see the war raging within him, his thoughts a battlefield of conflicting desires, pulling him this way and that. He was weighing his options. A furious spark ignited within me the moment I watched his resolve crack.

Electricity crackled around the room. Zipping back and forth between us as James took a step, then another, toward me. The air thrummed with anticipation as he stood close enough to touch.

"What are you doing?" I asked. The quietness of my words made me wonder if I'd actually spoken them at all.

"I don't really know," James replied as he reached out. His fingers, feather-light, traced the curve of my cheekbone. "I just knew I couldn't let our evening end so soon."

My eyes drifted to the windows overlooking the pool. The reflection of the lights on the blue water outside painted the night sky. "But Roxie and Sebastian?"

"Sebastian came back in for a second beer. I think they're going to be out there for a while."

His fingers dipped from my cheekbone, down to the

line of my jaw. Then the slope of my throat before tracing my collarbone. "You. Are. So. Beautiful."

He whispered each word into the quiet room.

"What are you doing?" I asked again. I froze, afraid of what was about to happen and afraid of when he'd stop.

"Touching you." His breath hit my neck, warm and slightly musky, as his nose brushed against my skin.

A nervous flutter pulsed in my fingertips as my hands shook, yearning to reach out and touch him. I'd been so shocked when he'd kissed me last week that I hadn't even reached out to run my hands over the hard planes of his body. But this time, James reached down and gently took my hands in his, the warmth of his skin a comfort as our fingers laced together.

I knew what was about to happen. I realized as James took the last tiny step forward, so our chests touched, that this was an inevitable ending for the two of us.

"Why?" Now it was my voice trembling instead of my hands.

"Because I've decided that I'm tired of holding back." James gently released my hands, his touch lingering, before cupping my face in his palms. "But I'm not making another move if this isn't something you want, too."

What did I want?

I wanted to write about things that I actually cared about.

I wanted to make enough money to afford a place that was bigger than the primary closet in this place.

I wanted to continue seeing all this world offered.

I wanted to be happy.

So I reached out, slowly at first. My teeth sunk into my

bottom lip, a nervous habit as my fingers brushed against the rough stubble of his jaw. A gasp escaped James's lips as I encircled his neck, and he froze, not daring to move a muscle. His eyes fluttered closed, eyelashes brushing against the apples of his cheeks.

"What am I doing?" I hadn't even realized I'd spoken the words until James replied.

"Touching me."

The silence stretched, a fragile thread connecting us.

As soon as I crushed my lips to his, the moment snapped, leaving a frenzy in its place.

20

James

The moment that Hallie's lips touched mine, life was breathed back into me. Kissing her was unlike any other experience I'd ever had. Both times I'd kissed her nearly brought me to my knees. Hallie was taking her time. Her hands exploring my chest. Then my back as her fingers dug into the muscles there. My hands shook at my sides as I did everything I could to be patient. To not reach out and scare her away by moving too quickly.

My chest ached and my heart throbbed as she pulled back, her eyes searching mine for something she apparently didn't find because she reached back up on her tiptoes to press her lips against mine again.

This time, it wasn't me devouring her. This time, she was voraciously consuming everything in her path. Just under one week after our first, I got to kiss Hallie Woods again and somehow it was impossibly better this time around.

Hallie's hands smoothed up my chest and back around to the nape of my neck, where she pulled at the hair just long enough for her to get a grip on. The moment she pulled me in closer to her, the rest of my resolve snapped. My thumbs found her cheekbones as our lips hungrily devoured each other.

We kissed.

And we moaned.

And we kissed some more.

I was nearly flying high above us as Hallie staked her claim on me. Tongues danced. Teeth nipped at my bottom lip. Her fingers sank further into my hair. The silence of the room stretching around us. The only sounds were our lips, our breaths mingling in the air between us, and the soft moans from Hallie.

After kissing Hallie last week, I hadn't realized that *this* was what I wanted. While she'd kissed me back the moment my lips touched hers for the first time, there had still been some hesitancy behind her movements. Now all her inhibitions had evaporated. No longer was there hesitation behind each of her kisses.

There was only *us*.

And I wanted more.

My hands smoothed over the curve of her ass, relishing in the way it fit in my palms. Then the backs of her thighs as I lifted her off the ground. Hallie wrapped her legs around my waist and the word *home* slipped through my mind.

"How is it possible for someone to be this incredible?" I whispered into her ear as I walked us toward the bed.

Desire was flooding my body, heating me up from the inside out. Fueled by the feel of Hallie's warm, soft skin beneath my fingers. The way our lips melded together *perfectly*.

But the moment that my thighs hit the side of the bed, and I lowered Hallie down to the mattress was like a douse of ice-cold water.

"Wait."

Hallie looked up at me from the bed. She looked beautiful. It made it nearly impossible for me to understand the words coming out of her mouth.

"We should stop. We *need* to stop."

A shiver ran the length of my spine as all the heat leaked from the room, leaving a chill in its place.

"What's wrong?" I took a few steps back, giving her space. The look in her eyes ripped a tear in my heart. It was one full of regret.

"We shouldn't do this." Hallie shook her head slowly. Her gaze remained fixed on my chest, and a second tear formed in my heart when she avoided my eyes. "It was never supposed to turn into this. We had a deal. This wasn't part of the deal."

The moonlight streaming in from outside highlighted a sheen in her eyes.

I took another step back.

She was right. This wasn't part of our deal. It was five dates for a review of my family's restaurant. That was it. We didn't agree to actually like each other. Attraction wasn't part of our agreement. Kissing wasn't part of the plan. None of this was part of the plan.

Fuck the plan.

But we both agreed in the beginning, and I wouldn't dare stray from our agreement if she wasn't in this with me.

So even though it pained me, I whispered, "Okay."

Then without another word or look in her direction, I backed out of the room, shutting the door behind me. Sebastian and Roxie still hadn't come back inside, so I disappeared into our bathroom. I was too numb to feel the water on my skin. Everything that had just happened replaying on a loop in my mind.

I leaned my forehead against the tiles of the shower, doing nothing to quell the heat that was still sitting just under my skin. She had been right there at my fingertips. Her lips had been on mine. She had been *mine*, if only for a few minutes.

My hand wrapped around my cock as I relived those blissful moments when I had Hallie in my arms. When she'd kissed me back. When she'd wanted me as much as I wanted her. I replayed those breathy sounds she'd moaned in my ear.

I tightened my grip as a moan of my own slipped out. My hand slipped up and down my length faster and faster as those stolen minutes with Hallie replayed again . . . and again . . . and *again*.

Until it became too much, and I came with the sound of her name on my lips.

A mixture of shame and desire twisted in my gut.

The regret in Hallie's eyes had nearly broken my heart in two. I couldn't stand to think that she wished she hadn't kissed me. That she wished she hadn't held me in her arms. I knew it was fear driving that regret. She was afraid of what it meant to let herself like me. To let herself be with me outside of the confines of our deal.

She had everything laid out. Five dates. Five articles. Then her dream job. She had never meant to keep me after those five dates. To have feelings for me outside of gratitude for helping her achieve her dream job.

But the only thing I truly knew was now that I had a taste of her, there was no chance I was going to let her go.

*

"When did you get to bed last night?" I asked Sebastian the next morning as we sat at the table by the pool, sipping our coffees.

"I think three?" Sebastian's forehead creased, a clear sign he was squinting, despite the sunglasses protecting his eyes from the sun.

"What's going on with you and Roxie?" When I left Sebastian's and my room this morning, their door remained closed, and no light seeped from under it. I wasn't sure if I should feel relieved or sad to have more time before I had to face Hallie after last night.

"Nothing's going on with me and Roxie." Sebastian's voice matched the stiffness in his shoulders at the mention of Hallie's best friend. "We were simply enjoying a beer together."

"Pretty sure it was more than one beer," I corrected him.

Sebastian waved me off. "Semantics."

"I'm not sure it's nothing when every time she stares daggers at you, you smile like you get some sort of sick joy from it."

Only proving my point that he was some sort of sadistic asshole. He smiled.

"Roxie fascinates me." He lifted a shoulder in a shrug. "That's all."

"Whatever it is, don't use her and toss her aside once you grow tired of her, like you do every other girl you've ever been with."

Sebastian clutched at his heart. "You wound me, James."

"And you act like I'm over-exaggerating."

The sound of dishes clattering drew our attention

toward the kitchen. Roxie and Hallie had finally emerged, showered and ready for the day ahead. "Roxie King is an enigma, James. One that I intend to understand. But what about you? What time did you go to bed last night?"

The lift of Sebastian's eyebrow was a sure sign that he wouldn't believe me if I told him I'd gone to bed after we'd returned from dinner. And while that *was* the truth, it was the truth with the most important moments of the night left out.

Normally, I shared everything with Sebastian. I bounced ideas and questions off him, with his vast experience with women. But those moments were between me and Hallie. They weren't for Sebastian to dissect or pass an opinion on.

I plastered on a smile and ignored the look on Sebastian's face that told me he knew I was lying. Thankfully, Roxie and Hallie saved me by joining us for breakfast before Sebastian could make me tell the truth.

"Good morning," Hallie greeted the two of us. I'd half expected her to avoid making eye contact with me after last night. But to my surprise, she smiled at me like she hadn't rejected me mid-make out.

"Good morning. How'd you sleep?" I watched her over the rim of my coffee cup. Waiting to see that same flash of regret I'd seen in her eyes last night. To see some semblance of acknowledgment of what had happened between us. Instead, she looked at me like last night had never happened. She smiled at me with the same sincerity she'd had before we'd arrived home from dinner.

It almost made me wonder if I'd dreamed everything

that had happened between us. Maybe my mind had just done a really good job of imagining how Hallie tasted. How her lips felt against mine. How her hands roamed across the muscles in my back and along my stomach.

"I slept great. Thanks for asking. So, what did you have planned for our second day?"

"I thought we'd take the sailboat out. Have either of you sailed before?"

Roxie perked up. She had yet to speak a word since joining us and her silence was off-putting. I'd come to know Roxie's vibrant energy during the past couple of months of shared moments, her cheerful voice a constant presence among us. While Hallie was still bubbly and outgoing in her own right, she always hung back when Roxie was in the picture. She followed Roxie's lead, never attempting to take the lead on purpose. It was like watching a well-oiled machine, their movements precise and effortless, a dance honed by years of friendship.

Roxie's usual confidence was gone the second we walked in.

"Roxie and I can go pack some sandwiches while you guys get the boat ready, if you'd like?" The smile that Hallie gave me had been hard enough to witness before without wanting to wrap her hair around my fist and yank her mouth to mine. But now, it was nearly unbearable.

"That sounds great." My voice came out softer than I intended as I stared at the girl who I'd spent all night thinking about.

The second that I'd closed the door to the primary behind me last night, leaving Hallie on the other side, I'd replayed everything that had just happened. Even after

Sebastian had stumbled into the room, plastered from how much he'd drunk with Roxie. Even after Sebastian had gotten up to puke his guts out. I'd only shut my eyes for a few brief hours before the sun broke through the curtains. I'd woken up with the same person on my mind, like an endless loop.

Watching Hallie attempt to flirt with my peers in Whiskey Locker had been torturous. Finally, getting to kiss the woman that I thought I'd have to figure out how to get over once this deal was done had been wondrous. Being forced to pretend that none of it had ever happened... I wasn't sure how I was going to get through the rest of this weekend.

21

Hallie

"So, you're telling me you and James made out in our room while I was outside getting hammered and just when things were about to get *fun,* you panicked?" Roxie stared at me in disbelief as I packed sandwiches, chips, and fruit for all of us into a cooler.

I glanced out the French doors, motioning for Roxie to lower her voice. Sebastian and James were down by the docks, far enough from the house, but the mere thought of James overhearing this conversation made sweat break out across my forehead.

"And we are *never* talking about this again," I stressed, glancing back at her. "You and I both know I can't keep anything from you. So, I'd rather tell you and we can both pretend it never happened."

Roxie stared at me like I'd lost my mind, and maybe I had.

I'd tiptoed down to the kitchen this morning, hoping to avoid any attention, especially from James. But when I saw James and Sebastian by the pool, I thought I could stretch out avoiding him a little longer. Instead, Roxie had walked into the kitchen and insisted we join them outside.

The forced smile plastered on my face and Roxie's sudden silence made it clear we were both hiding something.

"Hallie, if you think I'm going to pretend that you sabotaging your chance at happiness never happened, you are sorely mistaken." Roxie packed towels and sunscreen in a separate bag as she stared down from across the kitchen counter.

"Fine." I tilted my head, studying her. The woman standing before me now, packing for a day by the water, wasn't my best friend. She was acting strange, and I wasn't going to let it slide. "Then tell me why you're acting different since we arrived here? Since James first asked us to come?"

Roxie narrowed her eyes. But she didn't immediately deny her strange behavior.

"If you spill yours, I'll spill mine," I tried.

"It's Sebastian."

"Did something happen between the two of you last night?" I asked. Before this weekend, the two had only ever hung out once before. I had been sitting next to her the entire time at the bar when they had met. Nothing had happened then. So that couldn't explain why Roxie had been acting weird before we even arrived.

"Nothing happened between us last night." There was a finality to Roxie's words, leaving no room for me to question her.

"So, what is it?"

Roxie looked like she wanted to fire my own words back at me. But instead, with a sharp intake of breath, she dropped a bombshell, the words hanging heavy in the air. "I've known Sebastian for some time."

My mouth nearly unhinged. "What do you mean, you've known him for some time? The two of you introduced yourselves to each other at the bar."

"Well, because I didn't actually know his name." Roxie looked down at the contents of the bag she was packing. "We had a one-night stand a few years back. I'd met him out at a club. I think you were stuck at the office that night because you hadn't come out with me. It had meant nothing. Just scratching an itch. I'd never expected to see his face again until he walked up to us that day in the bar with James. That's it. That's all."

"Why didn't you tell me after we left the bar? Why didn't you tell me after James invited us here, and you knew you'd have to spend the entire weekend with him?"

Roxie laughed. "And give up the chance to spend Memorial Day weekend in the Hamptons? Not a chance."

"You spent a while with him last night," I continued. We always shared everything.

"We did. We had a conversation, Hallie. Just talked. About that night we met and about our lives. That was it." Roxie raised an eyebrow. "It sure gave you plenty of time to get busy."

"We're not talking about me."

"Well, we're done talking about me because there's nothing left to say," Roxie replied. "So, all that's left is you."

The moment that Roxie crossed her arms over her chest, I knew I would not get out of this one.

"I don't know what else there is to say." I sighed. "I'm not even sure what's happening. I can't make sense of it."

"Make sense of what?" Roxie walked around the

counter, reaching out for me once she was close enough. "Not everything has to make perfect sense, Hallie."

"We had a plan. A *deal*. Five dates. That was it."

It was the same excuse I'd given James last night. It rang false then, and it rang false now.

Understanding dawned on Roxie's face. "And growing feelings for each other was not part of that deal?"

"It wasn't part of the deal," I agreed.

"But that didn't stop them from happening."

"No, it did not."

James and Sebastian were making their way back toward the house from the dock. Their laughter carrying through the open window above the kitchen sink.

Roxie stepped closer and lowered her voice. "But you don't really care about any of that, do you? You don't care that you had a deal. Because you like him. You like him and that scares you, so you're using that as an excuse."

Before I could fire back at her, James and Sebastian walked through the back door.

"Are you ready? The boat's in the water." If I had thought that I could ignore my feelings for James, it died the second that he flashed me that stupid, gorgeous smile.

"Let's sail."

If I thought James was attractive in a suit or dressed down in linen pants, shirtless while sailing was another level of *hot*. For a man that worked in an office, he had a surprising amount of back muscles, the kind that rippled as he turned the sailboat in the correct direction to catch the wind. A golden expanse of skin bunched and stretched with every movement, making my breath hitch in my throat.

But it wasn't just about him. It was how *free* I felt, with my hair whipping around me and the salty scent of the ocean in the air. In that moment, I couldn't help but wonder why I had pushed James away the night before. Why couldn't I have it all? Why couldn't I pursue my dream position and enjoy a relationship with a guy I wanted to be with?

"Do you want to try?" James shouted over the wind, pulling me from my thoughts.

I blinked, momentarily distracted by the sun sparkling off his skin. For a second, I worried I might have said my thoughts out loud. "Try what?"

"The boat, Hal. Do you want to sail the boat?"

"Oh, no," I hedged. "I couldn't possibly. I don't know how to."

James turned, a hand outstretched. "Come on. I'll show you. Sebastian's on the sails. You don't have to worry about anything but catching the wind."

"Come on, *Hal*," Roxie said from next to me. "What's the worst that can happen?"

"I crash us?" I exclaimed incredulously. Roxie merely waved me off before she leaned in close.

"Catch the wind, Hallie."

Then she shoved me. Straight into James's arms.

"Woah, careful." James's arms tightened around me, and I couldn't help but remember how it felt to be held by him last night. "No need to throw yourself overboard just so you can be in my arms again. All you had to do was ask."

I wanted to roll my eyes and shove him off me. I wanted to feign annoyance at James's overconfidence.

Instead, I let him hold me for a few seconds longer than necessary.

"Alright, I'll give it a try. But if we crash and we all die, we can blame you for thinking this was a good idea."

James only laughed as he positioned me in front of the wheel. His thumbs swiped back and forth on my upper arms.

Once.

Twice.

Just the simple swipe of his thumbs against my skin distracted me enough that I nearly missed his directions as he explained what side of the sails I would want the wind to catch and how much I needed to turn the wheel to steer the boat.

"Are you sure about this?" I asked one more time for good measure.

James paused, his gaze steady on mine. His voice was low, a quiet question in the wind. "Is it okay if I touch your arms to help you steady the wheel?"

I swallowed, a warmth spreading through me at his gentle request. The fact that he'd asked—especially after last night—meant more to me than I expected. Nodding, I breathed out a quiet, "Yeah, it's fine."

James then picked up my hands and placed them on the wheel of the boat. "I believe in you, Hal." I half expected him to step away, taking his warmth and his signature scent of spices with him. But he didn't. His hands moved from mine to my forearms, his chest pressing into my back. It took everything in me to focus on the task at hand.

"This is my favorite part of sailing." James leaned in tight. His lips brushed against my head, just above my ear. "Trying to be so in tune with the wind that you know exactly how to steer. Listening to the world around you, letting it be your guide."

"I'm not sure how to do that," I told him.

His grip on my forearms tightened. "Just close your eyes and focus on the direction of the wind. Where's it coming from? You want the wind set up to go from right to left across the ship so it catches the sail. Close your eyes, Hal, and feel."

With a shaky breath, I let my eyelids drift shut and did what James said. I focused on the wind as it danced across my skin, blowing my hair back from my face, until I knew exactly the direction it was coming from. For a moment, the world fell away as my senses focused in on the crash of the surrounding waves. The sound of the front of the boat crashing in and out of the water and the roar of the wind in my ears. I'd spent the last seven years in the city and had forgotten what it felt like to feel this *free*. To not be chasing the next best thing. The next big story. The next big promotion. Everything that I had once thought was so important felt menial now, with such beauty and freedom stretching out in front of me.

It made me wonder why I ever felt like I had to do something I didn't want to, just to achieve a dream. Why I had to sacrifice so much to come up with so little? Suddenly, everything felt simple.

All I needed to do was steer myself in the right direction to catch the wind—to do the things I enjoyed. To be with the people that I cared about and that brought me happiness. If Anthea decided I wasn't the right fit for the job after this series was done, then so be it. I would figure out another way to achieve my dreams.

Sophisticate had always been my dream magazine to write for. But I loved showcasing great restaurants and people more. Reviewing food was the wind in my sails. I couldn't lose sight of that and steer myself in the wrong direction.

I gently turned the boat in the direction I thought was best for the ship to catch the wind.

Sebastian let out a whoop from the bow of the boat as the sails fully extended with the wind. Roxie cheered from behind us. James's laugh, a rich, deep rumble, echoed through the air as he let out a whoop that mirrored Sebastian's boisterous call. The boat leaned with the wind as we picked up speed and I nearly fell over with the sudden change.

"Easy. Keep your feet wide and your core tight." James pushed my feet apart to help give me a wider base as his hands dropped from my forearms to my waist to help steady me. "You're sailing, Hal!"

A startled laugh bubbled up from inside of me. "I'm sailing," I breathed as the boat tilted even further. "This is incredible!" I exclaimed.

Without thinking, I turned and threw my arms around James's neck. I felt him reach out to grab the wheel with one hand before he wrapped his free arm around my waist. I knew I was sending mixed signals after last night. I thought putting some distance between us would make things easier. But nothing about this situation was easy. Truth was, I didn't even know *what* I truly wanted.

The food critic position?

James?

The thing was, I'd just realized it might be possible to have both as I stood in James's arms on his family's sailboat. Although our backgrounds were worlds apart, and I'd initially judged him by his profession, his character consistently defied my expectations.

"Thank you," I whispered into his ear as I squeezed him a little tighter. He only hesitated for a moment before whispering back, "Always."

22

James

As I watched Hallie devour a crab cake Benedict at brunch on Sunday morning, I'd made up my mind. I wanted to date her. Without the deal we had struck. Without the fancy dinners and the trips. I wanted to stay in and watch a movie with her or play board games on a Saturday night. I wanted to know what she looked like when she woke up in the morning or how many steps her nighttime skincare routine was.

After sailing yesterday, and despite her pushing me away the night before, I was thinking that maybe she wanted that, too.

We were officially three dates into our agreement. Our time together was ending. In two more dates, Hallie would owe me a review for my family's restaurant and then we wouldn't have to see each other again . . . Unless we actually *wanted* to.

And I was so hoping that she would want to.

"There's a firework show and a party on the beach tonight, if the two of you are open to that," I told Hallie and Roxie. Sebastian and I had grown up going to the same party since we were kids sneaking out past our bedtimes to drink with the older kids. I wasn't sure there was anything more quintessential for a Memorial Day weekend in the Hamptons than a bonfire party on the beach.

"That sounds perfect," Roxie agreed. "I could use some booze to wash down all the food we've consumed this weekend."

"I'll make sure there's whiskey," Sebastian interjected, as a look passed between him and Roxie. One that only the two of them knew the meaning of.

"A party on the beach in the Hamptons would be the perfect way to wrap up my article," Hallie added.

Right. I'd almost forgotten for a moment why we were here.

"Do you think your boss will like your article?" I asked.

"*Like* it?" Hallie scoffed. "I think she's going to love it. I started writing some of it last night after we got back from sailing. I think it'll be my best one yet. Mr. Old Fashioned will make women around the country swoon."

While that was great for Hallie's chances at the critic position, I really didn't care if every woman in America swooned at the actions of the fictional version of me. I only cared if one woman did.

"Then it's settled," I declared. "We'll drink far too much and dance the night away."

"Now that's my kind of party," Sebastian exclaimed. "I can cheers to that."

The four of us clinked our glasses over the middle of the table, relishing what had been a perfect weekend thus far. There was only one thing that would make this weekend better than it was, and that was getting another chance to kiss Hallie.

"Are you going to actually tell Hallie how you feel about her or are you going to just continue on with this charade the two of you have going?" Sebastian asked me from the bathroom where he was getting ready for the evening.

"I don't know what you're talking about, Seb," I replied as I stared at the two shirts I'd spent far too long agonizing over.

Sebastian poked his head out of the bathroom, shaving cream still on half of his face. "It's cute that you think you can fake ignorance on this one. You've spent the entire weekend staring at Hallie with hearts in your eyes. If you wanted some semblance of plausible deniability, you should've tried a little harder to pretend you're not completely whipped for her."

I'll pick the dark green one. That feels like a safe option.

"Of course I like Hallie. How can anyone not? She's fun to be around."

Sebastian rolled his eyes hard enough I thought they'd get stuck in the back of his head. I had thought if I said the words out loud, it would convince not only Sebastian, but myself, that my feelings for Hallie were merely platonic. But who was I kidding? I was staring at two shirts, wondering which one would bring out the color of my eyes more. And it was all for her.

"Should I ask again?" Sebastian leveled me with a look.

"Come on, hurry up!" I tossed Sebastian's shirt into the bathroom. "The girls will never let us live it down if they beat us downstairs."

"It takes time to look this good." Sebastian Whittaker was one of the vainest people I knew, but there was no doubt he was one of the best-looking men in New York City.

"I'll meet you down there."

Hallie was the only one in the living room when I rounded the corner. She lay stretched out on one of my mother's prized sofas, balancing her laptop on her stomach as she typed. She reminded me of my mother on weekend mornings when we would come to stay here—the society persona she normally held in the city nowhere to be found.

"Working on the article?" Hallie jumped, a shriek sounding from her mouth as she grabbed for her laptop, stopping it at the last minute from smashing into the ground.

"Have you ever heard of announcing yourself?" Hallie asked me, clutching her chest.

"I just did."

She narrowed her eyes at me as she slid her laptop onto the coffee table. "I think you need to work on your idea of making yourself known."

I lifted Hallie's legs off the couch and replaced them on my lap as I sat down next to her. The article was still pulled up on her laptop and I reached for it.

Hallie smacked my hand before it could scoop up the computer. "Hey! No peeking."

"What do you mean, no peeking? The article is about me and what we've done this weekend. I think that makes it okay for me to proofread it before it's published."

She gave a firm shake of her head. "No. You can read it when it comes out."

"Are you afraid Mr. Old Fashioned will disapprove of what you're writing?"

"You're not Mr. Old Fashioned. Mr. Old Fashioned is a fictional character that I've based on you."

"Well, that's a disappointment," I drew out. "You really boosted my ego when you said that Mr. Old Fashioned made you feel seen after organizing a private cooking class with your favorite chef in last week's article."

Scarlet colored Hallie's cheeks. She diverted her eyes, which gave me the perfect opportunity to steal a long look at her beautiful face. Making Hallie blush was like watching the sun rise on a perfect morning without a cloud in the sky. She fumbled for some sort of excuse, but I cut her off before she could continue.

"It was a perfect article, Hallie. Just like I know this article will be perfect."

The barest hint of a smile spread across her lips and I knew one bat of an eyelash would be the end to my resolve. If it were up to me, I'd pick her up off this couch and wrap her legs around my waist. The bonfire would be an afterthought.

Footsteps pounded down the stairs, and I mustered all my willpower to gently remove Hallie's feet from my lap and stand. "Are you ready?" I offered her my hand.

She closed her laptop, shutting Mr. Old Fashioned away for the night before placing her hand in mine. "Here, let me help you up." With a little more force than I intended, I sent Hallie careening into my chest.

"Oof—" Her hands splayed across my chest and without thinking, I wrapped my arms around her. Just to hold her in my arms, feel her heartbeat racing in time with mine. A hungry sound deep in my throat broke the moment.

Hallie stepped back out of my arms just as Sebastian and Roxie rounded the corner.

"Ready?" Roxie threw her arm around Hallie's shoulder

as Hallie struggled for a breath. "You have your swimsuit, right?"

"Yes! I'm already wearing it." Hallie squared her shoulders, but she gave me one last parting look that lacked any hint of regret.

"Then let's go!" Roxie exclaimed, trying to herd us all out the door. "I'm ready to get drunk enough to regret it on tomorrow's drive home."

On the drive to the beach, I spared a few glances in the rearview mirror at Hallie when I thought no one was looking. The curve of her jaw. The slope of her nose. The way the sun caught her cheekbones. She was gorgeous.

I thought it would be years before I looked at another woman like that again after Cassidy. I'd sworn off women to avoid the heartbreak. To avoid the inevitable disappointment that always came with relationships. Yet somehow, Hallie Woods made me forget all of that. She was worth it.

Having this woman smile at me as I helped her out of the car once we pulled up to the beach was almost too much.

The beach was teeming with people, their bodies warm from the setting sun, the sand hot beneath their feet. Mismatched wooden tables and chairs were strewn haphazardly; the scent of salt and wood smoke mingled in the air as a bonfire crackled and roared farther down the shore. The DJ's music pulsed through the crowd, a rhythmic heartbeat against the backdrop of the ocean, while people danced on the soft sand. Waiters moved through the crowd of people with trays of various kinds of alcohol.

"How come rich people can't do anything halfway?" Hallie asked as she accepted a cocktail from the waiter.

"Who cares if we get to benefit from it?" Roxie asked as she grabbed two drinks for herself. She downed one before turning to Sebastian. "You—dance with me?"

"I think you meant to say 'please'." Sebastian leveled her with a look that didn't quite land convincingly. Because Roxie simply tilted her head with a smile on her face before turning on her foot and pushing through the throng of people. Sebastian hesitated for only a moment before he made up his mind and followed her.

"And then there were two," I drew out.

We hadn't been alone together for more than a minute or two since she'd thrown me out of her bedroom. If the obvious tension during the moments we had in the living room before we left was only a taste of what the rest of the night would be, I would lose my mind. Hallie had made it explicitly clear that we were to strictly follow our arrangement, despite the undeniable spark between us.

But if I thought Hallie was going to be reserved around me, I was sorely mistaken. "Do you want to dance?"

If, at the end of our five dates, I was going to have to walk away from Hallie, then fine. I'd walk away. But that didn't mean I wouldn't be greedy for every single second that she would be willing to give me.

"I wouldn't want to dance with anyone else." I placed our drinks on a passing waiter's tray before guiding Hallie to a spot in the sand where we wouldn't be bothered by drunken people enjoying their last day of the holiday weekend.

An upbeat love song blared from the speakers. I

watched Hallie, usually so controlled, let loose; her normally stiff posture relaxed, and a genuine smile spread across her face. With her eyes squeezed shut, she ran her hands through her tangled hair, the strands catching on her fingertips, then raised her arms, her body moving to the pulsing beat of the music.

A strange stillness came over me, and I stood transfixed, my eyes glued to her form. My heart hammered against my ribs, a frantic drumbeat that I feared she could see through my shirt.

I almost forgot people surrounded us as I debated on picking Hallie up and throwing her over my shoulder to walk us both into the ocean. Clothes completely optional.

"I thought you said you'd dance with me, James. Or are you going to just stand there and stare at me the whole time?" Hallie extended a hand toward me. Red fingernail polish shining in the sun as it set out over the horizon.

"I said I'd dance with you, didn't I?" *Fuck it.*

If Hallie wanted to dance, we were going to dance.

My hands gripped her hips, my fingers digging into her curves. Hallie's eyes widened as I pulled her in close. Close enough to feel her breasts press up against me. Now it was her turn to stand frozen, looking up at me.

I leaned my head down, my lips brushed against her ear. "Let's dance, Hal."

Her hands moved up my chest, slowly, almost hesitantly, before they found their place in the hair at the nape of my neck. It was almost like last night, when she had backed away, but now she was with me—fully present, not resisting.

No. She was fucking clinging to me.

My hands settled lower, daring to skim the top of her ass, but she didn't flinch. Instead, she moved closer, pressing herself against me, and for a moment, I lost myself in the feeling of her warmth, the electricity between us.

Her hips swayed with the beat of the music, and for once, neither of us needed to say a word. We were just two people, caught in the moment, moving together without hesitation. The world around us seemed to fall away, leaving just the two of us, feeling more connected than I had ever felt with anyone.

I could feel my heart pounding, but this time, it wasn't from the excitement of being close to her. It was from the way she made me feel, as if she was pulling me in, and I didn't want to fight it.

"Let's go, you two! Last one to the ocean sleeps outside." A naked blur flew past us, kicking up sand as they sprinted toward the water.

"Was that Sebastian?" Hallie blinked, completely stunned, her breath uneven like she'd just done an intense workout—or maybe that was from dancing with me.

Before I could answer, Roxie zoomed past next. "You heard the man. The water!" she whooped, removing her clothes as she bolted down the beach.

Hallie gaped at her best friend, eyes wide as saucers. "She's *naked*!" Her voice cracked mid-sentence as she clutched at my arm like she'd just witnessed a full-blow alien invasion.

I couldn't help the laugh that rumbled out of me. "I believe that's called skinny-dipping, Hal." I tried to keep a straight face, but her expression was too good—like she was caught between horror and the urge to cover her eyes. "If Sebastian is near a body of water, it's only a matter of time before he starts taking clothes off. I can only imagine the wager he struck with Roxie to convince her to do it, too."

"I really don't want to sleep outside," she muttered, still staring at them in disbelief.

"Oh, don't worry." I leaned in, my voice low and teasing. "I'd never let that happen. I'd sacrifice myself to the ocean before I let you take the floor."

She elbowed me, still flustered. "Not helping, James."

I grinned. "What can I say? Seb knows how to keep things interesting."

The sound of Sebastian and Roxie's laughter carried over the crash of the waves. Hallie glanced at me out of the corner of her eye, a myriad of emotions flickering across her face.

"We don't know anyone here," she mused. "Not really. And it's dark."

"I mean, technically, that's the perfect combo for making bad decisions," I said with a grin, already tugging my shirt over my head. "You heard Sebastian. Last one to the water sleeps outside."

Hallie's mouth dropped open. Those perfect red lips forming a circle that filled my mind with the dirtiest of thoughts. "Wait! Hold on. That's not fair! You said *you* would sacrifice yourself."

I took off running, laughing as her footsteps pounded the sand behind me. When I glanced back, she was right on my heels, her coverup discarded, leaving only a deep red bathing suit that knocked every coherent thought from my mind.

She overtook me just as the water touched our toes. Honestly? No complaints. Not when I got a perfect view of her swimsuit clinging to the curves of her ass.

"Where's your bathing suit?" Hallie shouted to Roxie, who was now neck-deep in the water.

"I left it in the car and Sebastian said I wouldn't skinny dip." Roxie glared over at the man floating on his back next to her. Fortunately, the ocean did us all the favor of hiding Little Sebastian.

Hallie stepped next to me, her fingertips brushing against mine beneath the surface. "Now what?"

Four loud booms echoed in the distance before the sky blazed with red, blue, and white.

"Now," I said, motioning toward the expansive sky around us, "we've got the best seat in the house for the show."

The sun had dipped below the horizon, and in the darkened water, Hallie turned to face me.

"James," she said softly, voice threading between the booms overhead.

I met her eyes, instantly alert. "Yeah?"

"I need to tell you something."

My stomach dipped. "Okay . . ."

She hesitated, her lips parting. "I-I regret telling you to stop. The other night."

My breath caught in my throat.

"I wasn't ready then. But I think I am now." She swallowed, cheeks flushed despite the cold water. "I just didn't want you thinking I didn't want you."

Before I could say a word, a giant splash sent a wave over our heads. Roxie shrieked behind us. "We're starting a chicken fight in thirty seconds, you two better get ready!"

Sebastian's voice followed, "Don't worry, I'll let James lose gracefully."

Hallie laughed, but her eyes didn't leave mine. "Later," she murmured, quiet enough that only I could hear.

Later, definitely. But not now.

Still, the truth of her words lit something inside me. When the chaos quieted again, and the fireworks picked back up, I couldn't help myself.

Fuck it.

That was the motto of my night as I pulled her against me and kissed her. Deeply. Fully. My control snapped the instant that her tongue pressed against my lips, begging for entrance to my mouth. Tongues danced. Teeth thrashed. Her hands slipped under the band of my underwear, fingers digging into the top of my ass.

"Maybe you're right," I groaned as Hallie kissed the curve of my jaw.

"I'm always right," she teased, her voice like honey in my ear. "What am I right about now?"

"That I'm not Mr. Old Fashioned," I murmured against her lips, breathless. "Because there's nothing old fashioned about what I want to do to you right now."

23

Hallie

Returning to work after a long weekend was always awful, but coming back from the paradise that is the Hamptons? That was a new kind of torture.

"Hallie!" Anthea's voice rang through the office, silencing the easy chatter of the other staff. She was a god among us mere mortals, and we waited with bated breath for her next move. "Come to my office."

Janelle gave me a thumbs up from the cubicle next to me.

My article went live on the magazine's website this morning and it was already the most shared of my entire series. Apparently, the idea of being taken to a mansion in the Hamptons for the weekend, learning to sail and eating at some of the hottest locations on the east coast really got all the matcha latte girls going.

Anthea glanced up from behind her computer when I knocked on her door. "Please, come in." She gestured toward the chair across from her.

I tried my best to sit as gracefully as possible. Being in the presence of Anthea made my brain short-circuit—all confidence leaked from my body the second that she looked at me from behind her red-rimmed glasses.

Anthea leaned back in her chair and steepled her fingers

underneath her chin as she studied me. The weight of the silence had me shuffling in my seat.

"The last time we spoke, I told you that you had a genuine gift for these kinds of columns." Somehow, Anthea sounded graceful even when she spoke. "Have you considered our conversation since then?"

Oh, yes. The conversation where she crushed my hopes and dreams?

"I've thought about what you said." I chose my words carefully. If Anthea was now leaning toward giving me a permanent column on the topic of relationships instead of the restaurant critic position, the last thing I wanted to do was encourage her. "I would still prefer your original proposition of writing these articles for the end goal of obtaining the food critic position."

Anthea's eyes narrowed.

"You know how many people would kill for your assignment—going on dates and being treated well by a nice, rich man? Women across the globe would sign on the dotted line for that experience. And just think, you could duplicate this experience and make a living off it. It could be all about dating in New York City. So many women would love to be back in their mid-twenties and have the freedom to date around this city. But you would rather spend your time reviewing food?"

I fought to keep my jaw from hitting the floor. *Sophisticate*'s food critic was widely respected in the industry. The kind of writer whose presence could make chefs drop their knives in panic. That position had launched careers, transformed neighborhood joints into global sensations, and helped restaurants earn Michelin stars in cities across the world. And now Anthea wanted me to give up ten-course meals, the best hole-in-the-wall diner food, and the people that made the magic happen back in the kitchen—for dating commentary?

Before I could muster another response in defense of my aspirations, Anthea started again.

"Have you seen the response to this week's article? I'm not sure I remember the last time a piece delivered this much foot traffic to the website. Marketing were saying something in our morning meeting about how it's started some sort of internet trend among women in the city trying to find their very own Mr. Old Fashioned."

"Has it?" I asked, caught off guard. "I haven't been on social media much lately."

I startled as an unfamiliar sound omitted from Anthea's mouth.

Was that a laugh? From Anthea Sparks?

"Of course, you haven't had time to be on social media when you've been dating Mr. Old Fashioned. My goodness, Hallie." Anthea pressed a hand to her chest and . . . *swooned?* "I'm not sure how you keep yourself from falling for him. He sounds like he's the perfect man."

If someone had told me two years ago that I would sit in Anthea Spark's office gossiping about boys, I would have assumed that they'd suffered a head injury. Yet here I was, watching one of the most intimidating women in journalism light up over a man that I'd grown real feelings for—and something in my stomach twisted.

Was that jealousy?

No. That couldn't be right. Yes, there was attraction—*God*, was there attraction. But there was a chance that

James was still just . . . keeping up appearances. Fulfilling his end of the deal. Fancy dates, charming conversation, the perfectly packaged Wall Street boyfriend for "Love on Wall Street". Just because he kissed like he meant it, like *I* meant something, or planned nights that felt tailor-made for me didn't necessarily mean . . . anything. Did it?

Except, it kind of did. At least to me.

And that was the problem.

Because we hadn't talked about it. Not once. Not after the night I told him to stop. Not after I told him I didn't want him to stop anymore. Not after he kissed me like I was the only person in the world worth touching. I didn't know if this was just some extended bit of method acting for the sake of a column that was going viral.

And I was scared to ask.

Because what if I already knew the answer?

James Rossi was the kind of man who belonged in penthouses and boardrooms. Who grew up ordering market-value items off menus and said things like "my family's estate." I was a girl from Ohio who still used coupons and knew how to stretch leftovers into four different meals.

Maybe that's why it was easier to push away. To pretend I didn't want more. Because just like the critic position, he felt like something I could *almost* touch, but never really hold.

"I'm not sure how you're going to do it—or should I say how Mr. Old Fashioned is going to do it—but I expect the next date to top this past weekend. Let's really strike while the iron is hot. We've got the attention. Readers are returning weekly for the next update. They're sharing their own attempts at finding *their* Mr. Old Fashioned online. This is a great opportunity for us to take advantage of a potential viral moment."

I nodded numbly. A single breath swept away the dreams I'd let myself believe over the past few months.

"Do you have any idea where you're going next?" Anthea leaned forward, excitement and something I could only describe as cunning in her eyes. Every piece of me felt pulled in a million directions at that moment. If I insisted Anthea held up her end of our bargain and considered me for the critic position, would that risk eliminating any chance I had at a career with *Sophisticate*—whether that be writing a dating column or reviewing food? That didn't even address the reservations I had about putting pressure on my dates with James. Dates that filled me with joy. Dates that had made me feel *seen*. Dates that made me reconsider everything I thought I knew about James Rossi.

"I do not know where we're going next." My phone screen lit up in my hand, screen flashing with a message from James asking to grab lunch. I stared at it, momentarily thrown. "He hasn't told me yet," I muttered, more to myself than anyone else.

The timing was freakishly perfect. Or maybe fate had a twisted sense of humor. Either way, it was like he knew I was talking about him.

"Well, I'm sure it'll be somewhere spectacular. A man like that is on a mission." Anthea sat back in her chair. "That's a man who knows what he wants and it's a wife. Why else would he spend so much time and effort trying to impress you with extravagant dates?"

Because he's trying to save his family's restaurant.

"Well then, you can look forward to next week's article, it seems. Maybe it'll surprise everyone." I stood from my seat, even though Anthea hadn't dismissed me yet. A sour taste filled my mouth. "I have another appointment I need to get to."

Anthea glanced at her computer and must have realized that she had spent more than her normal five minutes conversing with me because she waved a hand dismissively toward her office door.

"I look forward to what Mr. Old Fashioned has in store for us next," Anthea said as I texted James back, letting him know to meet me at a bistro that would be midway between our two offices.

James: Can't wait to see you :)

I stared at that text message all the way through my office and in the elevator to the lobby. Not once did the fact that we were meeting once again outside of our agreed-upon five dates cross my mind as I jumped on the subway to head south toward James. Only my growing giddiness as I emerged from the subway and headed toward the bistro was present in my mind.

After the fireworks on Sunday night, the two of us had wished each other good night once we arrived back at the house. Neither of us attempted to sway the other into either of our bedrooms, we just gave each other a shy smile and went our separate ways.

Not even during the car ride home did either of us mention the kiss—or kisses—we'd shared in the ocean. Roxie sat in the back seat wearing oversized sunglasses, grumbling about her hangover the entire time. Thankfully, Sebastian had taken his own car back to the city, sparing us any bickering between the two of them.

Besides Roxie's complaints about the brightness outside and the volume of the radio, the car was steeped in silence. Not tense exactly, just unresolved. Neither of us dared to bring up our multiple close encounters in the Rossi family house over Memorial Day weekend.

The bistro I was due to meet James in was busy, but not packed, as I checked in with the hostess.

"I believe your date is waiting for you," she told me. "He said he was meeting a 'cute brunette that would most likely be a regular here'. That must be you. I've seen you in here pretty much every week over the past two years."

Of course, James would guess I'd suggest a place I'd already reviewed and loved.

"Uh, yeah." I gave the hostess an awkward smile. "That's me."

"He asked for a table in the back."

James sat next to my favorite window that looked out on a small garden with a patio in the back. Lounging in his chair, an ankle propped on his opposite knee, and *The Wall Street Journal* unfurled in his hands. Gone were the linen shorts and button-up shirts I'd grown used to seeing him in over the weekend. In their place was his usual uniform of a perfectly tailored suit, shined shoes, and a tie that no doubt matched some subtle hue in his pocket square. His signet ring caught the light as he turned a page, and just like that, it was as if his armor had slid right back into place.

"I believe this is your table." The waiter gave me a wide smile before she left the two of us alone. James dropped the paper, a subtle smile playing on his lips as his eyes twinkled with mischief. Those eyes, dark and intense, slowly scanned me, lingering on every detail. Everywhere he looked, I could feel the ghost of his fingers trailing over my body.

We'd done this once before—met outside the parameters of our arrangement. And now we'd crossed that line again. No longer were we toeing it, dancing back and forth. We had dived headfirst into the unknown. Drenched ourselves in the ambiguity of it.

James stood once he realized I hadn't made a move to join him.

"How was work?" He leaned down. His lips brushing against my cheek as he slipped my work bag from my shoulder and slung it over one side of my chair.

"Anthea liked the article. I think she even laughed." James wrapped both of his hands around my upper arms. "I'm not sure I've ever heard her laugh before. Not a genuine laugh. Her fake laugh is this airy, haughty sound that she uses to pretend she's entertained by someone. But she gave me a *real* laugh today."

"I read the article," James said as amusement danced across his face. "It was good. I especially liked the part where you described Mr. Old Fashioned as a 'wet dream straight out of a romance novel' when you first laid eyes on him behind the wheel of the sailboat."

Heat flared across my cheeks as James gave me a knowing smile.

"Do you want to take a seat?"

I glanced at the chair across from where James had been sitting. It could be so easy to slip into that seat and have lunch with him. It wouldn't be any different from what we'd been doing over the past couple of months. But this *was* different.

I knew it.

He knew it.

Yet we were skirting around it just the same.

With every minute I spent with James, I wanted more. More of his smiles. More of his witty remarks. More of his playful bars. More of him. Maybe it was time that I made that known.

Once I'd gotten to know the real James behind the finance bro bravado, I was naïve to think that spending time with James would lead to anything other than this very moment. To think I could ever avoid developing feelings for him was almost laughable. It was time that I stopped avoiding reality and stopped ignoring the feelings that had taken root inside of me.

"I enjoy spending time with you."

James's eyebrows shot up, but he smiled. "And I enjoy spending time with you."

The heat that had started in my cheeks shot straight down to my stomach as his words settled in, lighting the blood in my veins on fire.

"So, we can spend time right now together," James drew out. "Over lunch."

"And what about when we complete our fifth date in a couple of weeks?" I asked, my feet still unable to take me toward the awaiting chair. "Will we still spend time together, then?"

Nerves twisted in my stomach, the same ones that usually kept me second-guessing myself. But the conversation I'd just had with Anthea—her swooning over *my* words, over *my* Mr. Old Fashioned—had stirred something inside me. A flicker of belief that maybe I was allowed to ask for what I wanted, even if my voice trembled while doing it.

Understanding dawned on James's face as he realized the reason for my current hesitation. His hands slid down my arms to slip into mine. Despite the chaos of the restaurant surrounding us, the two of us stood holding hands and all but careened toward a point of no return.

James's voice was a rumble that started low in his chest as he squeezed my hands. "I want to spend as much time with you as you'll let me, Hal."

The rest of the air in my lungs slipped out from between my lips as I let each of his words sink in, filling me with their own life.

"I swore off dating after Cassidy used me. She got everything she wanted and more, yet *I* still hadn't been enough for her. But when I look back on that time, I realize she had never made me feel like I wasn't a prize to be won. I had never understood what it felt like for someone to really see me and still want me. That was until you." James's eyes were nearly molten as he laid himself bare for me. "So yes, Hal. I want to spend time with you. This may have started with you and me on opposite sides. But I want it to end with us as a team."

I let out a small gasp, needing to fill my lungs with more of the very words that James was saying to me. Wanting to drench myself in the way they made me feel.

Light.

Airy.

Worthy.

"So will you sit down with me and have lunch now,

Hal?" James asked, that same amusement from before returning to his face. Then he leaned in and whispered in my ear something that set my entire body on fire. "Or do I need to clear the building so we can show each other how much we care with actions rather than words?"

"Lunch sounds perfect." The words came out on a squeak.

We sat down as if everything were completely normal and we hadn't just admitted our feelings for each other in the middle of one of my favorite bistros. A waiter came by shortly after to take our orders. James folded his copy of *The Wall Street Journal*. Every movement he made was confident. It was one of the things that I liked best about him, that unwavering self-assurance. Maybe it was rubbing off on me.

"I was thinking about our next date," James said, picking up the carafe of water from the middle of the table. He filled my glass first, then his own. "Something a little different this time. More low-key. Cozy. Less white tablecloth, more paper napkins."

I tilted my head, intrigued. "So . . . messy in a charming way?"

He grinned. "Exactly. Still finalizing the details, but I promise it'll be fun."

I nodded, trying to play it cool even as my pulse picked up.

Low-key, unforgettable, upside down—I didn't really care what the night looked like. As long as he was there, I'd show up.

24

James

"Oh, he's here!" my grandmother exclaimed as soon as she opened the front door of her brownstone. The familiar sounds of my family echoed down the long front hallway as they gathered in the kitchen, the heart of my grandparents' home. "James! *Nipote*. You look so handsome."

I leaned down to give her a kiss on the cheek, the top of her gray bun barely reaching my chest. My height had come from my mother's side of the family. "Nonna, you just saw me last week at family dinner. I can't look that much different."

"You have not been eating enough, James," she said, her hands gripping my biceps as she examined me like some fruit at the market. "I sent you home with leftovers last week. Did you not eat them?"

She gave me the same routine every Wednesday. My grandmother would answer the door. She'd pull me into a hug, tell me first I was handsome, then too skinny, then ask me if I hadn't eaten the armload of leftovers she sent me home with every week. I always split them with Sebastian whenever he came over. He was a fiend for Nonna's cooking. Then she would shoo me to the kitchen, where my mom and Aunt Maria were usually elbow-deep in flour, making pasta from scratch. I'd head to the dining room, where my dad, Uncle Tony, Brandon, and Emilia had already claimed their spots around the table, a deck of cards and a small pile of poker chips between them.

It was the same thing every week. But that was the best part.

No matter how the world changed around us, this part of life stayed the same. It was comforting, nostalgic. Even with all the quirks of the Rossi clan—my father's stubborn resistance to change, my grandfather turning a blind eye, my uncle's love for a heavy pour, and my grandmother's relentless scrutiny over everyone's eating habits—it would never get boring. It was where I was happiest.

But I'd started to wonder if the next time I met my family for dinner, Hallie would be with me. I wasn't sure what would be harder—their questions, their curiosity, or the way I'd feel exposing her to this part of me. Family dinners were predictable, yes, but they also revealed things about you that you couldn't hide. Things Hallie didn't know yet. And while it terrified me, it also shot a thrill through me at the possibility.

"James!" my uncle bellowed as I stepped into the dining room. "We'll deal you in next hand."

"The markets looked good today," Brandon said with a smirk. "Which should mean you have plenty to add to the pot."

I shrugged off my jacket as I slid into my usual chair next to my father. "For the millionth time, Brandon, just because the markets are good, doesn't mean I suddenly have millions in cash hit my bank account."

"Sounds like a waste." Brandon glanced at his cards before tossing a few poker chips into the middle.

Uncle Tony doubled Brandon's bet without blinking. "Still can't bluff worth a damn," he muttered, grinning.

"You haven't been around the pizzeria as much these past few weeks," my grandfather said, his deep voice halting the banter.

My father paused, poker chips in hand. Everyone read between the lines. That wasn't a question. It was a statement with an edge.

You have not been supporting your family, and you better have a good reason for it.

"I've been busy," I said. Which was true. But I couldn't tell them I'd spent most of the time with Hallie—taking her on dates, thinking about her, or trying to figure out what came next. What I could say though, was the intention I'd made clear to them already. "I've been busy working on solutions for the pizzeria, as a matter of fact."

Brandon snorted into his drink.

"It's true," Emilia said, jumping to my defense. She sat across from me, legs crisscrossed under her chair, wearing a volleyball hoodie. "James is going to make the restaurant go viral."

My grandfather took a thoughtful pull from his cigar. "Your father mentioned something about social media. Some app thing."

Tony snorted, but before he could say anything, a roll flew across the room and smacked him in the back of the head.

"Antonio, show some respect," Aunt Maria scolded, wooden spoon in hand.

"I didn't say anything, Maria!"

"Let your nephew speak," Maria said, pointing the spoon at him for emphasis. "We've talked ourselves in circles the past few months. Maybe it's time to try something new."

Every eye in the room turned to look at me. I'd given presentations to CEOs of Fortune 100 companies. I'd competed against some of the toughest sharks on Wall Street. Yet my family was easily the hardest group I'd ever had to convince of a business proposal.

"Well, Nonno," I began, turning toward the head of the table, "consumers live online now. They're looking for their next purchase, their next favorite restaurant, their next favorite store online. Whether they're looking at reviews or influencers telling them where they should spend their money. We are losing out on potential sales by only updating our single social media account once a month."

The room remained silent as Lorenzo flicked some ashes from his cigar into the tray next to him. While my father and uncle made the majority of the business decisions, as long as my grandfather was still alive, the final decision would always lie in his hands.

"Do you really think something like that could help our business?"

"I do," I said. "I have a food writer and photographer lined up already. They'll review the restaurant in the next few weeks, and if even one table books because of it, that's proof we're heading in the right direction. She also mentioned she could help revamp our social media. We can even hire someone for the position to maintain the accounts. I've already come up with how Dad can move the budget around to afford to bring someone in."

"I gave him the idea," Emilia added.

Silence fell over the entire house after I finished. My family spoke the language of food. That was what made the pizzeria a well-loved local joint in its neighborhood. I could talk about numbers until I was blue in the face, but they would never understand me. They did, however, understand a packed restaurant without a single table available for a walk-in.

"If you give me a chance," I tried again, "I promise weekends will be so busy again that you might even have to call me in to help."

My grandfather took a long sip of wine. "Alright," he said finally. "If this review brings in even one extra sale, we'll look at your budget and hire someone."

Brandon held a hand under the table for a subtle high-five. I didn't hesitate to slap it. Before anyone else could say a word, my grandmother's voice cut through the house.

"I think that's enough talking shop for the evening," she cut in. She started making her way to the kitchen, squeezing my shoulder as she passed. "Now, clear that table so that we can eat!"

Hallie answered her apartment door with her hair still damp and wearing Disney pajamas. The sight made me smile—so effortlessly her. Maybe I shouldn't have stopped by unannounced after family dinner, but I was too wired from the night to resist. I could've texted, called, even emailed her the update. But none of those options would've brought me here, standing in front of her, seeing the way her face lit up when she saw me.

A few minutes with Hallie were worth any excuse.

Not that I'd ever say that out loud. That would make me sound like a man completely wrapped around her finger.

Which I most definitely was not.

Oh, who was I kidding? I most definitely was.

"James!" She opened the door wider, stepping aside to let me in. "What are you doing here? I thought we weren't seeing each other until dinner on Friday?"

"I had some news that I couldn't wait until then to tell you." As we entered, I spotted the TV paused on a familiar film. "Is that *The Parent Trap*?"

Hallie's smile twitched the corners of her mouth as she glanced between me and the screen. "It just started."

The microwave went off in the kitchen, and I finally noticed the smell of butter filling the apartment. On the end table beside the couch sat a half-finished glass of red wine. "Popcorn and wine? You are really treating yourself tonight, aren't you?"

"Roxie's out all evening for a gallery showing. I think there are worse ways to spend a night, like sitting at a bar every weeknight at Whiskey Locker or any other bar in FiDi." She flashed me a knowing smile, then disappeared into the kitchen to grab the popcorn. "So, what's the big news?"

I glanced between the couch and the kitchen, not sure if I should make myself comfortable or just share my news and go. Suddenly, spending all my free time with Hallie had become the only thing I wanted to do.

"If you don't have anywhere else to be tonight," I called out to Hallie, who was returning with a bowl of popcorn. "I wouldn't mind watching a movie with you."

She didn't answer right away. Instead, she turned back around, disappearing into the kitchen for a moment. When she reappeared, she was carrying a fresh glass of wine—and a second one for me.

Hallie paused in front of the couch, her expression softening into a smile as she settled beside me. "That sounds perfect." She tucked her legs up under her, the bowl of popcorn resting next to her. "I've been wanting to watch this all week."

It felt like knocking off rust, like we were playing house. The last time I'd gotten this comfortable with someone, I'd also gotten my heart broken. I'd been too distracted, too caught up in the routine we'd created to realize that our routine had never been as perfect as I thought it was.

But instead of letting myself dwell on unresolved feelings, I kicked off my shoes by the front door and settled down on the couch next to Hallie.

"So, that good news you were going to share?" Hallie prompted.

"Right." I slung an arm over the back of the couch, and without thinking Hallie leaned back into me. The two of us both moving almost involuntarily, unable to fight against our bodies' desires to be close to one another. "Every Wednesday is Rossi family dinner. Tonight, my grandfather asked me about my ideas for bringing the restaurant into the modern era utilizing social media, influencers, and reviewers."

Hallie's attention was fully on me. I never realized how unfamiliar it felt to have someone genuinely interested in what I was saying. Rather than faking interest in me merely because it provided them a means to an end. The only people who ever gave me that kind of undivided attention were my mom and dad, and even then, it only happened when there wasn't some kind of family drama hanging over us.

"He was interested?" Her voice was full of excitement, and I felt the warmth of her enthusiasm radiate through me.

"Surprisingly, yes." A burst of laughter escaped from me, the realization of everything that had happened hitting me all at once. After all the time and effort I'd spent trying to convince my father of my plans, all I'd really needed to do was convince the head of the Rossi clan. "He brought it up before dinner and my father and uncle cut our conversation short at first. But my aunt insisted they let me speak, and he actually listened to me. He expressed he might not fully understand social media and how it could help the restaurant, but he was adamant about hearing me out. After I gave him a quick explanation of what I wanted to do, he was on board."

"James!" Hallie reached over to throw her arms around my neck. "That's great news!"

My hands slipped around her waist. Her palms moved to my chest as she leaned back in my arms. "I'll talk with Roxie about planning a day to go over to the restaurant together. That way she's free to take pictures and I can plan out a blog posting—"

I silenced her with a kiss. I didn't even hesitate. I was unable to resist Hallie's intoxicating energy any further. And when her fingers fisted the soft fabric of my t-shirt and she pulled me in closer, I knew I'd made the right move.

When I heard her moan into my mouth, I nearly splintered into a thousand pieces. There was no way I was going to walk away from her at the end of our five dates. I'd already mentally shredded our agreement in my head.

Hallie Woods was going to be mine.

25

Hallie

SUBJECT: THE SOCIAL EATERY—DUE BY EOD FRIDAY (YOU'VE GOT ONE CHANCE)

An email from Anthea sat at the top of my inbox Thursday morning. The subject line alone was enough to make my heart rate spike. The body of the email was even more cryptic—just a link to an article about the opening of a new restaurant in Soho that night, followed by a reservation for two that *Sophisticate* had already pre-booked. No message. No instruction. Nothing else.

I stared at the screen for ten minutes straight, wide-eyed and unmoving, as if even the slightest movement would make it disappear. After our last conversation, I'd written off any hope of landing the food critic position. But maybe, just maybe, this was Anthea's way of throwing me a bone. A chance to prove myself.

Hallie: Please tell me you're free tonight for a dinner in Soho?
James: A dinner in Soho sounds much better than the box of Mac & Cheese I was thinking about.
Hallie: Mac & Cheese, James? That's not very Italian of you. What would your Nonna say?

James: She'd hit me on the back of the head with her spoon. But I can't resist the cheesy goodness.
Hallie: So what I'm gathering from this is that you're free?
James: . . . yes.
Hallie: One catch.
James: Is this where you tell me you're inviting the other Wall Street guy you've been dating this entire time so the two of us can compete for your affection?
Hallie: No?
James: This is a sacrificial dinner?
Hallie: No.
James: Am I meeting your parents? Are you surprising me with a parental meeting?
Hallie: Will you just let me tell you?! Anthea wants me to review a new restaurant and got me a reservation for opening night tonight.
James: So, we're eating on *Sophisticate*'s dime? That's not a catch, Hal. That's a benefit.
Hallie: . . . I'll send you the address. See you there at seven.
James: As long as you add my review of their Old Fashioned in your coverage. You won't even have to credit me for the quote.
Hallie: You really are sooooo generous, Mr. Old Fashioned.

Did hanging out with someone for three consecutive days count as serious? I wasn't sure. Maybe I could ask the random man who'd ridden all the way from Midtown to Soho with me on the subway. He wore a gold wedding band, and his screensaver was a photo of his family at what looked like Coney Island in the summer. You can learn a lot about someone when you're crammed next to them on the subway for five stops. And surely someone in what appeared to be a successful marriage would know when a relationship started crossing into the land of serious.

Normally, New Yorkers don't talk to each other on the subway—it's practically blasphemy to do so. I'd rather line up for a bagel at Dunkin' Donuts than strike up a conversation with a stranger on public transit. But between the strange new confidence I'd been walking around with and the emotional spiral I currently found myself in, I was willing to break protocol. Desperation does that to a girl.

"When do you think a relationship can no longer be considered casual?" I asked the man once I'd worked up enough courage.

He startled, blinking at me like he wasn't sure if I was speaking to him or into the void. "Uh," he said, clearing his throat. "Have these two people been dating for a while?"

I shrugged. "Actually, dating for just about a month but have known each other for a couple of months."

He tilted his head thoughtfully. "And did hanging out multiple days in a row come on suddenly?"

I nodded. "Yeah. Popping by the other's place if they're in the neighborhood. Grabbing lunch or dinner just because."

The man snorted. "Then I'd say that yes, it's becoming serious."

The subway began to slow as a female robotic voice announced my stop.

"Thanks for your input," I said as I stood to leave.

"Does he treat you well?" the man called after me just as I stepped toward the doors.

I paused for only a second before answering. "Yes."

"Do you like spending time with him?"

"I do," I said, nodding solemnly.

"Then I'd say go for it." He gave me a wink as the subway doors slid shut, whisking him off to somewhere else in New York City.

Fairy godfather? Subway sage? I wasn't sure what to call him. But somehow, he knew exactly what I needed to hear.

I wasn't sure why I needed confirmation from a stranger about my relationship with James. Deep down, I already knew everything he pointed out. James treated me better than anyone I'd ever met, and the second our date ended, I was already counting down the hours until the next.

People swarmed around me as they moved toward the stairs, and I paused for a second to watch the train disappear into the tunnel. This was my favorite part about living in the city. Getting lost in the sea of strangers, all headed somewhere, all chasing something. New York truly was the city that never slept—constantly moving, living, *thriving*.

I fell in line with the crowd and let it carry me up the escalators and out into the hustle and bustle of Soho. With its cast-iron facades and cobblestone streets, the neighborhood felt like a beautiful contradiction—equal parts polished and gritty. Tourists flocked here for designer boutiques and high-end art galleries, but it was also the perfect place for a brand-new restaurant that, according to the article Anthea sent me this morning, could be a contender for a Michelin star by the end of the year.

Just a few weeks ago, I would've felt completely in over my head. But spending time with James when he made me feel seen, valued, and genuinely cared for had changed something in me. That, paired with the buzz around my recent articles and the subtle nods of approval from Anthea, had become fuel for a kind of confidence I hadn't felt in a long time. I was still figuring things out, sure, but I was willing to take the shot I was being given. And if the last few weeks were any indication, I had a pretty strong feeling I'd nail it.

The Social Eatery was more than a restaurant, it was a communal experience. Long tables designed for twelve meant you were sharing more than just food. You were sharing space, stories, and bites with strangers. Dishes came out family style, with overflowing bowls and plates to share and pass around. It was a bold concept, especially in New York City.

I'd been a little nervous that James might have imagined a white-table-cloth dinner for two accented with candlelight. But when I saw him looking through the arched windows with awe on his face, my worries vanished. And, okay, I had to fight off the overwhelming desire to kiss him.

"Maybe I should have said the catch was that we would be forced into conversations with strangers," I teased.

"Definitely not a catch," James said, leaning down to brush a kiss against my cheek. "How was your day?"

"Honestly?" I smiled. "Just standing here with one of the most sought-after reservations in the city makes it a pretty good day."

The line of people stretched around the block, all hoping to secure an unreserved table. A few weeks ago, I'd have been one of them. Now, walking past them to give my name to the hostess felt surreal, like stepping into someone else's shoes . . . or maybe finally into my own.

"Anthea's giving you a taste of what your future will be," James said, his hand warm and steady against my back. The simple gesture anchored me. This time, I didn't flinch or overthink it. I leaned into the calm it gave me, acutely aware of my body's response to his touch.

"She said this was my one chance to prove that I deserved the position or else she'll saddle me with a permanent column on relationships." I tried to keep my tone light, but we both knew how much that possibility weighed on me. Writing about love was never supposed to be more than a temporary assignment. The idea of turning it into a full-time identity made my skin itch.

What will James think if that happened?

What would it mean if my entire professional identity became *date me for a living*? Would he end whatever this was before it truly began because he felt like he was just another installment in a never-ending column?

A whisper in the recesses of my mind spoke something I never thought would cross my mind. *Maybe it's time to leave* Sophisticate.

That thought vanished the second the hostess, recognizing my name, seated us prominently at a table in the front. In a restaurant like The Social Eatery, the spotlight was the prize. Being seated at the central table on opening night meant influence. Reputation. Power.

Without *Sophisticate*'s reputation, securing this would require years of brand development on my part.

A waiter appeared almost instantly. I didn't need to scan the room to know we were surrounded by names people dropped at parties—people who didn't wait in lines outside or worry about splitting rent. The woman next to me was wearing this season's Vivienne Westwood and the man across from her was in Gucci, the subtle kind that still screamed money if you knew what to look for. I recognized the woman at the end of the table from real estate billboards all over Manhattan, and my heart actually skipped when I spotted Nola Simmons, an up-and-coming pop star just nominated for her first Grammy, sipping a cocktail like this was just another Thursday.

"In honor of The Social Eatery's opening night," the waiter announced, his gaze lingering on me before sweeping the table, "the chef will treat you all to a taste of his entire menu." He paused just long enough to let it land. "Tonight's meal is on the house."

Some guests whispered to each other about the revelation, while others clearly thought it was preferential treatment directed toward them. But when the waiter cast a look at me once more after taking drink orders, James raised an eyebrow like he was putting the pieces together too.

This was what it meant to hold the critic title at *Sophisticate*.

With every new tasting that landed on the table, the

beauty of this style of dining became the focal point of the night. James, a true socialite, had gathered all the information about the couple next to us before the main course arrived. I think I even saw them exchange business cards after James mentioned exactly which firm he worked for in the financial district.

Meanwhile, I took my time enjoying every flavor, every texture, every experience that the chef was delivering for us. Trying to pin down the words that would bring it all to life in print.

But for the first time . . . nothing came.

Even after everyone had scraped their dessert plates clean and the last of the wine had been poured, my mind was a blank page. Empty. Me, who could usually write three headlines by the second course—I was coming up short.

"What's on your mind, Hal?" James asked me as we made our way out.

"I'm at a loss for words."

He nodded, his eyes flicking to the restaurant's wooden doors behind him. "That was quite the experience. I'm not sure I've ever had a dinner like that before."

"No, I meant literally," I said, exasperated. "I've been trying all night to form how I want to showcase this for *Sophisticate* and I just . . . can't. This has never happened to me before."

This was supposed to be what I was best at. I spent my free time and passion on my own blog, reviewing restaurants just like this one. Sure, it wasn't usually on opening night, but I always knew precisely how to highlight the brand and *soul* of each restaurant or chef. But now that I had the weight of Anthea's expectation looming over me, and her terrifying stare behind those red-framed glasses etched into my mind, all my inspiration had dried up.

James held out his hand. "Let's get out of here, then. We'll find you some inspiration."

I hesitated. "I should really get home so I can try to start on this article. Anthea wants it by the end of day tomorrow."

He raised an eyebrow. "With what words?"

"I'll find them," I said stubbornly.

"Sure. But there's no sense in banging your head against a wall by yourself while you figure it out." His hand was still there, open and waiting. "Come on, Hal. I've got an idea of how to get those words flowing again."

"Are you trying to get me drunk, Rossi?"

He answered with a cocky smirk—a slow, deliberate curl of his lip that sent a shiver down my spine. There was no mistaking it . . . he wanted me.

But the look in his eyes, full of unspoken promise, did something to me. It made me feel bold. Excited. Alive. And for the first time in a long time, unafraid.

I closed the distance between us, breathing in the familiar scent of his cologne. There was nothing more than a mere breath between us, and the slightest movement of our heads would have his lips on mine.

"Then take me home, James," I said softly, looking up at him. "And help me find the words."

26

James

"I thought for sure you were going to live in Central Park West or One Waterline Square. At least one of the skyscrapers here on the Upper West Side. I definitely didn't see you in a brownstone," Hallie said as I unlocked the front door to my place.

"Can you imagine moving furniture up to the top of one of those skyscrapers?" I shuddered. "I'll pass."

"If you have enough money for a place like this, you have enough money to hire movers."

"But what if I find a cool couch on the side of the road and want to take it home with me?"

Hallie rolled her eyes, but a soft laugh escaped anyways as she followed me inside, her gaze already sweeping over the space, taking it all in. From the various wool coats I had hanging on hooks above the bench in my entryway to the pictures of my family that hung on the wall leading into my kitchen and living space. She paused at one in particular—a shot of me from my lacrosse days, back when I was still at that private school I'd attended from grade school through graduation. A Princeton hoodie was still thrown over the back of one of my barstools at the kitchen island from where I'd shed it this morning after my workout before heading into the office.

The brownstone had been bought with money left to me by my mother's father—part of a trust he set up before he passed. This place was his idea of a legacy. I hadn't planned to live alone forever, but for now, solitude felt like control. And I'd needed that, especially after Cassidy.

"That's what Roxie and I do," Hallie said, brushing her fingers over the sweatshirt. "Pick up furniture on the side of the curb meant to be thrown away. We bring it home, clean it up, and give it a new life. I highly doubt you're doing the same."

I knew what she saw when she looked at me—a kid from the Upper East Side, raised in privilege, private schools, nice clothes. And yeah, some of that was true. But not all of it.

"I don't think we are as different as you think we are," I said, guiding her further down the hallway to a picture of my family standing in front of Rossi Pizzeria last summer. It had been the first time all year that everyone could be at the restaurant together. One local that stopped in for a slice every day had snapped the picture.

"That's my grandfather and grandmother, Lorenzo and Giulietta. First-generation immigrants from Italy. They came here with nothing but a dream—to build something lasting for their family. And they did. Enough to give their kids a better life. But it wasn't easy."

I pointed to an old photo of my parents that was hanging on the wall next. "You already know my mom's dad didn't approve of my dad. But my father didn't care. He loved my mother and had no interest in trying to fit into her family's mold. Brooklyn is in his blood, and he made sure I knew what it meant to earn my way.

"My parents never handed me a dime. I have a trust fund, but I only used it for this place. My dad's rule. He wanted to know I could make something of myself without it."

Hallie didn't respond right away. Her gaze drifted back to the family photos. I could tell she was sizing it all up—me, this place, what I'd just told her. "My parents may not get my lifestyle, but they've always supported me. Helped with NYU. Made sure I had what I needed growing up." She gave a small shrug. "So, I guess we're not as different as I thought."

This conversation was a distraction from what either of us clearly wanted to do right now. After a few dates, we'd obviously both realized we liked each other and had more in common than we initially thought. But Hallie wouldn't have come home with me if she'd wanted to discuss our life stories.

Given how she pushed me away when we were finally getting close this past weekend, I wasn't going to be the one to make the first move tonight. Every time I saw her after the Hamptons, things seemed to improve. A tease. A kiss on the cheek after lunch on Tuesday. Making out on her couch after family dinner on Wednesday. Each time I waited for cues from Hallie, carefully watching her body language and listening for any hesitations in her voice to make sure I never crossed her boundaries.

"So, tell me about this loss of words you're facing," I said, instead of reaching out for her like I wanted to. "Is this recurring? Critical? Should we find a word doctor?"

Hallie let out a slow sigh. "I have no clue what's going on," she said, finally.

"That deconstructed banana cream pie nearly struck me speechless, too."

A reluctant smile tugged at her lips, and I felt a desperate need to keep that smile there, to be the reason for it. I ached for *her*. To be close to her. To have her in my arms like she'd been last weekend. To grip her ass in my hands. To hear that breathy moan again. To have that crimson mouth on *me*.

"The food was amazing," she said. "If I were to post about it, I'd highlight that tomahawk steak cooked to perfection. The plating was the most beautiful thing I'd seen in a long time. I'd focus on the community. That's what made it unforgettable."

She lit up when she talked about food like that—passionate, focused, real. It was when she was her most irresistible.

"So, what's the issue?" I asked.

Another sigh. "*Sophisticate*? Anthea? I'm not sure."

"What's so different about what they want and what you already write?"

"They feel like wildly different worlds," Hallie said. "The *Sophisticate* food critic has always sounded so polished, so established. I'm just . . . me."

"And that's not enough?"

She shrugged, "I guess not."

I hated that. Hated how small she looked in that moment when I knew exactly how big and bright she burned.

"Why can't you just be you?" I asked. "Why can't you write like you normally do? Anthea wants *you* to prove yourself for the position. Show her that your voice is what makes you right for the job, Hal."

The air crackled with tension as my words hung between us. I heard Hallie swallow before she murmured, "Please, just kiss me."

"What?" I froze.

Her eyes met mine. Steady. Certain. "I want you to kiss me, James Rossi. Matter of fact, I want you to take me to whichever of the many bedrooms in this place is yours."

Something inside me snapped within me.

I scooped her up into my arms, her legs wrapping around my waist instinctively. Her hand found my face, and she kissed me. It was a quick kiss. When she pulled away, she looked at me like this time she was waiting for *me* to stop *her*.

But I didn't.

I kissed *her*.

Again.

And again.

And *again*.

This wasn't like any time we'd kissed before. The quick, tentative kiss on the front steps of her apartment building. The hungry kisses in the Hamptons. The sweet kiss in her apartment last night.

Both of us wanted this *desperately*. There was no hesitation in our kisses, but we took our time to appreciate each other. Slow and deliberate in our explorations.

Her hands explored my chest, slipped around to press against the muscles of my back as I began our trek up the five flights of stairs toward my bedroom. My lips grazed her jaw, her neck, the hollow beneath her ear.

As we crested the second floor, I fisted my hand in her hair to gently pull her head back from mine. Only to trail kisses from the soft skin below her ear to her collarbone. If I wasn't nervous I would drop her, I would have sprinted the two of us up the remaining three floors.

Hallie's teeth sank into my neck on the third floor, and I groaned, the sound guttural and raw in the empty space. On the fourth, my hands gripped the curve of her ass, holding her flush against me.

When I reached my bedroom, I paused. "Are you sure?"

"Yes," she breathed. "I'm sure. I want to feel good. The last few months have been a mess, and I want to forget them. You make me feel good, James. You make me feel alive."

"I've been imagining this since the night I pulled out your chair at the dinner party," I confessed, setting her down gently. "I've thought about the taste of your skin. The sound of your breath. How you'd look falling apart beneath me."

I backed her up, one slow step at a time, until her legs met the edge of my bed, and she sank down onto the soft mattress. The look in her eyes was a challenge. A beat passed. Then she reached for the button on her pants.

"Make me feel good, James."

27

Hallie

"Are you sure?" he'd asked me.

I'd never been more sure of anything in my life. Last weekend I'd stopped us, too afraid of what it would mean if I let myself get carried away. If I let James kiss me senseless until we tumbled into bed and crossed that line I'd been toeing since the moment we met. Because if I gave in, if I let myself want this the way I *did* want it, it would make everything so much harder when it inevitably ended.

But I was tired of letting my fear rule me.

For one night, I just wanted to forget all the expectations I had to live up to. I didn't want to think about Anthea or what would happen if I didn't land the food critic position. I wanted to feel like I was someone's *first* pick for once. To be desired so deeply that all the noise in my head finally went quiet.

James backed me up one step at a time until the backs of my legs hit the edge of the bed. I careened backward until my body met the soft mattress. He hesitated for a moment. This was the moment when I could change my mind like I had last weekend. Tell him never mind and ask him to pour me a glass of wine. I knew he'd be disappointed, but he would agree and pour me that glass of wine just because he was that nice of a guy.

But I didn't want the *nice* guy tonight. So, I reached for the button on my pants.

Instead of unbuttoning his own clothes like I'd expected, James helped slide my pants down with slow, aching precision. His hands taking their time to squeeze my bare flesh before he tossed the clothing behind him.

Then—God help me—he dropped to his knees.

The way he looked at me, with raw hunger and reverence, made my skin burn. Like every blemish or imperfection I saw in the mirror was exactly what turned him on. His hands moved along my legs, over my hips, under my ass, then he curled his fingers around the band of my black thong.

"Can I?" he asked, his voice low and rough.

"Yes," I breathed, nearly moaning the word.

He peeled the delicate lace down my legs, slow enough to make me squirm. I thanked previous me for shaving last night, despite having no idea where I'd find myself only twenty-four hours later.

His nostrils flared as he took me in and to my surprise, he leaned down to place a single kiss right below my belly button. "You are a masterpiece."

I could have cried at the way he said it. Like he meant it. I'd never thought I was the prettiest girl in the room—especially being best friends with Roxie King. College nights out with her meant watching men start conversations with her first—that was normal for me. I found it difficult to believe a man found me attractive.

But not James.

James looked at me like I was *it*.

I gave James's shoulders a tug, he got the message and

crawled onto the bed with me. But there was only one problem. He remained fully dressed, unlike me, who was half-naked.

My fingers reached for the top button on James's shirt, but he shook his head, stopping me. The familiar fear of inadequacy returned.

"You do not know how much I want to have sex with you right now," James whispered. "I've been thinking about it since the first time I kissed you on the steps of your apartment building."

He kissed down my throat, dragging his teeth lightly along my jaw. "I had to stop myself from asking to follow you upstairs and ending our night *very* differently."

I gasped. That kiss had ruined me more than I cared to let on. I'd convinced myself it was just timing. Just for work. But I'd imagined him doing exactly what he described.

"The Hamptons was just the appetizer," he said. "A taste of the main course. I wanted to hear how my name sounded in that breathy moan of yours. I want to hear it right now. I want to hear it while I'm inside of you. But tonight I want something even more."

His lips brushed my ear.

"I want to taste you. I want to make you fall apart. Tonight is all about *you*."

Heat pooled between my thighs as James licked down my neck, leaving a trail of kisses in his wake as he crawled back off the bed. "I still can't believe there was a time I hated you," I said with a nervous laugh.

James kissed the inside of my thigh. "You never hated me," he said, looking up with a smirk. "Though, I'll admit, it was kind of hot when you glared at me like you wanted to set me on fire."

"James," I said, pushing at his shoulders, nerves settling in. "I just want to warn you it may take a while for me to come. It's not you—I'm just sensitive, and sometimes I get in my head and—"

"Hallie," he cut me off. "Stop talking."

He crawled up, kissed me deeply, then whispered, "I don't care how long it takes. In fact, I'm hoping it takes a while. This isn't a chore for me, Hal. This is dessert after the meal we just had, and I'm going to savor every last bite."

Could he be any more perfect?

"Now," he said, kissing his way back down my body, "tell me what you like."

I hesitated. But the way he looked at me, like there was no rush, like this moment belonged to me, gave me courage.

What *did* I like?

Any other time someone had gone down on me, it was a lot of squirming to help him hit the right spot. Or subtle head pushing so he would apply enough pressure. No one had ever made me feel as good as I could make myself feel.

"Circles. Not too much pressure, I'm sensitive." It felt uncomfortable talking about this, but the attentive way he listened, like he truly wanted to do what I wanted, gave me the confidence to keep going. "And ... I've always wanted to talk dirty during sex, but I felt too embarrassed to do it before."

James slid a hand under my shirt, fingertips dipping

below the edge of my bra as he squeezed my breast. A wave of heat followed his touch, leaving a tingling sensation on my skin. "Should I tell you how after I left your bedroom in the Hamptons, I had to get in the shower and fuck my hand?"

I was writhing on the bed. Every nerve felt flayed open. My skin felt like it had been set on fire. If I didn't find some sort of relief, I was sure to combust right here in this bedroom.

"Lay back," he murmured. "Let me take care of you."

He went back to trailing kisses on my thighs—growing closer and closer to where I wanted him to be. Where I *needed* him to be. I opened my legs wider, inviting him in closer. This time, I wasn't thinking about how I looked or if I was taking too long to finish. I just felt.

I gasped as his fingers slid inside me, slow and deep.

"Oh, sweetheart," James groaned. Gradually, his fingers began to move in and out of me, starting off slowly before quickening their pace. "Did I make you this wet?"

"Yes," I sighed.

"Do you want more?"

"Yes."

He smirked. "So needy."

Then his fingers were gone and his lips were next to my ear again. "Tell me what you want, Hal."

"*More*," I whispered, barely able to breathe. "I want more."

"Good girl." He kissed me hard, full of promise, and returned to his position between my legs.

His tongue replaced his fingers, and suddenly my body

wasn't my own anymore—it was a live wire. His tongue pinpointed every sensitive spot with precision. My legs started to close instinctively, but he held me open, kept me right there in that place that felt almost too good to survive.

I needed *something* to break.

And then I shattered.

I wasn't sure of anything at all. I'd lost the ability to think as all I could focus on was how he was making me fall apart.

When I could finally think again, James climbed back onto the bed and kissed me as my body turned to liquid. No longer containable.

"And how do you feel?" he whispered.

"I think I'm still in orbit."

He laughed, standing up and changing into a pair of sweatpants before offering me his hand. "But is it silent?"

"Is what silent?" I asked.

"Your head," he said, helping me into my own pair of sweatpants. "There was far too much going on up there for you to really hear yourself."

Now that he mentioned it, for the first time in days, I finally felt like my arrow was back pointing due north. It was no longer spinning out of control, leaving me unsure of what direction to go in.

"As a matter of fact. I think I know exactly what to write."

James grinned. "I'll pop some popcorn and crack open a bottle of wine. You can use my laptop."

As he reached the doorway, he looked back. "Are you coming?"

I crossed the room toward him. "Can you make a good Old Fashioned?"

That beautiful smile stretched so wide it crinkled the corners of his eyes. "*Can* I? Sweetheart, you're in for a treat."

Nothing seemed likely to eclipse the treat he'd just given me, I thought.

28

Hallie

"Do you think you could just . . . *not* go into the office?" I asked, snuggling deeper under the covers. I wasn't sure what thread count these sheets were, but they were so soft I felt like I was sleeping on literal clouds.

We'd spent most of the night watching reality TV and drinking Old Fashioneds while I worked on my review of The Social Eatery. James's suggestion to write authentically, like I did for my blog, had proven truer than I'd expected. I'd already carved out my own space within the food critic world—I'd found my own success. But when the opportunity came to write under the *Sophisticate* name, that success suddenly felt small.

The only solution was to do what I do best and be *me*. I wrote something I would be proud to post on my blog. James even contributed with his review of the Old Fashioned, which I included.

By the time I was done, it was well into the night. James offered me one of his guest rooms, but after everything that had already happened between us, sleeping in separate bedrooms felt far weirder than sharing one.

"I'd love to stay in bed," James said, his voice still thick with sleep as he pulled me against his chest, his arm strong and warm beneath my head. "But I have an important meeting today." Morning light was already starting to spill through the cracks in the blinds, casting a soft glow across the room and bringing with it the day's responsibilities.

The steady rhythm of his heartbeat beneath my cheek made it harder to let him go. Prior to last night, I'd done a good job of shelving my feelings for him, keeping things objective—measuring our connection like it was just content for the column. But after last night, the enormity of my emotions was too much to ignore.

James wanted *me*. And not just in some shallow, short-term way. He wanted me enough to respect my boundaries and understand my hesitancy to be with him. He'd taken the time to go slow, to make sure I was comfortable. With no expectation of reciprocity. And as I lay in these luxurious sheets, next to a shirtless James, I knew things were changing between us.

To fulfill Anthea's challenge, I knew I would have to date someone for a considerable time. Yet, I never thought I would find myself in this situation when I first started "Love on Wall Street". Lying in bed in a brownstone on the Upper West Side, beside a man who listened and cared.

"You are more than welcome to lie here all day if you want to," James murmured, kissing my temple. "If I didn't have this lunch meeting, I would be right here with you. Did you turn in your article?"

"I did," I said. "Haven't heard from Anthea yet though. So, no stamp of approval."

James threw off the covers and swung his legs over the side of the bed. I couldn't help but sneak a glance at him in his boxers. It had been too dark in the room last night for me to fully appreciate the view.

"Do you need her approval to feel like you turned in a good piece?" he asked as he crossed into his closet.

"I know I turned in a good piece."

"Then there shouldn't be anything else that matters." He walked back out of his closet, holding up two different shirts. "Which one?"

That was the thing about James. He was always so matter of fact. He didn't have a million different voices in his head, forcing him to second guess his actions. I couldn't possibly understand what that was like. To not be constantly wondering if you had done enough. If *you* were enough. To have the confidence that he woke up with every day would change my life. Being on the receiving end of his confidence, even for a few seconds, made a difference.

"The light-blue one," I said, smiling as he disappeared again.

"I'm thinking navy pants," he called out. "What suit jacket?"

"Do you have something tan or brown?"

He reappeared with two different jackets. I pointed to the brown plaid one. "How have you managed to dress yourself until now?"

"Is it such a terrible thing that I want to wear something you like today?"

I sank further into the bed, grinning. Judging by the number of times I'd blushed in his presence, I was pretty sure I had a good old-fashioned crush.

"You know I won't be with you today to appreciate that outfit," I teased.

James emerged fully dressed. And wow. He looked perfect—like a classy wet dream.

"No, you won't be there to appreciate how good my ass looks in these pants," he said, fastening his Rolex and sliding on his signet ring, "but I get to walk around knowing that you like how I look. That's enough for me."

For so long, I'd buried myself in my work. Food and my writing had yet to let me down. I'd convinced myself that something was wrong with me—that I wasn't pretty enough, funny enough, that I simply wasn't good enough compared to every other woman. I wished I could go back and tell my younger self that she was perfect. I only needed to wait for someone who could see that.

"Don't feel you need to rush out of here after me," James said, crossing the room again to fasten his cufflinks. "Take your time. Use whatever you want. I think I have a leftover breakfast casserole in the fridge that you can have. Do you want to spend our fourth date at my family's restaurant tonight?"

I blinked, caught off guard. "Dinner? With your family?"

James nodded, casual—but I didn't miss the way he paused to gauge my reaction. "I'd love you to experience the restaurant with the whole family vibe, so that you can really be immersed in the traditions and flavors which make it such a wonderful place. No pressure, though, if you don't want to go I can make other plans."

The invitation landed heavier than he probably intended. This wasn't just dinner—it was meeting his people. The inner circle. The ones who could make or break everything.

"I—yeah. I'd like that." I sat up straighter, the sheet falling around my waist. "You're sure?"

"Positive." He smiled, and it was that quiet kind of smile

that felt like a secret only we shared. "I'll pick you up. I don't want you trekking to Brooklyn alone. Plus, I can show you some of my favorite places on the way to the pizzeria."

I tried to play it cool, even though my heart was doing somersaults. "What time should I expect you?"

"Dinner never actually *starts* with dinner. There's always at least an hour of talking before any food hits the table. I'll get you around five—with traffic, that should work."

And that's when it hit me. Tonight wasn't just dinner. It was *meeting his family*. When he first suggested it, it had sounded casual. But now, on reflection? Now it felt a little like being invited into the fold. Into his world.

"And that's on top of our weekly Wednesday dinner! Sometimes we do that at the pizzeria," he added, shuffling through a briefcase. "Other times it's my grandparents' place, if Nonna's in the mood to cook. Either way, everyone shows up, and there's always way too much food."

I nodded my head absently, not trusting myself to do much more than that with the nerves pushing through me.

"I've got to head out," James said, grabbing his bag. "I need a few hours in the office before this meeting happens, so I can try to get some work done."

"Who's your meeting with?" I asked. "Some big client you're bringing on?"

James hesitated, rubbing his chin, gaze lowered. "It's not for Berkley Williams. I'm meeting a business acquaintance."

"So, a business opportunity for yourself, then."

He shrugged. "Potentially. I'm not sure. Maybe the start of being able to pursue my own thing."

"Then good luck," I said softly.

James paused before he crossed through the doorway. Only to backtrack across the room. "One more thing before I leave."

He leaned down and pressed the slowest, sweetest, tenderest kiss to my lips. I pulled him close, wanting to soak in a few more seconds in our little blissful bubble before we had to return to reality.

"I'll see you later," he said. "Promise me you'll have some breakfast before you leave?"

I lifted my pinky. "Promise."

"I expect a full review of it when I see you later." His face lit up with that perfect grin, the one I adored, a flash of pure joy.

That was the thing about James Rossi. He fought for the people he loved—his family when their restaurant was threatened, his friends when a girl writing an article about them came along, or me when I was my own worst enemy.

Thanks to him, maybe I was about to start fighting for myself.

29

James

I was falling for Hallie Woods, and I didn't know what the hell to do about it.

The moment I walked away after our first kiss, I knew. The weekend in the Hamptons only solidified it. But this morning? I woke up with her warm body tangled in the sheets beside me, and there was no denying it anymore. I'd crossed the point of no return.

She was still asleep when I stirred. Peaceful. Soft. The kind of tranquility I didn't know I'd been searching for until I found her. I reached for my phone, trying not to wake her, the glow of the screen casting light across her face. There was a text from Theo asking to meet for lunch. Said he had a business proposal and that a quick resolution would benefit us both.

For a minute, I considered ignoring him completely. Turning on Do Not Disturb and spending the rest of the morning exactly where I wanted to be—wrapped around Hallie, with no one else in the world to bother us.

But Theo rarely reached out unless it was important. So, despite every fiber of my being screaming at me to stay, I got up, got dressed, and headed toward the Financial District.

Even on the subway, I was completely calm. I wasn't checking the pre-market buzz or rehearsing elevator pitches in my head. My focus had shifted. Drastically. And all it took was a certain brunette I'd left alone in my bed—like an idiot—who had turned my whole world upside down.

Later, as I made my way from the Financial District up into Lower Manhattan to meet Theo, my phone rang.

"Mom, hi."

"You're still planning on coming to the restaurant tonight?" No greeting. Straight to the point—classic Eloise Rossi.

"Hello to you, too," I replied sarcastically. I could almost picture the exact eye roll I knew she was giving me right now. "Yes, I'll be there."

"Good. Everyone's going, so it would be pointless if you didn't make the time."

She was conveniently forgetting that I was the one who'd suggested we meet for dinner at the restaurant tonight. I'd thrown it out offhandedly, just looking to sneak in a visit and maybe some of the pizzeria's famous pasta. She'd thought it was a fantastic idea and had made a family event out of it, despite my attempts to dissuade her with the reminder that we had already met for family dinner on Wednesday. Twice in one week felt excessive, even by Rossi standards.

"I'll be there, Mom."

"Should we expect Sebastian?"

"Not tonight," I said, pausing for a second. Part of me wanted to mention Hallie. Part of me didn't want to open the door to fifty questions I wasn't ready to answer yet.

"Well, everyone's getting there at six," she said, "so be sure to leave the office early enough. I'm sure Berkley

Williams won't collapse if you left before it gets dark outside for once."

"Yes, ma'am." I grinned as I said it.

I stifled a laugh at my mother's groan. There was nothing she hated more in this world than being referred to as ma'am. She said it made her feel like she was one foot in her own grave.

"Don't 'ma'am' me, James Rossi."

"Listen, I've got to go. I have a business lunch to get to. I'll see you tonight."

There was a beat of silence before she spoke again, her voice a touch softer.

"I know you're always chasing the next big thing, and I don't mean to sound like I'm scolding you. I just hope you're not burning yourself out, honey. I worry sometimes that you're so busy building this life of yours, you forget to actually live it."

"Working hard lets me have the life I want, Mom."

"I know," she said gently. "I just hope you take the time to enjoy it, too. To really see the people around you, the ones who care about you. That's all."

Her words settled in deeper than I let on.

"I hear you," I said quietly. "I really do."

I didn't know where this line of questioning was coming from, and as I stood outside The Nest, I knew I didn't have the time to have this conversation. It was far more complicated than a five-minute conversation could unpack. "Let's talk about this later, Mom."

The lobby of The Nest was as empty as it was the first time I met Theo here. I half-wondered if they intentionally spaced out guest arrivals for maximum discretion.

"James Rossi, here for Theodore Drake," I told the concierge.

"Mr. Drake is on the fifth floor, dining at Bluebird," the concierge replied, presenting a lockbox. I did one last cursory check of my notifications and email inbox before handing over my phone.

"Thank you," I said, accepting the key card that would grant me access.

Bluebird was one of the many restaurants inside of The Nest and was known for being secluded and quiet. A hostess led me over to the table and, although it had only been a few months since I last saw Theo, he looked like he'd aged years. Dark circles stood out against his paler than normal skin. His face was marked by the same severe frown I'd seen in the handful of interviews he'd given, a frown that seemed like it had been carved into his features by months of stress.

"James, thank you for meeting me." Theo stood to shake my hand when the hostess announced my arrival.

"Absolutely," I told him. "I'm happy to make the time."

"Please, sit." He gestured to the table. "I took the liberty of ordering a few appetizers. I wasn't sure how much time you carved out for me, and I didn't want to take advantage of your busy schedule."

I kept my expression neutral. Last time we'd met, Theo had passed along information that had made me a king at Berkley Williams. It had also come with strings attached—strings I suspected he was about to start pulling.

"I wrapped everything up at the office this morning," I told him. "Cleared the afternoon just in case."

"Smart," he replied, dividing the appetizers between

our plates with meticulous precision. "I'm not sure how much time this conversation will take."

He had tousled his white-blonde hair, and his usually icy blue eyes looked far more tired than I remembered.

"I believe congratulations are in order," I said, raising my glass. He'd just been recognized by Rooster's board as the proper choice for the company's next CEO, despite early rumors that the board might look beyond the Drake family for the next person to put at the helm. But in the end, Theo had won them over.

"Thank you," he said.

"You used my information from our last conversation well," he added, voice low.

I nodded. Neither of us was willing to dig into that conversation. It had danced too far into a gray area for either of us to risk any illegal discourse.

"Well," he said after a beat, leaning forward slightly. "No sense in continuing the small talk."

I was used to Theo appearing aloof and unconcerned about the repercussions of his actions. But the Theo I was lunching with today appeared on edge. His leg bounced under the table and his fingers drummed against the white tablecloth.

Whatever this was, it wasn't just business. And it definitely wasn't casual.

"Please." I gestured in his direction, offering for him to take the lead.

"I'm sure you read the headlines," Theo began. "After my brother's hubris led to his own downfall, I scraped what was left of Rooster back together and am trying to carve something beautiful out of its remains. I fired every executive that had grown fat and happy under my brother's leadership. People that fired others who'd been the backbone of my company for years, just so they could pad their pockets with bigger and bigger bonuses. I've reallocated funds from irrelevant expenditures to benefit employees who have dedicated their lives to Rooster. But during my close examination of the health of the company, I've come across a unique problem that I think you have the skill set to solve."

It was impressive—listening to the way Theo had taken a scalpel to his family's company to cut away the excess fat. But for all his talk, I had no idea why I was sitting across from him.

"What did you find?" I asked cautiously.

"My brother has money set aside to start our own venture capital firm. But that was as far as he got. You, however," Theo leaned back in his chair, giving me the first glimpse of the business shark that I knew him to be, "you mentioned once that you wanted to start your own firm. Would you consider leading Rooster's venture capital firm?"

That may have been the furthest thing I would have expected Theo to call me here for today.

But what was even more surprising was the way excitement pumped through my veins at the idea of having that kind of opportunity. It wasn't just a job, it was an opportunity to shape something from the ground up. A seat at the table, not just another cog in the machine.

There was only one problem.

Hallie.

The last thing I wanted was to take on a new role that

would chain me to my desk to get it off the ground. It would sign our death certificate before we even started.

"I will consider it," I said slowly.

Theo dipped his head in understanding.

"But," I added, "I have a few things I would need in order for me to accept the offer."

"Now you speak my language, Rossi. Please proceed." Theo grinned, showing nearly all his teeth as he eagerly waited for me to lay out my proposition. "Let's hear it."

"Recent developments in my life would require for me to not spend all my hours at the office," I said. "If I take this on, I want to be able to work flexibly, and I expect the same for my team. I don't want anyone watching the sunset through a boardroom window five nights a week."

Theo raised a single eyebrow at my plan.

I charged ahead. "If we're really going to make Rooster into the kind of company people respect, then this firm has to reflect that. The financial industry's never prioritized balance, never cared about its employees' quality of life. I think we should be the ones to change that. Offer the best benefits. Attract the best minds. And still be the best at what we do."

Theo didn't respond right away. He just studied me, and for a brief second, I saw something that I could only describe as respect.

"Who is she?" he asked after a beat.

"I'm sorry?" I blinked, caught off guard.

Theo smirked, clearly amused by my confusion. "The girl. The one that's got you reconsidering your priorities."

"I'm not sure I know what you're talking about." I kept my tone even, careful. Just because I was considering going into business with him didn't mean I trusted him completely, especially not with something as personal as Hallie.

He waved me off. "Don't worry. I get it. If there's an incredible woman in your life, it makes sense that you'd want more balance. For what it's worth, I agree with you. That's the kind of future I want for Rooster, too. Not built on greed, not like what my brother turned it into. My grandfather didn't build this company to become a cautionary tale about ambition."

He leaned forward slightly, his tone softening. "Money warps people. If building something more human matters to you, then you have my full support. I never expected a decision today anyway. Go home. Think about it. Maybe talk it over with your partner."

Theo glanced at his phone. "Now I'm sorry to cut this short, but it looks like I'm needed back at the office. We will talk soon?"

I stood up with him. "Yeah, we'll talk soon."

As I left Bluebird, I found myself turning his words over in my head.

This morning, I'd woken up with every intention of staying in bed and wasting the day away with Hallie. Would I have regretted that choice if I had missed out on this meeting with Theo? Was this even something I wanted to consider?

There were a few things I knew—I loved what I did, and this opportunity would be incredible.

But I also wanted Hallie Woods. I just needed to figure out if there was a world where I could have both.

30

Hallie

"My grandparents have lived in the same rent-controlled brownstone for nearly forty years," James said as we crossed the Brooklyn Bridge.

I didn't make it to Brooklyn often, and seeing it with James's eyes felt like experiencing it all for the first time.

"My aunt and uncle live around the corner from them," he continued.

"So you and your parents are the odd ones out?" I teased, glancing at him.

From the moment that he picked me up, James had been keeping a steady stream of conversation going, and honestly, it was doing wonders for my nerves.

He'd asked me for my review of his breakfast casserole that morning. It was probably one of the best things I'd ever eaten: layers of fluffy eggs, crispy hashbrowns, spicy sausage, and it was topped with gooey cheese. I'd snapped a picture for my social media account before I even took a bite, and I hadn't been able to stop raving about it since.

Then I'd asked him about his business lunch, expecting a vague answer. Instead, I got a ten minute debrief of his meeting with Theo Drake, the famous heir to the Rooster empire. I might not know much about finance, but anyone who was vaguely plugged into current affairs had heard of the infamous Drake family. Theo was in the middle of taking over the company from his brother after the board had voted in favor of removing him as CEO. Following a few weeks of deliberation and interviews, the board had officially placed Theo as the new CEO of Rooster. His sweeping reforms had been all over the news, everything from massive changes within the executive suite and the salaries afforded to them, to cancellations of previous projects his brother had announced.

"So, he wanted consulting advice from you?" I asked, still trying to wrap my head around the fact that James was casually meeting with one of the most powerful men in business.

James tossed his head from side to side. "Yes, but not exactly. He knows of my ambitions to open my own investment firm. But he threw me for a loop with his request. He wanted to know if I would head Rooster's venture capital firm that he was looking at pursuing. I would get to decide on where the company invests."

"Wait, seriously?" I leaned in, excitement bubbling. "You'd be the one deciding where they invest?"

He nodded, eyes flickering with something between pride and hesitation.

"That's huge, James."

"It is," he said, but his tone had shifted. Gone was the lightness from earlier. "I asked for some time to think about it."

I frowned, unsure why he didn't sound more thrilled. "What's there to think about?"

He hesitated. "My dream is to open my own firm. I know it can be a huge risk. Especially to go from one of the largest firms on Wall Street to basically a start-up. The bigwigs would call me a cowboy. But I feel like I could make it work."

"This could be like the best of both worlds," I told him. "You'd be starting a brand-new investment company, like your own start-up. But with the backing of a large company behind you. Less risk."

He hesitated again.

"Don't you want to leave your mark on the financial world?" I pressed, channeling his usual way of pushing me to dream bigger.

"Of course I do—"

I immediately stopped him from going down the well-worn road of self-criticism and rationalizations—a path I knew all too well. "Then what else is there to consider?"

He paused. "I wouldn't be working for myself like I'd originally dreamed of. And ... Theo's a wild card. He took down his own brother to get the CEO role. Even if it was the right call, what's to say he wouldn't do the same to me?"

He took a breath and opened his mouth to say something else, only to close it once more after he must have thought better of it.

"What?" I asked gently. "What else?"

But whatever else concerned him about accepting Theo Drake's offer vanished as we pulled into the parking lot behind the building perfectly situated under the Brooklyn Bridge. The small lot, with only five cars, had spaces exclusively reserved for the Rossi family.

James crossed in front of the car to open my door for me. The building's architecture nearly distracted me too much to swoon. Nearly. There were still a few butterflies floating around in there as he tucked my hand into the crook of his arm.

"This place is amazing." I was in awe that James's family restaurant was in such a beautiful building.

"It was a bank in the 1800s," James told me as we walked around to the front of the building, giving me a better look at the large arched floor-to-ceiling windows that revealed an intimately lit dining space on the other side, filled with red-checkered tablecloths and old pictures hung on the walls.

My excitement about the restaurant nearly eclipsed the fact that I was meeting James's family. We stepped through the heavy old door that must have also belonged to the building when it was once a bank for Brooklyn centuries ago and a woman with beautiful black hair and a paler complexion than James came into view.

"James!" she exclaimed, hurrying around the stand to wrap him in a hug.

A scarlet blush crept into James's cheeks as he hugged the woman back before they pulled apart and her eyes landed on me.

"Oh, my. How rude of me." The woman turned to swat James across the chest. "Why didn't you tell us you were bringing a date, James? Your mother is going to be beside herself."

Us? I knew James's family ran the restaurant, but did that mean his *entire* family was here?

"Because I knew you, Mom, and Nonna would make a big deal out of it." James gave the woman a knowing look. "Like you are right now."

"Nonsense." The woman waved James off and turned to take my hands in hers. "It's so lovely to meet you, sweetie. I'm Maria, James's aunt."

"Hallie." I was acutely aware of the panic in James's eyes as he watched his aunt swoop me into a hug.

"Let me get a good look at you, Hallie." Maria held me at arm's length as she surveyed me from head to toe. James's face matched the red of the tablecloths.

"Aunt Maria—"

James's aunt silenced his pleas with a single look. "You are beautiful, Hallie," she told me with a wink.

"Thanks," I murmured, feeling completely out of my comfort zone already and we'd only just stepped inside.

"I'll let Tony and Lorenzo know you're here." Maria turned toward the dining room, scanning the area for someone in particular. "Brandon," she called out to a younger version of James. He was wearing a white apron around his waist and carried a notebook in his hand.

"Yeah, Mom?" Brandon asked once he was close enough.

"Can you take James and Hallie to the family table?" Maria asked.

Brandon eyed me curiously as he nodded to Maria. "I'm Brandon, James's cousin." He offered me his hand as the three of us entered the dining area.

The ceiling had gold-stamped tin tiles that I was positive were from the original bank architecture. Repurposed wine bottles formed chandeliers that hung around the space, creating the dim lighting which gave the restaurant a warm and inviting feel.

"I'm Hallie," I replied. Unsure how else to explain my presence, I left it at that, despite Brandon's curiosity.

Now I had a perfect vantage point for the pictures hung on the walls. They were black-and-white photos of Brooklyn—the surrounding neighborhood through the years and the people that lived there. There were stills of the Rossi family. I recognized Maria, though she was far younger in the pictures. She was standing in the arms of a man that had the same tan skin and dark features as James in front of the pizzeria. Next to them was a man that was the near spitting image of James with a woman in his arms. She was beautiful, almost ethereal in the way she held herself with such poise.

"That's my mother and father," James whispered in my ear when he noticed me studying the photo. "And that's my aunt, Maria, and my uncle, Antonio. They'd just taken over the restaurant from my grandparents that day—although in name only, it turns out."

"A true family business," I mused as I took in how happy they all looked for a few more seconds. "That's what makes restaurants so magical. The love that comes from people that care just as much about what they do as each other."

"That is exactly why I think people will love this place as much as I do. Tourists and locals alike. The people that live around here are loyalists. There are customers that have been coming in here for decades. But those are few and far between. We can't keep up with the flashy restaurants tourists love to go to. I just know that if they were to step in through those doors, they'd get the exact New York experience they wanted."

I looked again at the photo, wanting to remember exactly how James's description of this place's potential impact on NYC's food scene made me feel. And how honored I felt that he'd enlisted my help to do it.

"How are your finals going?" James asked Brandon, as we made our way through the dining room to a back table where five people were sitting.

"Good. I've got one more and then I'm done. Graduated." Brandon's pride was evident as we approached the table.

"You're in college? Where are you going?" I asked, postponing being the center of everyone's attention for a few seconds longer.

"NYU," Brandon said.

"Me, too. I graduated a few years back," I told him.

A smile broke out across his face. "No way! What did you study?"

"Journalism. What about you?"

"Business," Brandon said proudly. "I want to take this place over someday. Keep it in the family."

Everything about this restaurant was what made me fall in love with reviewing. It didn't have a Michelin star. Celebrities weren't trying to get reservations here. The chef in the back wasn't renowned on a global scale. But none of that mattered. Not when the backbone of this place was the *true* definition of Brooklyn.

"James!" an older version of the woman in the picture I'd just looked at called out. She still had the same ethereal energy.

"Hi, Mom." James leaned away from me to give the woman a kiss on the cheek as she wrapped her arms around her son.

"I thought you told me you weren't bringing anyone?" she asked, her voice tight as she gave me a smile.

James's mother had fair skin and white-blonde hair. Her skin was flawless, and she wore her age like it was its own accessory. She was the kind of woman I used to watch walk out of Bergdorf Goodman's in college with their arms weighed down with bags.

"I said I wasn't bringing Sebastian, Mom." I wasn't sure I'd ever seen James blush so much in one evening. It was charming knowing he was just as nervous about this situation as I was.

"So now I have to explain myself when I ask if you're bringing guests? How do you think she feels? Walking in here with your entire family staring at her like she's a zoo animal? Did you even tell her we'd all be here? I swear, I thought I raised you better than that."

"Eloise, come on now. You're only going to make it worse." The man that looked like an older version of James reached for Eloise to return her to her seat.

"Giacomo, Eloise is right. I would have made something for her to take home." An older woman at the table glared at James's father.

"We're at a restaurant, Ma. She'll probably have food to take home already."

I wanted the ground to open up and swallow me whole as they all looked at me expectantly. My family was much quieter and much more reserved than the bunch in front of me.

My lips opened, then they closed. Then opened again. I wasn't sure how many times I tried to find anything to say to these people that James cared about so fiercely, but nothing came out.

James rescued me.

"Everyone, this is Hallie," James said, his voice a blend of pride and something softer.

He went around the table, introducing his mother, Eloise. His father, Giacomo. His uncle, Antonio, or Tony. His younger cousin, Emilia, who had just come from a volleyball game. And his grandmother, Giulietta.

Eloise waved me over to the open seat beside her, the previous irritation she'd directed at James gone, replaced by genuine enthusiasm.

"Hallie, it's a pleasure to have you join tonight for family dinner." Then she dropped her voice to a stage whisper as I took the seat next to her. "I'm sorry about my son. I think he believes having us unprepared for his surprises is better, so we don't have an entire list of questions prepared." She rolled her eyes. "Men. What can we do? But I don't blame him. He's never brought a woman to the restaurant before, much less to a family dinner. So, you must be special."

James slid into the seat beside me and casually draped his arm across my chair, like we did this all the time. "This isn't *family dinner*, by the way," he added with a quick glance in my direction. "That's on Wednesdays at Nonna's house. This is just dinner with the family, totally different."

"And you brought her?" Emilia asked. "Are you two like together?"

"Oh, we're just—" I started to say, unsure how to define what this is.

"Dating," James cut me off, leaning around me to announce for the table. "We are dating. Just thought I'd get that out of the way before the salad is served."

"We could have guessed that the moment you brought her here, James," an older man grumbled as he walked up to the table with two bowls of salad in his hands. "I'm Lorenzo. James's grandfather."

I smiled nervously. Now it was my turn to turn the same shade of red as the baskets of tomatoes that were visible in the kitchen. While James wasn't lying, I wasn't sure how I felt leading his entire family to believe we were serious. Because while I was wishing we were, neither of us had properly broached that conversation yet.

"Hallie," I said, offering a polite smile.

"I think I'm the last one to join, so you won't have to introduce yourself anymore." Lorenzo took the seat across from us, but not before giving Giulietta a sweet kiss. Then he poured a glass of wine from one of the bottles on the table and offered it to me. "If you're anything like me, you're going to need this to get through this dinner."

James's shoulders shook with silent laughter beside me as he watched me accept the glass. Under the table, his hand found my thigh, his fingers giving a firm squeeze that sent a jolt up my spine.

"I'm sorry," he leaned over to whisper in my ear.

"Don't be," I whispered back.

There was something magical about being surrounded by the people who had shaped James—who had helped build the person sitting beside me now. The warmth, the noise, the stories passed across the table like bread baskets—it made me feel like, just maybe, there could be room for me here too.

31

James

I never thought I could love Hallie's laugh more. That was until I heard her laugh at one of my uncle's jokes that I'd heard a million times, the two of them in near tears by the time they'd caught their breaths again.

My grandfather unknowingly showed off for Hallie, having the kitchen send out nearly every appetizer the restaurant had. There was bruschetta and antipasto and caprese for all of us to share. I think I counted five times that Hallie sighed happily and closed her eyes after she tasted something new.

We hadn't even gotten to the best part yet.

"What is it you do, Hallie?" Nonna asked after the appetizers were cleared and the wine glasses were refilled.

"I am a writer for a women's magazine called *Sophisticate*."

"I know it! I've read it for years," my mother exclaimed. She and Hallie had really hit it off. I don't think I could recall one time that my mother had seemed interested in a single thing Cassidy had to say. But she had also pegged Cassidy for exactly what she was far sooner than I did.

"Is that the one that you cut that dating article out of the other day?" My grandmother asked my mother. "The one about the man with the nickname?"

I think both Hallie and I stopped breathing as we realized exactly which article they were talking about.

"Yes," my mother confirmed. "Mr. Old Fashioned. I don't know if I can remember the name of the writer on that article." My mother pressed a hand to her heart. "But it was like reading one of my favorite romance novels. The way that man treats her. She'd be silly to let that one go. I know she had some reservations in the beginning, but she'd be blind to think he wasn't head over heels for her. A private cooking class? The Hamptons? I'm itching to see what next week's article is."

Hallie's hand shook as she reached for her glass of wine. She took a large gulp. "I wrote those articles," she told them. Surprising not only me, but the entire table.

"What?" my mother asked her. Her gaze darted between me and Hallie as she pieced things together.

"But if you two are dating," my mother started. "That would make you . . ." she trailed off as her eyes landed on me.

"Mr. Old Fashioned, honey," my father supplied. "That would make him Mr. Old Fashioned."

"You know, now that you mention it," my aunt said, "when you take into account how James only seems to drink Old Fashioneds, and that he just got back from the Hamptons, and didn't he use your contacts, Eloise, to get a reservation at *Crepitio* a few weeks ago? It makes sense."

"So does that mean . . . your next article is about this date?" My mother looked back at Hallie, her expression unreadable. "About our restaurant?"

"Well, I suppose so," Hallie murmured. She had

retreated into herself. She was holding her breath as she waited for further questions.

"Well, I for one can't wait for the article." My grandfather spoke up for the first time since he greeted Hallie. "This is the publicity that this place needs. Didn't we all just have a conversation a couple of days ago about this?"

Suddenly the focus was off my family realizing they knew all about my dating life as they discussed how much of a positive having their restaurant mentioned in a magazine like *Sophisticate* could be. I watched Hallie visibly relax as my grandfather shot her a wink across the table.

Brandon leaned over, having ditched his apron for dinner, and whispered in my ear, "If Hallie could bring some extra attention to this place, it could really give us the edge we've been looking for. Plus, I'm not sure I've ever seen you like this before. Not even with Cassidy."

I had to give it to my cousin. He was quick as a whip and, despite his love for a good club in Dumbo, he'd do great things for the restaurant.

"I really like her, man," I told him. Because that was the truth. Fate and a copious amount of bickering over Old Fashioneds had brought the two of us together, and I hoped it was fate that would keep us together as well.

"I can't wait to bring Roxie to the restaurant. I can just imagine what she'd say about the food, and the pictures she'd take." Hallie had been nonstop in the car since we'd left. She'd been busy switching between writing her initial thoughts and raving about nearly every item on the menu. "And your grandfather came up with the entire menu?"

I nodded.

"I think I want to center my article around him. How he's built this amazing restaurant around two of the most important things in life—food and family." Hallie finally looked up from her phone long enough for me to see the bright flush in her cheeks and the shine in her eyes. She looked happy, wild. "Plus, I think we owe him for saving us from a potentially awkward conversation about 'Love on Wall Street'. I cannot believe your mother and grandmother have been following it weekly, like some kind of soap opera."

"I'm not embarrassed," I told her. "Honestly, I'm kind of relieved my mother basically knows the details of every one of our dates so far. That means she has less to interrogate me on."

During the rest of dinner, there was only one thing on my mind. How in the hell could I convince the woman sitting next to me we should date? Like officially. With titles and everything. Because the longer I hung out with her, the more I doubted my usual methods of charming would work. But during dinner, I was repeatedly reminded that Hallie was unlike any other girl I had ever dated. She didn't care if I had the smoothest pickup lines or knew exactly what to say. Words were more her thing anyway.

"I know you just stayed over last night, but I think it would be rude if I didn't invite you over after our fourth date."

Hallie's eyes lit up, relieving any worry I had. "I thought you'd never ask. I'd love to, but it also works out pretty well. Roxie texted halfway through dinner that she was having someone over. She didn't give me much detail, only asked if I could stay here again tonight because she wasn't sure if he was going to stay over all night or not."

My brows drew together in confusion. Roxie wasn't the type of girl to be shy about her conquests. "I didn't think Roxie cared if she had someone over while you're home."

"She normally doesn't," Hallie said with a shrug. "But who knows with her sometimes? She's been tight-lipped about whoever she's been going out with lately."

"Then to the Upper West Side we go," I declared as we emerged back in Manhattan off the Brooklyn Bridge.

"This is my favorite time of day," Hallie mused as she looked out the window as the skyline of Manhattan twinkled back at her. "There's so much excitement brewing for the possibilities of what a weekend in the city will bring."

The skyscrapers of lower Manhattan and the Financial District towered over us to our left. Random floors and offices were still lit despite the late hour. I used to be one of those people, wrapping up business late on a Friday night. But it had been weeks since I'd stayed past five on a Friday. The rest of the city that never sleeps was clocking out of their day jobs and checking in for their dinner reservations or lining up outside of a club. A few months ago, I would have just been arriving at Whiskey Locker to claim my normal corner booth with Sebastian. But now, there were other things I wanted to taste than just my regular cocktail, things only Hallie could offer me.

I pulled up in front of my brownstone, my blood roaring in my ears as I walked around the car to open Hallie's door. She gave me the same smile she always did when I did something so simple for her—pouring her a glass of wine, opening her door, walking on the part of the sidewalk closest to the traffic. I'd realized that she must have never had someone treat her with the respect and decency that she deserved.

It only made the pressure in my chest tighten, pressing down like it weighed a hundred pounds. Was I the right person for her? Could I give her what she wanted? What she deserved?

Theo Drake's offer was at the front of my mind. If he stayed true to his word, I wouldn't waste nights at the office away from her.

Was it even fair of me to ask her to start officially dating if I wasn't sure my circumstances would align with what she wanted from a partner?

"Penny for your thoughts?" Hallie asked me as I locked the front door behind me.

Fuck it. Why the hell should I let someone like Hallie slip away from me simply because of a bunch of what ifs? I said I was going to make her mine. It's time I put my money where my mouth is.

But when I turned to tell Hallie exactly that, my mouth grew dry again for a far different reason this time.

A pair of pants was the first thing I noticed. A pair of shoes. A shirt. Each article of clothing leading me toward the stairwell where Hallie stood in a black lace lingerie set. The moon shone in through the window next to her, illuminating her like she was a Renaissance painting.

Her curves were backlit, slipping in and out of shadow. I eyed the creamy expanse of her body. Nearly everything I'd planned to discuss with her slipped my mind.

"I'm not sure what I was thinking about," I drew out, nearly stumbling over my words like a teenage boy seeing his first half-naked girl.

"You know that cannoli didn't quite satisfy my sweet tooth." Hallie trailed a finger up the banister as she ascended the stairs, one step at a time. "What do you think? Do you still have an appetite?"

This was a completely different side of Hallie. I'd seen glimpses of her like this—wild, and unapologetically free—but never this vividly. And the fact that I made her feel safe enough to let that part of herself breathe? That was everything.

A light, melodic giggle echoed off the walls as Hallie watched me undo my belt, slipping it slowly through the loops before letting it fall to the floor. Next were my shoes. Then my shirt, landing in a quiet heap. I was down to just my boxers as I climbed the stairs after her, chasing her laughter.

"How do you not get out of breath climbing those stairs every day?" she teased, already stretched out like a goddess across my bed.

"I work out in my home gym," I said, suddenly struck with a strange kind of nervousness I didn't recognize. Shy was normally never a part of my vocabulary. The woman of every dream I didn't know I had was waiting for me, and I was frozen in the doorway like a fool.

"You have a home gym?"

"On the third floor," I managed, willing my legs to carry me forward. *Walk. Left foot. Then right foot. This isn't a hard concept, James.*

She arched a brow. "Are you going to just stand there staring or are you going to join me?"

You can talk to her about it in the morning. You will *tell her how you feel in the morning.*

Tonight, the only thing I wanted more than anything was to be with her.

My hands trembled slightly as I crossed the room, but there was no uncertainty in her eyes tonight. Only hunger. Desire. Trust.

She rose up onto her knees, level with me now, and the moonlight danced across the freckles sprinkled on her nose and cheeks. I traced my own patterns in my mind like a map I never wanted to forget.

Hallie leaned in and kissed me with a kind of abandon I hadn't known I craved. Giving herself to the moment and taking me with her. There was no hesitation in her lips. We melted into each other like we'd done this a thousand times in another life.

She took the lead this time, slipping her bra straps down, one by one, with a soft shrug, then reaching for the waistband of my boxers.

"I don't think I can wait any longer," she whispered into the space between us. "I want you. I *need* you. You may have wanted last night to be about me. But I want tonight to be about *us*."

She didn't need to say anything more.

I cupped her backside, drawing her flush against me as her mouth found mine again. Hallie drew a line of kisses from my mouth down to the hollow of my neck. She pushed my boxers down, and we both fumbled with a laugh as I kicked them away, joining her on the bed and helping her slide off her last remaining piece of clothing. Her laughter filled the room, and I realized it was my favorite sound.

I ran my hands along the curve of her ribs, feeling

the pounding of her heart and watching her heartbeat beneath my palms. She was beautiful in every light, but under the moon, she was breathtaking.

"Are you okay?" I asked as I hovered over her, brushing a strand of hair from her cheek.

Hallie nodded, her teeth catching her lower lip in a way that undid me. Her eyes drifted over me.

"If at any time you want to stop, just say the word," I said gently. "This is your pace. Your lead."

Her expression softened even more, and she brought her pinky up between us with a smile that melted every ounce of restraint I had. "I promise."

The moonlight danced across her body like it knew what a privilege it was just to look at her. Illuminating the dip of her stomach. The curve of her breasts. The slope of her neck. I felt the fire inside me surge, threatening to burn my resolve, but I held back.

I didn't want to rush this.

I wanted to remember every second. Every sigh. Every way her body fit with mine.

"Good," I murmured, my forehead brushing hers. "Because I want this to be something we both remember. Something that matters."

"James," she whispered, fingers threading through my hair, "there's no way I could regret this."

32

Hallie

James touched me like I was irreplaceable. His hands worshipped my body, mapping every inch as his mouth traced kisses over my collarbone, my neck, the slope of my shoulder.

I lay naked beneath him, and a hurricane of emotions was wreaking havoc within me. This wasn't sex born out of pure physical desire. This was something else entirely. Something that threatened to explode from my chest with every scrape of teeth against skin.

But instead of trying to inspect those feelings from every angle until I understood what they meant, I surrendered to them.

From the moment I saw him like this—completely, beautifully bare—I had to swallow the surge of awe that rose in my throat. I'd never seen a more perfect man, and still, somehow, he wanted me. Me.

My fingers traced the gold chain he always wore and then spread across the tan skin of his chest. He finally lowered himself between my legs, careful not to press his weight against me as his forearms bracketed my head, muscles taut. Need filled every inch of me.

His mouth captured mine again, and the kiss unraveled what was left of my composure. I couldn't get close enough. My legs wrapped around his waist, pulling him in. I wanted to feel every part of him. Needed to.

Normally, this would be the moment when my insecurities screamed the loudest.

Was my stomach too soft?

Was I too heavy?

Would he be comparing me to other women who'd given him head before?

Were my boobs big enough?

Or were they too big?

But not with James.

He silenced all those fears without a word. I was completely free, so utterly lost in this moment, lost in him. I'd never felt more beautiful.

James reached into the nightstand. I watched as he carefully rolled the condom down over his erection, completely entranced. My eyes devoured him—the way the muscles in his stomach flexed, the tension in his arms, the veins in his hands. Everything about him was raw, real, utterly captivating.

He paused once more to give me a meaningful look, one last chance to bail out, just like he always did. I answered him with a firm kiss. No doubts. No second thoughts.

Then the only sounds filling the room were groans and gasps as James rocked into me.

"Holy fuck," James cursed, his voice breaking as he buried his face into the curve of my neck. I rolled my hips to meet him, our bodies falling into rhythm like we were made to move this way. His hands fisted the sheets on either side of me, his signet ring flashing in the moonlight streaming in through the window.

The moment my fingers dug into his shoulders, something inside him shifted. As if James had been holding himself back all this time. His hands were everywhere, like he didn't know where to touch first because he wanted to feel everything.

Buried in my hair.

Pulling on my chin to press a punishing kiss to my lips.

Squeezing my ass.

A flick across a nipple.

The sensations were nearly too much. James was a master at turning me into putty in his hands, so overwhelmed by his touch. When his fingers found my clit, I nearly shattered. A cry escaped me, ragged and needy.

"You are so fucking beautiful, Hal."

He threw both of my legs up over his shoulders, giving him a better angle, and I couldn't stop the way my body arched toward his. I gave myself over completely. I didn't resist. I didn't think. I just *felt*.

My moans grew desperate as pleasure built, hot and wild inside me. James noticed and picked up his pace. He moved faster, deeper, keeping his gaze locked on mine.

"God, Hal. You feel amazing," he groaned.

And just like that, I came undone, the praise sending me over the edge. I broke into a million little pieces as James thrusted once more. His groans joining mine like the crescendo to a symphony.

He lowered my legs gently, letting them fall to the bed as he pressed his face against my chest. His six-foot-five body went soft against mine, no longer the towering man in charge of boardrooms. I threaded my fingers into his hair as my chest heaved up and down, trying to get air back into my lungs. He pressed a few kisses to the space between my breasts.

"You're perfect," he murmured, his blue eyes meeting mine. "You know that, right?"

"I don't know about that," I drew out. It slipped out like muscle memory.

"Well, you should," he whispered, capturing my chin in his hand and forcing me to look at him. "I wish you could see yourself the way I do. You'd never doubt just how beautiful you are for a single second."

He kissed the tip of my nose and slowly pulled away. Air rushed between us, the cool breeze kissing my skin. I instantly missed the way his arms had made the world feel quiet for the first time in forever.

"Come on." James offered me his hand once he'd removed the condom from his length. "Let's take a shower."

He scooped me up in his arm with a confidence that took my breath away. I expected him to be strong, sure, but nothing prepared me for the way he lifted me like I weighed nothing at all, like carrying me wasn't a strain but something he wanted to do. My head dropped to his shoulder, a tired laugh bubbling up as my limbs went limp with exhaustion and a sated happiness.

"Got you," James murmured, and I believed him in every sense of the word.

He took me through into the bathroom, flipping on the light with his elbow and nudging the glass shower door open with his foot. Steam began to curl into the air as he turned the water on, testing it with his hand until it was warm—just shy of hot.

He stepped into the wide marble shower, keeping me close to his chest as the water cascaded down his back.

Slowly, he set me down onto the built-in bench and crouched in front of me. He reached for a bottle of body wash, pouring a little into his palm, then lathered it into a gentle foam before he began to cleanse me. His hands moved gently, no teasing, no rush. Just long, slow strokes down my arms, legs, and over my shoulders.

He paused now and then to kiss my damp skin, to meet my eyes with a burning desire. When he leaned in and kissed my mouth—soft and steady, water strickling down our faces—it felt more like a promise than a kiss. One that I didn't know the words to yet, but I could feel the meaning of it all the way down to my bones.

He pulled back just slightly, his forehead resting against mine, and the water flowed around us.

Whatever promise he was making me, in that moment, I knew he was going to keep it.

"If I ever make my own blog with Roxie, I am going to have a 'Food James Makes Me' section. Just so I can review your food because, dear Lord. I don't know how you do it." I groaned as I took another bite of the Italian sub sandwich James had made me after our shower.

"Why don't you do it?" he asked me as he reached over to steal a chip from me.

"Hey!" I swatted at his hand. "Get your own."

"I ate mine," he replied around a mouthful of food.

"Then go get more."

James stood up to go grab the rest of the chips still on the kitchen counter. "Why don't you do it?" he asked again, as he made his way back to me.

"Do what?"

"Start your own blog, your own company," James offered. "Why not do it?"

"Honestly," I told him, "I've been asking myself the same question in recent weeks. I've been going back and forth on it. I leaned that way recently. But with this week's turn of events and Anthea's offer for me to write the piece on The Social Eatery, I think it would be stupid if I don't see the opportunity through."

James tilted his head from side to side. "Maybe. But maybe you should consider that you were nothing but upfront with your wants and desires with Anthea. You entered this entire agreement in good faith, yet she's gone back on that good faith by potentially taking that away from you."

The air hung heavy as James's words sunk in.

"If one door closes, another one opens." James leaned over to flick the tip of my nose. But not before he snagged another chip off my plate despite the open bag he now had.

"Hey!" I grabbed for the chip bag, but James held it out of my reach.

"Not until you finish your article. You still have to write about how amazing Mr. Old Fashioned is and how he brought you home to his family."

This time, I grabbed the closest pillow to me and sent it flying in his direction.

He batted it away with ease, a smug look on his face.

"Does this make us like *The Bachelor*? Did we just do a hometown date?"

"You're really full of it tonight, aren't you." I moved to straddle him, chips and sandwich forgotten. But he only pushed me back into my spot on the couch before placing my computer in my lap.

"No. No touchy until you're done." James reached over to my discarded plate to steal another chip.

"You really have to stop doing that."

I rolled my eyes at him but followed his direction. The words flowed out of me faster than nearly any other article I'd written for "Love on Wall Street". Between the food, the company, and the patriarch of the Rossi family, I had more than enough to work with. I described a family-owned restaurant built on the foundation of the American Dream. Hardworking folks that had a gift for flavors and creating a memorable evening. It was exactly what James had described—the perfect place for tourists to have a true New York City experience.

This article, paired with the blog post that Roxie and I would do, would provide enough press to spark some fresh interest in the pizzeria. By the time James finished his sandwich—and mine—I was ready to send the piece off to Anthea, feeling proud for the first time of one of these Wall Street articles. I let her know how sentimental this article was. How great the evening was. How amazing Mr. Old Fashioned's family was. I even added for her benefit—I told myself, at least—that this felt like a serious step in our relationship. A meaningful one.

My finger hesitated over the mousepad, daring myself to back out now. To keep this one to myself and tell

Anthea I'd changed my mind. Maybe the Hallie from a few months ago would have caved under the pressure, but I was just beginning to learn about this new *me*. Someone that wasn't afraid to go after what she wanted. I was teetering on the precipice of before and after. Before I became a food critic and *after*. My finger pressed down into my mousepad, and I watched my email to Anthea disappear into the ether. Some of the weight I'd been carrying since the moment I realized I had no clue where to start for this series lifted off my chest, flying away with the email. All I needed was to get out of my head and without James, I'm not sure I would have achieved that in time. Maybe eventually, but I would have let that insidious voice in my mind win. It was too easy to fall victim to its words. Or let it steal all of mine.

But not this time.

"Done," I announced as I closed my laptop. "What's my reward?" I was trying my best not to focus too hard on the panic starting to settle in.

What if she didn't like it?
What if she changed her mind?
What if all of this was for nothing?

James offered me the chip bag.

"I was thinking," I drew out as I rolled over on top of him, one thigh on either side of his, looking for the perfect distraction. "Something else?"

James's arms wrapped around my waist, pulling me down on his erection. Heat pooled in my core as I ground my hips down on him. He dropped his head back against the couch. His fingers dug into my hips.

"Round two?" I leaned in to whisper in his ear.

His hand wound its way into my hair and yanked it back, exposing my neck. Those baby blues were an endless ocean for me to get lost in. "This is a pretty big house. With a lot of rooms for us to try out. I think we have our work cut out for us."

This time when I kissed him, I sunk my teeth into his bottom lip. "Then we better get started."

33

Hallie

At work on Monday, my head was still in the clouds. I'd spent all of Friday and Saturday with James, and then woken up Sunday to an email from Anthea saying she *loved* my article on The Social Eatery, which had officially gone live on *Sophisticate*'s website.

Her praise put some wind back in my sails and gave me some hope that our original agreement was back on track. There was still a chance I could end up as *Sophisticate*'s food critic.

I'd squealed when I saw my name on the article—my *actual* name, printed on a review published by a magazine people actually recognized. Sure, it wasn't the first time my name had been attached to a food review, but this was the first time it wasn't buried on my personal blog. So many more people would read it than those my little blog reached.

Roxie had come charging into my room, wielding a frying pan, certain our mouse friend was back. When she realized that I was celebrating The Social Eatery article, she'd immediately discarded the pan in exchange for a bottle of champagne and some orange juice. For a moment, it felt like I was truly going to make my dreams become reality.

Then, earlier this morning, James messaged me to ask if I could swap our fifth Friday date for a full-day Saturday one instead. We'd fallen into an easy rhythm. Every morning I'd wake up to a text from James, wishing me a good morning and asking what my day entailed.

But I hadn't slept over at his place since Friday night, and he hadn't stayed at mine—probably for the best, considering Roxie could hear everything through our paper-thin walls.

Still, a tiny part of me was panicking over how I wanted to be around him. All the time. It had only been a month. And half of that had technically been . . . unintentional dating.

I didn't know what we were, not exactly. But my life was so busy that I didn't have time to spiral out about it. People slept with each other all the time without it being a *thing*. Right?

But could you still claim the relationship to be casual if there were feelings involved? Because this was definitely not a "no strings attached" situation. For me, or for James. I could just *tell* he was in as deep as me just from the way he looked at me.

"Hallie, that article you wrote on The Social Eatery was incredible," Janelle said as she leaned over our shared cubicle wall. "I can't believe you got to cover their opening night. Is Anthea considering you for the food critic position? I heard they were considering an outside food blogger, some big influencer, for the role."

Janelle's insight into my competition didn't even bother me. Not when I had the encouragement from Anthea over the weekend that my piece was good and the clicks on the article itself to back up its legitimacy.

For the first time in months, everything felt like it was falling into place.

"I've put my name in for it," I replied casually. "We'll see what shakes out."

My computer went off with a notification for my email.

RE: "Love on Wall Street" Article ETA Wednesday

Hallie,

We will be moving the "Love on Wall Street" article to this Wednesday. The magazine has a big feature story coming out on a celebrity wedding today. We want to make space for the exclusive and give it time to breathe.

X
Anthea

This wasn't the first time one of the "Love on Wall Street" articles had been bumped later in the week. But it was the first time I actually felt a pang of disappointment. Not because it was being pushed—but because it meant the world wouldn't get to read about Rossi Pizzeria *yet*. I was itching to help James get some tangible results to show his family that social media could make a real difference in their business.

Just as I replied to Anthea, letting her know I was fine with the article coming out on Wednesday, my phone went off.

James: How do you feel about gyros?
Hallie: I think they're a fantastic food. I have nothing against them. Honestly, I don't put them in my food rotation often enough.

James: Do you want to change that?
Hallie: Are you asking me on a date, James Rossi?
James: I'm asking you on a date-shaped thing. One that includes food and the company of a handsome man.
Hallie: I don't think there's another person in the world more sure of themselves than you.
James: I am sure of one thing. I'm sure that I'm about to have lunch with you.
Hallie: Just send me the address before this goes any further.

James was waiting for me at what he called one of his favorite Greek restaurants. It was closer to his brownstone on the Upper West Side. A hike for him coming from the Financial District. But he'd promised me that the trip would be worth it. He said he'd been dreaming about their gyros, so he took it as a sign that he needed to take me there.

As I walked into the restaurant, the aroma of garlic and oregano filled the air, mingling with the sound of sizzling meat on the grill. The soft glow of candlelight enhanced the cozy ambience, casting warm shadows on the rustic wooden tables. Vibrant paintings of Santorini adorned the walls, transporting me to the Greek island. A lively buzz filled the restaurant, created by the chatter of diners and clinking of glasses. James was at a small table in the restaurant's front window. Today's suit was navy—my favorite. It made his blue eyes stand out, drawing me to them.

"Hello, beautiful," James stood from his seat, setting aside the paper he was reading to kiss me on the cheek.

"Hi, how are you?" I asked, relishing in the feel of his lips against my skin.

"I feel like I'm turning over a new leaf this week. I can't explain it," James said. There was an excitement to his words. Like he was just as excited as I was for whatever life was going to bring next.

"You aren't planning on going back to the office after commuting all this way, are you?" I asked as I slid into the open seat across from him.

"No, I'm working from home for the rest of the day." There was an ease in James's body language. It felt like a striking change from when I'd first met him, but I realized it had been a gradual change over the course of the past few weeks. He was more relaxed. I think I even heard his phone go off in his pants pocket and he didn't make an immediate move to check it. That he was even working from home for a day instead of staying at the office until the market closed was unusual.

"Something on the horizon for you with work?" I asked. "Have you thought further about Theo Drake's offer to you?"

It had only been a few days since James's business lunch with the new CEO of Rooster, but surely that was enough time to think this over. Because, to me, it was a simple decision. I know James had been hoping to start his own firm, but this was almost better. James didn't have to invest his own capital. There weren't as many risks. But James obviously needed more time to consider what was seemingly obvious to me.

"I've been thinking a lot about it," James mused. "It's a big decision to make. I wanted to go out on my own and battle with the big dogs, but there's a lot of allure in trying something new. Venture capitalism could be rewarding."

"I know when to stick in my lane, so I won't try to tell you which choice is better. But I will tell you that the best decision is the one that feels right to you," I told him. "You'll know when it does."

"I've been meaning to text you, but wasn't the article supposed to post today?" James asked. "I didn't get an alert."

"Oh, I forgot to text you, too. Anthea said it was being pushed to Wednesday because of some celebrity's wedding that took priority."

"Damn celebrities," James joked.

But I was already going back to something else he had said. "Wait, did you say you didn't get an alert? Do you have web alerts on for my posts?"

James looked embarrassed for only a moment before he gave me a casual shrug. "They are about me, aren't they? I want to make sure that you do me justice."

Before I could fully make sense of what that meant, my phone buzzed on the table and Roxie's name lit up the screen. Normally, I would have ignored a phone call during a lunch. But Roxie never called me during the day. She was a strictly text-only type of girl. So getting a call from her in the middle of the day rang as an emergency.

"Do you mind? I think this is something urgent."

James waved off my concern about being rude. "Take it. Tell Roxie I said hi."

"Be careful what you wish for. She'll invite herself here by the end of the conversation," I told him.

I clicked to answer the call, already nervous about what Roxie was going to throw at me now.

"What's wrong?" I answered, cutting to the chase.

The sound of a taxi honking came through the line. "I have the walk sign, asshole!" Roxie shouted.

James raised a curious brow as he heard the tin of Roxie's yell.

"What's wrong?" I tried again.

"Why would you assume something's wrong?" Roxie asked once I finally grabbed her attention.

"Because you never call me in the middle of the day. You reserve that for emergencies only."

"We should really fix that, but you're right," Roxie replied. "This is one of those times."

I sucked in a deep breath, steeling myself for what was to come.

"I quit the art gallery." Roxie must have called me right after she left. I could tell she was on foot, and not even losing her breath as she walked the streets of New York City, most likely in heels.

"You quit?" I asked incredulously.

"Where are you?" Roxie replied, completely ignoring the panic in my voice. "I have so much to tell you. I think I could go for a drink, maybe five. Who's to say? Wow, I had no idea the kind of weight quitting would lift off my shoulders. I've got so much energy and have no idea what to do with it all."

"I'm at lunch with James," I told her. "Can we walk it back to when you said you quit?"

"Send me the address. I'll meet you there." Then the line went dead. I pulled the phone away from my ear and stared at my call log, like I needed proof it had even happened.

"What's wrong?" James asked. His brow creased with concern, and it was that concern *for* my friend that made my chest squeeze. Somewhere, in the chaos of this arrangement, we'd started to genuinely embed ourselves in each other's lives enough to care.

"Roxie just said she quit the art gallery," I told him.

"She quit?" James echoed, matching my shock. "Did she say why?"

"No, she just asked to meet me here." I hesitated for a beat. "Is that okay?"

James reached across the table and curled his fingers around mine. "Hal, your people are my people. Of course it's okay."

I smiled down at our hands, my heart doing that traitorous little stutter it had started to do lately whenever he said something that made me fall for him all over again.

Roxie was many things and impulsive was definitely one of them. But quitting the art gallery without at least *talking* to me about it first was the last thing I'd expected from her. She loved her job. The only thing she loved more was when she got to photograph beautiful food.

I ordered something for her when the waiter stopped by. If I didn't, I wouldn't hear the end. And thank God I did, because right when the food was being brought out, Roxie walked in like a storm sweeping through town.

"Who chose Greek between the two of you?" she asked. "Because good choice. Oh my gosh, I could eat a whole lamb's worth of gyros right now."

I could never understand how Roxie could walk

through life with no anxiety. Meanwhile, I lay in bed most nights thinking about things I'd said years ago and what the person I'd been talking to that day thought of it.

"Roxie, please. I can't take it," I told her. "What the hell happened?"

"Michelle Granger came in today while the gallery owner was in. I was going about my business, walking Michelle through the different pieces we had gotten in since the last time I'd seen her. The owner decided they were going to hijack the show and when Michelle bought a piece, I went to put my name on the sale so I would get my commission. You know, since my salary is pennies and all my money comes from commissions? And guess what? That motherfucker told me I didn't earn the sale. It was staying with the house because he did all the work. So, I walked out."

James and I both stared at her, slack jawed. Roxie was a master at letting no one know her next move.

"What are you going to do?" I asked, thinking about our very expensive rent bill that we'd just paid. Which meant Roxie had only a month to figure it out before we would have to pay it again.

"About that," Roxie said casually as she picked up a fry. "Remember our conversation about coming together to start our own business?"

"Roxie, that could take months for us to do! We have bills and other things to pay now."

But Roxie swatted my concern away like it was merely an annoying fly. "I know it could take months. I'll pick up freelance work in the meantime. But why not just take the leap?"

I could feel James's gaze on my face. Knowing how supportive he was of me was comforting. When he'd originally asked about this very topic after my clear frustration over Anthea not coming through on our agreement, he'd been nothing but encouraging. I'd almost taken the leap when I'd broached the topic with Roxie a few weeks ago, but when she'd put a pause in the conversation, I'd shifted my priorities back to *Sophisticate*. This felt like whiplash.

"Things are turning around at work. My review of The Social Eatery is doing well. Anthea really liked it. I have one more week of the 'Love on Wall Street' series and then I've fulfilled my end of the agreement with Anthea." James shifted uncomfortably at the mention of our fifth and final agreed upon date. I'd basically forgotten that our time together could end soon. Not after the turn of events that were these past few weeks.

"Do you want to see what shakes out there?" Roxie asked, unbothered that I was the one now turning down the opportunity to work together. That was why I loved her. There were rarely hard feelings between us.

But as the three of us continued to eat our lunch, I had a nagging feeling in the back of my mind that wondered if turning down the opportunity for artistic freedom and working with my best friend was the right move. Because what would happen if Anthea went back on another arrangement in the future? What if she promised me something that would change my career forever and then go back on it?

Despite those risks, I knew I had to see this through with *Sophisticate*. I had to do this for the little girl that used to cut out articles and pictures from her magazines and hang them on her walls. When there were moments when I wished I had an older sister and didn't always have to be the oldest sister, *Sophisticate* was there.

I couldn't just walk out on my younger self. I had to give it my best shot in the big city for the sake of the small-town girl I used to be.

34

James

"James, my sweet boy!" Nonna opened the front door, her apron wrapped around her waist and wooden spoon in hand. "That article your girlfriend wrote was magnificent. I asked your grandfather if we could go to The Social Eatery—once the crowd dies down, of course. That place has been packed every night."

I opened my mouth to correct my grandmother and tell her that Hallie wasn't technically my girlfriend. Not officially, anyway. But the words didn't come.

Because the truth was . . . she sort of *was*.

I had told my family we were dating because somewhere along the way, the lines blurred. We weren't just pretending anymore. We'd spent nearly every weekend together, texted constantly, shared meals, laughter, late-night talks. We'd fallen into something real without ever saying the words.

So I let Nonna call her my girlfriend.

Because if I was being honest with myself . . . I wanted her to be.

"Hi, Nonna," I greeted her with a kiss on the cheek. "I can see if I can get the two of you reservations. I think Sebastian knows the owner."

Hallie's review for The Social Eatery had gone out on

Sunday morning and was making its rounds. A few smaller media publications had picked up her article, drawing more attention to it than just *Sophisticate*'s audience.

"Where is Sebastian?" Nonna asked. "I thought he was coming tonight."

"He's on his way. He texted me on my way over here that he was a little behind leaving the office."

Nonna waved her wooden spoon in my direction. I kept my distance from her. I still remembered getting whacked on the backside with one as a kid. "You boys are wasting your lives away in those steel prisons."

"We're working, Nonna," I defended as I followed her into the house, where the same scene was always laid out for every family dinner. My uncle, father, cousin, and grandfather were playing poker. While my mother and aunt were in the kitchen. "We are doing exactly what you and Nonno did with the restaurant."

"But you are selling your souls to companies that do not care about you. They would toss you to the wolves given the chance." Nonna waved a dismissive hand in my direction before she returned to the kitchen to finish dinner.

I had to admit that she had a point. There were few companies out there that would sacrifice profits or padding their investors' pockets if it meant giving their employees a better experience. Berkley Williams was no better. They had perpetuated the idea that their employees couldn't have much of a life outside of work, or else they'd miss an opportunity for the investment portfolios that they oversaw. The CEO of Berkley Williams had gotten a large raise year after year, while the board continued to profit off the company's stocks. What else would you expect from a board for an investment company?

But there was one company that was making waves in recent weeks as it strayed from the status quo—Rooster. When I had told Hallie that I hadn't thought about Theo's offer that much since our conversation on Friday, I'd lied, and I had no idea why. Perhaps discussing my goals made me realize I was delaying my dream. Working for Rooster's new venture capital firm was nearly all I thought about during work hours.

With things working out in my personal life, maybe it was time to focus on other parts of my life. I'd even received a surprising email from Theo this morning asking if I'd thought anymore about our conversation at The Nest on Friday. I hadn't responded yet, but I knew a guy like Theo wouldn't wait around for very long.

"Hi, honey." My mother walked over to give me a hug and I leaned down to give her a kiss on the cheek. The minute she pulled away, I knew I'd somehow messed up. "Why didn't you bring Hallie tonight?"

Now I understood the look of disapproval she'd given me when I'd first walked through the door alone. My mother and Hallie had gotten on like two peas in a pod at dinner on Friday night. By the end of the night, my mother had nearly extracted Hallie's entire life story from her. She asked about her parents, her sister, her soon-to-be niece. I couldn't even remember if she'd ever bothered to ask Cassidy what her parents' names were. Yet there she was asking Hallie when her parents were next coming to the city because she'd like to meet them.

"She was busy tonight."

Which might not have been a lie necessarily. Hallie could have been busy. I hadn't wanted to ask her to come tonight after forcing her through a family dinner only a few days ago. Although I wanted to spend every evening with her, I worried I was moving too fast.

I had no one to blame but myself. I'd chickened out of making things official with her. When Saturday morning rolled around, I told myself I'd tell her at lunch the minute she kissed me awake. Then, when lunch came and went, and we remained preoccupied, I promised myself I'd tell her during dinner. But she left before I ever found the courage.

Which meant I was showing up to family dinner without a girlfriend, despite my family's differing opinion.

"She better be here next week." My mother raised her own wooden spoon at me threateningly. Most people saw that kitchen utensil for what it was. But in an Italian family, it had more than one purpose, and my mother had picked up that gesture over the years she'd been married to my dad. I raised my hands in mock surrender to avoid being on the receiving end of one of those purposes.

My phone sounded with the web alert I had for Hallie's articles. What better time to read this than with my family? They were going to benefit from this article. Even if most of the viewers flocking to it were there to read the next installment of Mr. Old Fashioned, like my mother and grandmother, they would read about the family restaurant that was the site for Hallie's fourth date.

I tapped into the alert just as Brandon called my name. "Are you coming? Nonno is about to beat Dad, so we can deal you in."

"Hey! Do you have no faith in me?" Uncle Tony glared over at his son. "You don't know what's in either of our hands."

"I know that Nonno has either a Royal Flush or a Full House. And I think you have maybe a three of a kind." Brandon gave a pointed look at his father. "So let's wrap this up."

"I just want to read this really quick. It may be the next round that you can deal me in."

"Is it Hallie's article?" My mother asked from the kitchen.

"The Mr. Old Fashioned article?" My grandmother exclaimed. "It's posted? I've got to message the group chat."

"What group chat, Nonna?" I asked.

My aunt poked her head out of the kitchen. "She's got some group chat with all the ladies from her book club. They open their meetings every week to talk about the newest article before they shift to their latest book."

The article had loaded onto my phone, and I had to do a double-take to make sure I was reading the headline correctly.

What Should You Do When They Run Out of Money? RUN!

By: Hallie Woods

When Mr. Old Fashioned brought me to his family's restaurant, I thought he'd made a mistake. I'd expected an upscale bistro, perhaps his parents had purchased it in the early noughties, and it had become a staple of the Upper East Side. So, when we crossed the river, I thought maybe he'd gotten the address wrong. Very, very wrong. Or maybe the restaurant he told me he was taking me to was a cool, avant-garde place in a basement in Dumbo, I could handle that at least . . . But an old pizzeria with red tablecloths to boot? Surely this wasn't it?

Well, it turns out that Mr. Old Fashioned wasn't exactly what he seemed. Because from the outside, he looked like the full package—wealthy, successful, and, almost most important of all, someone that had good taste. But apparently, the fourth date was now the new "meet-the-family" milestone, because how else could you explain him bringing me to a dingy pizzeria in Brooklyn and calling it a date?

He obviously wasn't as well off as he had made himself out to be during our earlier dates. His pocketbook had to have run dry, so he settled on a dive, trying to pass it off as sentimental by introducing me to his family far earlier than one should.

During most family dinners, the house could barely contain the noise. With my grandmother's record player incessantly playing Sinatra and my uncle's boisterous reactions, I was shocked that they'd received no complaints from neighbors. I suppose my grandmother had paid them off for years with her famous handmade ravioli.

But I couldn't hear any of that as the deafening roar of blood pulsated in my ears, echoing like a thunderous drumbeat that grew in intensity. The world around me seemed to come to a standstill, frozen in time, as I anxiously reread the title and the first two paragraphs repeatedly.

This can't be right.

There had to be a mistake.

Sound finally came back to me. First, it was a ringing sound, high-pitched and whining. Then it was the muffled sound of voices. The voices were garbled, as if someone had plunged my head under water and was shouting at me from above.

The room was spinning as my eyes slowly peeled away from my phone screen to look around the room. The first person I noticed was my mother. Her mouth was moving, but I still couldn't hear what she was saying. She crossed over to me from the kitchen in record time. Her hands cupped my face, her eyes wide with worry.

"What's wrong, James?" The world snapped back into place as I stared into my mother's eyes. My hands were shaking enough that the phone clattered out of my hand and onto the floor. "James, what's wrong?" The sound fell away, but this time I knew it was because the room had gone silent.

My mother bent down to retrieve my phone and after she took one look at my screen, she pulled me up from the chair I'd fallen into and ushered me out of the room. I was moving through the world completely frozen. The second I tried to even question what I had just read, the words never formed. I couldn't bring myself to consider that Hallie had written that.

"Speak, James." My mother's voice was insistent. Her gaze was intense as she forced me to look at her. "Tell me what's going on."

"You read it," I rasped. "I think you have a pretty good idea of what is going on."

She was still holding my phone, and she took another

glance at it when Hallie's name flashed across the screen. My mother held it out to me, a question in her eyes.

"No." I shook my head. "Decline it."

"What if she's calling you about the article? Maybe you should hear her out." Of course, my mother's suggestion was logical. But nothing about this situation felt logical.

Why would Hallie write that article? She knew what this meant for my family. Hell, I thought she knew what this meant for *me*.

The only thing I knew right now was how grateful I was that I hadn't yet asked her to be my girlfriend. I at least had the foresight to save myself the heartbreak.

"She's no different from Cassidy," I whispered. "I thought she was different. I really did. But here I am, disappointed again."

For one of the first times in my life, my mother was at a loss for words.

"How did you find Dad? How did you do it?"

She sighed as she squeezed my hand between both of hers. "He came into my life when I least expected it, but when I needed him the most."

"How did you know he was the one?"

My mother smiled as she thought about my father. "I knew he was the one the minute he told my father to fuck off."

Hearing my mother swear took me completely by surprise. "I'm sorry?"

"My father attempted to bribe your father when we first started dating. He knew your father would not walk away from me easily. So, he tried to bribe him with money to break up with me. Your father told him to fuck off. That was the start of their unlikely friendship, I think."

There were few people in life that had gotten away with saying something like that to my mother's father. The man had climbed the ranks of Wall Street and died one of the most powerful men in finance.

My phone buzzed again, Hallie's name popping up.

"Your father and I had to fight through many differences and obstacles to make our relationship work. But it was all worth it in the end."

"I'm sorry this didn't work out for the restaurant," I told her.

She shrugged. "She didn't name the pizzeria. No harm done."

When my phone went off for the third time, my mother gave me a sad smile. "I think you need to pick up and hear her out, James."

"Not right now," I told her. "I need some time."

My mother gave my hand a pat. "Let's go eat and celebrate having each other. We will figure something else out for the restaurant."

Grief filled my chest, wrapping around my ribcage, as I mourned losing the Hallie Woods I thought I knew.

35

Hallie

Wednesday morning came and went without my newest "Love on Wall Street" article hitting the *Sophisticate* website. Anthea emailed me, letting me know it would be up this evening. The celebrity wedding the magazine covered earlier in the week had caused a backlog in her editing schedule. The wedding, I realized, had occurred between two C-List actors and had been given barely a two-page spread in the magazine. But I didn't really think Anthea delaying my article for a two-page mid-level spread was strange until Wednesday evening, when the next installment was published.

"Do you want a glass of wine?" Roxie asked from the kitchen. "It'll cover the burnt taste of the chicken."

"Sure," I replied as I refreshed *Sophisticate*'s website for the tenth time in the last minute.

Roxie set a glass of wine and a dinner plate down in front of me. "I still don't understand why we couldn't order out."

"We've ordered out every day this week. I can't even remember the last time we used our oven. I'm pretty sure your purses are still in there for storage."

"We have limited closet space," Roxie reminded me. "Of course, I'm going to use what little storage we have."

"That's not the purpose of an oven, Rox."

Roxie cut a piece of chicken and brought it up to her nose for a sniff before she gingerly took a bite out of it. "Well, it's definitely not being used to cook good food. Because what is this?"

"I forgot to set a timer," I told her, explaining the charred poultry on our plates. "I was a little distracted."

"Anthea said the article would be up this evening, right?" Roxie asked as she switched to the salad that she'd prepared.

Most nights, we either ate out or ordered in. I couldn't remember the last time that we actually cooked a meal in our tiny kitchen that only one person fit in. But as the day bled into the night, my anxiety skyrocketed, digging itself deep enough in my mind to fester there. In order to distract myself from the article I was looking forward to being published the most out of this entire series, I'd decided I would try to use the skills I'd learned during my second date with James and cook.

That was clearly a mistake.

The pressure of showcasing Rossi Pizzeria had never felt greater until Anthea had pushed back the article. The anticipation only made it worse. I had made the choice to highlight the pizzeria's menu, the atmosphere that James's grandparents had carefully cultivated, and the picturesque location with the Brooklyn Bridge arching high over the top of the building. I put my heart and soul into the article. It was the first time that I meant every single word I wrote.

I'd also included just how James made me feel. How he introduced me to his family, and just how welcoming they were. I even went as far to mention James's invitation back to his home after dinner, alluding to our evening together, only to placate Anthea's desires to make these articles into something that women across the world could live vicariously through.

"Yeah, but she didn't say when."

I hit refresh one more time.

But this time, the website didn't return with the same article about the C-List celebrity couple and the taco truck they bravely decided to have at their wedding instead of a seated dinner.

"I think it's loading." Roxie spat out the chunk of chicken she was giving a second try and hurried to squeeze in next to me, so we both had a view of my laptop screen.

"Wait..." Roxie trailed off. "Is that what you wrote?"

Ice-cold dread gripped me as I stared at the headline, each rereading solidifying my worst nightmare. Rather than the article I'd written entitled "Mr. Old Fashioned is More Than he Seemed", I was looking at a headline that read "What Should You Do When They Run Out of Money? RUN!".

My body was in complete shock, my heart pounding in my chest like a relentless drumroll. Each thump echoed in my ears, drowning out any other sound. My hands trembled so violently I had to stuff them between my thighs just to stop the shaking.

I tried to focus on the words before me. Thoughts sluggishly formed and dissolved, like fragments of a puzzle struggling to fit together. I was so confused that I could barely grasp the seriousness of the situation.

Gone was the article that I had poured my heart and

soul into. Fear gripped me as I read the first paragraph, noticing changes to my writing that I hadn't made. Stripping away my appreciation for the evening and replacing them with thoughts of cynicism over the change in grandeur from our past dates.

My eyes scanned the screen faster and faster, hoping that whoever had made these changes had the forethought to remove the name of the Rossi's restaurant. Frantically, I scrolled through the rest of the article, searching for any remnants of my original work. To my dismay, someone had altered every line, erasing my carefully crafted prose. The once sentimental story had been transformed into a near hit piece on Mr. Old Fashioned. The only saving grace was whoever had done this was kind enough to remove any details that would give away the exact pizzeria that James had taken me to.

My heart sank as I realized the magnitude of what had happened. Someone had tampered with my article, deliberately sabotaging my story. Anger and frustration surged through me.

"Hallie?" Roxie had both of her hands on my shoulders now, jostling me gently to pull my attention from the article. "Hallie, what's going on? What's happening?"

"Someone rewrote my article," I finally got out.

A silent gasp escaped Roxie as her jaw dropped open.

"I can't believe someone would do that," she finally said, her voice filled with disbelief. To my best friend's credit, she sprang into action when she realized I was still frozen in shock. "But we'll figure it out, okay? We'll find out who did this."

"I just don't understand." My voice broke as I pushed

the last word out. Ever since I'd agreed to this ridiculous column, it had been nothing but whiplash with surprises around every corner.

Then I realized James would read this article right now, just like me. The article's content would completely blindside him. "Oh, my God. James."

Roxie's eyes widened as she realized what I was thinking. "Where's your work phone?"

She frantically searched the couch and coffee table, which were both covered in various magazines, books, and binders for Roxie's work that she was preparing to send out for freelance work.

"My room, I think."

In a flash, Roxie had dashed to my room. She came back, holding my phone firmly. "You should call him. Tell him what's happened."

With trembling hands, I reached for my phone and dialed James's number. Then I dialed it again. And again. As the ringing echoed in my ears, I couldn't help but wonder if he had deduced anything about the changes made to my article. Then, as the ringing stretched past when he normally answered, I worried he wouldn't pick up at all. Perhaps I was too hopeful in assuming James wouldn't find the published version of my article offensive.

"He didn't answer." I slowly took the phone away from my ear.

Then I dialed his number again. And again.

Hallie: This isn't what it looks like. They changed my article. They changed nearly everything I wrote. Please call me back so I can explain.

All the pressure building behind the dam in my heart finally broke, pouring despair and sadness out of the hole that was left in its place. My finger hovered over the send button, the text feeling like a futile attempt to reach him. But I still pressed down on my screen and watched the message appear in a blue bubble in our chat.

The seconds felt like hours as I anxiously waited for a response from James. Each passing moment only intensified my fear that he would never understand the truth. My mind raced with countless scenarios, all ending in disappointment and rejection.

I waited for the status under the text message to change from "Delivered" to "Read", but my hopes washed away on a river of grief as the seconds turned to minutes with no reply from James. I felt completely useless, a sense of helplessness washing over me as everything good in my life disappeared.

"He hasn't even opened it." I held my phone up hopelessly to Roxie before I tossed it to the side. "I think that says everything about what he thinks of the article."

"But you didn't write it!" Roxie exclaimed. "You said it yourself; almost everything was altered."

"It's still a betrayal. His family was relying on this article as the first of many for their restaurant. They had been so excited about the attention it could bring to the pizzeria. James cares more than anything about his family. This probably felt like an attack on that."

"But the article took out the pizzeria's name, right?"

I nodded. "Thankfully, or I don't even know what I'd do. If they'd left it in, not only would it have sent my relationship with James up in flames but it could have taken down a generations-old restaurant that had nothing to do with this, as well."

"Maybe he just needs a bit to cool down?" Roxie suggested. "That man is head over heels for you. And the two of you are dating, right? He'll call you back. I'm sure at the very least he'd want an explanation of what happened."

"He's not the only one who wants to know what happened," I told her. If it weren't nearly nine at night, I would have been on the first train headed toward Midtown, hoping Anthea would still be there. But I knew that, despite Anthea's workaholic personality, she would be long gone from the office. "But if we're being honest here, I'm not sure what exactly me and James are."

"Didn't he say that he wanted to date you?" Roxie asked me.

"Yes, kind of, but we never had the exclusivity conversation." It was a topic that had weighed heavily on my mind since I left James's brownstone Saturday evening. Things felt like they were heating up between the two of us. Yet I was in the dark on where any of it was heading.

"Well, we know one thing for certain," Roxie said as she reached over to take my hands in hers. She was a master at switching the conversation when she realized I was uncomfortable. "We need to figure out what happened with this article. We need a game plan for you when you go into the office and talk to Anthea."

"I'm going to need more than just a plan when I talk to Anthea," I mumbled.

"What do you mean?" Roxie asked.

"Well, when we consider who my editor is and who gets the last say on the article, all roads lead to her." There was no other way around the situation I was in. My boss had gone behind my back and changed an article with no discussion or input.

Realization dawned once more on Roxie's face. "Oh, no," she whispered.

"My thoughts exactly," I agreed.

"What are you going to do?" Roxie asked, her eyes widening with concern. I took a deep breath, considering the options before me. Confronting Anthea directly seemed like the obvious choice, but I knew it wouldn't be that simple. Anthea was known for her stubbornness and superiority complex. If I approached her with accusations, it could only lead to more conflict.

"This is the final straw," I said, my voice filled with finality. "I've been putting up with everything Anthea has thrown at me to get this food critic position, but she went too far with this. She's never changed anything I've done before. I do not know why she has now. I'm not sure any of this is worth it anymore."

Roxie wrapped me in a hug. "Just say the word and we'll start the blog and we'll do this together. I'm ready whenever you are."

I was ready, this was it for me. But first, I had business to take care of. If there was any chance of saving whatever was left of my relationship with James, I had to confront Anthea.

36

James

As the days ticked by, the void left by Hallie's absence seemed to grow deeper within me. I threw myself into my work, hoping to find solace in the busyness that consumed my days. The constant ringing of my phone, filled with her voicemails and messages, only served as a painful reminder of the gaping hole in my life. Each time it buzzed, I felt that familiar ache in my chest, the weight of my conflicting emotions pressing down on me.

But deep down, I knew I couldn't keep avoiding her forever. There were too many questions that needed to be answered. Part of me hoped I would wake up and these past few days would have been a dream—I'd roll over to see Hallie giving me a sleepy smile in my bed next to me. I needed closure to the questions that consumed my thoughts. But closure could wait. I wasn't sure I was ready to face whatever truths closure would deliver.

Instead, I reverted to some of my old finance industry habits—getting to the office before the sun rose and leaving long after it set. Financial reports and investment strategies became my refuge, a temporary escape from the void that Hallie's betrayal had carved inside me. Numbers didn't lie. Algorithms didn't leave. Their precision offered some semblance of control in a world that felt chaotic and unpredictable. It was the same remedy I'd turned to when Cassidy's betrayal had cut me bone-deep.

Sebastian, being perceptive as always, noticed a shift in my demeanor. He still extended invitations for our regular rendezvous at Whiskey Locker, and my polite refusals weren't anything to bat an eye at after I'd started dating Hallie. But he knew something was wrong when I'd declined his recent dinner invitation for Friday night.

He called me this morning, just as I was heading to work, his concern cutting through the usual sarcasm.

"Is there something big going on in the markets that I'm unaware of?" he asked after I'd picked up.

"No, why do you ask?" I replied, weaving through the crowd on the sidewalk as I hurried toward the subway station near my house. I opted for the subway most weekdays, saving my car for special occasions on the weekend. The fewer opportunities I had to rage at other New Yorkers on the road, the better.

"Because you're working overtime, which hasn't happened in months. Not since Rooster's stock took a nosedive before Theo took over. So, if nothing big is happening at work, what's going on?"

Car horns blared, brakes screeched, someone yelled something far too expletive for this early in the morning, and the scent of street meat mixed with exhaust fumes made me grimace. I caught sight of the food truck on the corner—the same one Hallie had covered on social media months ago. I'd only started frequenting it after stumbling across the review during my initial deep dive into who she was. Funny how quickly she'd infiltrated so many parts of my life, and now she was gone.

"Nothing's going on," I said, the words ringing as false as they sounded.

"I'm going to give you another chance to tell me the truth," Sebastian replied.

I nearly pretended to lose connection with him as I descended into the subway. It wouldn't be that far of a stretch, but faking loss of cell phone service and actually losing cell phone service were two different things.

"Fine," I sighed, dropping down into one of the cracked plastic seats just before the train jerked forward. "The article for 'Love on Wall Street' came out on Wednesday."

"Okay?" Sebastian drew out. "Like it does every week. What? Did Hallie tell the entire world that Mr. Old Fashioned color codes his suits?"

"No, Seb."

"Then what's the problem? Didn't you take her to the pizzeria? I recall you telling me I couldn't go last week because you were taking Hallie. Which we need to talk about. Having a girlfriend doesn't mean you can ignore our relationship. Who am I supposed to take to Whiskey Locker when I'm trying to pick someone up, or who am I supposed to tell when I *take* someone home?"

"These are truly life's biggest questions," I murmured, letting my head fall back against the cool subway window.

There was a pause, long enough that I knew Sebastian was reading between the lines.

"She didn't screw you over in the article . . . did she?"

"I took her to the pizzeria." Flashes of Hallie's face as she met my family, joked with my grandfather, and tasted the pizzeria's food for the first time played through my mind. What she wanted to do with the article, and what was actually published, were completely different. "I'm just going to send you the article. Hold on."

I shot the link over to Sebastian and waited patiently for him to finish reading it.

Two girls sitting across from me, not much younger than me, clad in expensive leggings, were holding matching matcha lattes. They were giggling together about a date one of them had just gone on that hadn't ended the way the girl had imagined. It reminded me of Hallie's first column, "Overheard in NYC". How she had sat in the subway, listening to the surrounding people divulge pieces of themselves for her to use.

Everything in this goddamn city had pieces of her in it I couldn't ignore.

A low whistle came across the line. "Holy shit."

"Yeah," I sighed.

"Have you talked to her?" Sebastian asked.

"Not yet. I've actually blocked her number—for now," I admitted, my voice low. "I just . . . I'm not sure I'm ready for a conversation."

Like the voice of reason, Sebastian argued back, "But you don't have the full story. Maybe there's a reasonable explanation for all of this."

I paused, rolling his words around in my head. Maybe he was right. Maybe there was more to the story, an explanation that would make sense. Or maybe, she was just doing her job.

But the thought of confronting her, seeing her face, hearing her say it out loud—it made my chest tighten.

"I should talk to her," I admitted finally. "It's just . . . it's hard. I thought I knew her, but this article feels like a betrayal."

Sebastian's voice softened. "I get it, man. Really. But Hallie isn't Cassidy. That girl looked at you like you were the sun in her sky. You can't throw that away without hearing her out."

I stared out the subway window, the tunnels whipping past like static.

"I don't even know if I care enough to fight for that balance in my life," I said quietly.

"What do you mean?"

"Theo offered me a job," I told him. "To lead their investment division. It would be a huge undertaking."

Sebastian let out a laugh. "That's huge."

"Yeah," I said, my voice flat. "I told him that the only thing I wanted was flexibility because of Hallie. Working that much would not have been good for a new relationship." A pause. "But now? I'm not sure there's anything left to balance it with."

Sebastian let out a slow breath. "That's the grief talking. You're hurt, man. You're allowed to be. But don't build a whole damn life around it."

The train screeched to a halt. I stepped out onto the bustling platform, blending in with the crowd of people all heading to their own destinations. I climbed the stairs out of the Wall Street station and into the Financial District.

This place used to give me such a thrill. I loved seeing everyone in suits hustling to the many metal skyscrapers looming up toward the clouds, waiting to make their mark on the world.

But the thrill had dulled. It had been gradual, my growing disengagement from the career I'd once loved. For so long, my career had provided me a predictable rhythm, a routine I could count on. The moment I seriously considered going out on my own, that structure began to shift.

My conversation with Theo had only cemented it. Theo Drake—already a rising name in tech—spoke about innovation like it was a living thing. He didn't just see what was, he imagined what could be. Walking through the Financial District with Sebastian still sitting on the other end of the phone, I couldn't stop thinking about it. Theo had opened my eyes to a world beyond the confines of corporate life, where ideas led the charge and built creativity and room to breathe.

And Hallie . . . she'd shown me something else entirely. Something I hadn't known I'd been missing. Her presence had cracked open a part of me I'd kept tightly sealed. With her, I'd glimpsed the possibility of building a life filled with more than just success. A life with someone to come home to, someone who didn't need perfect, just real.

For a second, I'd believed I could have both—a career worth waking up for, and a relationship that didn't feel like a performance. But now? I didn't know where things stood.

A couple months wasn't much time, but her absence felt like a physical blow. Maybe I'd been wrong about her. Maybe her ambition outweighed whatever was happening between us. Maybe, deep down, she was just like Cassidy—putting herself and her career first, no matter who got hurt.

There was only one thing in my control.

"Seb, I've got to go," I told my best friend, hanging up before I got a response.

I tapped Theo's name on my list of contacts. The phone rang twice before I heard his voice on the other end.

"James, what a surprise. To what do I owe the pleasure?"

There was only a split second before I could bail on my decision, but I knew I wouldn't take the way out.

"I'll take the job, if you'll still have me."

Theo said nothing. Maybe he'd changed his mind. Maybe I'd waited too long to accept the role, and he'd offered it to someone else.

"Took you long enough," he drawled after what felt like ages. "I thought for a minute that you were icing me out to see what more I'd give you. I just asked my assistant to write up a new offer with higher pay and some more auxiliary benefits—like a membership to The Nest."

"Oh, that's not—"

"She'll send it over shortly. Read it over, sign, and get it back to me."

"Theo, you don't have to—"

"It's going to be a pleasure working with you, James. I just know it."

I halted a few steps before reaching the Berkley Williams entrance. "I'm glad you think so, Theo. I'm honored you thought of me for the job. I'm excited about what you're doing with Rooster and about the company's larger ecosystem."

Theo blew out a breath. "What I'm doing for Rooster is only the beginning. I have my sights on the larger industry. The possibilities are endless, Rossi."

"Wherever the destination is, I'm excited about the journey."

Theo laughed. "Save the cheesy lines for your speeches. I'm sure you'll be having to give plenty of them soon for our events. Now, I don't want you to feel like you need to jump from one shark tank into another. There's no need to rush into your new position. I need to wrap up a few things with Rooster and the disaster my brother caused. So how does a month sound?"

"That gives me plenty of time to wrap things up with Berkley Williams too."

"No, that's not what I meant. I meant you should put your two weeks in and then enjoy a vacation before you start."

Everything about working with Theo Drake felt foreign. Not feeling like I was competing against everyone else over who could work themselves into the ground the quickest would definitely be a bit of a change. The free time made me nervous. I wasn't sure if I was up for it yet.

"I don't think I need a vacation," I started.

"Didn't you mention that you're seeing someone?" Theo asked. "Take some time and spend it with her."

Her. My mind raced, trying to come up with an excuse. I wasn't ready to share my personal life with Theo, especially not the complicated mess that was my relationship with Hallie. But there was no escaping the truth.

"I *was* seeing someone," I admitted reluctantly. "But things between us . . . they're not exactly smooth sailing anymore."

Silence stretched down the line. "Well, that's even more reason for you to take some time off," he said firmly. "Relationships need nurturing, James. Sometimes a little distance can help bring clarity."

His words struck a chord deep within me. Maybe Theo was right. Maybe a break from the chaos of work would give me the space I needed to figure things out with Hallie. And if it didn't work out, at least I would have recharged and refocused.

I sighed. Theo had a point. "Alright, you win," I conceded. "I'll take that vacation."

Theo chuckled. "Deal, Rossi. Just make sure you come back refreshed and ready to tackle whatever challenges lie ahead. Rooster is counting on you."

As I walked into Berkley Williams, I couldn't help but feel a mix of excitement and trepidation. The road ahead was uncertain, both in my personal life and in this new chapter of my career.

Yet part of me still hoped that maybe, just maybe, everything would work out in the end.

37

Hallie

I walked into *Sophisticate* like a woman on a mission. Even Janelle gave me a double-take as I marched past my cubicle and hers on my way to the print team. I desperately needed to direct my anger into something. So, what was better than understanding who changed my article and ruined my life as I knew it?

"I was sorry to read about your date with Mr. Old Fashioned, Hallie," Janelle called after me.

"Yeah, so was I."

Janelle gave me a sympathetic look, completely misjudging the furiousness in my gaze. "Maybe it was just too good to be true. Nobody could be *that* perfect."

Mabel was the head of the print team and had been with the company for ages. She was retiring at the end of the year and looking forward to chasing her grandkids across the country for their various hobbies. Their pictures covered her desk. Her record player crooned Boy George.

"Hallie!" Mabel exclaimed. "Your latest column has been so much fun to follow along with. Such a shame how it ended last week, though."

"Well, that's the thing, Mabel," I started. "It didn't end that way. In fact, I'd written a completely different article detailing a wonderful night. You wouldn't know anything about that, would you?"

Mabel clutched a hand to her chest. As if I'd accused her of something quite terrible. "If you think I had anything to do with it, Hallie, I promise you I didn't. In fact, I remember your first article. I thought it was so romantic. When Anthea stopped me from going to print with it, I just assumed something had happened with you and Mr. Old Fashioned after your date."

Her eyes grew wide as realization dawned across them. "Are you saying that Anthea changed your article?"

Anthea changed the article after it had already been sent to print?

"Mabel, has anybody told you how important you are to this office?"

Mabel smiled warmly, her eyes crinkling at the corners. "Not nearly enough, Hallie, but it's always nice to hear."

My mind raced as I left Mabel's office and made my way toward Anthea's. I'd gone through the stages of grief over the past few days. I'd spent the first night in a state of denial that James was icing me out. Then the next day in a state of anger that he wouldn't take the time to hear me out, despite how bad the optics were. But confronting Anthea that day would've been reckless, with all the raw emotions still bubbling inside me. So instead, I took a long weekend. I cried on Roxie's shoulder, ranted over takeout, and reread the article more times than was probably healthy. Somewhere between the tears and the carb-loading, I found the clarity I needed—not just to face Anthea, but to do it without burning my entire career to the ground.

I didn't move on from the anger stage—just redirected

it to Anthea Sparks. There wasn't a chance I was going to be bargaining with her today. I'd already done plenty of that after asking for a fair shot at the food critic position. Which was exactly how I ended up in this situation.

Anthea had a pair of glasses perched on her nose as she stared at her computer screen. I was certain that she didn't need those glasses, and they were purely an accessory. Totally deceptive, just like her.

I hesitated with my hand on the handle to the door of her office for only a minute, watching her. I used to be so terrified of her, but I wanted to be her at the same time. Her tenacity. Her wit. Her industry knowledge. Her reputation. They were all traits that I aspired to have. But now my view of her felt tainted. If she was the person who had changed my story without consulting me, which was the most likely option, all my respect for her and this place would cease to exist.

Not giving myself any further time to back out, I knocked on the door and opened it without waiting to see if it was alright to enter.

"Hallie," Anthea said. "What can I do for you?"

If it weren't for the anger blinding my judgment, I would have turned around and walked out. But maybe the anger was allowing me to see clearly for the first time.

I took a deep breath and stepped further into Anthea's office. Every change that was made echoed in my mind, reminding me why I was here. I knew that once I did this, there was no going back. This would likely be the last time I set foot in *Sophisticate*. But I owed it to myself and to the Rossi family to sort this out.

With a firm voice, I looked Anthea straight in the eye and said, "You changed my story without my consent."

Surprise flickered across Anthea's face for a split second. She adjusted her glasses. "Well, first and foremost, the contract you signed when you came to *Sophisticate* stated that the company could take creative liberty over your work and shape it how we see fit. Hallie, I understand your frustration, but I assure you, it was necessary. The readership that 'Love on Wall Street' has grown isn't looking for something soppy and boring. That kind of sentimental stuff will not get the same clicks and shares that the other installments of the column have. They come to *Sophisticate* to escape their boring lives and read about a life of glamour. If you want the food critic position, you better get used to stylizing articles. I did you a favor."

Her words hung in the air, attempting to justify her actions. But I wasn't about to back down. "A favor? You broke my trust. I poured my heart and soul into that piece, and you didn't even have the decency to discuss it with me. That isn't something a good editor would do."

I held my ground, refusing to let Anthea's attempt at justification sway me. There was no going back now. All the hard work I'd poured into this magazine deserved to be honored.

"A good editor would have communicated with me," I continued, my voice steady. I had idolized this woman. I'd put her up on a pedestal, only for everything I'd believed about her to turn out to be false. "We could have discussed alternative ideas, found a compromise that respected both the readership and my vision. For you to think that our readership isn't looking for a happy ending to vicariously live through is your biggest oversight yet. They would have eaten my original article up."

Anthea shifted uncomfortably in her chair.

"I understand the need to cater to the readership's desires," I acknowledged, trying to maintain a level of understanding despite my anger. "But there are ways to do it without sacrificing artistic integrity. As an editor, it's your role to guide and support the writers, not to manipulate their work for the sake of popularity."

Anthea opened her mouth to speak, but I held up a hand, silencing her.

"I didn't come here seeking an apology or an explanation. I came to reclaim my voice, to remind myself why I started writing for *Sophisticate*. This place has led the industry in its innovation. It has covered stories that truly *matter* to women. I thought I had found my forever home with this company, but I'm realizing now that it was only an avenue for me to find myself."

With each word, the weight of my decision lifted from my shoulders. The realization that I had outgrown this place, that my potential lay beyond these walls, fueled my determination. I straightened up, staring directly into Anthea's eyes.

"Today is my last day at *Sophisticate*. I will send you my resignation as soon as I get home," I declared. "*Sophisticate* deserves more than somebody who wants to put its reputation at risk by fabricating articles for clickbait. That definitely isn't a publication that I want to be a part of."

Anthea's eyes widened. She opened her mouth to protest, but words seemed to escape her for once. I could see the realization dawning on her face—the loss of a talented writer, the consequences of her actions. The room fell into a heavy silence, the air thick with tension. But there was nothing left to say. Nothing left to do that could fix this.

She knew it.

I knew it.

"Hallie," Anthea called just as I reached the door.

I paused, hand on the knob, and turned back toward her.

"I know whatever you'll do next in your career . . . it will be magnificent."

I wanted to be angry at her for thinking she could compliment me *now*. After she'd upended my entire life. After she'd taken away everything that I had been working for. But I'd come to realize in the moments I stood in front of her that she was merely misguided. Clouded by her own judgment of what the world wanted—glamour, power, wealth. When all most people really wanted was connection. I couldn't fault her for coming to that realization, even if it was at my own expense.

"You're not going to ask me to stay?" I was shocked I'd even asked the one question that was bouncing around in my head.

Anthea pursed her lips. "You are one of the best writers here and with the popularity of 'Love on Wall Street', you will be missed by our readers. But I'm not sure *Sophisticate* is where you truly are meant to be. I think we've both known that for quite some time."

That should've felt like a lethal blow. There was a time that I would have died for this place and what it meant to me growing up. But there was no denying the truth in her words.

"Bye, Anthea."

And this time, I didn't look back.

I dialed Roxie the moment I walked out the doors of *Sophisticate*.

"This is your resident unemployed roommate speaking," Roxie said as she answered the phone.

"I guess that makes two of us," I told her.

There was a pause, then a gasp. "What? What happened? Did that bitch fire you for standing up for yourself? I know an excellent lawyer, Hal. I think you'd have a good case for wrongful termination."

"Easy there, Rox," I laughed. "Anthea didn't fire me. I quit."

Another pause.

"You *quit*?"

I understood why Roxie was shocked. Neither of us ever thought I'd leave *Sophisticate*. Even when I brought up the idea of our blog, I think both of us thought it would always be a pipe dream.

I guess all it took was Anthea crossing a line for me to finally act. The thought of spending my days churning out soulless clickbait pieces, whether that be for relationships or food, forever at the risk of her completely rewriting them without my consent, had become unbearable.

"Fuck yeah, we are going out tonight to celebrate," Roxie exclaimed, her voice buzzing. "It's about time we made our blog a reality."

"This is going to be a long, hard slog, Rox," I warned, my voice heavy. "Are you sure you're up for this?"

Choosing to walk away from a stable job and into your own venture was terrifying. There was no way around it, and part of me might have hoped that Roxie would back out. Say that this was too risky and quell all my anxiety, but who was I kidding? This was Roxie.

"You know that I'm in, Hal. We will make such a splash that restaurants will *beg* us to cover them," she replied, her words laced with determination. "And I know just the place to cover first."

I didn't even have to see Roxie's face to know a smug smile played on her lips.

"Roxie, you remember what happened this last week, right?" I asked, ignoring the pang in my chest that was there every time I thought about James, which was a near constant. "I don't think that's a possibility."

"You made a deal with James, didn't you?" Roxie asked me.

"Well, yes."

"And you hold up your end of deals, yes?"

I could see where Roxie was heading with this, but part of me wondered if I could even stomach showing my face in front of James's family after what had happened. What if he told them? What if his mother and grandmother read the article like they had all the others? How was I supposed to waltz back into his family's pizzeria and have a meal, intending to review it? Would they even want me there?

Despite all the questions circling in my mind, I knew Roxie had hit the bullseye. She knew me well enough to know that I couldn't possibly walk away from my deal with James, even if we weren't speaking right now. He'd gone through with four incredible dates, and while I would no longer be getting what I needed out of our deal, that didn't mean he couldn't.

"Okay, fine. We can go by the pizzeria and have our first review be Rossi's."

Roxie squealed on the other end of the line and while I wanted to join her in celebration of the start of something potentially great, all I could think about was James.

38

Hallie

I was fairly certain I hadn't changed my underwear in almost three days. Tissues and various old bowls of popcorn littered the couch. Wine glasses and empty plates sat on the coffee table. I was sure I looked absolutely pathetic, but the moment I got back from *Sophisticate*, it was like the floodgates had opened. I mourned the loss of my job and my potential relationship all at once. The second I crossed the threshold into my apartment, the tears started, and four days later, they were just drying up.

Roxie came out of her room, barefoot and wearing one of her old NYU sweatshirts. She looked at me for a moment, holding something behind her back.

"Before I hand this over," she said, her voice softer than usual, "can we do a quick check in?"

She stepped into the living room, now cautiously navigating a minefield of tissues and wine-stained glasses. "Do you need help with rent this month? Or bills? I know you didn't expect to walk out of *Sophisticate* like that, and I don't want you stressing over money on top of everything else."

I blinked at her, dazed from another afternoon spent face-down in a blanket cocoon. "Rox, you quit your job, too."

"Yeah," she said with a shrug. "But I've got a bunch of photography gigs lined up this month—weddings, engagements, a branded shoot for a restaurant. It's more than enough to cover everything if you need me to float us for a bit."

My lip quivered at her kindness. "I . . . I think I'm okay for this month," I managed, voice scratchy. "But I'll let you know. I promise."

"Okay." She nodded and set something on the coffee table—it was a fresh glass of water and a small stack of Saltines. "Now," she said, pulling her phone from behind her back, "I have someone on the line for you."

"Who is it?" I croaked.

"It's your mom." Roxie held out the phone, her expression somewhere between sympathetic and no-nonsense. It was clear my time wallowing on our couch was over.

I hesitated, my throat still raw from days of crying. Taking a deep breath, I reached out and reluctantly accepted the phone.

My mom's voice, filled with concern, wrapped around me like a blanket I didn't realize I needed.

"Hallie? Are you there?"

Hearing her made my chest ache. I missed being little, when a hug from her and a grilled cheese sandwich could fix everything.

"I'm here," I whispered. The words wobbled out of my mouth.

"Roxie said you're having a hard time?" she asked gently. "What's happened, honey?"

"I screwed up, Mom," I sobbed.

Roxie handed me another tissue and I blew my nose

into it with the kind of dramatic force that could have scared away wild animals.

My mother listened patiently as I spilled my heart out, sharing mine and James's story. From meeting at the dinner party, to our agreement, to my utter surprise when I realized I was developing feelings for him. I told her how, for a split second, I felt like everything in my life was finally working out. Only for the universe to laugh in my face, as if I could be that lucky.

"And James won't talk to you?" she asked gently, once I finally paused for breath.

"No, he hasn't even opened up a single text I've sent him." Defeat weighed heavily on my shoulders. I simply couldn't fathom that the two of us were over, just like that.

"Oh, honey . . ."

Her voice cracked slightly, and somehow that made the tears return, freshly sprung from a well I thought I'd emptied.

"Everything happens for a reason, Hallie. You may not understand it all now, but days, weeks, years from now, you will. All of this has happened to put you in a position that future you will benefit from."

"But why does this kind of stuff have to hurt so much?" I sniffled.

"The best kinds of things in life don't come for free." My mother sighed, as if she knew intimately the pain I was going through. "And if you want my advice, if James won't listen to you, and you really do like him, then make him listen."

These were the moments, when life felt too hard to carry by myself, that I wished I lived closer to my family so they could shoulder some of the weight. But my parents raised me to be strong. She reminded me that even in the darkest of times, there is always a glimmer of light waiting to guide us forward.

I glanced over at Roxie, who was adding to the mood board we'd created for our website, realizing I knew just the thing to do with what my mom was suggesting.

"Thanks, Mom."

"You're welcome, sweetie. Now pick yourself up. You're stronger than this. Just know that your dad and I love you. But most importantly, we *believe* in you."

As I hung up the phone, a spark of determination ignited within me.

I stood up from the couch, ready to face the world once again. The tissues and popcorn bowls scattered around the room suddenly seemed like remnants of a past that no longer defined me. It was time to clean up the physical mess and, more importantly, my emotional mess. It was time I did something about it.

I took a long, overdue shower while Roxie started on our apartment. By the time I stepped out of the steamy bathroom, I felt brand new.

"So, what's the plan?" Roxie asked me as she loaded the last of the dishes in our dishwasher, one of the prized possessions of our tiny New York apartment. Between the two of us, I was normally the organized one, the one with a plan. While Roxie moved with the wind and made decisions based on "vibes".

"First, we need to complete the website. I know you've been working on it over the past few weeks. But if we can get it to a place where we are happy with it, then we can get our first review up. Which means, we also need to take a trip to Brooklyn."

Roxie's eyes sparkled. "It's about damn time."

Roxie was practically salivating as our taxi stopped in front of Rossi Pizzeria. Her eyes took in the late-eighteenth-century architecture, her fingers itching toward her camera.

"This place is amazing," she murmured, pressing her nose against the taxi window.

"Just wait until you taste the food. It is the full package." I could practically taste the tomatoes, garlic, and perfectly baked pizza dough already.

Just as before, the gold-tin ceiling, wine bottle chandeliers, and roaring wood-fired ovens in the back kitchen greeted us upon entering. The restaurant was still far emptier of customers than it deserved to be. I hoped that mine and Roxie's work would change that.

My stomach was nearly in my throat as we stepped toward the empty hostess stand. I didn't know who was working today, if I'd come across James's aunt, his cousin, his father, his uncle, or Lorenzo, his grandfather. They had welcomed me with open arms over dinner two weeks ago. Now, I wasn't sure they would do the same.

"Hallie!" James's aunt, Maria, stood up from a table in the back where she and Brandon had been having lunch.

Her surprised expression was expected. Part of me wondered if they'd chase me out of the place with pitchforks after what Anthea had done to my article.

"Are you here for lunch?" Maria asked me. She greeted me with a warm smile, like nothing had happened.

"Actually, we were hoping to do a review of the restaurant." I motioned to Roxie, who was holding her camera next to me. "It was something James had asked of me when we first met and I want to make sure I follow through on it."

I saw it then—the quick, fleeting look of fear I knew would come was etched into her features for a moment. A pit of shame filled my stomach.

I reached out and softly touched Maria's arm. "You have to know that the article that came out in *Sophisticate* was not the article I wrote. It's a long story and not worth rehashing. But I left the magazine after I figured out what happened. I have every intention of putting a positive spotlight on this restaurant. You can trust me on that."

Maria's eyes flickered over to the kitchen where Lorenzo was sprinkling some parmesan and oregano on top of a pizza. "Let's get you to our best table. The light on one of the tables at the front by the windows would look good in pictures, don't you think?"

She didn't question my revelation any further as she led us over to one of the many empty tables at the front of the restaurant. I knew it would be hard to show my face here again, but it was nearly unbearable to feel the tension in the air.

"I'll let Lorenzo know you're here and send Brandon over to get your orders." Then she was gone before I could ask her how James was doing.

Maria disappeared into the kitchen, and my apprehension only grew as I watched her speak with Lorenzo. James's grandfather looked in our direction, but his expression revealed nothing. I glanced at Roxie, who seemed unaware of the inner turmoil I was dealing with, her eyes fixated on capturing the essence of Rossi Pizzeria through her camera lens.

As we settled into our seats by the window, a familiar face approached our table. Brandon, with his signature mischievous grin. "Hallie, long time no see! So, you're here to review the restaurant? James mentioned you have a big social media account for that kind of stuff."

"Actually, Roxie and I are going off on our own to do our own thing. The website is still being finished. We have some developers who we are working with, but we want the pizzeria to be the first restaurant we post about. I know we're not a big, fancy food critic bringing a ton of attention to this place, but I hope it makes a difference. Roxie's excited to try everything. I've been raving about it since I last ate here."

There was an awkward pause as understanding passed between me and Brandon because the last time I was here, I came as James's date.

But the moment passed as quickly as it came. Brandon's eyes twinkled with excitement. "Well, you're in for a treat, Roxie. My grandfather has been tinkering in the kitchen this week. He thought if we bring a new signature pizza to the menu, that might help draw in some traffic. Our newest pizza creation, the 'Rustic Italiana,' is my new favorite. I'll make sure it's on its way to your table shortly." With that, he disappeared into the kitchen.

"Well, this ought to be interesting," Roxie mused. "Everyone's dancing around the very obvious elephant in the room."

"I didn't think showing my face here again would be easy."

Roxie reached across the table to squeeze my hand. "You're doing the right thing."

As I observed the restaurant's few patrons, I took in their genuine smiles as they ate their pizzas. Some of them were familiar faces from the last time I was here. Despite the sparse crowd, there was an undeniable warmth that emanated from the place, a testament to the love and passion the Rossi family poured into their craft. The success of Rossi Pizzeria meant everything to them, so much so that James was fighting hard for this place, and I was determined to showcase that in my review.

Right after Roxie walked away from the table to capture the restaurant through her camera lens, Maria returned, accompanied by James's grandfather, Lorenzo. His eyes twinkled with a mix of wisdom and mischief as he joined us at the table. It was what had made me feel so welcome the first time I had dinner with all of them. "Hallie, welcome back," he said. "I heard you're here to document the magic of our pizzas. Brave of you, dear."

Heat flared across my cheeks. My mouth dropped open, then closed, then opened again. But still no words came out.

"How is he?" were the first words that finally slipped through my lips.

Lorenzo's eyes softened.

"He's been quiet this past week. But I saw how hurt he was when he read that article."

I nodded my head. I could imagine the betrayal that James felt. The betrayal that he didn't want to experience again after Cassidy.

"Maria tells me you did not write that article?" Lorenzo's deep voice held an air of softness.

"No. The published article was nothing like what I'd originally written. My editor changed it all. She thought my article was too sentimental and wouldn't have generated the readership that the magazine needed."

Lorenzo shook his head. "I don't know what the world's come to that we focus on trying to draw the attention of people on the internet. Yet, here we are. Have you told James this?"

I sighed. "I've tried. But he doesn't want to speak to me. Rightfully so. From the outside it looks like I strung him along and then disrespected him."

"Well, if it's meant to be, then the two of you will figure it out." Lorenzo reached out to pat my hand. "Now tell me about this business you and your friend are starting."

I smiled. "Roxie and I are starting our own blog. We are still working on getting everything off the ground. She and I are taking some freelance jobs in the meantime to help fund everything, but once it's up, we would like the first review on the site to be Rossi Pizzeria."

Lorenzo mulled over my words for a moment. "And you think this will help the restaurant?"

I took a deep breath. "I truly believe it will. Rossi Pizzeria has a story to tell, a story that will resonate with so many other hardworking families across the country. I want our blog to showcase places like this, places that pour their heart and soul into the food they serve to their customers. Between my previous social media account and the connections from the freelance jobs we've taken over the years, we have enough of an audience for the restaurant to see a difference."

"I'll bring everything on the menu over for you two. I look forward to seeing what this does. James was so passionate about this, and I have the utmost confidence in my grandson."

I only wished James were here to see how much his grandfather trusted him.

39

James

"God, I missed this." Sebastian sighed as the two of us sipped on our drinks at Whiskey Locker during Monday's happy hour. We'd decided to celebrate the end of my time at Berkley Williams after I'd handed in my resignation.

I twirled my Old Fashioned in circles on the table. This should be a day of celebration. I was on the verge of starting something new, something exciting. But the last thing I wanted to do was celebrate. Not when nearly every waking moment was haunted by Hallie. She waltzed into my life with a stubborn attitude that I couldn't get out of my head. I developed feelings over the next few months of getting to know her, only for her to show her true self. Part of me wanted to be grateful that I'd realized before it had gone any further. But a bigger part of me refused to believe that Hallie could be that calculated. It felt completely out of character for the woman I thought I knew.

A few of the men I knew from different financial firms had come up to me after hearing the news that I was leaving Berkley Williams. Most of them were trying to figure out where I was going next. I kept quiet about my new position at Rooster's venture capital, which wasn't to be announced for another week. I was too distracted by reliving all those nights I'd spent trying to disrupt Hallie's carefully crafted plans to find a man in this bar. Neither of us had expected that the man she had been looking for all along was me.

"Dude, if you're going to be a fucking bump on a log, you could have just told me you didn't want to come," Sebastian said. "I've been trying to get you to come out with me for over a week, and you've been turning me down left and right. Is this still about Hallie?"

Sebastian's normal antics had never bothered me before. I couldn't remember if he'd ever fallen head over heels for anyone before. His relationships usually had a twenty-four-hour expiration. He couldn't fathom why I was still reeling from everything that had happened with Hallie. In his eyes, I should have gotten over Hallie by getting under someone else. But that was where he and I differed. Hallie wasn't a girl one could simply get over. The girl I thought I knew was now just going to be the one that got away.

"Of course this is about Hallie. How *couldn't* this be about Hallie?" I downed the rest of my drink, relishing the burn it left in my throat. It provided some relief from the constant focus on the ache in my heart. "I think I'm in love with her, Sebastian. Or the person I thought she was. How in the hell am I just supposed to get over her? Nothing makes sense. I still can't figure out why she would do something like this."

"And you still won't reach out to her to find out?" Sebastian asked. "For someone so smart, I would assume you'd want all the facts. This isn't like you."

Sebastian was right. It wasn't like me to act so emotional.

It was why I was a numbers guy. I made decisions based on facts and provable scenarios. But there was no way of making sense of all of this. Which was why I'd avoided Hallie's texts, calls and voicemails for so long. If I just ignored it, my brain didn't have to turn it into logic.

But for once, maybe Sebastian was right.

I hesitated for a moment, then pulled out my phone. My thumb hovered over Hallie's contact—the one I'd blocked days ago in a moment of anger and hurt. With a deep breath, I tapped unblock.

Almost immediately, the unread messages poured in.

It was tempting to ignore them, to pretend they didn't exist and keep moving forward with my life. But a small voice inside me whispered I could never move on, not without understanding what had really happened.

I opened the first one. Hallie's words spilled out, a mix of apologies and explanations. She swore she hadn't written the article that was published. That what I read wasn't hers. Her messages were filled with disbelief and desperation. She claimed her original version had been changed by Anthea, who didn't think the piece was "strong enough" and had replaced the heartfelt tone with something far more cynical.

As I scrolled, a part of me wanted to believe her, to give her a chance to explain herself. But another part—the part that was still bruised—wasn't sure if I could trust her again.

Sebastian leaned closer, his eyes scanning the messages on my phone. "What did she say?" he asked, his voice laced with curiosity.

"She said the article that published wasn't hers," I

replied, my voice tinged with uncertainty. "She said that her boss changed the entire article without her knowledge."

Sebastian's eyebrows shot up in surprise. "Do you think she's telling the truth? I know she really wanted that food critic position. What if her boss shot down her first article and asked her to put out the one she wrote instead, without telling you about it?"

I took a moment to gather my thoughts, weighing my options. The logical part of me screamed to walk away, to protect myself from further pain. But deep down, a flicker of hope burned, reminding me of the connection we had shared.

"I think I need to talk to her," I finally answered, surprising even myself. "I need to understand why she did what she did, and if there's any chance for us to move forward."

Sebastian nodded. "Good for you, man. Go get your girl."

I tapped into Hallie's contact to call her despite how loud it was getting in Whiskey Locker. Things were just getting going for everyone looking to enjoy a night out. I covered my ear, trying to block out some of the noise as I put the phone up to my ear. My heartbeat was nearly in my throat in anticipation. Far more nervous at the prospect of hearing Hallie's voice for the first time in over a week than I'd expected. But just as I expected the phone to ring, I instead heard a long beep, indicating a disconnected line. I tried to send a text message instead, which immediately failed to deliver.

Before I could question what was happening, my web

alert for Hallie's column flashed across the top of my screen. I'd almost forgotten that it was Monday, when Hallie's articles normally came out. My finger hesitated over the link. Now that she and I weren't going on dates, would her boss have made her go out for her last article? Or would she have had to come up with it all by herself?

"Jesus, are you going to share anything?" Sebastian asked. "You're leaving me in the dark over here."

"Hallie just published an article."

Sebastian's brows furrowed, mirroring my confusion. "But you two didn't go on another date."

"Exactly." I clicked into the article, only to see "Overheard in NYC" instead of "Love on Wall Street" and to make matters even stranger, a different journalist had written it.

I shot off another text to her—only for it to bounce again. Then, like the definition of insanity, I tried to click on her number again. The disconnected tone sounded once more.

"Damnit." I clutched my phone tightly in my hand, remembering that Hallie had only given me her work phone number. If the number was disconnected, could it really be that she'd left *Sophisticate*? "Seb, I think Hallie might have been telling the truth about her boss. I think she quit her job."

"And she's not answering your calls or texts?" he asked.

"I think she gave me her work phone number when we first met, and she never gave me her personal."

I realized, just as Hallie did, that someone had changed the article. Then she had been trying to reach me that night, only for me to shut her out.

"Don't you know where she lives?" Sebastian asked me as he casually sipped at his drink.

"That's a great idea, Seb," I said, already standing up from the table.

"Wait, you're leaving now?" Sebastian asked as he shot straight up.

"Yes," I told him as I tossed some cash on the table. "You can come with if you want, but you don't have to."

"Well, fuck." Sebastian downed the rest of his drink. "Of course, I'm coming. What else am I going to do? This is far more entertaining than anything that's been going on in my life recently."

"Are you sure you're not just tagging along in the hope that you'll see Roxie?" I asked as the two of us walked out of the bar. I tried my best to ignore all the curious glances thrown in my direction as we walked out the door.

"Now, why would you think that?" Sebastian asked me with a mischievous smile.

Sebastian called a car to take us uptown toward the West Village. He was many things, but a man that took the subway was not one of them. But of course, there couldn't be any more traffic than there was on a Monday night after work. Which only made the anticipation feel that much more serious as we inched across the city.

If Hallie had quit her job in response to what had happened with her boss, that told me a lot of what I needed to know.

I was already out the door before the car came to a full stop outside of Hallie's apartment. Sebastian was nearly ten steps behind me as I pressed the buzzer to the correct apartment.

"Hello?" a woman's voice crackled across the speaker.

"Roxie?" I asked, instantly recognizing Hallie's best friend. "Is Hallie home?"

"James? What are you doing here?"

"I need to speak to Hallie. Is she here?" I asked again.

Roxie sighed down the line. "Hold on. I'm coming down."

Sebastian stood on the sidewalk, just before the stoop, behind me. But I watched his shoulders straighten when he heard Roxie's voice.

It only took a minute before Roxie pushed open the front door—without Hallie in tow.

"I tried to call Hallie, but I think she gave me her work phone number. All my texts are failing, and her phone is disconnected." I didn't waste any time getting to the point. If Hallie had sent Roxie down here to send me away, I would not go down without a fight. I wanted a chance to speak with her.

"Yeah, she had to turn her work phone and laptop back in when she quit *Sophisticate*," Roxie replied.

"She really quit?" I asked. "Why?"

"Because Anthea Sparks has no integrity," Roxie spat. "She changed Hallie's article without her consent. Hell, she basically published an entirely different article with Hallie's name attached to it."

"But what about the food critic position?" I couldn't believe that Hallie would walk away from her dream just like that. Not after the lengths she'd gone over the past few months for it.

"She and I are finally starting our own blog together. We're still working with our website developers and finalizing branding, but our first review should be up in the next few weeks."

Pride bloomed in my chest for Hallie's bravery. It was inspiring to see her refusing to let someone else dictate her success.

Sebastian, who had been listening attentively, broke the silence. "Congratulations, Roxie. I know that was something you'd been hoping you could do."

Roxie peered over my shoulder down at Sebastian, who was now standing sheepishly with his hands shoved in his pockets. She let out a long sigh that I couldn't quite read.

"Do you think Hallie would be open to talking to me?" I asked, my voice filled with a mix of hope and apprehension.

Roxie looked at me, her expression softening. "I can't speak for her, James. I know she tried her hardest to reach you, to explain, and when you shut her out, the guilt nearly overwhelmed her. She barely got up from our couch for nearly a week, if I'm being honest. I thought I was going to have to call reinforcements in to help me peel her off the cushions and force her to shower. *But*," Roxie paused, a small smile playing on her lips, "she hasn't stopped talking about you."

"Is she home?" I asked for the third time.

Roxie shook her head. "She's out doing a freelance project while we wait for our business to get off the ground."

My shoulders sank. I wasn't sure I could go another day without speaking with her.

"I have an idea, though. How do you guys feel about going to Whiskey Locker tomorrow night?" Roxie quirked an eyebrow.

"When aren't we there?" Sebastian piped up again.

Roxie acted like she hadn't heard him. "I can make sure Hallie is at Whiskey Locker tomorrow night. If that's something you'd want?"

"Yes," I replied fiercely. "I want a chance to clear the air, to start fresh."

"Then let's make that happen. For the both of you, because you also look miserable and it's a real vibe killer, if I'm being honest."

With a renewed sense of hope, I stepped off the stoop of Hallie's apartment building. The same stoop that I'd first kissed her on.

"Hey!" Roxie called out once Sebastian and I were halfway to the car. "You know she went to the pizzeria to do the review she agreed with you to do? She wants it to be our first review on the new website. She asked your family not to tell you until it was published, in case you'd be mad. But now you're here, well I think it's okay that I tell you."

I was so overwhelmed all I could do was nod. If there was one thing I wanted more than anything, it was to have Hallie Woods back in my life.

40

Hallie

"The last thing I want to do is go to Whiskey Locker tonight," I told Roxie as I watched her get ready in her room. I was still in my pajamas and Roxie was casting wary glances my way when she realized I still hadn't attempted to change to go out with her.

I propped my laptop on my chest as I put the finishing touches to the freelance work I'd done the night before. A new Indian restaurant had reached out through a private message to my social media account. I'd taken the job while our business was still being developed, so Roxie and I didn't end up on the streets of New York City.

"I have an article to finish." Once our new website was live, my old blog would reroute to the new one. We recommended city restaurants and tagged them with my old reviews. "Plus, I don't want to go pretend I'm happy when that couldn't be further from the truth. I don't even know if I can stomach walking into that bar. Can't we go somewhere else? There are so many other places to get drinks."

I'd finally started coming to terms with the fact that I may never see James again. The last thing I wanted was to go to a place that reminded me of him.

"Just for old times' sake," Roxie pleaded. "I heard

they have karaoke tonight. Can you imagine a group of inebriated men in finance singing along to 'Girls Just Want to Have Fun'? You may not need something like that for content anymore, but why not enjoy the entertainment?"

She and I both knew that if Roxie wanted something, she was going to get it eventually. Roxie threw a top at me from her closet.

"Wear that. You'd look *amazing* in that."

"I'm not going, Roxie," I argued again.

She rolled her eyes at me, knowing just as much as me that soon I would be in a taxi with her on our way to the Financial District.

"I want to celebrate our new website." Roxie stuck her lower lip out, giving me her best puppy dog eyes for good measure.

"Fine," I sighed, reaching for the top Roxie had given me before rolling off her bed to go change in my room.

It would be like saying goodbye. It was the closure that I would never get from James. But even as I attempted to persuade myself of that, a little voice in my head whispered that maybe, just maybe, he'd be there. Maybe if we saw each other, and I had a chance to explain, everything would finally be okay.

I held on to that tiny seed of hope as the two of us rode across the city in the back of a taxi. We used the time in traffic to discuss outstanding business issues.

Which font did we want our logo to be in?

Did we like the pastel orange or the pastel red?

The amount of tiny details to stress over were endless. I did not know how difficult starting our own business would be, but neither of us was deterred. The universe had laid the path, and it was now up to us to follow it.

The cab stopped in front of the familiar bar, one that I had spent weeks in boring myself to death attempting to find the perfect finance man. Only to realize that the perfect man had been the one smirking at me across the bar the entire time. Roxie was halfway to the front door of Whiskey Locker by the time I finally got the courage to step out of the taxi.

Flashes of the night James and I had made our original agreement played across my mind as I followed Roxie inside. I didn't regret making that deal despite how everything ended. Without it, I never would have had the chance to feel seen and appreciated, how James had made me feel.

I spotted a few familiar faces hanging around the bar. The first guy I attempted to talk to—Mark. Then there was Graham, still lingering near the dart board. Even that bastard Henry who was now trying to flirt with another woman that hadn't picked up on the ring tan line on his left hand. But the one familiar face I wanted to see was nowhere to be found.

I wasn't sure if the feeling pooling in my stomach was one of relief or disappointment.

"What do you want to drink?" Roxie asked me.

For a split second, I almost asked for an Old Fashioned before I thought better of it. Was I trying to make myself miserable? "I'll take a glass of white wine."

"Grab us a couple of seats at the bar?" Roxie asked me before she sidled up to the bartender, Joey, who gave me a smile and a wave when he recognized me.

"Sure."

Oddly, this place felt like a second home after all the time I'd spent here over the past few months. But I felt like a completely different person since the first time I had stepped inside. Back then I would have done *anything* to claw myself into Anthea's good graces. Now I was taking matters into my own hands.

"Should we play a round of darts?" Roxie asked, eyeing Graham's friend, who, I'm pretty sure, was devastated because Roxie hadn't given him her number that night.

"I think I learned my lesson last time," I said as I took my glass of wine from her.

"If you say so," Roxie sang as she scanned the room.

My eyes drifted toward the entrance of the bar as I was wondering when we could leave, only to see a familiar face walk through.

6'5".

Blue eyes.

The most handsome man in all the financial district.

All the air seemed to leave the room, but my gaze stayed glued on James.

He was here.

Then, like something out of one of my favorite romance movies, his eyes found mine across the room.

My heart stuttered. I forgot how to breathe. And then James was walking toward me—confident, familiar, impossibly handsome—his smirk soft but unmistakably *him*.

"Hey," he said.

"Hey," I breathed, my voice barely above a whisper, as if speaking too loudly would break the spell between us.

The air shifted. It was heavy with everything we hadn't said. With hurt and hope. With all the words we'd carried in the silence.

"Can I buy you an Old Fashioned?" he asked.

That warm smile I had grown so fond of flickered across his face.

"I would love an Old Fashioned," I replied, and he signaled to Joey, who nodded in understanding the minute he saw James.

"It's really good to see you, Hal." That familiar nickname that I once hated was like music to my ears.

It was strange not being able to reach out to him.

"Hi, Hallie," Sebastian's voice broke the moment. He slid onto the barstool next to Roxie, offering a little wave. I blinked, noticing how easy he and Roxie looked together. Much more at ease with one another than the last time I'd seen them together in the Hamptons. Roxie totally avoided my gaze as she turned to Sebastain, asking about his day with the innocence of someone who hadn't just orchestrated an entire romantic ambush.

"How are you?" I winced the second the words slipped from my lips. Because I had a feeling I knew exactly how he felt. *Betrayed.*

"Maybe the better question is, how are you doing?" James asked. "You're no longer at *Sophisticate*?"

"You're right," I said. "I left *Sophisticate* after I found out that my boss had published a completely different article under my name."

I tried to choose my words carefully, worried I might offend James and end our conversation before it started.

James tilted his head slightly, concern filling his eyes, but he didn't interrupt. Didn't pull away.

"What was your article meant to be about?" James asked.

I hadn't dared to send it to him before. I'd been too afraid of rejection. Of more silence. But now . . . I didn't hesitate. I pulled out my phone, opened the document, and handed it to him. The *real* article. The one where I took a risk, laid my heart bare and talked about just how much that date and meeting James's family meant to me.

He took my phone from me, his brow furrowing in focus as he read. Every flicker of his expression hit me like a wave—until finally, he muttered under his breath, "Goddamnit."

My stomach sank. "You didn't like it?"

He looked up quickly, eyes wide. "No! Hallie, it's *incredible*. This would've been your best piece. The way you wrote about us, about that night . . . There's so much heart in it. I feel like people would've really *felt* it."

I gave him a sad smile. "I guess we'll never know, will we?"

"That's not your fault," he said. "You couldn't control what your boss did."

"No," I murmured. "But I should never have brought you into this mess."

His expression shifted. "And that's what you truly think? That you shouldn't have met me?"

"No. God, no," I said quickly. "You're the first person who ever really saw me. Who understood me. I don't regret one *second* of it. But I still feel terrible that you got caught in the fallout."

"I don't," he said, his voice certain. "It was the best few months I've had in a long time. I think it was the catalyst I needed to step away from the grindstone that is Berkley Williams and do something out of the ordinary."

"You took the job with Rooster?" I asked, eyes wide.

He nodded, grinning now. "I did."

"James!" I exclaimed, throwing my arms around him before I could second guess myself. "That's incredible."

It wasn't until I felt the warmth of him, his arms winding around me, that I realized what I'd done. I started to pull back, awkward and apologetic. "Oh, I'm sorry—"

"Don't be," he said, his voice fierce as his grip tightened, holding me close. "I missed this. I missed *you*. I'm sorry I didn't reach out to you. To let you explain sooner. It felt like I had the rug pulled out from under me, like what happened last time with Cassidy. That wasn't fair to you."

I tilted my head back to look at him. His eyes were full of everything we hadn't been able to say.

Was he going to kiss me?

God, he had to kiss me.

But he didn't move right away. He just *looked* at me, as though memorizing every detail, every piece he thought he'd lost. My heart pounded so loud I thought for sure he could hear it.

And then, finally, he leaned in.

Soft at first, tentative. But after a few moments, everything we'd been holding back finally broke free. The kiss deepened, slow and consuming. Longing poured behind every movement. The world narrowed down to just this—the smell of his cologne, the press of his mouth, the way his hand slid up to cup my cheek like he was anchoring himself to the moment.

The cheers startled me.

We pulled apart, just barely, and realized the entire bar had erupted around us.

Even the guys I'd attempted to get dates from—Graham, Mark, even Henry—were lifting their glasses. Regulars at the far end of the bar were clapping. Joey winked at me from behind the counter and mouthed, *finally*.

I blinked through the laughter and surprise, then turned back to James. His eyes were still on me, unwavering.

"I want to make this clear, Hal. I *like* you. A lot," he said, when we pulled apart. "These past couple of weeks have been awful without you. But this? Seeing you tonight? It's reminded me how much better everything feels when you're part of it. You make me excited to go to build something new. To come home to someone who actually gets it—gets *me*."

I laughed softly, teary-eyed. "James . . . I don't just like you. I think I'm in love with you."

"Damnit," he whispered, pulling me closer. "I wanted to say that first."

His thumbs brushed my cheeks, and he looked at me like I was everything.

"You didn't need to," I told him. "You showed me. In every way that matters."

And then he kissed me again. Long and slow. As if he had all the time in the world.

The cheers echoed in the background. But I didn't hear a single thing. It was only me and him in the middle of the bar where it had all started.

Because as far as perfect moments go, I couldn't think of a better one. After months of searching, I'd finally found my man in finance.

Epilogue

James

A Year Later

"James!" my aunt exclaimed as Hallie and I walked through the door. "We have your usual table ready."

"You need to stop saving that table for the two of us, Aunt Maria," I said, leaning across the hostess stand to kiss her cheek. "There's a line out the door."

"We will always save your table, James. The two of you are family." Aunt Maria reached over to squeeze my chin between her thumb and forefinger. "I'll let your father and Tony know you're here. And you look as gorgeous as ever, Hallie."

Without hesitation, she pulled Hallie into a hug, and Hallie melted into her arms like she'd always belonged. After we'd made up, the Rossi clan had welcomed Hallie back without hesitation. They'd seen the magic between us and kept their faith in us when it looked like there was no coming back. They claimed her as one of their own from the start and the Rossis never gave up on family.

"Is Nonno in?" I asked, as Maria led us to a small table nestled near the window between the dining room and the kitchen.

It was the only one draped in white linen. The others all wore our famous red-checkered cloths. A single candle flickered at the center of our table, casting a soft glow.

"I thought we said no candles," I teased as I pulled Hallie's chair out for her.

"Your Nonno insisted," Maria said, her voice sweet and a little smug. A twinkle shone in her eyes that made it clear this had been planned long before we arrived.

I glanced toward the kitchen to see Lorenzo, where he appeared less and less these days as he enjoyed a proper retirement. His trusty peel in hand as he pulled pizzas out of the brick oven and replaced them with fresh ones. Once the restaurant had gotten busy enough to afford double the staff, my grandmother convinced my grandfather that it was okay to let go.

When he did, he finally let my dad and uncle take full control of the business, just like everyone had hoped. But the surprise came when he handed me something more.

After Hallie and Roxie's glowing review brought the restaurant a flood of attention—mentions in major critic columns, a few national lists, even a short feature on a travel food show—I finally asked to be more than just the grandson who helped out when he wasn't stuck in finance meetings. I wanted to be part of it for real. To have skin in the game. My grandfather, who never gave anything away lightly, pulled me aside and offered me his stake in the company.

When I wasn't busy building something great with Theo Drake and Rooster, I was here, helping the pizzeria cement its legacy.

Now Lorenzo spent his mornings meeting up with his

friends at a coffee shop down the street, and his evenings hosting poker nights in the dining room.

"James. Hallie." Brandon appeared at our table. He was still working at the restaurant waiting and bussing tables, but after expressing an interest in the business side, my uncle and father gave him a seat at the table so he could learn the ropes. "Do you want your usual? It's on the house tonight, per Nonno. Congratulations, by the way."

Hallie gave me a soft smile.

"Thanks, Brandon. The usual would be great. Where's Emilia?"

"She has practice tonight. Are you guys coming to her game this weekend?"

"We wouldn't miss it," Hallie told him.

My cousin bowed his head before disappearing into the kitchen where I could see him speaking with our grandfather.

"How would you feel about a night cap at Whiskey Locker?" I reached across the table to take Hallie's hand in mine.

I couldn't believe the stroke of luck I'd had with Hallie Woods. How she'd swept into my life like a storm that I'd originally pegged only for destruction. But what I didn't realize was that she was making me a new man. Stripping away all the hard-headedness I'd tried to disguise as commitment to my job.

"I think it's only right that we end the night there. It is where it all started, after all."

"I think Sebastian will probably be at our usual booth tonight. He sent me a congratulatory text message.

Honestly, I was surprised that he remembered what today was."

Brandon stopped by to drop off one of the pizzeria's best bottles of wine and a bruschetta platter, one of Hallie's favorites. "Nonno said to bring antipasto by the table before the pizza. So that should be out soon."

"Thanks, Brandon."

Hallie didn't hesitate to dive into the bruschetta, sighing contentedly as she bit into the toasted bread. But she waited until my cousin had disappeared back into the kitchen before lowering her voice and continuing. "Well, Sebastian has made some *very* noticeable changes as of late."

I raised an eyebrow as I reached for the bottle of wine and filled her glass. "And I wonder why?"

We shared a knowing look, laced with something close to amusement.

"I think he's trying to prove something," she said. "Like maybe he's finally realizing that he can't keep skating through life charming everyone and everything around him."

I leaned back in my chair, watching her. "Do you think Roxie gave him some kind of ultimatum."

Hallie hesitated, then gave a small shrug. "Knowing her, probably. But not in a dramatic way. More like . . . a quiet line in the sand. She's not one for games."

"She doesn't seem like she's into him," I replied.

"That's the point," Hallie murmured. "She's trying not to be. Roxie doesn't trust people who are too smooth, and let's be honest—Sebastian is practically bottled and labeled *'for short-term use only'*."

I laughed, but Hallie's expression stayed thoughtful.

"She likes him," she added. "I know she does. But she also knows better than to fall for a guy who says the right things but won't show up when it counts."

I considered that. Sebastian had always been good at the chase with his easy charm, desire for low stakes. But lately he'd been different. Asking about Roxie when she wasn't around. Turning down dates with women he would've casually flirted with six months ago. Even his wardrobe had shifted—less flash, more intention.

"And what if he means it this time?" I asked. "What if she's the one who makes him want to show up differently?"

Hallie gave a small smile, the kind that didn't quite hide the worry beneath it. "Then he's going to have to earn it. Roxie's not a girl who falls for words. She waits for actions. And if he messes it up . . ."

"She'll shut the door for good," I finished.

Hallie nodded. "Exactly."

There was a beat of silence as we both stared into our glasses, the candle flickering between us.

"There's the couple of the hour!" My father, appearing rarely on the dining room floor, stopped at our table. "Happy anniversary to you two."

"Thank you, Giacomo." Hallie accepted my father's hug.

My father had gotten onboard with my plans for the restaurant after seeing an uptick in foot traffic after only a few weeks of Hallie and Roxie's review being live. He immediately put out job ads for a new social media manager and asked for Hallie's help in vetting the perfect candidate. Hallie had helped him find Eliza, who had just graduated from college after majoring in marketing. She had her finger on the pulse of the social media trends and had gotten a few posts to go viral within her first month on the job.

And the rest was history.

Rossi Pizzeria had embedded itself firmly back into the very fabric of the New York food scene. In under a year, it appeared on almost every tourist-oriented list of top places to visit in the city, and it continued to draw local customers.

"Thanks, Dad," I told him when he turned to give me a hug next.

"Hallie, are we still expecting your family next Wednesday for family dinner?" my father asked. If I had known the two of us would be subject to multiple rounds of questioning from my family, I would have picked anywhere other than here for our anniversary dinner.

"Yes! They get in this weekend." Hallie smiled up at my father, completely unbothered that my boisterous family had no sense of boundaries. "They are excited to meet everyone. It's been a while since they've visited the city and with my sister's baby, I'm sure it will be eventful."

"Eloise is excited to have a little one around for a few days. I'm sure she will be more than happy to take your niece while you show your family around."

Thankfully, he spared us from any pointed looks. Hallie and I had only been dating a year, and we were both focused on our careers, which were at their peak. We still had time to think about everything that came after. We were taking things slowly and enjoying each milestone of our relationship.

My father clasped his hands together. "I'll let you two enjoy your anniversary dinner. If I don't see you before next Wednesday, I love you both."

"We have more than just our anniversary to celebrate." Hallie lifted her wineglass in my direction. "I believe congratulations are in order for you. Officially official, now that the resignation letter has been sent in."

"Now we just have to hope Rossi Equities lasts longer than a year," I joked as I clinked my glass against hers.

"It will."

Hallie's undying faith in me was part of the reason that I had finally mustered up enough courage to take the next step—again. I wasn't walking away from Rooster entirely. Not yet. I'd shifted into more of a consulting role while Theo and I searched for someone to take my place full time. It was Theo, after all, who gave me the space and confidence to figure out what I wanted—to think about what kind of legacy I actually wanted to build. While I'd helped Theo get the new division of Rooster off the ground, I think he saw that I was itching to claim something that was *fully* my own. He was the one to approach me and suggest I look into chasing my dreams.

I hadn't realized how rewarding it could feel, investing in a small business that just needed a little capital and the right kind of belief to grow. Those days were my favorite. It cut up the monotony of making lucrative business decisions.

I'd learned from the best about taking risks in your career after watching Hallie leave *Sophisticate*, which was once her dream company, only to achieve far greater things than she ever would have if she'd stayed. If she could do it, why couldn't I?

"You said you had an interesting email today?" The nerves were growing as the little box in my pocket pressed into my thigh, reminding me that it was there.

"I did." Brandon stopped by again, this time with the pizzas. Each hand-thrown and fired by my grandfather. "Someone from Odd Hour Films, that production company, emailed me about an idea for a series they've been thinking about. Something about eating around the world."

"And they want you for it?" My excitement was almost uncontainable. This was more than Hallie had ever imagined—getting to become a figure in the food industry.

"They said I'm on the short list." Hallie was trying her best to keep her own enthusiasm under control.

"Hallie!" I really wished I'd decided on that home-cooked meal instead. "That's amazing. You are more than deserving of it."

"I'm trying not to get my hopes up in case they don't pick me."

"They'll pick you."

Now it was my turn to show Hallie my undying faith in her.

"I'm going to show you just how proud I am of you when we get home." A deep red colored Hallie's cheeks as she glanced around to see if any of the surrounding tables had overheard me. But I didn't care if they had. I'd climb to the top of the Empire State Building and announce my love for Hallie Woods if I could.

"James, this dinner is enough of a celebration."

"Well, there's more."

"We already gave each other our gifts," Hallie protested. She was right. We'd exchanged gifts at my apartment before leaving for dinner. I'd surprised her with tickets to Mexico, her number one bucket list destination, so we could hop all over tasting some of the best food the country offered. While Hallie had gotten me hand-blown whiskey glasses imported from the province in Italy my family came from with "Mr. Old Fashioned" inscribed on them.

"There's just one more." I pulled the box from my pocket. It was a little square box that fit in the palm of my hand. But what lay within it carried more weight than the plane tickets I'd given to her earlier.

Hallie glanced nervously between me and the box in my hand before she reached out with trembling hands to take it from me. For a moment, I thought she'd give it back to me before she even opened it. But after steeling herself with one big inhale, she lifted the lid on her box.

"This is a folded-up piece of paper," Hallie deadpanned.

"It didn't feel right just asking you or handing the piece of paper to you. I had to dress it up a bit."

"And give me a heart attack in the process?" She rolled her eyes. "You and I both know there are only a few things that come in little boxes."

"I wanted to watch you squirm, just a little," I admitted with a mischievous smile.

As she opened the note and read my hastily scribbled question, I held my breath.

"Wait, are you serious?"

"Roxie's moving out, and I know you aren't looking forward to finding a new roommate. So I thought, what if you just didn't? And we moved in together instead?" I never thought I would be this nervous. I'd even rehearsed this moment in my head earlier today, but nothing prepared me for her big, brown eyes staring at me while the moment continued to stretch between us. "You've got me on the edge of my seat here, Hal."

The corners of Hallie's lips pulled upward and the nerves that had been about to spill over subsided. "As long as you make room for my wine glasses next to your whiskey glasses."

I stuck my hand out across the table for her to shake. "You drive a hard bargain, Hallie Woods. But you have yourself a deal."

On a station platform, with nothing to read,
and a four-hour train journey stretching ahead of him...

That's where the story began for Penguin founder Allen Lane.
With only 'shabby reprints of shoddy novels' on offer,
he resolved to make better books for readers everywhere.

By the time his train pulled into London, the idea was formed.
He would bring the best writing, in stylish and affordable
formats, to everyone. His books would be sold in bookstores,
stationers and tobacconists, for no more than the price
of a ten-pack of cigarettes.

And on every book would be a Penguin, a bird with a certain
'dignified flippancy', and a friendly invitation to anyone who
wished to spend their time reading.

In 1935, the first ten Penguin paperbacks were published.
Just a year later, three million Penguins had made their
way onto our shelves.

Reading was changed forever.

—

A lot has changed since 1935, including Penguin, but in the
most important ways we're still the same. We still believe that
books and reading are for everyone. And we still believe that
whether you're seeking an afternoon's escape, a vigorous debate
or a soothing bedtime story, all possibilities open with a book.

Whoever you are, whatever you're looking for,
you can find it with Penguin.